They were the brave and passionate
ancestors of humanity,
struggling in a savage time—
embarking on the first
and greatest adventure of all. . . .

TORKA—Fit and strong at forty-seven, he had passed the time when most men went to walk the wind, but his fate was to lead his clan on one last adventure in this strange and hostile land.

LONIT—Torka's brave and beautiful woman, she would follow her mate through every hardship—even if it meant exile to the realm of shadows.

UMAK—Torka's first-born son, his blood burned with passion for a beautiful maiden he would do anything to possess—a passion that would drive him to make the most tragic mistake of his life.

MANARAVAK—Umak's twin brother, he was kidnapped and raised by the brute wanawut only to return to the clan more beast than man—his savage heart hungering for his brother's woman.

NAYA—Granddaughter of a powerful shaman, her rare, sensual beauty was working an evil magic of its own—creating a bitter rivalry between two brothers that could destroy the entire clan.

DEMMI—Graceful, tall, and fierce, she had the heart of a hunter and only one love greater than her husband and son—her obsession for her wild brother, Manaravak.

THE
FIRST
AMERICANS

WALKERS OF
THE WIND

WILLIAM
SARABANDE

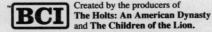

BCI Created by the producers of
The Holts: An American Dynasty
and **The Children of the Lion.**

Book Creations Inc., Canaan, NY • Lyle Kenyon Engel, Founder

BANTAM BOOKS
NEW YORK • TORONTO • LONDON • SYDNEY • AUCKLAND

WALKERS OF THE WIND

*A Bantam Domain Book / published by arrangement with
Book Creations Inc.*

Bantam edition / September 1990

*Produced by Book Creations Inc.
Lyle Kenyon Engel, Founder*

DOMAIN *and the portrayal of a boxed "d" are trademarks of Bantam
Books, a division of Bantam Doubleday Dell Publishing Group, Inc.*

ISBN 0-553-28579-3

Published simultaneously in the United States and Canada

*Bantam Books are published by Bantam Books, a division of Bantam
Doubleday Dell Publishing Group, Inc. Its trademark, consisting of the
words "Bantam Books" and the portrayal of a rooster, is Registered in
U.S. Patent and Trademark Office and in other countries. Marca
Registrada. Bantam Books, 666 Fifth Avenue, New York, New York 10103.*

PRINTED IN THE UNITED STATES OF AMERICA

OPM   12 11 10 9 8 7 6

To Laurie Rosin—one in a million!

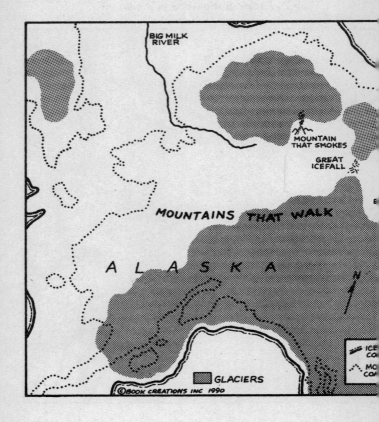

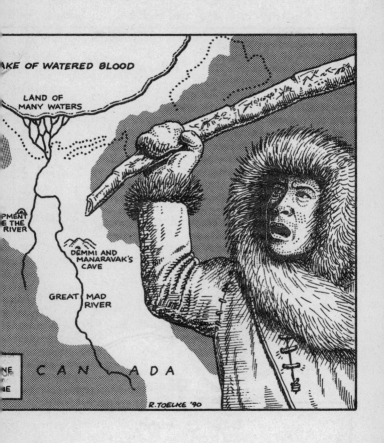

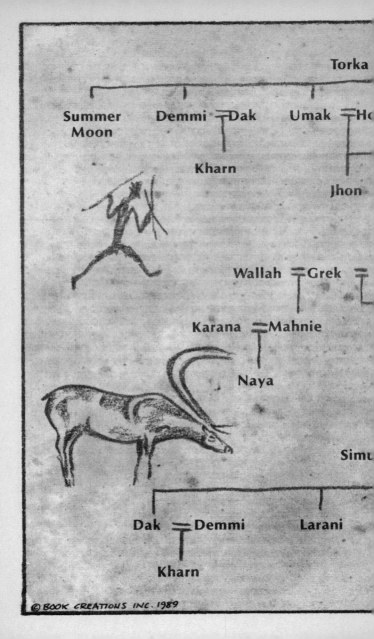

Torka

Summer
Moon

Demmi —Dak   Umak —Ho

Kharn

Jhon

Wallah —Grek

Karana —Mahnie

Naya

Simu

Dak —Demmi   Larani

Kharn

© BOOK CREATIONS INC. 1989

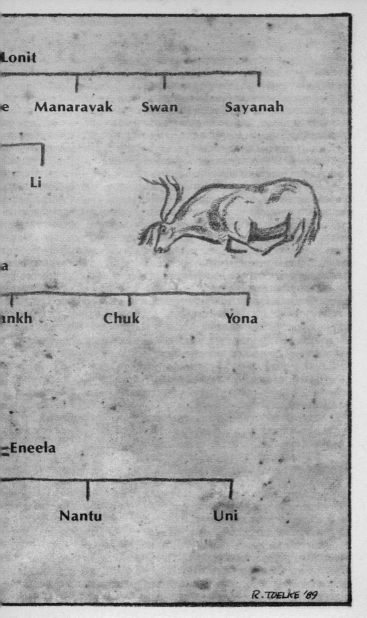

Lonit

e   Manaravak   Swan   Sayanah

Li

a

ankh   Chuk   Yona

Eneela

Nantu   Uni

R. TOELKE '89

PART I

THREE PAWS

1

The land burned—not with flame, not with heat, but with the raw, savage colors of the Ice Age autumn. The girl seemed to burn with the tundra as, knee-deep in the dry, wind-whipped grasses of the rolling Arctic steppe, she deliberately slowed her pace and allowed old Grek to lead the other girls and women on. With their heavily laden gathering baskets hefted on their hips and the children and dogs trotting at their sides, they were far too busy chattering to notice that Naya had fallen behind. They leaned into the wind, their dark hair streaming behind them. The bone, shell, and stone-beaded leather fringes of their garments flapped, tangled, and clicked noisily as they hurried on with never a backward glance.

Naya stopped, waiting for old Grek to sense her absence. When he did not, she smiled. She had made a careful game of her sudden need to be alone. No one had missed her. On and on walked old Grek, proudly assuming the role of woman watcher, aggressively stabbing the wind with his bone-shafted, stone-tipped spears. Loudly and respectfully he appealed to the lions, bears, leaping cats, and wolves. The wind carried his deep voice to Naya; she could hear it clearly.

"The women and children of Torka come, yes!" he cried. "Grek leads them now to the lake, yes! The women and children will drink! The women and children will bathe! Look not with hungry eyes as they pass, for Mother Below has made the lake for all creatures who live upon her skin. Let us come safely through the country of the flesh-eaters."

It occurred to Naya that she should be afraid to stand alone in the country of the flesh-eaters; but the sun was so warm and the day so fair that not even fear could chill her—only pity could do that, and did. The men of the band were hunting bear in the far hills, and she wondered if her grandfather resented being with the females instead of with the other hunters, who were tracking the great three-pawed bear that had been raiding the winter storage pits of the People. Grek gave no sign of resentment. He walked arro-

3

gantly ahead of his charges in his timeworn shaggy leggings and long-haired black shirt cut from the skin of an adult bison. It took a big man to wear such a heavy hide. Grek *was* big, and the shirt made him seem even bigger. With his massive head bent and his broad back humped against the wind, Naya understood why the children of the band called him Bison Man.

A cloud passed before the sun. Naya looked up. Shadows swept across the world, then vanished as the cloud was consumed by the hard, dry wind. The euphoria that had brought Naya to pause was gone. She felt tired now, irritable. The fringes of her lightweight coltskin dress were tangled from the wind, and she did not savor the prospect of separating them. The morning's gathering of lichens, fungi, tubers, and the seeds and berries of the dying summer had wearied her.

Naya scowled. She was all too easily wearied these days. Was it any wonder? Soon the thirteenth winter of her life would begin. *Thirteen!* The concept staggered her. It seemed an enormous number of years for a girl who had yet to come to her first time of blood.

True, the spirit of a woman's life would come to a girl in its own good time, and she was not the only girl in the band to come late to womanhood. Many a chant and medicine smoke had been offered to the forces of Creation on behalf of Swan, the headman's youngest daughter, and Larani, daughter of the hunter Simu; yet neither girl had come to her first time of blood even though they were the same age as Naya.

She frowned as she thought about this. The girls' slow maturation had prompted the older band members to whisper with concern. Naya had seen the women seeking omens in the organs of female animals taken by hunters. The women assured the headman that all boded well for the "new women to be," but saw to it that Naya, Swan, and Larani shared equally in the small, fatty glands that were cut from above the kidneys of every kill. It was well-known that rare and wondrous spirits lived in these little glands—spirits that favored women and had the power to bring girls more quickly to their time of blood.

Naya made a face of revulsion. She did not like the taste of the little glands, but she always dutifully ate her portion. Swan found them pleasant enough, and Larani actually liked them. Nevertheless, while Swan and Larani were visibly blossoming toward impending womanhood, the granddaughter of Grek still looked like a child.

She sighed wistfully. Swan had grown tall during the last long winter, and Larani actually *looked* like a woman under her clothes. The hunters of the band were gazing at her with new eyes. Soon gifts would be brought to her parents, and she would become some man's new woman.

Naya sighed again. No man looked at her as they looked at Larani. She would always be called Little Girl because she *was* little—a small, bird-boned, skinny sprout who would never bleed as a woman bleeds, never be looked at by the men of the band, and never be given gifts by those who would wish to invite her away from the fire circle that she had shared with her grandfather since the death of her parents so many long years ago.

Old Grek promised that someday she would win the finest gifts of all because she was the daughter of a great shaman. He had told her that she would be mated to one of the headman's sons. But Naya was not certain if she believed him. Unlike Swan and Larani, she was not growing up—she was simply growing *old*! Soon days and nights would pass and one morning she would wake to find that her entire life had gone by. She would limp around camp, mumbling about the past, and sucking food through the rubble of her teeth.

The girl's eyes widened as she realized that the distance between her and the others was much greater than before. "Grek! Everybody! Wait!"

The wind blew the words back into her round little face. Her small, perfectly matched, but oddly serrated upper teeth chewed her lower lip thoughtfully. The others walked on, not looking back. Not even Squirrel Killer, her favorite among the dogs, had missed her. Vexed, she hurried on.

Now a wild dog—or was it a dire wolf?—yapped somewhere in the tawny, windswept hills to the east. Naya turned, startled, to stare across the open, rolling steppe toward the hills and the vast, tumbled, ice-ridden mountain ranges that lay beyond. She could see no sign of dog or wolf, but that did not mean that one or more of these animals was not there.

She held her breath and listened, straining to see. To become a straggler was asking to become meat for the watching yellow-eyed carnivores of the wide, savage steppe.

Yet, somehow, she did not feel threatened. The most unusual sensations were sweeping through her body and mind, as pleasant as they were disconcerting. She had never felt like this before.

Her right hand strayed to her throat and rested there on her newly strung necklet of berry beads. In her gathering basket was a generous collection of the seedy, summer-dried little fruits, which she had at first mistaken for craneberries. Thinking them pretty, she had made a necklet of them while the other women and girls had been busy with their own morning's gleaning. With a bone needle taken from the feather-shaft quill case that she wore like a tiny ornament inserted through the base of her nose, she had carefully strung the berries onto a slender thong ripped from the fringes of her knee-length dress. The result had been a pretty adornment, and Naya liked pretty things.

Now—and not for the first time since stringing the berries—she absently raised the strand to her mouth and nervously moved the tip of her tongue against the slick, oily skin of the tiny orb of fruit. Although nearly completely dehydrated, the berries still oozed a little juice. The taste was subtle, decidedly sweet, and pleasant.

Her pulse began to pound and leap. She laughed, then stifled the sound. She was behaving so strangely!

Now her small right hand drifted downward . . . lightly, questingly, to her newly budding breasts. Larani would have laughed to see them; they were not really breasts at all, not when compared to the wondrous swellings upon the chest of the daughter of Simu and Eneela. No, these were the breasts of Little Girl; no larger than the minute shells that were sometimes found along riverbanks. These were nothing to boast of.

Her mood suddenly shifted. Awash in the sunlight, she was euphoric again, at perfect equilibrium with the moment. The berries were a warm, moist embrace around her neck. The world trembled before her. Her dress suddenly felt hot, suffocating. In one fluid motion, she peeled off the garment.

Naked save for her necklet and calf-high moccasins, Naya felt so much better that with a sudden laugh she raised her arms and began to dance. She whirled faster and faster until her long, plaited hair spun outward, whipping and singing in the air like twisted sinew.

Dizzy, she stopped. The world went on spinning. Her braids coiled around her face, slapping her, rousing pain as, crying out in surprise, she staggered, then fell.

It took a moment for the world to stop moving. Puzzled by her own behavior, Naya clambered shakily to her feet and wiped her bruised knees with her palms. For the first time since deliberately falling behind, Naya's head cleared completely. She felt a chill, a warning of winter.

Soon the time of the long dark would come to the northern world. Hares, ptarmigan, owls, and foxes were already changing color. Soon the great herds of grazing animals would follow the sun over the edge of the earth, and many a wolf, wild dog, and fox would follow. Soon horses, camels, and mammoth would leave the tundra to winter with moose and deer within the wind-protected hills. Bears and lions would seek their dens. Pikas, voles, squirrels, and lemmings would go to ground. Rivers and ponds would turn to ice, and fish would either seek deep water or freeze. The sky would whiten with clouds and migrating geese, and when the last of the winged ones was gone, Father Above would close his yellow eye, wrap himself in robes of storm darkness, and seek winter sleep in the arms of his sister—the moon. Then the days of endless night and cold would come. Then the People and the animals of the world would go hungry as Spirit Sucker hunted the earth, feeding upon the lives of the old and the weak . . . and occasionally upon the young and the strong.

Naya trembled. Why think of winter when the wind still sang of summer as it blew warm and hard across the world? Entranced by the splendor of the moment, Naya wanted to prolong the glorious day so that its memory would warm her in the long dark times to come.

Moments passed. Again the dog yapped, a deeper sound now, more threatening. Naya jumped, turned, and saw nothing, but she felt eyes watching her. It was definitely time to go.

"Wait!" she cried. "Wait for me!"

Umak laughed. In the high, sun-scorched grasses beside him on the hill, Companion, his wolflike hunting dog, cocked its gray head and put back its ears in puzzlement. Then, not to be outdone, the dog lifted its head and howled as though in contest with the man.

Far below on the rolling grassland, Naya looked back over her shoulder as she ran, tripped, then went sprawling. In a moment she was on her feet again, screaming as she stumbled on, abandoning her dress and leaving her gathering basket and its hopelessly scattered contents where they lay.

The young man was the wolf who had deliberately set dread into Naya's heart; it was his fault that Little Girl was running in panic. But what else could he have done when she had fallen behind the others? He had wanted to shout a warning, to ask her what in the name of the forces of Creation she thought she was doing there alone, sucking on her berry beads and dancing naked beneath the sun. But if Naya discovered that he was following, she would reveal it to old Grek. And if Grek found out that he had not been trusted to be sole woman watcher, his pride would shrivel. Not a man in the band would wish such shame upon old Grek. And so, by the "luck" of a secret draw, Umak, elder of the headman's twin sons, was hiding, shadowing the old man, the women, and the children instead of where he wished to be—tracking bear with the other hunters.

The words of Torka, his father, echoed in his head: *In protecting our women and children there is much honor!* They were strong words, as powerful as the headman himself. *The man who is chosen to protect the women and children of the People holds the future of the band in his hands.*

"Yes, yes, of course," Umak muttered impatiently now as he moved resentfully forward through the grass.

In his lightweight summer tunic and leggings of caribou skin, Umak's lean, powerful young body cut a narrow swath through the tawny hills as he moved forward, being careful not to stand erect lest Naya turn and see him. He lengthened his stride; Little Girl was faster than he had thought possible, and she had put herself beyond the protective range of his spears. Until he was able to close the distance between them, she was completely vulnerable.

"Either slow down or run faster, Little Girl!" he muttered, wishing that he could shout the words. He howled instead—a loud, deep, vicious howl.

Naya screamed.

"There!" Umak said, satisfied. "That will put fire beneath your feet and speed you on your way to safety." He would have added more, but Naya tripped and fell again.

Umak stopped, ducking low within the dry, stony depression of a streambed. The dog stopped beside him, panting now, tongue lolling and slobbering. Umak's long, earth-eating stride had lessened the distance between him and the girl considerably.

"Silly Little Girl. If only you knew that it was Umak, and not a wolf, who pursues you."

Naya was such a gullible child—amusing and clever and always unpredictable, except when it came to satisfying her appetite for food or pretty things. Everyone smiled upon Naya. Everyone was amused by her. But everyone worried over her increasingly headstrong nature. Grek pampered her excessively, and it was not a good thing to spoil children; eventually little ones had to grow up and assume their full responsibilities within the band. What Naya had done today was irresponsible and dangerous to herself and to those who might be forced to risk themselves on her behalf.

Troubled by his thoughts, Umak edged his way downhill. The lay of the land allowed him a view beyond the rise that stood between Naya and the others: The females had reached the reed-choked shore of a small, shallow lake that shimmered in the wind. It was beautiful. Umak smiled with pleasure at the sight of it. Several of the women were already racing ahead, casting off their garments as they sloshed into the cool shallows. The children and pups and big, rangy dogs followed to turn the water brown with their splashings. It was evident that in the excitement of the moment, no one had missed Naya. Umak frowned. Grek should have noticed her absence long before now. He nodded to himself. Torka had been right to send a man to keep an eye on the old hunter—Grek was obviously not the man he used to be.

Crouching low, he sought the concealment of grass, then moved downward across the face of the hill, flat on his belly with his spears extended forward and held in both palms. He paused close to a scrubby tangle of craneberry bushes. The sight of the fruit caused him to salivate. The berries were much larger than usual, dark and half-dried from the effects of wind and sun. Nevertheless, Umak had not tasted water since dawn, and a craneberry was a craneberry. Even the most desiccated bit of fruit would help to ease his thirst.

He reached for a handful of berries, tossed them into his mouth, then instantly spat them out, recoiling. Whatever the fruits were, they were *not* craneberries; a closer look at them and the shrub that bore them affirmed this. Still spitting particles of seed and half-dried pulp from his tongue, Umak castigated himself for carelessness. Many summers and winters had come and gone since the five-year-old son of the hunter Simu had eaten the flesh of an unfamiliar fungus, but Umak still cringed at the memory of the bloated little body, the grotesquely swollen face, and the pitiful, gasping cries of the dying child.

A sudden crack of thunder startled him. The sound seemed to have come from directly overhead, but he had seen no lightning, and the sky was clear. He frowned. How could lightning strike out of a cloudless sky? He looked across the wide, rolling river of golden steppeland. Clouds were gathering over the distant ranges like herds of woolly, growling black animals. The thunderbolt had come from the west. The clouds were massing now, forming into squall lines, gradually extending their range to shadow the foothills and the distant reaches of the summer-parched plain. Soon the tundral lake would be in shadow. Soon it would rain—at long last!

As Umak stared across the distances lightning veined the sky and sent probing fingers of white-hot light deep into the skin of the earth. The wind was growing much stronger now, whipping the grasses and causing them to lash his face. Remnants of golden pollen rained upon him and caused his eyes and nostrils to itch fiercely.

He stifled a sneeze. It was a wasted effort. Companion sneezed with him—followed by another that was twice as loud. Umak quickly curled his fingers around the broad muzzle lest another such sneeze reveal his presence to Naya.

The girl was facing toward him now, with her back to the wind, listening and alert, tensed to sprint from danger. Umak held his breath. Only after the longest, most searching pause did she whirl and begin to run again.

Had she seen him? For a moment he could have sworn that their eyes had met. Something was different about her stride—it was so intensely and unexpectedly sexual that he stared after her in shock and amazement. A moment ago he had been looking at a child. Now the sight of her bare, shapely little bottom winking away in panicked flight reminded him of the upturned tail of a doe antelope racing provocatively across the steppe, inviting all ready bucks to follow.

Warmth stirred within his loins. What a tiny thing Naya was, all legs and nearly breastless, yet she was heart-stoppingly lovely. His woman did not look like this. No. Honee, the mother of his two little ones, was fat, with layerings of skin in places where flesh should lie smooth. . . .

The dog whined and nuzzled Umak's free hand, urging him to move on, but the young hunter paid no heed. He stared at Naya until his eyes burned, and even though the sun was beating on his back, heating his hunting tunic until his skin seemed to be liquefying beneath it, he made no attempt to move or to look away. Unlike the sun, a man could look at a woman without going blind.

Or could he? Naya was not a woman! She was a child! But she would be a woman someday. And when that time came, she would be his brother's woman. It had been decided long ago: Naya was for his twin, for Manaravak. Umak had no right to look at her at all.

"And what or *whom* does Umak hunt, lying on his belly in this deep grass?"

Flustered, Umak looked up in embarrassment as his brother Manaravak elbowed through the grasses to lie at his side. Companion thunked his tail in happy greeting.

Umak's face flushed with shame. "I . . . uh . . . the granddaughter of Grek fell behind the others. I've been seeing to it that she comes to no harm. How long have you been trailing me?"

"Too long." Manaravak's handsome features settled into an expression of speculation as he clucked his tongue in affectionate admonition. He was bigger and broader than Umak, longer of limb and with more of their father than mother in his face. His eyes narrowed thoughtfully—black eyes with all of the reflected warmth and color of the sunlit plain shimmering beneath dark, straight lashes. "Umak keeps an eye on Naya, but who keeps an eye on Umak?"

"Umak needs no one to keep an eye on him! Umak is Shaman!"

"If this man were a lion, Shaman's life spirit would be in Manaravak's belly, and Manaravak would be spitting out his brother's bones by now!"

"Ha!" There was no amusement in Umak's exclamation. "Companion would have alerted me to danger—but not before I sensed it myself!" He stopped. There was no duping Manaravak—he could smell uncertainty in a man as readily as a wolf perceives fear in its prey.

Umak's eyes narrowed as he met his brother's piercing

gaze. It was not surprising that Manaravak was, in many ways, more a beast than a man: A strange fate had ripped the second born of Torka's twins from his mother's arms, to be raised as an animal by the elusive beast that men called wanawut. Furred and fanged and more terrible than any other carnivore, the wanawut was man and beast combined, with the look of the former and all of the power and killing potential of the latter.

When at last the forces of Creation had conspired to kill the beast and reunite Manaravak with his family, ten long autumns had passed and Manaravak was as wild and savage as the creature that had raised him as its own. Now, nearly another ten autumns later, life within Torka's band had gentled him. He had learned—if not mastered—the language of his people. He no longer howled at the moon or pounded the earth with his fists when he was angry, nor did he move in the long, ambling gait of the wanawut, with his knees bent and his head extended grotesquely forward.

Whether walking or in repose, he now had an easy grace about him, and when he ran, it was with all of the lean, fluid power of a hunting lion. He used a spear with ease and a dagger with pleasure, but he still preferred his food raw, was afraid of fire, and all too often chafed under the authority of his elders.

Now as Umak lay beside his brother, he sensed the watchful, wary, and elusive wolf in Manaravak—in the tension of his body and in the set of his long, expressive mouth and in his eyes.

"Why are you not hunting with the others, Manaravak?"

Manaravak shrugged affably. "If Brother Umak cannot hunt bear, Manaravak will not hunt bear, too. Torka and Simu, they go off one way. Dak and Demmi and Nantu go another. This man Manaravak thinks that his brother cannot be happy watching women, children, and an old man while others hunt bear. I think that it will be a good thing if together Manaravak and Umak watch over Bison Man."

"You are considerate, my brother, but Torka will be angry. We are a very small band, Manaravak, and every hand that is not needed to guard the women and little ones will be needed against the great bear."

Manaravak did not appear to have been listening as he stared off through the grasses at Naya. "I see now why you watch. Maybe she is not so little anymore. Maybe she is asking to be mated."

The autumn sun was not half as hot as the wave of jealousy that seared Umak just as the inner wind of Vision suddenly rose to speak through him:

"Before the time of the long dark turns the world white, the child in Naya will die. Out of this death a new woman will be born. . . ."

"Manaravak's woman!"

Umak stared at his brother; were it not for the happily lecherous look on Manaravak's face, he would not have been certain if he had just spoken aloud at all. The whispering Vision was dissolving like vapors above the river at the rising of a winter dawn. Like birth and death, the Seeing Wind came as it would, when it would. But it had come to Umak often enough for the People to name him Shaman. It had made him Wise Man before he had become a man.

Yet now, although he was nearly twenty and a member of the council of elders, he felt young and as ill at ease as he always did when Vision came to him, unbidden and unwelcome. It was one thing to know when the caribou would come through the passes or when the first wedges of waterfowl would fly out of the face of the rising sun to become food for the People. It was another thing when the Seeing came without being sought, consuming his thoughts and rendering him completely vulnerable to his surroundings and to the nightmare of his childhood—the old fear that he was not his father's son at all, but the child of rape, the offspring of the consummately powerful and evil shaman, Navahk, who by some dark and vicious magic implanted him within his mother's womb against her will . . . to take root before Torka set the seed of life into Manaravak. Just thinking of it made him sweat.

"Look, Umak! Little Girl is catching up with the others. Let us move closer before she enters the lake and cannot be seen."

Deeply shaken, Umak realized that Manaravak had risen and was making his way through the grasses, with Companion following close at his side.

"Come, Umak! A better look is what we need."

Umak did not move. *Yes. Soon Naya will be Manaravak's woman.*

Why should he care? Why should he feel sick at the thought of it?

The great three-pawed bear ambled across the wind-scoured Arctic hills. Even here there was the subtle, inescapable smell of Man—a stain upon the wind or within the memory of the animal; the bear could not tell. Hunters had driven her here—out of the grassland and up onto this high ridge, where the skeleton of the earth lay exposed and broken by the elements. Slick-bottomed, uneven shards shattered by frost slipped away beneath her massive paws and sent her clambering desperately for purchase. The steep slope would have allowed her none even if her left forepaw had not been mutilated by the crushing jaws of the big, grizzled male that had blundered into her hunting territory the previous spring. He had attempted to eat one of her cubs, but she had eaten him instead. It had not mattered that he was one of her own kind or that he had sired her cubs. The cubs had grown fat on his flesh.

But that was long ago. Spring and summer were far behind her now, as dead as the male bear whose distant bones lay cracked, scattered, and bleaching in the autumn sun . . . as dead as the left paw that dangled uselessly at the end of her left forelimb. The ruined paw had prevented her from hunting all but the slowest and most dim-witted meat and had set her to raiding the cache pits of Man. She was lean now, as were the two cubs that trudged wearily behind her.

The great bear lost her footing, and close to eight hundred pounds of bone, muscle, blood, fat, and scarred, time-yellowed hide went sliding down the side of the ridge. The cubs bawled as they suddenly found themselves rolling head over bottom amid the dust of the rockslide that their mother had spawned.

The fall ended where the ascent of the ridge had begun—at its base. The huge bear came up angry, irritable, and shaking dust and stones from the fur of her massive shoulders. This was not the first time that she had lost her footing and slipped since she had begun her walk upward across the talus-scabbed skin of the hills. Irritability was nothing new to her, nor was anger. They came with the pain that lived in her paw. No amount of licking or gnawing had been able to make the pain anything but worse. Now, as the cubs saw her blunt snout twitch and her vast, sloppy lips draw back to reveal enormous plaque-thick teeth, they scampered out of her way. Each remembered that there had been three of them once; their mother had cut their number to two when, in a blind rage against the pain in her paw, she had chewed the offending member to bone and gristle and then, without warning, had suddenly extended her great jaws to render the skull of her littlest offspring into the same.

Now, from a safe distance, the cubs stared at her as she raised her mass to its extreme. Standing eleven feet tall on her hind limbs, she shook her head and turned into the wind to drink it in. She slobbered with frustration and hunger at the scent of that which lay far below within the grassland: the scent of meat! The scent of Man. Of Man on the hunt. They for her . . . she for them.

But the hunters that had driven her and her cubs into the hills were on the southern side of the ridge. It was not their smell that rode foremost on the wind. The great, growling bear now began to follow the smell of the small, naked form that ran sweating with terror across the western grassland.

2

Naya ran on, clasping a tiny hand across her mouth lest her laughter reveal her knowledge that she was being watched and followed by . . . Umak! *And* Manaravak!

As long as the twin sons of the headman were near, no harm could come to her.

Why did they follow? For how long had they been watching her? Had they seen her dance naked beneath the sun? Had the sight of her childlike little body been so amusing that the sound she had heard was not a sneeze but an attempt to stifle their own laughter?

Without warning, the thong ties to Naya's right boot came loose, tripped her, and sent her sprawling. She lay still, unhurt, and cast a glance back over her shoulder. Yes. The twins were still within the grass now, with the dog between them. The corners of Naya's lips turned upward with satisfaction because Demmi was not with them. The twins' older sister was too big and too bold for a proper female. No doubt she was off tracking the bear with the other hunters. Summer Moon, the headman's eldest daughter, showed none of these faults, and neither did Swan, the youngest of the threesome. Demmi was Manaravak's constant shadow, and Naya half hoped that the young woman would run afoul of the great bear and never return to the People.

Manaravak! His name formed upon Naya's tongue, as complex and beautiful as the man to whom it belonged—a man who would be her man someday, when and *if* she ever grew up! With the berry necklace held between her teeth, she sat up, tied her moccasin thongs, and ran on toward the lake. She could see Grek and the others and hear their laughter. How cool the water looked! Naya hurried on, wondering if the brothers were still following her.

She stopped, turned, and planted her little feet wide. Yielding to laughter, she put her hands upon her hips, thrust her minuscule breasts forward, and worked her hips as though movement might cool the sudden, unfamiliar, and deliciously pleasant warmth that was throbbing within her loins.

"Naya!" Pure anger heated old Grek's tone as he roared out at her.

Turning, she frowned. So her grandfather had seen her at last! It was about time! On either side of him, nine-year-old Tankh, and eight-year-old Chuk, the bear-bodied boys whom he had sired through his much younger woman, Iana, clutched their boy-sized spears and looked up at him, amazed by the strength and resonance of his roar.

"Naya, how long have you been alone? Where are your clothes and your gathering basket, Little Girl? Answer!"

Below the crest of the ridge, the hunters paused as their headman dropped to one knee and laid his hand upon the earth.

There it was again—the sign of the bear, and of something else. He watched, listened, and waited, but no matter how hard he tried to define the warning within his brain, it refused to reveal itself.

"Torka? What is it?"

He raised a hand to silence the hunter Simu. A moment passed. Whatever had raised the hackles on his neck was gone. And now a real and immediate danger threatened them all: the great, plundering bear. All day he and the others had

been searching for it. He rose and walked across the ridge
until he knelt again, and with his left hand upon the earth
and his right hand curled around the hafts of his spears, he
saw that bear sign was fresh. The newly scattered scree
revealed a massive imprint that lay bared to the sun, unmarred
by the crossing of insect tracks or by the settling of dust.
Beneath that massive print lay another—a much smaller,
human, imprint that turned him cold with dread.

At his back, his daughter Demmi stood beside Simu and
his sons, Dak and young Nantu. Silent and motionless in the
wind, the foursome awaited his word.

It came: "Here the great one slipped, fought for footing,
and fell. She slid and then rose again, followed by her cubs,
into the country of much grass."

"But that is where Grek has led the women and children!" Nantu's exclamation was as full of fear as it was loud.

"Silence!" Simu's reprimand withered his eleven-year-
old son.

"I'm sorry," the boy said. "I did not mean to speak."

Simu, not a man well-known for patience, gave his younger son a hard shove to the shoulder. "Do you think that the
headman of the People needs a boy to remind him of the
whereabouts of the women and children of his band?"

Demmi came forward to kneel beside Torka. "Is there
sign of Manaravak?" Her voice was tight with stress.

Torka looked into Demmi's worry-shaded dark eyes. He
saw much of his beloved woman, Lonit, in the face of his
daughter: the wide brow; the narrow, high-bridged nose; the
round, deeply lidded eyes that were so like those of an
antelope. These features Lonit had shared with all three of
her girls, as well as with Umak, the firstborn of her twins. Of
Torka's children, only Manaravak and Sayanah, seven winters
old and the son last born to Lonit, resembled the headman.
Their fourth daughter had lived just long enough to be named,
but Torka had looked upon her face and known that if the
forces of Creation allowed her to be born into the world
again, she would carry the look of her mother. A cold, fleeting mist of mourning chilled him.

Demmi leaned closer and put a strong, sun-browned
hand over his own. "Father, is there sign of Manaravak?"

The mists within Torka's mind cleared. He nodded but
could barely find the heart to speak as he looked into her
distraught face. Demmi, even more than Lonit, had taught

Manaravak to speak, live, and think as a human being when
he had first returned to his people from the wild. From the
moment that she had set eyes upon her long-lost younger
brother, the girl had been fiercely protective and possessive
of his affection. It was not unusual for them to know each
other's thoughts, as though their ability to communicate transcended the bonds of flesh, as though their blood was one
blood, and their spirits, one spirit.

"Father, please, have you found any sign that he has
come this way? One moment he was behind me; the next he
was gone. It is not like Manaravak to leave my side without—"

"*Your* side?" Dak's query was pincer sharp. "He left us
all, woman! Forgive me, Torka, but if we had needed
Manaravak, where would he have been, eh? And you, Demmi,
what is the matter with you? Soon Manaravak will take a
woman of his own! It is about time that you stopped mothering him."

She glared at Dak coldly. "I am of the People. Manaravak
is my brother. Ours is a bond of blood and heart and spirit.
You . . . what are you to me? I sit at your fire only because
this is a small band that needs children to assure its future,
and it seems that a woman cannot make them by herself!"

"Demmi!" Torka sent her shrinking back like a scolded
child. "Enough! This is no time for you and Dak to set to
your endless bickering." Beneath his headband of lion skin,
Torka's brow furrowed as he appraised the young hunter.
Dak was as solidly put together as a well-made sledge and,
like Simu, his father, every bit as useful to the band. He was
an exemplary hunter and had proved to be a caring father to
Kharn, the little son Demmi had born to him three long
autumns before.

But although Dak was strong of arm and fleet of foot,
steady of hand and disposition, at twenty he was two summers younger than Demmi and only a single summer older
than the twins. Unfortunately, as far as Torka was concerned,
Simu's elder son had yet to exhibit any imagination and was
overly possessive and resentful of his woman's affection and
concern for her brother.

"Come, Dak," Torka invited. "Kneel beside me and
Demmi. Use your eyes *and* your head, man. Do you see it?
The track of the man is overlaid by the imprint of the bear.
Your woman has just cause for concern on Manaravak's behalf."

Dak glowered down at the ground, leaned low, then nodded solemnly. "The bear *follows* Manaravak!"

"Yes," confirmed Torka. "And Manaravak follows Umak, who follows Grek, the women, and children."

"And now we will follow them all!" blurted Nantu.

"Nantu is right," said Torka, rising and loping forward into the wind without looking back. "Come. Hurry! We have no time to lose!"

3

Naya hit the lake at a run, sloshing into the reeds, laughing as she dove past Iana, Lonit, and Eneela. Larani and Swan called out her name, but she ignored them. She bottomed out in less than two feet of water and came up spitting mud to sit waist-deep in the reeds with her legs stretched before her. She splashed handfuls of water happily into her face.

It was a moment before she realized that everyone— including the dogs—was staring at her.

"What's the matter?" she asked. "Have you never seen a girl sitting in a lake before?"

"Not with her moccasins on!" Iana said angrily. "Where have you *been*, girl? And where are your clothes and your basket?"

Naya ignored her grandfather's woman. The light-headed bliss that she had experienced earlier was with her again. She looked at her feet, protruding from the water, and was surprised to find that Iana was right. She *was* still wearing her moccasins! She wiggled her toes. They looked silly to her.

Squirrel Killer came bounding across the shallows, leading the dog pack to pounce upon her. Pummeled by paws and tongues, Naya hooted in delighted protest and wrapped her arms tightly around Squirrel Killer's sodden neck lest he knock her flat. The other dogs closed ranks, and one of the pups, tail up and throat full of growls, nipped at the tip of one of Naya's moccasins.

"Get away!" Summer Moon shouted at the dogs, kicking

water toward the animals while little Kharn, her sister Demmi's son, rode high upon her bare hip. The three-year-old boy hefted a pudgy arm to point an equally pudgy finger at Naya. "N'ya!" he gleefully shouted. "N'ya funny!"

Everyone except Iana seemed to agree. "Perhaps if Naya had sewn her own moccasins, she would not find her carelessness so amusing. It took this woman many days to prepare the hides and stitch them into boots. It is not enough for Naya to slosh around in the water and mud while wearing them. Now she feeds them to the dogs."

"They are not my only pair," Naya pointed out from somewhere within the mass of licking, yapping dogs.

"Yes," snapped Iana. "And I have made them all!"

Iana was the eldest woman in the band, with over forty summers of life. She was still a handsome woman. Men had fought and bartered for her in her youth, and more than one of these had loved her. Old Grek still did, despite her everwidening midriff and the many long, thick-shafted strands of gray in her hair. Seven infants had drawn the milk of life from Iana's well-worn breasts. Three of these, all by Grek, still lived. Her two boys—Tankh and Chuk, at nine and eight, were so close in age, appearance, and disposition that they might have sprung from her womb at the same time. Her six-year-old Yona, a strong little girl, was neither too pretty nor too plain but somewhere pleasantly in between. She seemed oblivious to Grek's preferential treatment of Naya, the granddaughter who shared the fire circle of his little family as though she had been born to rule over it.

If Naya had only looked more like the handsome but forbidding shaman Karana, her dead father, Grek might have raised her differently. But she looked like her mother, Mahnie, and thus reminded Grek of the only child that he had ever had with Wallah, his first woman and first love. To Grek, the spirit of his beloved dead wife lived on in Naya, and so he favored and indulged the girl, pampered her as though she could do no wrong.

Iana found herself nodding against the weight of troubling memories. The girl was not perfect. Huggable, sometimes kind, and occasionally solicitous of others, she was more often willful, selfish, and impetuous. Iana worried that one of these days, Naya would unthinkingly bring serious trouble to herself or to the band.

Grek's woman could find nothing amusing in Naya's

behavior, nor could she feel anything but annoyance with the others for encouraging her recalcitrant silliness. Even Lonit, woman of the headman, was smiling at Naya's humorous predicament with the dogs.

Lonit rose from the water—tall and lean and a pleasure to the eyes even though she was the mother of six and well over thirty summers in age. "Ho, dogs! Ho and back!" she cried, unwinding her bola from her brow.

"Out of the way!" cried Honee, Umak's woman, reaching protectively for her children. A pair of panicked pups went racing between Honee's flesh-pebbled legs, knocking her off balance and sending her backward to land in a spread-eagled splat. Water whooshed up as Honee went down; the sound was explosive. For a moment the fat woman sat stunned.

Making no attempt to stifle their laughter at Honee's expense, sag-breasted Eneela, and Larani, her bounteously bosomed young daughter, sloshed to her rescue and drew her limp and sputtering from the water as the children continued to shout and splash at the fleeing dogs.

"Do you see what your spoiling has accomplished!" cried Iana at Grek. She glared at her man.

The women and children were startled into silence by her disrespectful outburst.

Iana clearly did not care. "Has there ever been a more thoughtless girl? Lagging behind like that, and then running after us! Who knows what predators might have followed her?"

"Wolves followed me," Naya said, a mischievous twinkle in her eyes. Her pointed little chin jabbed skyward defiantly. "Yes, wolves. Two of them—big, young, and bold. And a dog. I saw them clearly in the grass." The girl looked away from her grandfather and spoke to the dog—or was it to the old man? "What sort of woman watcher are you? You must be more alert, or the People will think that you are going blind and deaf with age, and of what use to the band is an old, deaf, sightless dog?"

"Naya!" Lonit's tone was an unmistakable rebuke.

Naya seemed genuinely puzzled by it.

"Wolves, you say?" Grek looked worried and vaguely disoriented. His great head was cocked, and the long, graying strands of his time-brittled hair whipped around the crags and promontories of a face that was as grooved and rough-ened by time as the frontal lobes of a glacier.

Somewhere far off within the deep grass to the east of the lake, one of the dogs yipped once. In that single cry had been surprise and fright, terror and pain.

Everyone in the lake tensed as Squirrel Killer rose to all fours and, without bothering to shake himself, stood beside Naya with his tail tucked. He growled low as the wind turned and blew briefly from the east—and in that moment, the smell of blood caused them all to know that death was near.

"Did you hear it?" Umak's voice was the merest exhalation of a whisper as he stared through the grass toward the lake.

"I heard," Manaravak affirmed darkly. He would have risen, but his brother's hand stayed his movement as surely as Umak's other hand kept Companion from racing off into the grassland.

"Wait," whispered Umak to both dog and brother. "The cry of the pup placed it well to the east and well behind us."

"Yes. Little dog runs into big bear."

"How can you be certain?"

"It is bear, Umak. The dying dog spoke its name. You should know these things, Shaman. It may be the bear that the others seek."

"You cannot be sure of that."

"No." A dark brow rose toward Manaravak's hairline. "For that knowledge I must be closer . . . must see better." Again he started to rise.

Again Umak stayed his movement. "Not yet. If old Grek sees us—"

"He will be assured that he does not have to stand alone against an attacking bear."

"From the sound of it, the bear—if it is a bear—has killed the pup. It might not move toward the lake. Perhaps even now it eats and is content."

"But perhaps not. Listen now, Shaman: Deep in the grass, the other dogs are circling wide, seeking that which made one of their pack cry out. The bear will have smelled them by now. Only a stupid beast would not abandon what may be left of its little feast in order to avoid the dogs."

"Stay low, Manaravak. All we need do is get a little closer to the lake, within better spear range just in case whatever is there should come forward, and if Grek cannot drive it off, we can—"

"Kill it." A smile moved upon Manaravak's mouth.

"Maybe yes . . . maybe no. Have you not heard our father say that to kill the great one that walks on three paws will take the combined effort of all the hunters of the band?"

"Is Umak afraid?"

The question stung. "Is Manaravak *not* afraid?"

"Fear can be sweet. Fear can heat the blood and make the hearing sharp and brighten and extend the sight."

"When you have a woman and two little ones of your own, Brother . . . when you know that your spear arm may well be all that stands between them and starvation in the depth of the winter dark, then you and I will talk about the meaning of fear."

Manaravak looked hurt. "All the women and children of the band are my women, my children, my people."

"It is not the same."

Manaravak's expression revealed that he did not understand. He had taken no woman of his own.

It was, Umak conceded, to Manaravak's credit that he had offered to wait until Naya, chosen for him by consensus of the council of elders, came to her time of blood; in the meantime, he made it clear that he was used to sleeping alone and, because he preferred his meat raw, had no need of a woman to tend his cooking fire. When need of a man's release came upon Manaravak, in the way of the band since time beyond beginning, an older woman would be sent to ease him.

The wind turned, as did Umak's thoughts. For a moment the air was unnaturally still, then the wind gusted hard from the north. Beside Umak, Companion trembled against his restraining hand.

Manaravak raised his head to scent the wind in the manner of a wolf. "Listen. The dogs come closer now. The bear hears them. It walks on three paws, and the little bears that follow are still hungry." Manaravak's handsome face expanded into a smile that made him look purely carnivorous. "We go now! We show the dog eaters what it means to come up against the sons of Torka!"

"No, Manaravak!" Umak was emphatic as his hand pushed his brother's forearm down and held it fast to the earth. "It would kill Grek to know that he is no longer trusted. We will move closer but not show ourselves unless the bear moves toward the lake. The women and children are safe for now."

"And Naya, too."

"Yes, and Naya." Umak was suddenly dry-mouthed and breathless. Had the wind turned cold? No. It was only his heart and its desperate desire for Naya.

Naya had ducked under the water lest she burst out laughing at the look on her grandfather's face. Her hands rose to tent her mouth and nose, and laughter bubbled through her fingers, tickling her palms and her mood until she was choking and gasping. She rose to her feet, surprised to find that Squirrel Killer had run off and that she was no longer the object of everyone's attention.

Why were they all so suddenly serious? The boys had taken up the short stabbing spears that they had carried out from camp. They stood boldly, yet she could see the unnatural pallor of their faces. The little girls clustered around Summer Moon, Honee, and Eneela. Lonit, clutching her bola, sloshed out of the water and clambered onto the embankment, where she reached for her wolverine bag.

"What are you doing?" Grek demanded.

The headman's woman did not look up. She emptied the bag's stones and shells into her palm and rapidly began to arm her bola. "You hold your spears ready. I will do the same with my bola."

Wide-eyed, Naya looked at Lonit. She was ready to stand against an attack, but from what? She started to ask, but Iana hushed her with a hiss. Naya frowned, annoyed with Iana. The woman had been far too critical of her this day. The girl was about to speak out anyway, to inform everyone that two armed spearmen hid within the grass ready to stand with Grek to their defense. But Lonit raised a warning hand and fixed Naya with narrowed black eyes that were so hot and sharp that the girl actually felt burned by them.

"But—"

"Silence, Naya!"

"For once do as you are told, Naya!"

The echoing admonitions came from an unexpected source—from Swan and Larani, her best friends!

Naya stared at them with surprise and hurt. But as she looked at them, standing together, stark-naked and dripping wet, she swallowed hard against a bitter truth: Swan and Larani were on the brink of womanhood while she herself remained a child. Her light, dizzying euphoria was gone. Her hand moved to what was left of her necklace, but she was disappointed to discover that her submersion had rendered it a thong without berries.

The wind was turning all around now, and again in the wind was the smell of blood. Naya's eyes widened, and she felt sick with understanding.

Iana was staring at her. "Yes," she grated. "Something out there has killed the pup and may now well be stalking us. The other dogs have taken off after it. Whatever the predator is, your scent has drawn it here. It has followed you, and whatever happens next will be your fault!"

4

Torka led Simu, Dak, Nantu, and Demmi down from the hills.

"Umak watches the woman watcher," Simu reminded, attempting to ease the strained look from Torka's face as he jogged beside him. "If Manaravak has joined him, what bear would not turn away at the sight of those two standing against it, eh? Perhaps we worry too much. The bear kind does not often come against the People when it can avoid it."

"True, but this sow has been clever enough to elude our snares and raid our cache pits. I have the feeling that this bear is a grave danger to us all."

The hunters went on and on. At last they came to the place where the tracks of man and bear crossed those of the women and children.

"The bear *is* following," said Simu, reading the prints.

Torka nodded his agreement.

"They seem to be headed for the lake," said Dak.

Again Torka nodded. The lake of which Dak spoke lay beyond a rise.

"Old Grek has led them far from the encampment," said Simu, his face a mask of ill-concealed worry.

"Too far," Dak's voice snapped with resentment. "Grek takes too much upon himself these days, and now because of Torka's compassion he risks the women and children."

Torka's head went high as he met the younger man's challenge calmly and without anger. "I have lived long enough to know that nothing in this life is completely predictable, Dak—not men, not beasts, not wind, not weather, not even the ways of the forces of Creation themselves. Now let's go."

Torka moved on without looking back. Although the others followed without hesitation, terrible uncertainty pummeled his gut. Was Dak right? Had his compassion for Grek clouded his judgment?

No! Umak was strong, bold, and wise for his years. If Grek proved unable to stand against predators, Umak would know what to do. And Torka was also certain that Manaravak had joined his brother. Manaravak was as swift and as strong as a running lion. He used a spear with a skill that nearly equaled Umak's, and even though he had never mastered the use of the spear thrower, his years among beasts had taught him things about hunting to which only animals were privy.

Bending his head into the wind, Torka willed himself to breathe more slowly. The pounding rhythm of his heart relaxed. His breath came as effortlessly as his ability to rationalize. His jaw tightened, compressing the long, straight rows of his strong, even teeth until he felt the smoothness of them—the slickness of the grinding edges that revealed forty-seven winters of wear.

Coldness touched him. Man, like any other animal, lived only as long as his teeth. And if Torka was growing old, what then should be said of Grek, who was so much older?

He led them forward with infinite caution; just as the deepest, most treacherous depths of a river are to be found in the fast-flowing channels that run farthest from shore, so it was with the broad, rolling terrain, where the grasses grew so thick and tall in shadowed troughs that they could easily conceal even the largest of carnivores. They walked with their spears at the ready, just in case something big and hungry should leap at them from out of the walls of grass through which they passed.

Naya's discarded dress and basket lay ahead. Torka gestured the others forward. No one spoke. It seemed that no one even breathed. They stared wide-eyed at these well-known things, as though they were looking at the remains of a corpse.

"There is no blood!" Demmi said hopefully and, after a

consenting nod from Torka, went forward to pick up the basket and dress. "Nothing is torn!" She smelled the dress. "The bear has been here—I can smell its spittle. It is feverish, this bear, and where its flesh has touched the garment there is a stink of a wound gone bad. But from the tracks, Naya was long gone by then, and running from the look of them. But it would seem that the twins were following her more closely than was the bear."

A sigh of relief was exhaled from every mouth, and Torka nodded in approval of his daughter's skill; he had taught her well, and although in years past there had been criticism of his willingness to instruct a female in the skills of the hunt, he had no regrets. His woman and daughters could track and take game. In times of need, they were an asset to their men.

The wind resumed its hard thrust from the west. Torka stood against it in his garments of lion and wolfskins. Once again his mouth went so dry that the back of his throat and nostrils felt singed by an ill-made fire. He wished that the wind would hold steady long enough to allow him to grasp its warning.

Torka shook his head as impatience swept through him. A man could scent the wind and know what it was about or he could not! Never had he doubted his abilities as a tracker. He hissed in self-deprecation, telling himself that this was no time to doubt himself. The wind would speak to him in its own good time.

5

Surrounded by leaping, snarling, harrying dogs, the great bear rose to her hind legs while her cubs cowered close to her flanks, seeking protection. It did them no good. The dogs were on them now, charging in to bite and tear and then back off, only to charge in again, careless of their safety in the frenzy of their attack.

Towering eleven feet tall above the grasses, the great bear extended her forelimbs as she shook her head and lifted her slobbering lips to show her massive teeth to the dogs.

The taste of the flesh and bone and blood of one of their kind still lingered in her mouth, and remnants of the animal lay beneath her feet. Enraged by the bawling of her confused and terrified cubs, she used her one good forepaw to swipe down and out.

All the power of her back and shoulder was in that swing. She felt her claws rake flesh. Two dogs that each weighed as much as a woman were lifted and spun away as though they were no more than blackflies. Blood and guts were in the air.

The bear threw back her head and shook it as she roared at the yapping dogs, which backed off and circled wide. Only one of her tormentors ran off in bloodied flight, tripping over its own intestines, its once-gray body red now and laid open all along its right side. The other dogs stayed.

A big, grizzle-coated male kept them circling, feinting in and then back, and snarling. The bear dropped to all fours and roared in sudden rage as pain flared within her ruined paw. She charged away.

The dogs broke and scattered, staying maddeningly just out of range as they circled back upon her. She wheeled and charged again. The dogs broke and scattered again and, working in a pack, harried her, provoked her into blind, raging fury. Two more dogs died in a spray of blood and hair. Her cubs were gone. She could hear them tearing off through the grass. She stood again—a living mountain of flesh and hide and power that towered over the dogs, which circled her and refused to break off their attack, no matter how she menaced them.

Deep within her brain, bear logic was working to confuse her. These dogs were not behaving like dogs at all! Why had they not taken off after her vulnerable cubs? Why did they stay even after she had killed several of them?

"Hold! Easy now!"

Umak's commands went unheeded as every hair upon the spinal ridge of Companion's back went straight up. The hunter tried to soothe the dog and might have succeeded if Squirrel Killer's yelp of anguish had not rent the air. Umak felt Companion stiffen within the fold of his arm. He tried to hold the dog, but Companion was close in size to a wolf and was just as strong. The dog's head snapped back, and his teeth threatened. Umak released his grip. Companion was off through the grasses in defense of his own kind at a snarling, slathering bound.

Umak did not mean to leap to his feet; he and Manaravak were still between the bear and the lake, in a good position to drive the bear off if the dogs did not do so first. He could hear his mother and Grek calling for the dogs to return to the lake, but it was in their blood to stay, to place themselves between danger and the People. Umak's need to stop Companion from rushing to its death was a purely reflexive action. The pup had been with him since its birth. So now Umak was on his feet, up and running, brandishing his spears. And Grek had seen him.

Manaravak rose, and howling and yapping like the most aggressive of the dogs, he raced toward the fray to save the life of his brother.

Naya screamed. "Somebody stop the bear! It is killing the dogs!"

Little Girl's cry, more than the sight of the twins bounding toward the bear, visibly shamed old Grek.

Honee, beside Naya in the shallows, wheeled and knocked the girl down. "Dogs! Is that all that concerns you? Manaravak and my Umak are in danger, and you scream about the dogs?"

"Manaravak . . ."

It was not Naya who moaned his name; it was Larani, daughter of Simu and Eneela. She exhaled it with such longing and fear for him that Lonit, amazed, turned to stare at the girl.

Larani's fine, curvaceous young body glistened in the sun as one graceful hand rested over her heart and the other pressed her lips as though to keep herself from making another sound.

She cares deeply for him, thought Lonit. *And he is for Naya . . . who is more concerned for the dogs!*

Anger at Little Girl pricked Lonit's heart, but she knew full well that this was no time for such thoughts. The headman's woman turned back toward the open steppe. If Manaravak was hot on Umak's heels, it was because Umak was desperately attempting to catch up with Companion. The dog was more than halfway to the bear, however, and the distance between him and the twins was widening. Nevertheless, Umak kept after the dog, shouting its name.

Lonit gasped with relief as Manaravak tackled Umak and pulled him down by his ankles. After a moment of ferocious wrestling, Umak was up and off again. Lonit was aghast. Manaravak's advantage of height and weight had always rendered Umak the loser.

But now, as she watched, Manaravak sat stunned; then he was on his feet and following Umak at a run. But Lonit had never seen Umak run faster—his love for the dog drove him.

Her heart seemed to be beating in her throat. *Where is Torka?* she wondered. *Where are Simu and Dak and my brave Demmi?*

A terrible, sinking feeling of helplessness tightened in her belly. Her own spears lay back in camp. Although the women had brought their bolas, none had any real weapons with them. If the bear broke from the grasses and came toward the lake, they were all in danger. Anger overwhelmed her fear. Blame for this situation belonged with one small, thoughtless girl who had deliberately lagged behind her people.

Arming her bola, and commanding those who had bolas of their own to do the same, Lonit drew in a deep, steadying breath. The twins were running wide of one another now, hooting and shouting in raging bravado, shaking their spears as they circled the bear, signaling and yelling out their strategy in a plan to bluff the bear into fear of them as they tried to drive it away . . . or make a fatal wounding.

Lonit's chest ached with a mother's fear and pride.

"Does my mother believe that my brothers will be able to do what the dogs have not?"

Swan had come to stand tremulously beside Lonit, with her own bola armed and ready.

"We must all ask the forces of Creation to grant them that gift!" replied Lonit, wanting to sound strong and unwavering, but her voice had cracked. She stood a little taller. For the sake of all, especially for the little ones, she must set a brave example.

Lonit realized that the wind was blowing steadily out of the north, and it was no longer sweet with the scent of grass. It seemed warmer and acrid with a subtle, dusky smell that made her think of cooking stones and fire pits and roasted meat.

A terrible sound suddenly issued from Grek. She had all but forgotten he was there.

"Stop!" Beneath his shaggy robe, the old man's massive shoulders trembled as a tortured growl of frustration came out of him. "You will all stay here in this safe place! Grek is woman watcher! Grek will tell the others what to do!"

Without another word, he burst forward with a whoop and a shriek of such savage determination that little Kharn, still astride the sleek hip of Summer Moon, burst into tears.

Grek did not look back. Brandishing his spears and shouting at the top of his lungs, he warned the great bear to run away before it was too late.

Lonit found herself instinctively lunging forward, grabbing at his furred, shaggy arm and half dragging him to stop. "Wait! If my sons fail to drive the bear away, we will need you here to protect us, Grek!" She stopped, brought up short by the look on the old man's face.

"Is that right?" he asked bitterly. "Bah! Do you think this man is stupid? Umak and Manaravak are the wolves that my Naya saw! You and your man and all of the others think that old Grek is not wolf enough to be woman watcher!"

Lonit was struck to her heart by the anguish that she saw in his eyes. "No . . ." She hesitated. It was not in her nature to lie. "You do not understand, Grek. You must—"

"Must *what*? Ah, yes, Grek understands. And because he understands, Grek must show you what this old man can do! This man *is* still a man!"

"Grek! Please!" Iana, stumbling across the shallows, reached out toward her man. "Think of Naya and the children!" She stopped, silenced by the withering look that he gave her.

"Have I ever done anything but think of Naya and my children and my band? And of you, Iana. *Yes*. It is a man's pride to think of his women and children. And so I tell you to stand back! Grek will not be shamed—not by you, not by the woman of Torka, not by the *sons* of Torka. And most assuredly not by himself!"

Old Grek ran out across the golden land. Umak and Manaravak stopped and stared in amazement as the old man waved them away and told them that the kill was his.

Meanwhile, Lonit put the children at her back and gathered the women and older girls into a protective half circle around them. The headman's woman saw to it that each woman armed her bola and was ready to sling a hail of stones at the great bear if all else failed.

At that very moment Torka and the others appeared on the crest of the rise—too far away to do anything but stand and stare as Grek stood to his full height and raised his arms wide.

Only the wind moved, beating at the old man's back, as the bear stood and cocked its head and tried to decide what manner of mad beast had dared to come before it.

In that moment Grek charged the bear. With his head lowered and his spears extended outward from his armpits, his broad limbs pounded through the grasses. His voice was raised in a ululating bellow that seemed to have the strength of a rolling thunderbolt.

With the old man roaring directly toward it, the bear stood taller and made ready to swipe downward with its one good forepaw. Suddenly, spears flew from the hands of Umak and Manaravak. The bear whirled around just as two spears glanced off the fur and hide of its shoulder. The beast's movement allowed Grek to get in close enough to place what might well have been a killing blow. But the bear suddenly dropped to all fours and charged after the two young hunters with Grek's two spears protruding from her rump.

Manaravak and Umak ran deep into the cover of the grass, with the smell of death hot in their nostrils. A quick look over their shoulder showed it was the end of one of them. They both knew it. There was no time for words. Without breaking stride, they touched hands briefly, then broke off in different directions, each hoping to draw the great bear away from the other.

Umak pounded away, the grasses lashing his face. Suddenly he fell, tripped by his own terror. He sprawled flat on his belly, splayed wide like a skin stretched by the women for fleshing.

He could hear the bear crashing after him, with the dogs barking and slavering and growling after it.

"Father Above, Mother Below, make it a quick ending!" His prayer to the forces of Creation was a half-choked sob.

Soon he would be torn apart, gutted, chewed. The image was more than he could stand. Somewhere deep within him, terror burst wide open and bled into a red, blinding rage.

"No! Not that easily!" He gnashed the words as he

realized that he still had one of his spears. With it gripped in his right fist, he rolled violently into a crouch and faced his death head-on.

It came. It passed. The bear literally ran over him and kept on going, the head of Umak's spear broken off in its shoulder and the dogs still in hot pursuit.

Stunned and battered, the young hunter found himself flat on his back with the air knocked out of him and more bruises than he wished to think about. But he was alive. *Alive!* He stared up at the sky and laughed aloud. "Thank you!" he said to Father Above, Mother Below, and to all of the forces of Creation that had allowed him this moment.

He closed his eyes. Life was sweet. Yes! Moments passed. He heard his mother and Honee calling his name. He would answer in a moment. Now he was too weak with relief. It was good to lie still and feel the wind flowing over him as cool shadows drifted across the face of the sun.

He opened his eyes, frowning. Strange: The wind actually felt hot. He noted that the blue skin of Father Above was gray and that the yellow eye of the sun was obscured by high clouds that smelled of smoke.

Once again terror burst to life within him. He heard his father's voice calling from the rise and speaking the one word that no man wished to hear when he was far out upon the dry summer grasslands and a great distance from the encampment.

"Fire!"

PART II

DAUGHTER OF THE SKY

1

It was Father Above who made the fire, in anger, with the stinging tip of his silver spear of lightning. As Naya sat alone on the embankment apart from the others who were gathered on the opposite shore, she knew in her heart that Father Above had set the fire because he was angry with her. It was all her fault—the coming of the great bear, the dead and wounded dogs, and now the distant but ever-advancing wildfire! If only she had not fallen behind the others! And it had been a very bad thing for her to have wished death to Demmi, the headman's daughter. Yet now, she almost wished it again as she looked up and saw Demmi sloshing across the lake toward her.

Only a few moments before, Torka had led Demmi, Dak, Simu, and Nantu to join the others at the lake. It had been a somber reunion. Manaravak and Umak had met them halfway across the plain, and somewhere on their way to the lakeshore they had taken the time to search out and, with their spears, put a merciful end to the mortally wounded dogs. The other dogs had kept on in pursuit of the great bear. Maybe they would return to the People. Maybe they would not.

Stern-eyed and reproving, Demmi stopped before her. "I found your dress and your basket. Here, take them."

Naya stared up at the second daughter of Torka. Demmi towered over her, making her feel small. The repudiation in the woman's eyes and in her deep, husky voice gave Naya a headache. She looked for sympathy on Demmi's face but could find none.

As she looked past the headman's daughter she saw that Manaravak was coming toward them. With Umak at his side, Manaravak was smiling broadly at her . . . or was he smiling at Demmi?

"Manaravak . . ." she whispered.

Demmi turned, saw her brothers, then turned back and shoved the basket and dress into Naya's hands. "Get dressed,

Little Girl! There is much to do before the fire reaches our encampment. I can't even begin to imagine what possessed old Grek to lead you all so far from home!"

"Grek is strong and brave!"

"Grek is old! His judgment has failed him."

Manaravak and Umak had come to stand in front of Naya. Both were eyeing her with wide grins. Embarrassed, she snatched her belongings from Demmi and held them against her body. And to think that she had found pleasure in having their eyes upon her! Now she felt unworthy of their appraisal. Oh, how she wished that her head would stop aching!

"Do not be so hard on Little Girl," Manaravak admonished Demmi. Like Umak, his eyes were on Naya, and his expression was of unconcealed sexual speculation.

Naya lowered her eyes. Manaravak's gaze caused her scalp to tingle and her face to flame bright red. She could not look at him or at Umak.

With a contemptuous sneer, Demmi stepped forward to put herself between Naya and her brothers. "Both of you, leave Little Girl to dress. Let us get back to the others."

"You go back to them. This man and Umak must go on now!" Manaravak informed her ominously.

"Where? Why?" Demmi asked.

Umak replied. "Our father has said that the encampment is too far for the women and children to go, especially by night. Manaravak and I must return to it before the fire destroys everything. We will carry what meat and hides we can across the shallows, if there is time—or bury them if there is not."

Demmi stood so straight that it seemed to Naya that her back would snap. "I will go, too!"

"No!" Umak told her emphatically. "Torka says that all the women and children must stay. It will be safe here."

"But if it catches up with you before you reach the camp and the river, you will have no shelter against it." Demmi's voice was as stiff as her back.

"It will not catch us," Umak assured her. "Soon the time of the long dark will come, Sister." His voice was as calming as his eyes. "If the snows come early and the winter supplies of the People have been eaten by the fire, how will we live without shelter? How will we find food to keep us from starving in a land that has been scoured by flames?"

"Umak is right," said Manaravak. "Fast runners are the sons of Torka! Together Umak and Manaravak will save the meat and winter stores and tent hides, and then together we will run back to sit with the People in this lake before the fire comes! You will see! It will be so!"

Demmi, furious, slapped Manaravak hard across his upper arm. "And to think I feared that the great bear had eaten you! Hmmph! It would have choked on your arrogance!"

Manaravak laughed out loud and pulled his sister into a tight embrace.

Demmi closed her eyes and buried her face in the long, deep hollow between his powerful neck and shoulder. "Oh, Manaravak, I was so frightened for you when you left the hunt without a word to me! Do not go off again without me. Promise. Please? Promise?"

Naya's frown deepened. Her headache was a mean, tight, throbbing knot. Demmi was different when she was with Manaravak. Her voice had grown so gentle, her manner so open and vulnerable and imploring. And Demmi was standing in Manaravak's embrace as though she were his woman and not his sister!

With a hard, perfunctory kiss to the top of his sister's head, Manaravak peeled Demmi's clinging arms from around his neck. "I am no longer a small, wild boy. I am a man now, all grown and strong. I will go where I want, when I want. I do not need a sister at my side worrying all the time. You have a child. You want to worry, you go watch over your little boy."

"Good. And well-spoken!"

Naya blinked, startled. She had been so absorbed in Manaravak that she had not noticed that Dak came from the far shore to join them. Kharn rode atop his brawny shoulders. The three-year-old boy giggled with pleasure as his father swung him down. Dak, stopping in front of Demmi, looked at his woman with open hostility as he thrust the child into her arms.

"This is called a *son*," Dak told his woman. "He is hungry for his mother's breast."

"Good! And well-spoken!" Demmi mimicked Dak. "You keep him, then!" She thrust the uncomprehending boy back into his father's hands. Then she stalked off to stand alone in the middle of the lake, hands on her hips, hair flying back, eyes slitted and glaring into the wind as she tried to cool her temper.

Dak cursed under his breath and drew his son closer as he asked the twins, "What bad spirit eats your sister's heart?" But before either brother could respond, he continued, "There's no talking to her these days. Why does she suddenly hate me? We were so happy once."

His lament was brought short by Torka's summons. Naya looked to the opposite shore. The headman's arms were up, and he was calling his people to gather around.

"We must go on now," Umak said to Dak.

Dak mumbled a begrudging acquiescence. "Yes, yes. You two go on. Save our belongings! There's a long, dark, cold, and hungry winter ahead! All the omens promise it: a summer without rain . . . bears raiding the cache pits . . . herds going lean . . . young girls unable to bleed as women . . . our great mammoth totem gone from the land . . . and one miserably small band alone in a world and no way back into the land from which we've come. Ah, what's the meaning of it all? Maybe it'd be best if the fire took us all!"

Umak's face expanded with rage as he took hold of Dak's arm and pulled him so close that their noses almost touched. "You want to recross the Forbidden Land? Do you remember nothing of the horrors that we have left behind? Go back, then! But go alone, Dak, because I would not let my sister or her son go with you. And go *now*, for if you stay among this people and I hear you risk the wrath of the forces of Creation by speaking such blasphemous words again, there will not be enough of you left to walk the wind forever . . . and your life spirit shall spend eternity trying to find itself amid the refuse of your bones!"

The words settled like a rockslide, leaving stony echoes to linger on the wind.

Umak and Dak faced one another eye to eye, like two stags braced together with antlers locked. In the increasingly ash-sullied wind, Kharn, squeezed between them, began to fuss and arch his back, but neither Umak nor Dak seemed aware of the hapless boy.

Naya was stunned by Umak's outburst. It was not like Umak and Dak to argue like this; as spear brothers, they were raised from earliest boyhood to hunt together as a team. They had made their first kills together and had endured the rituals that had made them men of the band together.

"Hey, hey, stop this now!" Manaravak tried to draw his brother back, but it was no use.

"Take back your words," Umak demanded.

Dak glared with a belligerence that showed no sign of weakening.

With a snort of anger and impatience, Umak suddenly gave Dak a shove that sent him reeling back. The two young men stood staring at one another. The tension was palpable until Kharn, wet faced and sobbing now, wrapped his arms about Dak's neck and cuddled close.

"Da . . ." the boy whimpered.

Dak closed his eyes. A deep breath went out of him. "I take back my words," he said. "You were right to be angry."

"You have no right to forgive him, Umak," Demmi called out from the center of the lake as a lifetime of love and affection allowed the men to clasp hands. "The forces of Creation will have to do that! Why not take the boy and go, if you feel that you must, Dak? I, for one, would find little to miss in the absence of either of you!"

"Demmi!" Lonit's voice rang out with shock and anger from the far shore. Close beside her, Dak's parents, Simu and Eneela, glared at Demmi with an animosity that was as hot as the distant grass fire while their daughter Larani shook her head sympathetically.

Naya looked toward the headman. For a moment Torka did not move. He stood very tall and straight, and for a moment the girl saw so much of Manaravak in him that she caught her breath at the pure power and beauty of him. His hair was as thick and black as a youth's, his belly as flat, his hips as lean, and his thighs as well muscled. Torka pointed at Demmi, scalding her with the heat of his dark eyes. "More and more you distress and shame me, Daughter. The People are *one*! No one mocks the unity that gives strength to the few and hope to the future! No one! Especially not a callous and thoughtless woman! But there is no time for this now! You and Dak and your boy will come with your people. Together we will prepare to stand against the coming night of fire while Umak and Manaravak run ahead of the wind to do what must be done. Go now, you two! Go swiftly and ask the spirits of the wind to grant you speed!"

They ran together, side by side, measuring their pace so that they could maintain it over the long distance that lay ahead. They did not speak. Yet Umak found himself wondering if Manaravak thought of Naya as he ran—deep, hungry thoughts of how it would be with them . . . someday . . . soon. He swallowed down his jealousy, acknowledging it for what it was and berating himself because he knew that he had no right to it. Besides, there were more important things to think about now.

At the base of the rise, bear and dog sign veered north. Umak and Manaravak stopped and exchanged meaningful glances. The bear was leading its cubs and the dogs *toward* the fire! Umak found it difficult not to tremble as he tensed against apprehension.

Companion! Where are you, my old friend? Let the bear go! She does not matter now!

Umak raised his voice in a long, summoning, doglike wail into the tide of the wind.

He and Manaravak waited, facing into the wind, squinting into the vicious, onrushing air current from out of the north. They could taste ash and smoke and smell evidence of distant heat and scorched stone and death—yes, the death of grass and shrubs and of burned hair and hide. . . .

Umak winced against his thoughts. "The dogs have the same instinct to survive as we," he said strongly, wishing that he believed it. "May the forces of Creation be with them now, for we cannot. We must go on. The lives of the People depend on us."

They went on again, uphill now, pausing briefly at the top of the rise to look around. Manaravak's eyes were unnaturally round and wide with the pure, instinct-driven terror of a wild animal that is on the brink of panic, for in the broad, lowland passes between the mountain ranges to the west and north, the fire was burning high and advancing along the entire curve of the horizon, forming an ominous smoking squall line as dark and tall as the clouds that stood over the peaks.

"So big this fire. All the north country burns!"

Umak was so preoccupied with the immensity of the fire that he took no heed of Manaravak's words or tone. He stared toward his people. He could see the women and children from here, tiny forms clustering along the shore. Torka was talking with the men and boys. The women and girls were gathering reeds. The children were scampering about as though they had not a care in the world. It suddenly occurred to

Umak that everyone that he loved was there: mother, father, children, sisters, brother, friends. . . .

"They will be safe in the lake," he said, almost to himself.

Manaravak's head swung in slow and somber incredulity. "Will they? It is such a small lake. Will the shallow waters keep the People safe from such a fire as *that*?"

No! The word exploded within Umak's mind and almost escaped unbidden from his lips. As Umak stared at the advancing conflagration, his eyes narrowed. He was not at all comfortable with his father's decision to stay at the lake. But who was he to say that a great headman such as Torka might be wrong? He drew in a deep, steadying breath. He was a loyal and loving son. "Of course they will be safe! Torka would not risk the lives of the People! The band is everything to him."

"But look at the clouds!" Manaravak pointed off. "Torka cannot see them from where he stands."

Umak felt suddenly sick and cursed himself as a fool. The clouds were growing, expanding, boiling, and climbing angrily into the sky.

He realized that they were the *same* clouds that he had seen earlier in the day. The fire must have been burning unseen behind the peaks for hours, adding fuel to the rainless, late-summer squalls that had been building high over the mountains since well before noon.

An upwelling of disgust made him scowl against the bitterness of self-revilement. In his pursuit of Naya across the grasslands, he had not thought to analyze the clouds with the alert, well-trained eyes of a hunter or a shaman . . . but of a female-bedazzled male, of no use to anyone.

There was death in those clouds. Umak felt it. He could taste it. He could smell it. He stared ahead without blinking, enduring a premonition that nearly struck him down as the Seeing Wind swept through him without mercy: The fire was too big; the lake was too shallow. He saw the waters boil. He saw his people surrounded by flame, suffocated in a rain of cinders as black smoke closed in upon them even as their flesh cooked and fell away from their bones like meat within the hide boiling bags of the women.

He heard his son, Jhon, and his little daughter, Li, cry out to him. He saw them melt . . . he heard them scream. . . .

He gasped. He would have fallen, knocked flat by the

devastating power of the vision, had Manaravak not caught his arm.

"What is it, Brother?"

For a moment he could not breathe. He dropped to his knees and hung his head and forced himself to inhale as the Seeing Wind fell away into quiet transparency.

"You must go on, Manaravak. You have far to go if we are to save those things that will mean life or death to the People this winter."

"I? What about you?"

"I will follow. With the People."

Manaravak frowned. "You will challenge our father's decision to remain at the lake?"

"I must challenge him. If I do not, he will die . . . and all our people with him."

◆━━━━━━◆

2

◆━━━━━━◆

Torka stood dead still in a darkness more ominous than any he had ever known. It was brought down upon the world by wind-driven clouds of smoke and fire, and in this unnatural night, as the children whimpered in fear and his people gathered close around him, Torka was afraid.

Have you erred in this? Should you have led the People away from this place? The sickness of despair was on him. His instincts were raging at him. *You must go, before it is too late! But what if it is already too late, if the wind intensifies and the fire catches up with us on open grassland?*

"My father!"

"Umak?" He was startled to see the elder of his twins coming through the smoky gloom. "Why have you come back? Where is your brother?"

"He goes on to the encampment. You and the others must go, Father. If you could see the fire and the smoke from the rise, you would know there is no safety for you here."

"If Torka has said that it is safe, it *is* safe!" proclaimed Grek, doubly bold now since his encounter with the bear.

"The fire has *changed*," Umak interrupted. "The fire has

grown. I speak as Shaman, with the voice of the Seeing Wind. We cannot stay in this place."

Torka knew now and unequivocally that the instinct that had been driving him to rethink his decision had been right, for as his eyes met Umak's he shared the Seeing Wind . . . and the vision of holocaust.

The headman's woman came forward under the rain of cinders that had begun to fall. "Before we go, we must all do one more thing!"

Lonit had already insisted that everyone work together to hastily assemble capes of sodden, mud-slicked reeds. Every man, woman, and child had donned a cape. Now, as Torka watched with knitted brow, Lonit began to gather handfuls of mud from the lake bottom, and as she told the others to do the same she started to slather a thick paste of brownish ooze over her head and face and hands.

"If the forces of Creation are willing," she explained, "this may protect us from the rain of fire until we reach the far river!"

No one argued; all saw the wisdom of her words.

How swiftly the long distance had passed when the day was young and there was no need to hurry. How slowly the expanse fell away now, when the day was done and darkness had fallen upon a world that had gone mad with wind and fire.

Under choking clouds of smoke that continued to rain ash and cinders upon them, both men and women took turns carrying the youngest children while the girls and boys raced on ahead, led by Nantu, who thought himself a man and said as much whenever the others fell behind.

There was a deep, maniacal, occasionally explosive roaring behind them now. It was the raging voice of Fire, Daughter of the Sky—or so the ancients called her. The band tried not to listen, for it was said that in order to live, fire must feed upon the skin and bones and children of the earth.

Naya wept for the dogs and for all the other dying animals as she ran, half stumbling, until Larani caught up with her and took hold of her arm.

"Hurry, Naya! This is no time for tears. Run with me now! You must be strong and brave, and you must not look back!"

"But I am not strong! I am not brave! I am—"

"The granddaughter of Grek! And the daughter of Karana, the greatest magic man of them all! He watches you now from the world beyond this world. Would you shame him? Would you shame us all? You keep insisting that you don't want to be Little Girl anymore. Well, now is your chance to prove it! Run, I say, run fast and far!"

This said, Larani lengthened her stride and left Naya behind to stumble on, crying harder than before. Larani inadvertently flushed a family of steppe antelope from cover directly ahead of her. They leaped upward out of the grass, wild-eyed with terror as they made high, frantic nick-nicking sounds of panic. Larani raced on with them as though she were a member of their herd. When they tried to turn and circle back, she waved her arms and drove them on.

"What is the matter with you?" cried the daughter of Simu and Eneela. "You must run forward unless you want the Daughter of the Sky to burn you alive!"

Gulping down her tears, Naya was shamed by the sight of her friend. If Manaravak could see the way Larani was behaving, he would never smile at Naya or want her to be his woman when, with only a word to the council, he might have Larani instead. Drawing in a breath of hot, smoke-tainted air, Naya began to run faster. Larani was right. She *must* go on! She must give the others no cause to find fault with her.

And so, willing strength and swiftness into her limbs and bravery into her heart, she ran. But despite her best effort, she *was* a little girl, and the years of pampering that had nurtured happiness in her heart had not nurtured endurance in her body. In a few minutes she was panting and weak-legged.

"Run!" she cried in frustration, urging herself onward.

Iana came up from behind with the long, steady stride of a woman half her years. Naya found it difficult to keep up with her, even though she soon began to suspect that Iana was holding back, being careful not to run ahead of Grek, who plodded heavily to her right with little Yona clinging to his back.

Naya told herself that his heavy breathing had nothing to do with his age. He was only plodding and wheezing to make her feel better, for her own step was flagging. It was growing harder to breathe—there was a terrible stench in her nostrils, of thick, foul-smelling steam. A horrifying understanding exploded within her: *The fire has reached the lake! The stench*

*is of the lake's shallow water turning to steam, and living
things are dying in it. Oh, what would have become of us had
Umak not returned from the rise to warn us away?*

She sobbed, horrified by her thoughts, and was almost
overcome when a cinder burned through the dried and cracking mud that caked her scalp and caused her to cry out again,
this time in pain and in terror. The fire was getting closer.

She pulled her steaming cape of reeds over her head and
ran on, gasping for breath.

"Hurry, girl! The others are well ahead of us now. We
will be at the encampment soon! We can rest later, when
we've reached the river's far shore!"

Naya was grateful for Iana's encouragement. She gritted
her teeth and resolved to run faster so that she and not
Larani would be the first into camp. She would make
Manaravak see that she was indeed a woman of strength and
courage.

"Ummph!" The sound that came out of Grek was that of
a big animal struggling for breath.

Naya turned her head, expecting him to fall, but he kept
on running, even though his face was contorted with strain
and his eyes were bulging. "Yes . . ." he huffed. "Got . . . to
. . . keep up . . . the pace . . . yes!"

They ran under rolling, choking black clouds until Grek
stumbled. Iana cried out in despair. But before Torka and the
others came back to stand around him, Grek was on his feet
again, shaking his head and steadying his breath and cursing
a nonexistent stone.

"Are you all right?"

Grek growled at Torka's question, and his brow settled
over the sunken bridge of his time-battered nose. "Of course
I am all right! Why would I not be all right? Have you never
tripped before? Ummph! Under such a sky, in such a foul
blackness and heat, I am surprised that not more of us have
fallen!"

Yona was sitting on the ground at his feet, her round,
mud-darkened face streaked with tears as she reached up
toward her mother. "Carry me!"

Grek prevented Iana from going to the girl. "You think I
cannot carry my girl? You think Grek is too old? You think
Grek will trip again?"

"Yona, go to your father," Iana commanded.

The child obeyed, blubbering as the old man lifted her with one big hand and hefted her onto his hip.

Grek arranged her spindly, mud-painted legs so that they gripped him firmly around his lower back and belly, under the protection of his reed cape. As the girl settled herself in the fold of his arm and curled her fingers into the long hairs of his bison-skin robe, he glared down at his sons. "What are you staring at? You want this man to carry you, too? Do you think that I could not!"

In unison Tankh and Chuk stepped back from their father.

"I am no baby to be carried!" Chuk's voice was tight with constrained resentment.

"And you, Tankh. Does your brother speak for you as well?"

Tankh glared up at Grek. "I have seen the coming and going of nine summers. I need no younger brother to speak for me, and no man needs to carry me anywhere!"

"Good," Grek approved. "But do not think that this man, who has placed two spears in the great bear's backside, could not carry you if there was need!" His gaze found Naya. "And you, Granddaughter? There is always room in Grek's arms for my poor, lost Mahnie's child. Come. Weariness is in your stance and in your eyes. Grek will carry both of his little girls!"

"No!" Naya stepped back. "I am almost a woman, my grandfather. I can run."

They went on, hurrying to make up for lost time, and although no one spoke the words, all of them were secretly glad that Grek had stumbled. In the time that he had taken to rise, steady himself, and regain his dignity, they had all been able to rest their muscles and try to catch their breath.

It was all but impossible. Breathing required a conscious effort, and even then it failed to sustain them. The air was filled with smoke and heat, and a terrifying, suffocating darkness was closing in around them. The children began to falter, and old Grek was soon wheezing like a dying bull.

Torka was growing increasingly worried. He had never witnessed a fire like this. The wind, gusting viciously, was at his back one moment, blowing hot and hard straight out of the north, then it dropped abruptly almost to nothing, only to rise again from all directions. Eddying, violent, swirling funnels of heat and ash and bits of torn grass and shrubs—and charred remains that he had no wish to identify—descended out of the clouds to come directly at the People, slapping and pulling at them as though invisible hands were trying to carry them away into the sky.

A woman's scream caused him to wheel around in time to see a funnel of superheated air descend directly over Honee. In disbelief, he saw it rip the cape of reeds from her hands. The heat-dried reeds exploded into flame as the wind tore the cape apart and sent its pieces flying away. Honee collapsed in shock and terror. Her boy, Jhon, and all the women gathered around to make certain that she was all right. Summer Moon and Swan worked with Eneela, Larani, and Naya to get Umak's woman to her feet again.

Honee was having a difficult time catching her breath. As she struggled to rise Umak came to help her. The woman bravely wiped the cinders from her smoking head and resolutely waved away the attentive ministrations of Lonit and the other women. Torka found himself touched by her valiant heart.

"No fuss! No fuss!" Her voice was a rasping croak as she clasped a hand to her throat and winced against pain; it was clear from her expression that it hurt her to breathe, let alone speak. "I am fine! Daughter of the Sky is welcome to my cape. Come now, everyone, we must go—" Realizing that the headman was watching her, she lowered her head in deference. "It *is* all right to go on?"

He nodded. "Yes, Daughter. It is *imperative* that we go on."

Honee's face split with an expansive smile. Torka suspected that she was blushing beneath the mud. Honee's color always rose when he called her Daughter. The fat woman urged Umak to hurry as she began to move forward as fast as her short, thick legs would take her. Torka saw Umak roll his eyes, then snap at her to stop nagging.

"Father?" It was Sayanah, his small, strong palm hot and sweaty as it curled around Torka's hand. "Where is the river, Father?"

"Ahead," the headman said, swinging the boy up onto his shoulders. Sayanah offered no protest.

"Will the great mammoth totem be there with Manaravak and the dogs, waiting to bring luck back to the People?" The boy's voice was drained of strength as he wrapped his arms around Torka's neck and leaned his face against his father's head.

"We will see!" said Lonit as she came to stand at her man's side with Swan and Summer Moon.

Torka took the lead again, gradually lengthening his stride into a lope.

"Soon we will reach the camp and the river," he said to the strained intake of Lonit's breath and the exhalations of relief from his daughters.

But on and on he ran. And now the fire was closing on them, roaring and screaming, hurling debris overhead until, suddenly, the grassland straight ahead exploded into a wall of flames, driving the People back in horror. Torka stopped dead. There was no hope of reaching the encampment now.

Swan dropped to her knees in despair. He pulled her to her feet by her hair. "The river!" he cried, his voice raging to be heard above the flames. "Turn south, and we *will* reach the river!"

And so, in the rain of fire, they turned south and ran until old Grek fell again, and Torka turned back to help him as he commanded the others to go ahead.

No one moved except Iana. She put Yona into Naya's quaking arms. "Take Yona. You and Chuk and Tankh run for the river! I will not leave my man."

Everyone hesitated until Torka's words flailed out at the girl and made her jump. "Go, Naya! And you, too, Iana! Grek and I will follow!"

Only Grek moved. He sat up, rasping for breath, and found enough of it to allow him to shake his head and urge Torka to leave him.

"You will have your wind again in a few moments, you old bison! In the meantime, do not tell Torka what to do!"

Simu shook his head and cast a fearful eye at the sky. "He is old, Torka! If you wait for him, you will die!"

Torka leveled a dangerous look at him. "Lead the others to the river, Simu. I *command* you to go! But I will leave no man of this band behind to burn!"

Simu's face had the look of a cornered wolf. His dark eyes were full of fire and an emotion that struck Torka to the heart. "What would the river gain us without you to lead, Torka? Here, together, you and I will help Grek to find his feet."

The old man shook his head, but neither Simu nor Torka

paid him heed. They hefted him by his elbows and, without another word, led the others on.

"When you two grow weary of his weight, Dak and I will ease it for you," Umak offered.

"I am no sucking child to be carried along by any of you young—"

"Prove it!" Torka challenged the old man. "You are big and bold, but by the forces of Creation, Grek, you are also *heavy*! So take pity on us and stop arguing!" Torka and Simu had not carried the old man more than fifty paces when, with a grunt and a snort, Grek was running on his own again.

But for how long? wondered Torka.

Daughter of the Sky was screaming at his back and raining fire upon his head, and Simu was running beside him, portending blackly:

"Find the river, old friend, find it soon. Or soon there will be no People left to get across it!"

3

It was the howling of beasts pounding close behind her that caused Naya to look back over her shoulder and stumble.

"Wanawut!" she shrieked as the forms went running by through the fiery gloom.

She lay stunned upon the earth. No one had heard her scream. It had been a while since fatigue had forced her to put Yona down. Iana had swept the girl up and carried her away. Once again Naya had fallen behind the others, and she was alone with the smoke, the fire, and the wanawut. Her heart stopped in terror, then began to beat again as the dark, crouching beasts ran ahead without even looking her way. They ran like massive, hairy, deformed men knuckling the earth with enormous hands, screeching and sounding to one another as they vanished into the wind-torn smoke as though they themselves had been made of nothing more than mists.

"Get up, Little Girl!"

The shaman lifted her to her feet with one strong hand.

"Umak!" Naya was shaking with fear. "D-did you s-see them?"

"I saw something," he acknowledged. "Beasts ran ahead of you, and several bears, I think. No matter. Escape, not hunger, drives the animals and the People this night. Come now, Little Girl, you must move faster!"

Naya sagged against him, nearly swooning with exhaustion. "I am so tired, Umak!" Her legs felt as though they were melting, yet his strong arm held her as he urged her on, following the band in the direction in which the beasts had run. "Oh, Umak, they say that wanawut feed upon the flesh of people. Will they cross the river?"

"Unless they wish to be cooked they will."

She started to cry. "I am so afraid."

His face gentled as his arm tightened around her and drew her close. "Don't cry. Umak will not leave you here to feed the flames!"

She buried her face in his chest. She could feel his heart beating, strong and hard and very fast. Then suddenly, she heard a deep sigh go out of him, and even though Jhon was on his back, he lifted her into his arms.

"Do not be afraid, Naya! I would never let you come to harm—never." His voice was hoarse with smoke and strained from his run, but it was as powerful and comforting as his arms as he carried her to safety as though she weighed no more than the smoke through which they ran.

Torka found the river at last! But the fire storm had forced them well south of the broad shallows below the encampment. He did not know this part of the river, and he did not like what he saw through the smoke-shrouded, fire-shot gloom: On its run to the south, the river had found a mate, and now a new river stood between Torka's band and the far shore—an immense body of water that ran fast and deep between high, clifflike embankments. Animals were fleeing out of the smoke and plunging forward over the cliffs, only to be swept off by the current.

He turned to face his bone-weary band and looked into their streaming eyes. "We cannot make a safe crossing here."

They went on, exhausted and afraid, with the river running on one side of them and the fire closing from behind. Torka saw no safe shallows where the band might cross the river—only wide, tumultuous, boulder-islanded deeps in which drowned and drowning animals rushed by on the current like pitiful, bobbing refuse. It seemed that the world was composed of two colors, black and red, a roaring, raging inferno that was reflected in the water and in the People's eyes when they looked at one another and tried not to think of death.

The wind was gaining strength, bonding with the thousand streaming channels of night wind that were flowing downward from the high peaks and out of the canyons and stream drainages.

And now, with a great, cracking roar, a huge body of fire leaped over them and exploded in midair to rain not ash or cinders but flame upon them. As Torka ducked away and waved his arms to ward off the falling fire, he saw his people doing the same, performing a terrible dance of terror, whirling and stomping their feet, casting away their burning capes of reed and slapping at the flames that seemed set upon consuming them.

Simu's voice was raised in anguish. "No! Come back! Wait!"

Torka squinted through the raging inferno to see the hunter pass his youngest child, Uni, to Eneela and, without looking back, race forward in pursuit of their daughter Larani.

The girl was running toward the river—running and screaming—and as Torka looked on in horror he saw that she was still wearing her reed cape even though it was blazing high upon her back. Simu was raging at her to fling off the garment.

Torka swung Sayanah down from his back and placed him at Lonit's side. The headman was running now, and Demmi appeared abreast of him. Umak had put down Grek's granddaughter and little Jhon to run beside them.

Torka lengthened his stride in pursuit of the running girl, threw back his head, and bellowed a roar that was a curse of frustration against the unspeakable unfairness of it all. There was something about Larani that had always pleased him and made his spirit smile—a certain easy self-assurance that, even as a toddler, had set her apart from others and made her Simu's pride and joy. Again he roared.

He was running so fast that he had left the others behind. He was closing on Larani. The sparks and bits and pieces of her cape were flying back at him, stinging his face. He could smell the stink of burning hair and knew that more than Larani's cape was afire.

Suddenly, as he reached out for her, a cyclonic eddy of searing wind descended from out of the blackness to lift the girl off her feet and into the clouds. The force of the blast knocked him flat, and as he lay sprawled and staring in incredulity he saw Larani hurled like a flaming brand into the river.

Under the roaring fallout of fire, it was Grek who went after her, shoving Simu and Dak aside to plunge into the rushing torrent as though he had no fear of it.

"No!" shrieked Iana. "Larani is lost! Let her go! You will drown, Grek!"

Torka's ears were ringing from the blast. He fought his way to his feet. Umak and Demmi, he saw, had also been felled by the tornadic wind. His heart sank as he saw his children lying motionless upon the earth. Then Umak cursed and leaped up, slapping at sparks that were burning his scalp and the backs of his hands. Honee was helping him; too aggressively, apparently, for he stopped slapping at himself and instead batted away his woman until she backed off and bumped into Dak, who was lifting a semiconscious Demmi.

"Torka." Lonit was beside him, touching him tentatively, as though she was not certain if he was truly still alive. Her face was twisted with remorse as she looked up at him. "Always and forever, Torka, we have been together, and we *will* be together, even now, at the end."

"End?"

Yes . . . the word swam in her eyes; along with sadness and regret and surrender that cut him to his soul.

"No!" His heart was pounding. "The forces of Creation have been with us this far! Why would they abandon us now? I will not believe that they have done so! I will not accept this!" He could not bring himself to speak the word *death*. His spirit seemed to be swelling within him, feeding upon a rush of blood drawn upward from some inner well of resolve that made him feel suddenly light-headed with the power of pure intent. He turned, stared back at the way they had come, and then ahead.

Lonit was right. Despite his protestations, in another moment it would all be over. The fire was all around them. The river lay ahead. The river—too deep to cross, too dangerous even to try. And yet in the fire there was certain death. Was there not in the danger of the river at least some small hope of survival? He doubted it.

He fixed his eyes upon the river, and as a visibly stunned Simu knelt upon the embankment wailing his lost daughter's name, Torka watched in horror as old man Grek was swept away and away and then, incredibly, found his footing.

Torka started. Was he imagining it? No! Armpit-deep in the onrushing current and fighting for every step, the old man was well out from shore, but he was not drowning or being carried away.

"Look!" Simu was pointing.

"Do you see that?" Umak's voice cracked like an adolescent boy's as he shouted in excitement.

They all saw it: Grek was on his feet and battling his way downriver to where Larani's body had been washed by the current and now lay lodged between several large boulders, which rose like a jagged-toothed island amid the torrent.

"He has reached my girl . . . my poor burned and drowned girl!" sobbed Eneela.

Even as the woman of Simu spoke, Torka saw Grek reach the boulders, then slip and disappear under the rushing waters.

Beside him, Lonit hung her head and whispered Grek's name softly, in an incantation of grief and loss.

But just when the headman was certain that Grek was lost, Torka caught his breath. The old man had surfaced on the other side of the boulders. He flailed his great arms, propelling himself toward the rocks. When he gained the boulders, he hung draped over the rocks, resting, catching his breath. Then, like a sodden bison levering himself out of a deep wallow, he struggled up, found solid footing once again, and clambered over the boulders to stand upright.

He raised a beckoning arm to them all. "Come!" Grek cried loudly and proudly. "The current will carry you, yes! It is shallow here—a good, safe place to wait until Daughter of the Sky is tired of eating up the dry land and its children! Use the bolas to tie yourselves together so no one will be swept away! The forces of Creation are smiling upon the people of Torka, yes!"

Torka's head went high. It would be a dangerous crossing, but in danger there was hope!

"Come!" Grek called again, gesticulating wildly. "For what do you wait?"

Torka's heart beat in his throat as he turned to stare back at the way they had come. There was one more favor to be asked of the forces of Creation before he led his people into the river.

"Father Above, Mother Below, be with my son Manaravak. If he still lives, he will need all of your magic to get him through this night alive."

Manaravak had crossed and recrossed the river. Still his people had not come.

Sometime during the first crossing, the dogs had joined him—a bedraggled pack of six led by Companion, Squirrel Killer, and the little gray bitch that the people called Snow Eater.

Manaravak had known from their stance and the confused, empty look in their eyes that the animals were all that was left of their pack. They were droop tailed and exhausted, but except for Squirrel Killer's missing left ear and Companion's bloodied snout, they were all in one piece.

Manaravak had been grateful when they came to his side and helped him move the camp of the People, yielding to the weight of subsequent packs and to the drag of a fully loaded sledge. Man and dogs had worked together until all felt the need for rest. By then it was night. They sat in the rising wind on the far shore of the river amid the things they had labored to save. In troubled silence they had listened to the raging roar of the fire and watched it advance. Deep within both man and dogs, the beast of panic stirred.

"The People will come," Manaravak had said.

Companion put up his battered snout and loosed a howl. Knowing that the dog was calling to Umak, Manaravak had joined in. Man and dog howled together, then waited, listening for an answer. There had been none.

"Come," he said, rising and heading for the shallows again. "There is still more to bring across the water. One more crossing is all I ask. By the time we have returned to this shore, the People will be here."

The dogs did not agree.

Restless, Manaravak recrossed the shallows alone, knowing that work seemed to keep panic at bay. There was one more hut to disassemble . . . one more series of bone thongs to yank from the earth, one more ridge pole of camel rib to drop, one more quick search for precious tools and leather bags of oil and fat and dried meat, and one more hasty spreading of waterproof floor cloth over the remaining hide tent covering.

A blast of hot, searing air flew overhead like a flaming, screaming bird. He took no note of it. At last, with his eyes burning and tearing and his lungs screaming for air, all was assembled before him. These were the things that would mean life or death to the band in the coming long dark days of winter. He had saved them all!

His people would rejoice to see what he had done. Hefting the staggering weight up and across his shoulders, he rose, stood against the wind, and looked east across the shallows. He stared in disbelief. The fire had leaped the river, and the far shore was ablaze!

Panic formed a fist that struck him hard in the belly and roused the nauseating chill of dread as he instinctively wheeled around to stare westward . . . westward . . . in the direction from which he had come . . . westward in the direction from which his people would come to join him.

What he saw caused him to drop his load: An unbroken wall of roaring wind-whipped flame towered before him. His heart seemed to fall into his gut. His people could never come through such fire, and if they had tried, they were dead. All dead.

"No!"

The word seemed to enrage Daughter of the Sky. Windborne, she leaped overhead, turned her body inside out, and as Manaravak stared up, in an explosion of power and heat and white-hot flame she knocked him flat. Stunned, he lay sprawled on his belly, facedown and burning.

It was the heat of flames touching flesh that roused him instantly. He cried out in anger and was on his feet, running and screaming as he hurled himself into the cold shallows, where he rolled and howled like a mindless animal until the strong teeth and jaws of another animal grabbed him by the back of the tunic and, before he could right himself, dragged him downstream and into deeper water.

PART III

IN THE LAND OF THE BURNED MOON

1

All that night they stayed upon the rocky islet in the cold rush of the river. Huddled in shivering, frightened family groups, the adults clutched their little ones to them and faced downstream with the largest boulders at their backs lest they be swept away by the river that flowed blood red with reflected firelight. The night roared with the explosive power of fire storms, and Daughter of the Sky ate freely of the dry land.

Nothing, Naya thought, curled protectively within the sodden lap of old Grek, could hope to escape the fire's ravenous feeding frenzy unless it had dared to seek safety within the river. From all around her came the distant cries of the dying animals: bleatings, mewings, screamings, terrible roarings, and fear-crazed howlings.

She felt sick with loss. *Manaravak, where are you? And Squirrel Killer and Companion and all of the dogs! Oh, please be safe!*

Burying her head in the wet strands of Grek's bison-skin robe, Naya wept as she heard the low and terrible moans of agony that came from Larani.

"Better perhaps if this man had not pulled that one from the waters." The old man's voice was flat with sorrow. "Her back and her face—her poor, pretty face—so badly burned . . ."

"It should have been me, not Larani!" cried Naya, overcome with guilt. Without another word, she left old Grek and went carefully to where Larani lay in Simu's embrace.

Eneela knelt close by, haggard and beyond tears. "What is it, Naya?"

"I . . ." The words stuck in her throat as she looked down at her friend. Simu's arm lay over the girl, shielding her from the constant fall of wind-driven ash, but Naya could see that he had swathed her in bandages made of strips of buckskin cut from his own tunic. Soaked in river water, they must have cooled her burns. Nevertheless, she was moving her limbs restlessly and plucking at the air with her hands as she mewed and moaned like a wounded animal.

Simu looked up at Naya out of a face stretched taut by grief. "What do you want, girl?"

"To . . . be of help," she stammered.

Under the burning sky, Simu seemed about to weep. Instead he snarled as he drew his arm away and gestured Naya closer. "Look before you speak, Little Girl! You may have been instructed in the healing ways by your grandmother, but for my Larani there can be no healing, no help, and no comfort!"

Naya's eyes widened. Until now she had not been able to bring herself to venture close enough to see the extent of Larani's burns. She stepped back, sickened and relieved beyond measure that it was the daughter of Simu and not the granddaughter of Grek who had been burned. In abject misery, she turned and fled back to the comfort and consolation of Grek's lap.

After the bottom fell away under Manaravak, the water was suddenly colder, the current faster. The river took a sharp turn and carried him and the beast clamping onto him into an area of deeps between high rocks that sent water eddying ferociously and spray flying high.

Companion held him as long as possible, but by the time Manaravak recognized his savior and tried to get an arm around the big dog's neck, it was too late. If Companion barked in fear, Manaravak did not know; his own howling was far too loud. The river changed course again, and the water flowed fast and dark, first through narrows and then through wide stretches of open country. He could see the fire burning on both shores, reflected in the water and in the frenzy-wide eyes of the dog as the whirling current spun them into a series of eddies, then smashed them over and against a rough shoal of boulders that angled steeply out from the far shore.

Manaravak recognized shoreline and cried out, grabbing desperately for dry land only to fall short of it. He lost sight of Companion, but other animals, large and small, were helpless in the wild course of the twisting rapids. Some were dead—burned and drowned, even as he was burned and drowned.

The beast of panic had consumed his spirit. He was no longer Manaravak, the son of Torka and Lonit. He was wanawut, son of the beast, only one more animal fighting for life, raging and flailing and howling until another of the river's many sharp turns sent him smashing onto a sandy spit of land where he lay gasping and weeping with exhaustion and relief.

Something with small paws ran over his back, then something with hooves, and then something with paws again. He turned and saw a squirrel and an antelope skittering off after a small, scorch-eared hare. And then he heard a horse neighing in agony, and levering up onto his palms, he looked up to see a stallion plunging down from the stone walls of a high cliff. The horse, afire as it fell, scattered flames and burning hair and flesh as it landed. Manaravak rolled away just in time and heard the sickening snap of its forelimbs and neck as it rolled forward, rump over head, and came to rest on its side. It moaned once, then died beside him, its mane and tail still aflame, its body burned black, its eyes oozing fluid.

Suddenly maddened by the horror of the moment, Manaravak was on his feet. His limbs were bruised and battered, but he was running, away from the burned and broken horse, away from certain death along the river, clambering and falling over boulders, racing inland. He was an animal, a savage, purely reflexive beast running in fire-maddened fury until he could run no more, until he could not breathe and fell upon his knees, then his face, gasping in the choking, boiling cloud of smoke that lay upon the land. The smoke-thick air that he drew into his lungs was killing him.

The land was black and smoking on both shores, but the wind was down and a steady rain was falling out of a gray and heavy sky. The fire was out. Daughter of the Sky would feed no more upon the earth this day.

"We cannot stay in this place," Torka declared. "With the rain, the river has already begun to rise. Soon these islets will be underwater."

No one argued. The terrifying night had brought them rest if not ease, and although all were suffering from smoke inhalation and fatigue, they knew that the headman was right.

In silence the band members did what they could to comfort the little ones and the cruelly burned Larani, then prepared themselves to go back across the river in the same way that they had come. Torka surprised them with his command:

"We must go *with* the current, not against it."

"Downstream? But how?" asked Dak, obviously not liking what he heard. "The water runs too fast and too deep."

Torka silenced him with a wave of his hand. He stared downstream for many long moments before, at length, he spoke evenly: "Look downstream. The river is pocked with islets much like this one. With luck, what worked for Grek last night should work for us again now."

"But how?" pressed Dak again. "Last night half of us were nearly swept away as we followed Grek's lead. Even with the little ones tied to our backs we nearly lost them."

From where she crouched alone atop the tallest boulder, Demmi sneered down at her man. "You have the heart of an old woman, Dak! Do not boast of it!"

Torka ignored his daughter as he eyed Dak sternly. The young man had been questioning his decisions much too readily these days. He wondered if he had given Dak cause to doubt him or to chafe against his will. Despite Dak's lack of innovativeness, his very stolidness occasionally proved a steadying force. Now, however, the ultimate responsibility rested upon Torka's shoulders, and with the rain intensifying and the river rushing by, he knew what he must do.

"We cannot stay here," he said firmly. "The other islets angle shoreward until that last and farthest one, which nearly touches on dry land. With luck—"

"We have not had much of that lately," reminded Simu sharply as he looked up at Torka from where he knelt beside Eneela over the curled form of their daughter Larani. Indicating the girl with a single downward nod, Simu glared openly at the headman. "Or is it possible that you would call *this* luck?" His voice was as hard as the boulders of the islet.

Torka's voice was harder. "With care and in a proper encampment, Larani's burns will heal. In time she will be well again."

"And scarred, forever scarred!" Eneela sobbed against her grief.

Anger flared hot within Torka. "She is alive, woman! We are *all* alive! And yes, Simu, I *do* call this luck! There was a time last night when I was not certain if any of us would live to see another dawn! If the fire storm had not hurled Larani into the river, she would have burned to death, and we would never have found this refuge from the flames."

"The forces of Creation were with us last night," the shaman reminded the others.

Torka turned to see that Umak had come to stand beside him.

"Were they?" Dak challenged. "Where is your brother, then? And your dog? Where are any of the dogs?"

Umak's eyes narrowed defensively as his head went high. "I cannot say," he replied unflinchingly. "But the People are one. Torka and the forces of Creation have brought us through the fire and—"

"Umak speaks truth!" The volatile exclamation came from Honee. She was looking proudly and adoringly at her much younger man. "Umak saw the danger to us in the lake! He spoke with the voice of the Seeing Wind! If Umak says that the forces of Creation have been with Torka and this people, then it is so!"

Umak's face remained set and expressionless. He stood as Shaman, with his arms raised and his face set, impervious to the falling rain as he spoke:

"Let no man or woman forget that the forces of Creation walk at Torka's back! We must put our faith in them and in Torka, who has not failed us in the past."

The People stared and murmured. A sobered Dak kicked at the waters that swirled around his ankles and turned away.

A moment later Umak lowered his arms and faced his father. No one but Torka saw the wink that lowered the shaman's right lid.

"Well?" Dak pressed the headman. "Do not keep your wisdom to yourself, Torka! How are the forces of Creation going to get us across the river?"

Torka's eyes narrowed as he looked at the young man and saw through the deception of his abrasive challenge. Dak was tired and afraid.

"We will cross the river," the headman said, "as we crossed the burning land: with courage and strength!"

Only a few of the band made the move to stand.

"We will need to make the longest, strongest rope that we can possibly devise," Torka continued.

"A rope?" Dak's brow came together over the bridge of his nose like a gathering storm cloud. "Of what possible use will a rope be to us now?"

"Be still, Dak!" Torka commanded. "I am your headman, not your woman! You will not bicker with me!" He whirled around, sensing Demmi's smirk. "You will not say a word or offer insult to your man! You will do as you are bidden, both of you!"

"What would you have us do, Torka?" Lonit's question calmed the moment.

He commanded his people to cast off their clothes and to cut them into long, wide strips. Following his instructions, they fashioned a rope of the still-sodden strips of hide. The women set aside strips of thong from the main body of the rope; with these they were to bind their children to their backs. The work, shared by all, was finished quickly.

"I will go first," Torka said. "Once I reach the first islet, I will secure my end of the rope, and with the other end secured here, you will all be able to follow, clinging to it. When the last man comes across, we will rest, then go on again, using the rope to guide us from one islet to the next until we—until the forces of Creation and the spirits of the river carry us all in safety to the far shore."

Lonit's eyes remained full of fear, but she was wise enough not to voice her misgivings.

"The smaller boys must be carried—I will hear no argument about it. Simu, you will carry Larani upon your back."

His way would be dangerous, but it was the only way. It was raining harder now—already the water level around the boulders was noticeably rising.

Torka tested the river. He was naked except for a length of thong, which was cross laced over his chest and shoulders to bind his spears laterally across his back, and a single twist of rope, which was wound around his waist, securing his bludgeon and spear hurler to his side. Grek and Simu held on to the other end of the rope, feeding it to Torka as needed.

The cold of the water attacked him, penetrating his skin until he was certain that his entire body was on the brink of shattering like brittle ice.

Stunned, Torka grasped for purchase. His fingers were torn by contact with the rough surface of the stones, but he managed to pull himself from the water. After he clambered onto the rocks, he sat awhile, head down, arms resting on his bare knees. He could hear his people cheering. Simu and Grek were shouting enthusiastically as they waved and held up the other end of the rope. He was too exhausted to wave or call back, but the tug of the rope against his skin was gratifying. The rope had held!

With the rain falling on his bare back, he found himself smiling with sweet irony as he noted that only one twist of the knotted line remained around his waist. There had been just enough of it to bind him to those whom he had left behind . . . just enough to form a link between the islets . . . just enough to give his people a chance.

Just enough. It was all that any man could ask for.

In the hours that followed, with Torka steadying the line that meant life or death to his people, the band crossed to the second islet, and not one of them was lost to the river, even though cold and exhaustion weighed heavily upon them. The little ones wept against the terror of the additional crossings that were still required of them.

From one rocky islet to another, Torka led his people on until he found a long tongue of shallows that led to the far shore. And there they sat, clustering and rubbing one another for warmth as they looked back at the way they had come and, through chattering teeth, gave thanks to the forces of Creation, to the spirits of the river, and to luck for having granted them their lives.

Later, in the long Arctic twilight, Torka and his people sat shivering themselves warm within raw, uncured skins taken from the many drowned animals that littered the river shores.

Beneath a still-bloody moose hide, Umak was distracted by the raised voice of his sister Demmi.

"He lives!" she cried to the hunters. "I know that he lives! How can you all just sit here when he is lost? You must get up and help me find him!"

"Sit down, woman!" Dak's voice was heavy with fatigue. "We must regain our strength. By that time, if he *is* alive, he will probably have found his way to us!"

"But—"

"Demmi, do as you are bidden!" Torka's command silenced her. "Your man speaks for us all."

Umak was grateful. The last thing he needed now was to listen to the endless bickering of Demmi and Dak. He did not understand them. They had once been such a happy couple. But he was too tired to think about that. Even a shaman needed his rest. He folded his arms around his knees and tried to sleep. It was no good; Umak was also worried

about Manaravak. Had he survived the conflagration? Had he
managed to cross the river, and if he had, were any of the
dogs with him?

Companion. Where are you, old friend?

Almost in answer to his unspoken question, the sound of
howling rose out of the distant hills. Fire-shot images flared
in Umak's mind as he recalled the smoke-blurred forms he
had glimpsed at the height of the fire. *Wanawut.*

Now he listened to the distant howls and wondered if it was
was wanawut that he heard. For so many years the People
had believed that there were no more wanawut left in all the
world—and then they had found their sign, and all but
Manaravak had trembled in fear of them. Had the strange
beasts that seemed to be half bear and half man survived the
fire and crossed the river? Were they out there now, howling
at the sky until their sounding was lost in undulating hills and
pummeled into the earth by the falling rain?

Umak's eyes grew heavy. He dozed until a single wail
awoke him. He looked up. No one else seemed to have heard
it. But it was there, resonating in his heart long after the
sound itself was gone: the cry of a man. *Manaravak . . . ?*

Umak was sitting upright now, wide-awake, and his heart
was beating very hard. Had he heard his twin? Was his
brother howling with beasts in the far and unknown reaches
of this burned land? He waited for the sound to repeat itself
and was glad when it did not.

Somewhere deep within himself, guilt stirred. What kind
of a brother was he? Manaravak was his twin! Did he not
want him to return to the People? Of course he did! But . . .
if Manaravak did *not* return, who would speak for Naya when
at last she came to her time of blood? He swallowed hard. He
would not allow himself to think this way. He was dishonor-
ing himself and his brother and the girl.

Honee began to snore beside him, her girth a restless
mound beneath the warmth of the charred elkskin that he
had skinned for her. Li and Jhon were curled up asleep in the
warm protection of her fleshy arms and breasts. He smiled to
know that they were both safe, but the smile was short-lived.
If only Honee were not so fat! If only Honee were . . . Naya.

2

They searched for Manaravak along the river. No trace of him was found. Then the weather worsened, and the pounding rain obliterated all hope of picking up any sign of him.

"We must go back." Torka's voice was bleak.

"No! We must go on!" insisted Demmi.

"When the weather clears," the headman told her. "There is no way that we are going to find anything in this."

For two days they rested on the scorched embankment, recouping their strength while a driving, sleet-stinging rain fell. Wolves sang songs of death and sorrow from the fire-blackened hills.

Harder and harder fell the rain, and the band knew that if Manaravak were alive, he would have to find his way to them.

"I told you that we should have gone on when we still had the chance!" Demmi's accusation stung them all.

Lonit stood tall and resolute against a mother's worst fears. "He who is lost has been lost before," she said, betraying none of the inner turmoil that was tearing at her heart. "He has come back to his people from across great distances, from out of the arms of a beast, and from across time itself. And so we must have hope. It would be an insult to the spirits to assume otherwise."

But hope was drowned in the pummeling rain as the families watched the islets disappear in the rising river. Swollen animal corpses floated past the embankment—hare and wolverine, horse and lion, sloth and leaping cat, antelope and lynx and mouse—carnivore and herbivore had become prey to the river.

Because of the animals' death, Torka and his people were able to survive. There was meat for the taking, which the band ate raw—no one wanted to see fire again, even in the most controlled circumstances, for a very long time. They cut the skins from the animals for sleeping skins and crude shelter.

In one such lean-to, Dak lay on his side, with Kharn asleep in the fold of his arm. Sleep would have come easily to Dak had Demmi not been stretched out on her back beside him, wide-awake and staring up into darkness.

"We will find him, woman," said Dak quietly, knowing that her thoughts were with her brother.

"You are no shaman!"

"No. I am only your man, trying to ease your heart."

Her breath was a ragged pull of pain as she turned toward him and whispered desperately, "Find him for me, Dak. You are a fine tracker, a steady hunter."

"I would if I could, Demmi," he assured her. "If it would make you smile at me once more." His arm moved across the sleeping boy to touch her cheek, to trace slowly the contours of her face and to push back the strands of her long hair and let the ends slip through his fingers. "What has happened between us, woman? Why do you scald me with your tongue and turn your back upon me in the night when we once found such pleasure in one another?"

A tremor went through her as her hand rose to rest upon his. "He is out there somewhere, Dak . . . alone, as he was before, with no one to care for him, no one to love him."

Resentment hardened his tone. "He is a strong and capable man now, Demmi. He will survive until we find him or he finds us."

Demmi propped herself up on her elbow. Even in the darkness Dak could see that her eyes were bright with hope. "Together we could find him!" The tension of her body changed to become supple and vibrant. "If we left now, no one would know until—"

"The weather is foul, Demmi. Until we have a chance to replace our lost clothes we—"

"Clothes! I do not care about clothes."

"Even so, Demmi, my sister Larani is badly burned. I would not leave her. Besides, who would care for Kharn?"

"You are not his mother!"

The statement took him aback. "No, but *you* are."

"Bah! I have given birth, but I am not much for mothering. There are enough women in this camp for that. Swan loves to watch Kharn . . . almost as much as she loves to watch you!"

The unexpected teasing lightened his spirit. This was the Demmi he had loved since boyhood. He smiled, reached up, and touched her mouth provocatively with the backs of his fingers. "Swan is a girl. You are a woman. My woman."

She brushed his hand away, and hostility flashed in her eyes. "Not now, Dak! I will *not* stay in this camp while Manaravak is lost. If you and the other hunters are not man enough to take up the search again, I will go alone!"

Awakened by his mother's shout, Kharn sat up and began to reach for her.

"Be still, you! Go back to sleep! I am done with nursing you! It is time you were weaned!" Demmi pushed the boy away.

Kharn burst into tears and sought safety against Dak's broad chest.

Dak laid his wide hand upon Kharn's back and eyed Demmi as though she were a stranger. "I don't understand you," he said quietly.

With a tremulous exhalation that somehow hinted of regret, she lay down and turned her back to him. "No need," she said at length. "Manaravak does."

The rain continued. Days passed. Within their lean-tos, the adults reassembled the necessities of life. When enough sinew was extracted from the carcasses of dead animals, they fashioned awls out of whittled bone and set to the task of piecing together rough garments. The fumbling fingers of the men and boys generated small smiles of weary amusement that proved to be good medicine for the People's troubled spirits.

But there was no medicine to help Larani. She lay alone within a special lean-to that Simu had raised for her so that she might recuperate from her burns in peace. Poultices were made of moist squares of still-bloody, tissue-slick hide. Eneela soaked them in the river and impregnated them with pounded fat and marrow that would quicken the healing of the girl's burns, but Larani knew none of this. She knew only the excruciating, endless pain.

Someone was always with her. She was dimly aware of quiet comings and goings and low, muted whispers. She could feel herself being watched. Somehow the pressure of staring eyes hurt her skin and made her moan. The whispers were a soft, irritating hum that beat upon her eardrums and made her want to scream. When she did, the watchers fell silent, and she was glad. In silence she was alone, able to lie motionless, breathing deeply, concentrating on the slow, rhythmic pull and release of each and every breath. It was the only way to control the pain: to think of one thing, to concentrate so hard that nothing else existed.

But now Simu was breaking her concentration.

"How is it today, Larani? Not so bad as yesterday?" His voice sounded far away, as though he were looking in the opposite direction as he spoke to her. Everyone seemed to do that, but Larani did not ask herself why. She only wished he would stop talking because his words stirred the air and caused her skin to hurt.

He kept on, his voice strained by his attempt at an uncharacteristic levity. "Naya and Swan just left. They told me that you aren't eating, Larani. You *must* eat, Daughter. Your mother is beginning to worry about you, you know! No need for that, I said to her. Why, with Larani's two best friends hovering close by, our girl will soon be up and eating and talking away about all the things that young girls love to talk about. You *will* be well soon, Larani, and . . ." His voice cracked. When he spoke again, it was with an edge of desperation. "I wanted to go after you! You must know that, Larani! The old man took me by surprise when he shoved me back. He is stronger than I thought possible! And then, afterward, it seemed that the river had swept you away, and there seemed to be no sense in . . ." His voice broke. "Larani, can you forgive me for not being the one to save you? Larani, can you hear me?"

"Forgive?" The query cost her, as had the opening of her eyes. Even so small a movement as the parting of her lips or the raising of her lids set the beast of agony loose again. The pain was so intense that it blinded her. She did not know what her father was talking about, nor did she care. Her memories of the fire were her own. They ended not in flame and terror but with the dark, cold, explosive embrace of the river as it had carried her away from her pain and into oblivion. She yearned for that now. The pain was so excruciating that all she wanted was to be away from it. "Let me die!" she cried. "Please, Father, let me die!"

"Oh, my poor burned girl!" Eneela entered the lean-to and knelt next to Simu. "Be brave! Be strong! We have all searched the land for unburned stalks or leaves of willow, for the spirits that eat pain live within willow trees, and sooner or later we will find some to ease you, dear child. We will! We *must*!"

"Be brave, Daughter. The pain will soon pass," promised Simu. "In the meantime, Umak has made offerings to Father Above and Mother Below, to ease the pain of Larani and to bring Manaravak safely back to the People. Let our shaman's magic ease your spirit as you thank the forces of Creation for sparing your life."

"Manaravak . . . is lost?" A small burn-blackened hand curled and tightened around Simu's broad wrist as Larani's body convulsed against agony. "Has Daughter of the Sky taken us both? Oh, let me go to him, then. Let me walk the wind with him! Please! Take my life! It hurts so much that I do not want it anymore!"

Her words struck Simu to his heart. The girl was right. A burned girl . . . a scarred girl . . . what sort of woman would she be? Ugly. Deformed. No man would look at her. She would be of no use to the band. There was no sense prolonging her pain. He knelt over her.

"Larani . . ." He whispered his daughter's name for the last time as, with her hand still holding his wrist, Simu's fingers closed about her slender throat. Tears were welling in his eyes.

"Yes . . ." the girl consented, smiling for the first time since the fire—a twisted, pain-racked smile that was meant to encourage him. "Please, my father . . . please . . ."

He would have strangled her then and there. Death would have come quickly, mercifully. But little Uni began to cry, and Eneela's sudden heartrending wail of anguish brought the headman racing to their shelter.

"What is it? Is something . . . ?" Torka stared in from the rain, with Umak and Dak behind him. Understanding dawned instantly on all three faces.

"No!" Dak's exclamation was of disbelief, then of terrible acquiescence as he turned away, realizing that his sister was about to die.

Umak's face was set. "I have implored the spirits on Larani's behalf. Can you not wait?"

"She is in pain!" Simu's voice broke with despair. "Let it be done!"

"Wait!" Torka's word allowed no argument as he bent and entered the little lean-to on his knees. Gently he drew away the poultices that covered her and tried not to show his revulsion at the sight that filled his eyes and the stench that assailed his nostrils.

She lay on her right side. Her shoulder and upper back as well as her entire left arm and the side of her face had gone black. Her hair lay in patches, in places crisped and gray like a matting of fibrous ash; in others it was as though fingers of flame had extended across her brow and cheek, leaving deep gouges in the soft young flesh and altering the composition of her hair, so that the once long, thick, and lustrous strands had melted and congealed into the glutinous cap that was the upper left quadrant of her scalp.

But the burns were confined to only a portion of her body. The rest of her was beautiful to behold, pale and newly come into the form of a woman . . . soft, almost white in the gloom and shadow of the little tent. Her thighs and breasts and hips were fully rounded, and the sight of that part of her could not help but stir the man in him, for despite her burned face and arm and shoulder, Larani possessed the body of a bearer of life.

"The future of the People lies here," he said quietly. "Larani must not die."

Manaravak looked up through the rain. Before him, the bloated, sodden bodies of collapsed animals littered the riverbank. A caribou calf rose from its mother's side, staggered forward, and then fell into a heap. There was also a badly burned badger next to a dead leaping cat; he stared at the creature, knowing just how weak he was when he felt no desire to take the cat's fangs. Of what good was adornment to a dying man or to an animal—and at this moment Manaravak was both.

He dropped his head, panted like a dog trapped in an airless hut, and then, through slitted eyes and blurred vision, he saw Squirrel Killer lying motionless on its side. He moved forward, seeing a friend in the dog, finding comfort in the nearness as he buried his face in the dog's wet fur. But comfort twisted back on him. There was no movement in the rib cage— no breath, no heartbeat. The dog was cold and dead.

A wail of remorse drained out of Manaravak, and a terrible weariness filled him as he sighed and rested his head upon the body of Squirrel Killer. If he must die, he would die here with a friend. Naya's friend.

Naya. Lovely, silly, adorable Naya. *I am sorry that you will not see this dog or this man again. It would have been good between us.* He smiled a little just thinking of her. He drifted out of consciousness, following the vision of the naked girl into the sun and beyond until something small and pawed ran over his back.

He swatted up and sideways. When he felt wet fur bounding past him, he opened an eye in time to see the scorch-eared hare that had run across his back once before. Strange to see it twice, he thought, then realized that there must be many a hare with scorched ears. The animal seemed to know exactly where it was going. In long, leaping strides it ascended the side of the high, dark embankment and disappeared. Intrigued, Manaravak sat up. Above the river at the height of three or four men together, a dark shadow cut laterally across the face of the embankment. It was into this shadow that the hare had disappeared.

For the first time since the fire, the young man felt hope. He was on his feet in an instant, following the hare. And then, with a wolflike howl of pure triumph, he saw what he had known that he would see: a cave! He was no stranger to caves; the wanawut had raised him in one. And this one had an opening large enough to welcome a man.

He went in, scenting for carnivorous occupants. His nostrils drew in only the scent of wet river rock, old hare droppings, and nest material. Bending low, he went on along a wide, deep corridor. With renewed hope of survival, he took little note of the walls of gravelly scree or of the seepage that oozed from between the stones. The deeper he went, the cleaner and cooler the air. He found it delicious and nourishing and breathed in and out until he was light-headed.

Dizzy, he stopped, brought short by common sense and total darkness. He was surprised that he had come so far inside. With a sigh, he began to edge his way back. It was slow going, but at last he reached a place where he could see dim light. He seated himself and turned about. But in that moment, there was a rumbling in the earth above him as a herd of panicked animals fled toward the river. The rumbling seemed to shake the world to its roots as the roof of the cave began to collapse around him.

The rain stopped at the end of the third dawn. It was the absence of its sound that woke Umak. From beneath eyelids heavy with need of sleep, he watched his father, armed with spears and bludgeon, emerge from his lean-to and stand tall beneath the glow of the rainless dawn. The young man rubbed his eyes. It had been his turn to guard the camp from predators. Now he expected Torka to take a turn at keeping watch.

But Torka made no move toward his son. Instead, the man surveyed the camp as though he might never see it again, then he turned and walked off toward the northeast.

"Wait!" Umak intercepted his father. "Where are you going?"

"Back." Torka's face was haggard and drawn. "The land is dead, Umak. We must leave it. We must seek and follow the great mammoth into the face of the rising sun. Our luck lies with our totem. But first I must search once more for my son."

"We have all looked for sign of him. There is none!"

"I will go farther upriver this time, to where our encampment stood . . . and beyond, if it comes to that. If there is no sign of him, in five days' time—the length of time that a life spirit stays within a body and the dead must be watched lest they come back to life again—I will return. Then we will go on our way."

"You cannot go alone!"

"I have walked alone for much of my life, Umak. I will not risk the other hunters to this trek. It is my son who is lost."

"This son will go with you!"

"No, Umak. You have a woman and two children to care for. And if for any reason I did not return, the People will need their shaman more than ever, and your mother and little brother will have need of a man to hunt for them."

"If he lives, do you not think that he would have found his way to us by now?"

"Yes. Unless he is hurt. Unless he cannot."

It was as though a rock had been dropped into Umak's gut. He had thought of his brother's absence only in terms of life and death. It had not occurred to him that Manaravak might be hurt and lying helpless somewhere.

"Tell the others where I have gone, my son. In the meantime, make what 'magic' you can for Larani. Naya may be able to help you. I know she's a light-witted, scatterbrained little creature, but like her grandmother Wallah, she has always taken an interest in the healing ways."

"I . . . yes . . . I will talk to Naya."

"And ask Father Above and Mother Below to smile upon this man so that I may return with the one who is lost!"

"Granddaughter of Grek . . ."

Startled by Eneela's whisper, Naya raised her head. She was still sitting cross-legged beside the fitfully sleeping Larani. Her neck ached, and her back felt sore. How long had she been asleep? When she had dozed off, Umak's chanting had filled the night air. He was not chanting now.

It was very dark within the little lean-to. The stink of Larani's burns was all-pervasive. Naya willed herself not to be bothered by it.

"Listen . . ." Eneela's voice was barely audible. "The beasts are closer now. Do you hear them? Demmi has disappeared, and Dak has gone after her." She shuddered.

Naya listened. Wolves were singing in the distant hills across the river. They sounded like lost and lonely men . . . like hunters far from camp with no way of returning home again. The thought made her cringe. *Manaravak is out there somewhere, too . . . if there is anything of him left to be found!*

Something else was howling now. With the sound came the recollection of her sighting of the wanawut disappearing into the black smoke of the burning land.

Eneela shivered. "It will be dawn soon," her whispering continued. "The wolves and wanawut will seek their lairs. Go now, Little Girl. You, too, must rest."

"I would rather stay with Larani. Iana is not happy with me."

"I will tend to Larani now. Thanks to you, we have both slept. Wallah would smile if she could see how much her granddaughter had learned from her. The shaman Karana would be proud to know of his daughter's healing ways. May the forces of Creation smile upon you, Little Girl, in gratitude for your compassionate heart and your gentle hands."

"I do not deserve your gratitude, Eneela." It was not compassion but guilt that had forced her to tend Larani's burns. It was dark enough to prevent Eneela from seeing the truth in her eyes, but it could never be dark enough to hide it from herself. Iana had been right. Everything bad that had happened was her fault. As long as Naya lived, Larani's burns would be etched into her memory, for she was responsible for them.

She could not breathe. Her heart was pounding. With a sob, she scooted forward on her knees and in a moment was outside the shelter standing shakily beneath the light of stars that was fading with the dawn. The wolves and wanawut were silent now. She snuffled as she walked not toward Grek's lean-to but toward the nearby riverbank. She reached the river's edge and paused to stare down at the water.

"Naya? Why are you crying?"

She gasped, startled. She looked up to see Umak standing beside her, in silhouette against the hills.

"Are you all right, Naya?"

The words that followed burst from her throat in a torrent of emotion that took them both off guard. "I am sorry, Umak!" she cried, and threw her arms around him.

"Sorry?"

"For everything! For all that has happened. Ever since I fell behind Grek and the others as they walked to the lake, everything has gone wrong. Oh, Umak, it *was* I the great bear was following, and it was because of me that—"

"You could not have known that the bear was there."

"No." She closed her eyes and rested the side of her face against his chest. His breast was bare and warm against her cheek. She pressed closer and felt his arms enfold her and draw her nearer still. It was good to be in Umak's embrace—steadying, calming.

"You are very often thoughtless and careless, but if you have learned from your last mistake, then we will all be served by it."

"I have learned, Umak. You'll see. You won't have to watch me again."

"It is no trouble to look out for you, Naya. I will always be there for you. Why did you fall behind, Little Girl?"

"To string pretty berries for a necklet. I thought that they were craneberries, but they weren't, and once they were strung, I just wanted to stand alone beneath the sun . . . to dance, to laugh, and then—" Her eyes opened. "And then I thought terrible thoughts that must have angered Father Above. Oh, Umak, I am so sorry!"

"I know, I know." He moved slowly, rocking her, holding her more tightly. "We are all sorry. But truly, you cannot blame yourself. The signs and the omens have been bad for this people for a long time now."

She sniffled again. Could he be right? Of course he could. Umak was Shaman! A wan smile tugged at the corners of her mouth. "Umak does not think that it is all Naya's fault, then?"

"Umak doubts very much if either Father Above or Mother Below could ever be so angry at the granddaughter of Grek."

"And is Umak angry at Naya?"

"Naya fills my heart with many things, but anger is not one of them."

She hugged him hard. "I am glad. Oh, Umak, tell me what to do to make the spirits smile. What can I do to make Manaravak come home again? If he does not return, who will be man for me?"

He stopped moving. She felt his heartbeat quicken. "I will be your man," he said.

"Oh, Umak!" she exclaimed in amazement, and once again she hugged him. This time she nuzzled his chest and kissed his bare skin in gratitude for his expression of kindness. She liked the feel of a man's arms and the warmth of a man's breath blowing softly across her scalp, and most especially she liked the sound of her name as a man exhaled it as a loving whisper. "I *will* be a woman soon. When Manaravak comes back, you must make him ask for me! Oh, Umak, he is the most beautiful man. At his fire, this girl *will* be a woman!"

The change in Umak was instantaneous. Tension filled his body.

"The dawn is rising, Little Girl, and you must go to the lean-to of your grandfather. When Torka returns, we will leave this place—with or without the one who is lost."

3

Beneath the cold light of a scar-faced moon, Demmi
walked determinedly upriver without looking back. Dak would
be furious when he discovered that she had left the encampment, but she did not care. Her spear was gripped in her
hand, and her bola was wound around her brow, but prickles
of dread ran up her spine. She knew she must find Torka if
she was to stay alive long enough to locate her brother. She
gritted her teeth when she recalled her brother's chanting in
the miserable camp of lean-tos.

"Chant all you want to, Umak! That will not bring our
brother home! If my Manaravak lives, Torka and I will find
him."

But where was Torka? Suddenly disoriented in the acrid
fog that lay upon the land, Demmi paused, aware of the
feeling of being watched.

She peered through the swirling vapors of the thick,
foul-smelling ground fog that enveloped her. It had formed so
slowly at first, oozing out of the charred, rain-saturated earth
to grow thicker and thicker until now it confounded her every
step.

"Manaravak! Where are you? Father! Can anyone hear
me?" The fog absorbed her words.

Totally lost, she realized that the river must have forked
and that she had followed an unfamiliar tributary into even
more unfamiliar country.

"Hmmph!" She snorted bravely, attempting to shrug her
fears away. How could anything, man or beast, be watching
her in this fog? She could barely see herself in it!

Nevertheless, the sinew-wrapped haft of her stone dagger was gripped tightly within her left hand, and her favorite
throwing spear was balanced in her right. She turned slowly,
trying to remember the last time she had been out upon the
land alone and unable to find her bearings.

"Never," she hissed through clenched teeth. She was

never alone; she was always with the band, or with Dak, or with her father and the other hunters . . . or with Manaravak.

"Fog spirits that walk the night, can you not let this woman see a little?"

And then she caught her breath, amazed, for in that very moment a soft wind stirred, and the fog shifted and seemed to grow lighter. She laughed aloud with pleasure and relief. She raised her arms and shouted for joy.

But with the lifting of the fog, she was able to see the thing watching her . . . the thing that had been following her. A scream lodged in her throat—she was too terrified to release it. Instead she hurled her spear, but even as it flew she could not bring herself to speak the name of the thing that stood before her: wanawut.

It was cold and damp and completely dark inside the cave. Sounds from the outside world filtered through the blocked entrance and through the flesh of the earth itself . . . of wind and flame, of pounding rain and flood, of death . . . until now.

Now there was no sound at all for Manaravak, except for the increasingly shallow exhalations of his own breath. He lay very still, curled on his side with his arms wrapped tightly about his knees to keep himself from shivering while his large, dark eyes stared straight ahead into blackness. He was dying. He accepted it. He had gone beyond thirst, beyond hunger, beyond caring. His hands and shoulders were raw as a result of attempting to dig and lever his way through the debris of stone that littered the cave's entrance. He had given up wondering what had happened to the hare. Perhaps it was trapped as he was trapped, dying in some deeper portion of the cave, alone and frightened. Had it attempted to backtrack past him, he would have grabbed it and sucked it dry of blood.

Thinking of moisture, he salivated. His throat hurt from calling out to his father and brother for help. No one had heard him except the dire wolves that prowled the world above. He held his breath, listening. He knew that he must be very near the entrance to the cave because he could hear the wolves coming close again.

His heartbeat quickened. He could smell them! The cold, heavy night air was settling out of the sky to carry their scent downward through openings between the fallen stones.

They were sniffing out the smell of him, whining to one another and briefly digging before snorting in boredom, urinating, and then walking away.

"Wait! Do not go! Do not leave me!" In desperation, he yapped and howled and made all the wolf sounds he knew in hope of calling them back, but the sound of their padded paws ceased to be a weight upon the world, and he knew that they had gone their way.

Weeping, he howled in frustration and named himself a fool. Even if the wolves had managed to loosen the stones and dug their way into the cave, he did not know if they would have greeted a brother or claimed a ready meal. He would not have cared; either way he would gladly have dealt with them, for as he breathed in the hot stink of their urine, he knew that it was the smell of life.

Panic leaped within his bones. Snarling and growling, he tried once more to dig himself free. It was no good. The flesh of his fingers was worn through to the bone. Exhausted and bloodied, he lay still and cried like a baby until he fell asleep. But in sleep there was no rest, no peace, for he dreamed of fire and flood and death. He saw his people perishing in the flames, and with them the dogs and the horse and the great bear—and the beast wanawut. It thumped upon a massive chest as it called his name. *"Manaravak!"*

He awoke. Listened. There was nothing but the sound of his own breath and heartbeat and the sibilance of the river. Even the wolves were silent now. He lay still. And although his eyes were open—in the way of an animal—he somehow slept and dreamed again and made low, hurtful whimperings in his throat as, somewhere beyond the stone-occluded entrance to the cave, a dog barked and a man called his name; but Manaravak walked with the wanawut in his dreams and did not answer.

For all of a day and a night, Torka had walked upstream through the burned and ruined land. Twice he became lost when the river forked, then twisted back upon itself. There was no sign of Manaravak. Again and again he called his name. There was no answer except from the wolves.

He charged at every gathering of carrion-eating birds that he came across, shouting and shaking his spear at them as they feasted upon the dead. Bloody-beaked and squawking in confusion at his audacity, they hopped away or whipped their wings threateningly but always allowed him the view he sought . . . never the one he feared.

He went on and on. At last he reached the place where the shallows should have been. Had it not been for the contours of the scorched and steaming hills, it would have been impossible to recognize the place. Staring to the other side, he looked for the conical huts of his people, but where there had once been a meticulously assembled cluster of well-made shelters, there was only a burned and smoking plain stretching and rolling away to the hills and to distant ice-mantled ranges. It was as if the encampment had never existed. It took him a moment to accept the fact, but at length he nodded, acknowledging the harshness of the truth.

"Manaravak!" Again and again and again he called the name of his son, until the rapid movement of a hare caused him to look down.

The little animal darted suddenly from beneath a mound of blackened rubble close to his feet. As Torka bent to take a closer look at the debris, a rush of emotion nearly staggered him. He was completely amazed to realize that beneath an overlaying of thick, rain-congealed ash was a sizable pile of scorched tools as well as the long bones the People used as their huts' wall braces and ridge beams. Briefly, he looked for other bones—the bones of his son—and nearly wept with relief when he found none. So Manaravak *had* reached the encampment and managed to bring his people's belongings across the water! But where was he now?

The charred, oblong shape of Lonit's favorite cooking lamp caught his eye. With a start, he realized that he was kneeling beside blackened remains from his own hut. Gone were the many bladder flasks of precious oil and the fermented brew of summer's end. Gone were the lengths of scoured intestine packed tight with pounded fat and the stacks of pain-eating willow leaves and the sprigs of healing artemisia. Ruined and brittle were Lonit's fishing trident, fur comber, antler straightener, and the lightweight, perfectly balanced bow drill with which she had kindled many a cooking fire.

His eyes strayed again to the soapstone lamp. He lifted it and was not surprised when a portion of it cracked away in his hand. The lamp had been broken long before the fire. Torka smiled, touched by memories. Of all of her belongings, Lonit treasured this lamp the most. It was one of the first things that he had ever made for her. In its light Torka's little ones had learned the history and ways of the People. He closed his eyes and drew the lamp closer. Given the extent of the crack along its side, he did not know why the vessel had not exploded into numerous unsalvageable pieces. Perhaps Fire, Daughter of the Sky, was not such a merciless creature after all.

The sound of a barking dog caused Torka's memories to collapse. He was suddenly an aging man holding an old lamp, remembering the past when he should be looking for his lost son. He opened his eyes and, still holding the lamp, stared across the ruined land. He cupped a hand around his mouth and called his son's name.

"Manaravak!"

And this time he had an answer. It was not what he expected. It was Demmi's scream that had him running downriver with his spear in one hand, the lamp in the other, and his heart in his throat.

Standing upright before Demmi in the fog, the wanawut looked like a huge, stump-legged, slouch-shouldered man. It watched her out of small gray eyes that glinted like polished pebbles above a long, cylindrical snout.

She saw it all in an instant: the massive musculature of its furred body, the shaggy mane bristling along its upper back and shoulders, the short, thick neck, and the arms that were nearly as long as the beast was tall, so that the knuckles of its clawed·and hairy hands rested on the ground. And its face: the projecting brow ridge humping up out of the sloping, flattened cranium; the pointed, yet grotesquely manlike ears set low at the side of its head; the wide, flaring, hairless nostrils; the broad-lipped mouth that was pulled back to reveal canines as broad and long as a lion's as it extended its head and drew in her scent.

It was in this moment that Demmi screamed. She threw her spear with all of her considerable strength, but the fog congealed, and the beast was lost to view. She heard a huff of surprise followed by the scuffling of feet and an angry exhalation.

Breathless and afraid to advance, she stood her ground, certain that she had struck the beast. But had she killed it? She loosed her bola, armed it with stones from a small bag at her belt, and held the weapon at ready. Dry-mouthed, she heard it moving in the fog, breathing hard, and sucking air through its teeth. She felt sick. It was riled, and it was coming for her.

She took a step back and whirled the bola. Around and around hissed the thong arms and then, just as she loosed the stones with deadly force, she shrieked and nearly fainted because the thing that emerged from the fog was not the wanawut but Dak, storming toward her with her spear in his hand.

He threw himself to the muddied earth as the projectiles from her bola barely missed his skull.

"Dak? Is that *you*, Dak?" Completely confused, she watched him get to his feet and angrily wipe mud from his face and garments. Where was the wanawut?

"Didn't you hear me calling you?" he shouted. "Why didn't you answer?"

"I . . ." She frowned. "Where is . . ."

"Where is *what*?" snapped Dak, spitting mud.

She looked directly at him and formed the word *wanawut* with her lips without speaking it aloud. "It was following me."

He made a rude noise of derision. "Nothing has been following you except this man!"

Had she been so frightened that she had not known the face and form of her own man? As she appraised his broad, muddied, somewhat crookedly assembled face, she was amazed to realize just how much that face meant to her. What had changed her feelings toward him? She frowned. Odd . . . she could not say.

"I am sorry. I did not mean to. . . ." She stopped. Her voice surprised her. It had sounded so tender, so caring, so full of loving regret. She saw the defensive look in Dak's eyes turn into a look of love and gladness to have found affection in her once again. She stiffened. She did not want to be affectionate toward Dak. Not now. Perhaps never again. Manaravak might be dead; and if this were true, then she would never love anyone again.

"You should not have followed me," she said coldly.

His expression became purely defensive again.

"Had I not, you would have said that Dak was not man enough to find his woman and bring her safely back to camp when she was lost."

"I am *not* lost!" The lie embarrassed her. She looked around. "At least not anymore."

His eyes narrowed, but he spoke kindly. "I will help you."

"I do not want your help!"

It occurred to her that she was being obstinate and foolish. Dak was a fine tracker, so she stood a better chance of finding her father and brother with him at her side. She closed her eyes, conjured a vision of her lost brother, and held it tight and safely captive beneath her lids. *He must be found! By all the spirits of this world and the next, let me find him alive!*

"Demmi?"

She kept her eyes tightly closed, refusing to allow Dak to intrude into her thoughts of Manaravak.

"Demmi!"

She opened her eyes and glared at him. It was all that she could do to keep herself from striking him for having interrupted her silent prayer to the forces of Creation on Manaravak's behalf.

"Are you all right?" Gently he drew her closer.

"No!" She held her ground; she would not be drawn nearer to him. "I am *not* all right!" She slapped his hands away. "Until I have my brother by my side again, I will never be all right." She did not regret the words or the obvious pain that they caused him. "What are you staring at? Go back to camp, Dak. Kharn must have missed you by now. Coddle *him*, not me! You make a better mother than I do."

Dak's eyes went wide, then narrowed as he tried in vain to prevent the anger within them from spilling out. He snarled like a riled wolf, grabbed her wrists, and took her down. He straddled her, pinned her flat on her back, and held her pinioned. "You are my woman!"

A perversity of emotions flooded her, leaving her breathless with pride that he was her man and that he cared enough to come after her . . . and yet she could not help snarling back at him, wanting to hurt him. "In another band I would not be your woman! In another band there would have been more men to choose from and I would have chosen another."

He struck her, causing her to cry out as pain flared within her skull and a wide, expanding dizziness carried her away into momentary unconsciousness. Stunned and immobile, she heard the high, excited barking of a dog coming closer and closer as she awoke—not in pain—but to a kiss. It was a deep, slow, probing kiss of love and passion, and somewhere beyond her consciousness Dak murmured through the kiss.

"I'm sorry, Demmi. I'm sorry."

Her mind filled with the image of the one she loved as she returned the kiss without restraint, moving her body and arching upward against the warmth of the man who lay over her. Half in a dream, she whispered, "Manaravak . . ."

Dak broke his kiss and drew back. He struck Demmi hard across the face with his open hand and would have struck her again, this time a backhanded blow that might well have broken her jaw had Torka not intervened.

"Stop! Stop this at once!" Throwing aside his weapons and the lamp, Torka grasped the scruff of Dak's hunting tunic and pulled the young man off Demmi.

Dak did not resist. He stood limp armed, glaring down at his woman as he wiped the bitterness of her kiss from his mouth.

Torka eyed them sternly. "I heard my daughter scream and thought she was being attacked by a beast. And here, after running all this way, I find that it is only you!"

"He *is* a beast!" Demmi declared, rising to her feet as she touched her face with cautious fingers, moving her jaw tentatively, as though uncertain that it was still in working order.

Dak's face was set and hard. He allowed her accusation to settle without framing an argument in his defense.

"Why are you here?" Torka demanded of his daughter. "I did not give you permission to leave the others."

"Nor did you deny it," she said, wincing against the pain in her jaw.

"I left camp before you could have asked. My action was statement enough that this was a trek that I wished to make alone."

"I had to come, Father. I had to!"

"No, Demmi," Torka said coldly. "You did not have to come. Your first responsibility is to your child and—"

"Nothing and no one is more important to her than Manaravak," Dak interrupted.

Torka was unsettled. The young woman's need to find her brother had become an obsession. True, there had always been an inordinately deep bond of affection and understanding between the siblings. But now, as he focused upon the fixed and fiery look of resolution in Demmi's eyes, he wondered if it was a good thing for a woman to put her love for a brother above her love for her child and her man.

Torka was not given the time to pursue the subject. Dogs were barking up-country. He had heard them before, while racing to respond to Demmi's scream, and he had thought: *If Manaravak lives, he might be with the dogs!*

The dogs were close now and getting closer.

Suddenly, as though from nowhere, a hare with scorched ears burst from the cover of a nearby grove of burned, semiflattened willows to run for its life across the land. Startled, Torka recognized the animal just as two dogs broke through the same thicket, scattering ashes and blackened, brittle stalks in all directions as they pursued the hare downriver.

Torka's heart sank. Manaravak was not with them.

Snow Eater raced on after the hare without looking back. But Companion stopped, turned, and lowered his great wolflike head in puzzlement as he met Torka's gaze and let loose a single yarf that seemed to say quite clearly: "Follow!"

4

They followed the dog, the dogs followed the hare, and the hare led them to the one who was lost.

It was no easy thing to dig Manaravak from the cave, but dig they did, and when at last they found him, he lay delirious, making the low, mewling sounds of an animal. The hare with the scorched ears lay panting upon his chest, and even when they drew him out of the cave into the light of day, the animal made no move to run away and the dogs did not harry it. It lay passive and exhausted upon the man.

Kneeling beside her brother, Demmi touched Manaravak's face and the backs of his hands with tenderly questing fingertips; he was burned but not badly—just enough to rouse pain and cause him to moan. She withdrew her hand and kissed Manaravak's brow as Dak looked on jealously.

The moment was sacred to Torka. "The little one with the burned ears is Manaravak's helping spirit," he intoned. "The first time I saw this hare, it showed me where Manaravak had been. The second time, it risked its life to show me where he was. Now it stays with him as though it were his brother. When he is well again, the hare will leave him. You will see—it will be so."

Dak smiled, but there was no humor in his eyes as he said caustically, "My father taught me that in the far country a man sometimes had several helping spirits in his lifetime. I would guess that up to now, Manaravak's has been the beast wanawut. Now there's a fitting totem for him: half man, half animal."

"Watch what you say of my son, Dak!" Torka shook his head with paternal admonition. "You are hopeless, both of you! Lend a hand now, before you wear each other away with your constant bickering, and I have no one left but the dogs to help me bring my son home!"

Umak stood with his sisters Summer Moon and Swan before the shelter of the headman. He saw Naya running toward him, and instinctively he reached out for her.

She flung herself against him. "Oh, Umak, thank you for being such a wonderful shaman! Thank you for asking the forces of Creation not to be angry with this silly girl! Thank you for making Manaravak safe!"

With one little hand splayed upon his chest, she stood on tiptoe, planted a quick, hard kiss on his chin, then pushed back from him. With the bladder flask of healing oil dangling from her free hand, she was suddenly on her knees and scooting forward to disappear into the lean-to of the headman's family without asking welcome of them.

"Silly girl," muttered Swan dourly.

Dizzied by her display of affection, Umak thought almost blissfully: *Yes, she is silly. But she is also so adorable that Torka, Lonit, and Manaravak will not be able to send her away any more than I could.*

Swan rolled her eyes. "Only Naya could get away with barging in, uninvited. Our father should send her scuttling back outside with a good scolding."

"Torka will scold no one on the night that he has brought Manaravak back to the People," said Summer Moon evenly. "Besides, Naya will be our brother's woman soon. She assumes that she has the right to take certain liberties with manners and tradition."

"She behaves with the carelessness of a spoiled child," said Swan hotly of her lifelong friend. "What is happening in this band, anyway? Demmi obeys no one but her own whims! Naya does as she pleases! Has Torka not taught us all that the good of the band must always be considered if the People are to survive?"

Umak was startled by the unexpected passion of young Swan's outburst. "Yes. Torka has taught us this."

She nodded, pleased with his affirmation. "Then isn't it time that someone reminded Naya that she is not exempt from this teaching? For her own sake and for the sake of Manaravak, I will talk to Naya."

Summer Moon's right eyebrow arched upward as she looked at her younger sister speculatively. "Will you also talk to Demmi for Dak's sake?"

"I . . ." the girl stammered.

Umak shot a look at Summer Moon. Her teasing had obviously wounded a tender portion of their younger sister's heart. Swan . . . and Dak?

Swan's head went high. "Demmi does not care about him."

Summer Moon smiled in the slow, secret way of mature women when they listen to the voice of youth, innocence, and naïveté. "Do not be so certain, little sister. Besides, when Naya becomes a woman, all she will need to cure her impetuosity is a strong and steady man."

"Manaravak is more impetuous than she is," countered Swan.

"Yes," agreed Summer Moon, and looked directly at Umak. "He *is*."

It was as though her spirit saw into his. He resented the intrusion and bristled against it. "Naya will listen to Manaravak when he is her man," Umak told his sister, hating that she smiled at him in the same benign, all-knowing way that she had just smiled at Swan.

But more than this, he hated the way that his mouth turned down when he spoke the words. Manaravak was his brother. His heart had soared with gladness when Torka and Demmi and Dak had brought him home . . . until Naya had come running to his arms.

*   *   *

"Oh, Manaravak! You are alive!" Naya was a small, breathless form leaning close.

He was puzzled by her words—a statement of the obvious, completely irrelevant. Of course he was alive! If he were not, would his eyes be open and would his breath be causing his chest to rise and fall beneath the sleeping form of the hare? But like all of his people, Naya had need of words at a time when he could see no use for them. Had it been anyone else leaning over him, Manaravak would probably not have spoken. But her face was so small and lovely that he said, "I am alive."

She smiled and sighed with pleasure. "Oh, Manaravak, I am so glad that you are alive! I am so glad that you have come back to us!"

Naya's repetition of so many useless words both wearied and irked him. Of course he was alive! Of course she was glad! All his people were glad! He had been glad, too; but his gladness had shriveled away the moment he had come from the cave and had seen again all the dead and dying animals. He closed his eyes. He remembered the dead leaping cat, the dying caribou calf, and the screaming horse leaping to its death with its body and mane afire. He remembered the animals that had been swept away by the raging river. Manaravak thought of the wanawut that had raised him, and a terrible loneliness overwhelmed him as he wondered if any of its kind had survived the wrath of Daughter of the Sky.

Beneath the protective cup of his palm, the little hare stirred and sighed erratically as it lay upon his chest. His fingers flexed, stroked the slender back, and felt the hard, rapid, arrhythmic beat of the animal's heart pounding within the meager protection of its rib cage.

"Listen to the way it breathes. It's sick. You should kill it."

Startled, Manaravak opened his eyes and looked up to see that Sayanah had come to peer at the hare over Naya's shoulder.

"I would not kill you if you were sick," responded Manaravak.

"Of course not. I am your brother!"

"All of the living creatures of this world are my brothers, Sayanah," he said; then, as he looked at his brother, he wondered if a man who had been raised among animals could ever be anything but an animal.

Sayanah's forehead furrowed in thought. "Yes. But that hare is suffering. You should kill it out of kindness."

"No!" cried Naya.

To Manaravak's surprise, the girl reached out, took the animal into her hands, and drew it close against her breast. "I will heal your brother, Manaravak," she whispered passionately. "I will make your helping spirit well again so that the spirit of my man will be strong!"

He frowned; he had forgotten that she was to be his. As he observed her tenderly stroking the hare and cooing softly to it, the darkness left his mood. She was such a pretty girl. The sun was shining within his memories, and a small, golden girl ran wild and naked across the pathways of the past . . . toward the future that warmed his loins and made him smile. Naya would soon be a woman. *His* woman. Thinking of this, Manaravak was glad to be a man.

—◆—————◆—

5

—◆—————◆—

No one saw the lions that circled the camp in the rising mists that dawn, but they could smell and hear them prowling close until the hunters' shouts caused the beasts to move off snarling.

"They are still close," said Grek.

"Close enough to be a danger to anyone who strays from camp," confirmed Simu.

The headman did not flinch. "We can stay no more in this country."

There was more plea than suggestion in Grek's weary voice as he spoke against moving on. "We could hunt these lions. We could eat of their meat and rest while we grow strong and—"

"No, old friend," Torka told him. "Our hunters are few. I will not risk you or any other man or boy against lions. We have meat enough to see us through as we break camp and travel to the east. We may find the great mammoth totem— and our luck again—in a land that has not been slain by Daughter of the Sky."

* * *

In the days that followed, Torka led his people due east, away from the river and across the ruined land. They transported Larani on a sledge made of hide that was stretched across the long bones of a camel. Companion walked easily in the braces, pulling the girl as though she were no burden at all, while the much smaller Snow Eater trotted at his side. The People trudged on with the tightly rolled hide coverings of their lean-tos secured to pack frames that were contrived of the same bones that supported the little shelters whenever they made camp . . . which was often, for after the second day the weather changed, and the sky bled a cold, intermittent rain that made traveling miserable.

Nevertheless, Torka kept them moving from one damp, foul-smelling camp to another in the hope of finding game and fresh meat. On and on they walked, looking for a land that had not been ravaged by fire, until it seemed that the entire world had been burned and all of its living creatures had died except for them and the carrion eaters of the sky.

The landscape changed. The grasslands narrowed and funneled through low, shouldering hills. Distance slipped away, but beneath the feet of the travelers, the skin of Mother Below remained charred and blackened.

Lying upon her sledge, Larani looked upon the world and then closed her unbandaged eye as she wept. "Oh, look at it. It looks like me," she whispered her grief. "Why has Spirit Sucker left me alive?"

"There is already too much death in this land!" Manaravak snarled.

He startled her. When had he come to walk at the side of her sledge with Naya?

"Manaravak has come to see how you are feeling, Larani," Naya told her. "Look: His burns are nearly all healed, and I have healed the hare that he carries. Soon you will be well again. You will see."

Larani saw only one thing—and that was Manaravak. Even in her pain and despair, her heartbeat quickened. But now her heart stopped, then half leaped out of her chest as, without warning, he reached down and drew aside the oil-moistened buckskin cloth that covered the burned side of her face and head.

"No!" she screamed. "Do not look at me!"

It was too late. He had looked. He had seen. And as his

long, fine mouth drew back in open horror and revulsion at the sight of her, Larani snatched the buckskin bandage back over her head and knew that the pain of her burns had been nothing to the agony that her spirit felt now.

That night Manaravak sought solitude beneath the wide, cold, compassionless vault of a clouded sky. If there was a moon, he could not see it. If there were stars, their light was dulled by the clouds. He knelt in a low, whispering wind, hunkering on the balls of his feet. With the tip of the first finger of his right hand he began to incise points and circles into the charred, blackened surface of the earth— points to represent the stars, a circle for the moon. He stopped. He stared down.

There! he thought, satisfied with his work. He had saved the stars and the moon from being digested by the carnivorous earth! Or had he? He looked up again. Clouds still concealed the sky; he would have to wait until the wind carried them away before he would know for sure if the stars and moon were still there.

He could still remember sitting naked as a child on the broad, bone-littered floor of the wanawut's fireless cave, sounding happily to himself as he made his drawings. The beast wanawut had not approved of this. She had screeched at him and had sent him to his corner whenever she caught him at it, and then she would sniff and show her teeth at his markings, pound at them with her fists, rub them out with her feet, and defecate upon those that she could not erase in any other way.

Nevertheless, a need was a need, and Manaravak knew that his mood had always been soothed when he carved or traced images in the surface of the earth. Except tonight, because the earth was dead. No markings in the skin of Mother Below would change this, nor would they restore the ruined face of the girl Larani.

He trembled, not only with revulsion but with pity as he thought of her.

"Why?" he asked the pitiless night. "Why?"

There was no answer.

Like a gutted wolf, he threw back his head and howled his rage at the cold, lifeless, compassionless forces of the infinite.

*   *   *

In the lean-to that she shared with Dak and Kharn, Demmi awoke with a start. Dry-mouthed and breathless with panic, she came up out of her dream and for a moment thought that it was the howling of the beast wanawut that had awakened her.

The moment passed. The nightmare images vanished. She lay still, listening, relieved when she realized that it was only a wolf until she caught her breath and knew that it was her brother. She started to rise. "Where are you going?" Dak demanded, pulling her back.

"To Manaravak. Listen to him. He needs me."

"Go back to sleep. Let Torka or Lonit, or the girl who is to be his woman go out to him if someone is to give him comfort."

"But I—"

"You will do as I say, Demmi. Or by all the powers of this world and the next, this time I *will* break your jaw!"

Naya was up and out of Grek's lean-to and on her way to Manaravak before the old man or his woman could tell her to stay, but Lonit was already returning from Manaravak's side and intercepted her.

"No, Little Girl. He would be alone. Sometimes comfort cannot be given. Sometimes sadness demands release through solitude. Since he has come to live among his people, this has been the way and the need of Manaravak. We must let the wolf in his spirit speak. Perhaps, by releasing its voice, he will eventually let it go."

The next day, Torka led his people on. They searched for game and found none, although now and again they heard the distant sound of elk in rut—the crack of antlers clashing, the high, ear-piercing, whistling screams of stags in the full battle frenzy of the mating season.

"How can they think of mating in a land like this?" asked Dak as he paused and leaned forward to ease the burden of his pack. He was surprised to find himself longing for the first hard freeze of winter that would make tracking and traveling easier.

Demmi glared at him, wanting him to see the resentment that had been building in her since the previous night. "How could *you* think of mating in a land like this?"

He glared back at her with equal resentment. "Manaravak

is not the only man in this band to have need of your comfort, Demmi! He may need a sister's solace now and again, but as your man I need more than that from you."

Standing beside them, Swan blushed in embarrassment and, wanting no part of their argument, called out for Summer Moon and Sayanah to wait for her and hurried on.

"Mating is good in any land!" Lonit declared. She had fallen back to relieve Demmi and Dak of her grandson for a while. Kharn clung to her side with his legs about her waist and his hands grasping the shoulder thongs that secured her pack frame to her back. She turned her head and gave the toddler a resounding kiss, then looked squarely at Demmi and Dak. "Mating is especially good in a land like this! It is proof that the living things of this world—including you two— still believe in their future!"

"Hmmph! That is what *you* think!" exclaimed Demmi, stalking off after Swan with her nose in the air and her lips set into a scowl.

Dak's expression of belligerence melted. He looked sick with hurt and disappointment as he stared after her.

Lonit measured him thoughtfully. "You should let her see that look once in a while, Dak, instead of shouting and glowering at her all the time."

He willed the look from his face. "I do not shout!" he shouted. "I do not glower!" he said, glowering. "Besides, when I took Demmi as my woman, you advised me to be forceful with her!"

"I told you to be forceful. I did not tell you to *use* force. No woman will long smile upon the man who strikes her."

"Demmi does not smile at me at all."

"Why?"

"I don't know!"

"Find out. Look at her with love—with an expression that says she is your woman and the mother of your son, and no matter what happens or what may be troubling her, your lives are one. And because you love her, you will not allow her to make your future together less than a good thing!"

That night the dogs were restless and the children were fretful. Wanawut howled with wolves, and Manaravak howled back. Umak painted his face with ash and mud and made supplications to the forces of Creation on behalf of his people's need for fresh meat as they ate of their dwindling, increasingly putrid provisions.

That night the headman dreamed of mammoth and awoke to hear them thundering in the distant mountain passes to the east. He rose, pulled his sleeping skin around his shoulders, and went out into the dawn.

A storm had left the blackened earth covered with a thin, dry dusting of snow that would be gone before the morning; both land and sky were still too warm to hold snow captive. He stared eastward. The wind had blown itself out over the distant ranges. With the sun rising behind them, they seemed like a great, snaggle-toothed, impenetrable black wall. He stared. Again the sound of trumpeting mammoth reached him.

Lonit came out to stand beside him, breathless with excitement.

"Did you hear?" he asked her.

"Yes! Was it Life Giver, do you think?"

"It was *mammoth*! And where mammoth graze, there will be grass and spruce wood. And where there is spruce wood and good grazing, there will be meat!"

A pass through the mountains opened before them. It was a dark, forbidding, hungry, and sleepless passage, but at length the mountains fell away. The bulk of the great range elbowed southward as Torka led his people east across high, open, rolling hill country—but still the surface of the land remained blackened by fire.

Over the next few days circling teratorns occasionally guided them to carcasses that still possessed enough gristle to invite the predation of carrion-eating birds. The women and girls got close enough to brain a few small birds with stones loosed from their bolas, and three times in as many days the men of the band speared larger quarry, and the heartened people shared the meat of eagles and a teratorn.

They thanked the spirits of their kills and the circling teratorns that had led them to their little feasts. They saved the hollow bones and feathers, for these were sacred things that linked the people with the spirits of the sky and to their ancestors who walked the wind forever.

But in a band of twenty-four people, the flesh and blood of birds did not go far. They lived off the meat that they had prepared and packed for traveling in those first days after the fire when the flesh of the corpses that they had found along the river's edge was still fresh. But the meat had been prepared quickly in the sodden days of little wind and no sun in which to dry it properly, and had thus not kept well. It had transcended the tang of rancidity and the cloying sweetness of mild spoilage to grow soft and ripe with a stench that appealed to only the most tolerant palates.

"Eat, eat!" Grek urged his woman and children enthusiastically as they settled in to a family meal at day's end under a carelessly assembled lean-to of his devising. "Why do you make such faces at your food? In the far country, this man Grek has seen men and women draw lots to win such well-aged meat as this!" He smacked his lips appreciatively as he gulped a wedge of putrid fat and followed it down with a strip of something that had once been a filet of red meat; it was blue now and so far gone with decomposition that it looked as though digestive juices had already been at work on it.

"You make a joke, yes?" Chuk's face was contorted with revulsion.

"No joke! It is good meat, yes!"

"It smells bad, Bison Man," whimpered Yona, wrinkling her nose.

"It stinks!" proclaimed Tankh, dubiously eyeing the skewered lumps of greening fat that his mother Iana proffered to him.

"It is the best we have," she told him.

"We could eat the dogs," suggested Tankh.

Iana struck him so hard that he fell sideways with his nose spurting blood. "The people of Torka do not eat dogs!"

Iana's face was flushed as she shouted at him, but she had already set down the skewer of fat and was kneeling next to her son, helping him up, checking to see what damage she had done.

Tankh sat up, touching his nose, then stared at his bloody fingertips and shook his head to clear it. "Why? We do not name them totem."

Iana took up the edge of her skirt and, ignoring his protests, wiped his face. "The dogs that walk with us are the children of Aar. Since the days of Torka's grandfather, old Umak, they have carried our loads and have hunted at our sides across greater distances than a woman of my age cares to remember. Men of many bands have called us magic makers because of our dogs—perhaps they were right. When Three Paws came to feed upon the women and children at the lake, who was the first to race to the attack? The dogs. When the helping spirit led the headman to his lost son, Torka and the others would never have followed it had Companion and Snow Eater not led the way. More times than this woman can count have the dogs led us to animals and helped us to bring down game so that all might eat together—man *and* dog, feeding as brothers. Eat them, you say? Would we eat each other?"

The premise left the boy white-faced.

"People do not eat people!" blurted Chuk, openly appalled.

Iana and Grek exchanged long looks.

"Long ago, in the far country it was so," informed Iana solemnly. "In the deepest, darkest, coldest times of the winter dark, when the bands gathered in starving camps and Spirit Sucker rode on the back of the wind looking for the dying spirits of people to eat, the flesh of newborn babies and the bodies of the dead were meat for some bands."

"The flesh of dead *children* who would not eat when and what their parents told them to!" added Grek with dire emphasis.

His offspring suddenly fell eagerly upon their food as he had known they would.

Only Chuk refrained, staring with disbelief at his mother and father. "You would not . . . eat us?"

"Never!" Iana's face twisted with the intensity of her emotions. In the far country, with other bands and as a slave to marauders, she had seen her babies abandoned and killed. In the violent horror of these memories, she trembled as she spoke with a passion that stunned her children. "In Torka's band no one eats of the dead or of their newborn babies! That is why he walks alone in a country where there are no people. That is why we have chosen to walk with him! And that is why you must obey your father and eat the food that is put before you, so that you will be strong when Torka follows his totem into a new land where there will be good hunting and plenty of fresh meat for all!"

PART IV

EVER = CHANGING WOMAN

1

Under the broad wings of a soaring white-headed eagle the People crested a long, stony rise and knew that at last they had reached the place where Daughter of the Sky had died. In this place the wind had turned the fire back upon itself. The skin of the earth was black beneath their feet, but ahead of them only a few charred islands of blackened stubble stood amid otherwise undisturbed communities of rough grasses, mosses, and miniature, weather-prostrated shrubs.

Umak raised his arms and cried out in thanksgiving to the forces of Creation while Honee sat down and tried to breathe without pain as she looked at him and smiled with love and pride.

As they stood together, survivors of fire and flood and the long, hungry trek across the devastated land, more than one woman wept happy tears. Sayanah and Jhon ran about and jumped for joy before withering looks from Nantu and the older boys caused them to remember their dignity.

Naya and Swan joined hands with the little girls and danced in a happy circle while the hunters of the band embraced and slapped one another upon the back as they hooted with pleasure and relief.

Lonit looked adoringly at Torka as he stood tall and resolute in the knowledge that he had done the right thing in leading his people east.

Simu and Eneela held their daughter Larani so she could "look ahead and see the country that offers hope."

Larani sighed, closed her eyes, and lay back into ever-present pain upon the sledge. "To you, yes . . . not to me."

Dak reached for Demmi's hand and told her that in the new land things would be better between them. But she stepped away from him and went to stand beside her brother. Manaravak paid no heed to her, for as Demmi came to his side, his helping spirit leaped from his shoulder and bounded off, leading the People down from the rise and into the land where the great mammoth totem Life Giver stood grazing alone while others of its kind drank along the shore of an enormous river that sparkled blue and silver in the face of the rising sun.

The river was the dominant feature of the land. They had all seen big rivers before, but this giant was wider than any they had ever imagined. It muscled its way north through a vast, braided valley that stretched grass gold, tundra red, and willow yellow between blue and purple hills and dark forests of arctic spruce, tamarack, and autumn-denuded hardwoods that fingered tenuously upward across the broad, stony laps of the surrounding mountains.

"*Deh Cho* . . ." murmured Grek in the language of the band into which he had been born so long ago.

Torka nodded. It had been years since he had heard the old man speak his mother tongue, but the languages of the nomadic big-game hunters from beyond the Sea of Ice were of one root. Some words were so similar that they were virtually interchangeable.

"*Dehcho*," the headman confirmed in the dialect of his ancestors. Great River. No other name would suit. Delighting in having the thick, resilient tundral skin of Mother Below beneath their feet once more, they moved on with lighter hearts and barely felt the weight of their pack frames as they gazed across the Valley of the Great River.

"It is beautiful!" exclaimed Lonit.

No one could disagree. But there was something infinitely more beautiful than the view of the land itself—and that was the sight of the game that walked upon it. Moose browsed in tundral ponds. At the edge and upon the surface of several pristine lakes, waterfowl still lingered to fatten upon the northland's last berries before beginning their migration over the great white ranges that stood to the southeast. A herd of striped, tawny horses moved fetlock-deep across one of many sun-bright tributary streams that emptied out of great dark mountain canyons to glisten like veins of liquid mica on the massive floodplain of the valley floor. A rivulet of hook-nosed antelope darted ahead of a predator that remained unseen and silent in the cover of the tall grass, while a family of musk-oxen plodded stolidly over the crest of the talus slope that seemed a promising place to keep in mind when the men of the band later set themselves to search for stones that would be suitable for shaping into blades, projectile points, and scrapers.

They paused and prepared to make camp along a sparsely wooded tributary creek in good south-facing country well above and inland of the river.

"Willow!" cried Naya with delight. "Look everyone! We have found willow trees at last! Now we can make medicine for Larani!" With Swan at her side, she immediately set herself to picking the greenest branches.

Iana's brow arched thoughtfully. "You would think that she is the only female in the band to know anything about healing. A regular little medicine woman!"

"Just like her grandmother before her," Grek added proudly.

"And her grandfather Navahk," reminded Iana darkly.

Grek scowled at his woman. "I am her *only* grandfather! The other is dead, and the only medicine he ever made was bad medicine, to bring pain instead of solace, to take life rather than restore it. Do not speak his name in this camp! Look at Naya! She is her mother all over again!"

Iana's brows lowered. "Your blood is strong in her, but sometimes I can see his as well. Look how she smiles . . . her teeth, so much like Navahk's and Karana's and—"

"Stop, I say! I will not hear it."

His tone was so crushing that Iana had no choice but to obey.

"Isn't this enough?" asked Swan, pausing as she worked with Naya to look off toward where the People were beginning to assemble the new camp.

Naya appraised the stack of leafy branches that she and the youngest daughter of Torka had gathered. "Yes. This will do. Now we will need a good hot fire in which to heat stones for a boiling bag."

"Why? The pain-eating oils of the stalks will dissolve in Larani's mouth when she chews them. We can make a hot drink for her later with the leaves, but now we should help the others with the new camp."

Naya frowned. Setting up huts was hard work. "The medicine I will make is best when boiled," she informed Swan.

Then, suddenly, all thought of Larani evaporated as Manaravak came to stand alone just upstream. How handsome he was! He seemed to be staring after something. Puzzled and then concerned, Naya saw that the hare was nowhere in sight. Without so much as a word to Swan, Naya went to him. "Where is your helping spirit?" Naya asked Manaravak when she saw that he was loosing the thongs that held his pack frame to his back.

He dropped the pack and pointed toward the woods along the creek. "There. Now that we have found our totem, he will seek his own kind. Little Scorched Ears will seek his woman before the long winter dark comes down."

"Do you think so?"

"He told me."

"Really?"

"Not all things are told with words, Little Girl," he said, and with the entire band looking on, he drew her close and kissed her deeply on the mouth.

"Away! Away I say!" warned Grek, hurling a spear toward the embracing couple.

Iana shrieked in dismay. It was a strong throw, obviously wide but deliberately close enough to cause Manaravak to release the girl and for Naya to cry out.

"This is not the time for that!" Grek shouted at Manaravak. "Until Little Girl bleeds as a woman and accepts your bride offerings, you have no right to do that!"

Manaravak was more puzzled than disturbed by the old man's display of emotion. "Yes," he conceded. "But *soon*," he added with an emphasis that made Naya blush.

Before the sun was down the lean-tos were up and Naya's medicinal brew was made. For the first time since the Daughter of the Sky had hurled Larani into the river, she slept without pain as the People gathered around a high, boldly crackling communal fire of driftwood. The dogs were here, and even Honee was feeling well enough to join the band as the last of the putrid traveling rations were eaten.

With the next dawn the hunters went from camp in search of elk and found what they had never even dared to dream of: the wintering grounds of the caribou.

Since time beyond beginning the meat, hide, bones, and antlers of the caribou had been the preferred sustenance of the nomadic hunters of the northern steppe. Since time beyond beginning, Torka's ancestors had followed and hunted the caribou beyond the Sea of Ice. But this was a new land, a new world. And this herd of caribou—autumn-fat, autumn-sleek animals—had never seen a man, let alone an entire hunting party of human beings.

"Speak softly," urged Torka, lying flat on his belly with the other hunters and dogs on either side of him. "We don't want to startle them before we can get within killing range."

Lying to his father's right, Manaravak raised his head into the wind. "There is no scent of fear in them. They do not know our kind. They do not speak to one another in warning."

"How can you know that?" Umak, lying at his father's left, sounded annoyed.

Manaravak shrugged. "I just know."

"So many, yes!" Grek licked his lips.

"Have any of you ever seen anything so beautiful?" exhaled Dak.

"Umak, Manaravak, you two hold back with the dogs until I call for you," Torka instructed. "The rest of you follow me."

The headman rose and, one meticulously paced step at a time, led the others into the wind. Bending almost double, he moved slowly, paused often, and made a great show of pretending to graze in the manner of caribou as he held his spears upright, their tips jabbing skyward, over his head like a pair of antlers. He moved on, then paused again, this time by a fresh mound of caribou droppings. He knelt, lifted a handful, and slowly began to slather it over his arms. This was the way of his father and grandfather and of a thousand generations of grandfathers before him. Now, if the wind turned, his prey would catch no scent of him. Now, since he smelled, walked, grazed, and had antlerlike projections, it was more than likely that the caribou would take him to be one of them.

Closer and closer to the herd he led his fellow hunters until a young cow stared at them fixedly out of mild black eyes.

Torka stopped. He knew that the men and boys behind him had done the same. His heart was pounding. His hands tensed around the bone shafts of his spears. All along his shoulders and spine and the backs of his thighs, his muscles quivered and tensed. Still the cow did not move or blink. Only her jaws kept working until a late-season blackfly that had somehow survived the early snow landed on her left ear. The fly drew blood. The caribou's ear swiveled and the muscles along her neck, haunch, and shoulders rippled. Yet still her eyes remained fixed. Calmly, with her tail up and her left ear still twitching, she began to advance toward the strange, long-antlered caribou that crouched before her.

Other animals were following her! Some were in range of his spear now. And still she came toward him, closer, ever closer. Torka held his breath. A few more steps and he would be able to take hold of an antler and, leaping out, twist her head back until he felt the snap of her neck.

She paused, looking right into his eyes, and then, to his amazement, through his eyes and into his spirit. He exhaled in surprise at such unexpected invasive eye contact. She was letting him know that curiosity, not fear, was drawing her toward one that she perceived to be of her own kind. He should have looked away, for as she allowed him to see into her nature, so, too, did she see into his.

He was wolf!

No!

He was bear!

No!

He was lion!

No!

She blinked. Confused and frightened, her head went up, and her nostrils went wide. Every muscle in her body stiffened as she was suddenly alert to the realization that this strange-looking caribou was not a caribou after all. He was something that she had never seen—but he was everything that she feared.

He was Predator!

And had he hesitated for so much as a fraction of a second, she would have leaped away and sounded a warning to the entire band, but already the other caribou were reacting to the change in her stance, so Torka did not hesitate. Her beauty and her trust and her vulnerability had not failed to touch him, but he *was* predator and she *was* prey, and in the lean-tos by the creek the women and children of his band were hungry.

They killed and killed again.

Long before the day was done, the new encampment in the Valley of the Great River was piled high with skins and meat and bones, and each lean-to had a tangled stack of antlers before it to signify that the man who dwelled within was a fine hunter and provider for his family.

There was no moon that night, but that did not matter. The stars and the tremulous glow of a green aurora were light enough for the people of Torka as they built their fire high and joined to celebrate their first hunt in the Valley of the Great River. They feasted. They sang.

The men boasted of their bravery and skill. The dogs took their place by the fire, where prime cuts of meat and fat were theirs. The descendants of Aar were celebrated in the boasting of the hunters, who sang of how Companion and Snow Eater had pursued the fleeing caribou to harry their prey, confusing and frightening the caribou until they turned and fled back into the men's waiting spears. The children watched in wonder and delight, sucking on caribou eyes and scooping the green, tangy, puddinglike contents from the generous cuttings of caribou intestine that had been portioned out to each of them.

The women glorified the tales of their men with "oohs" and "ahhs," and portioned out the blood meats to all and saw to it that the young girls—including Larani—had a generous share of the glands.

But Larani refused to eat hers. She waved away her mother's offering as she stood on shaky feet close to her own little shelter, well into the shadows so that she could not be seen by others, and so far back from the fire that not even the most wayward cinder could reach her. A lightweight sleeping fur lay over her right shoulder and fell forward to cover the front of her body and her ankles. Her left shoulder, arm, and upper back were bare; it was too painful to place even the thinnest garment against her still-raw, oozing flesh.

She drew in a cautious breath. Despite her weakened condition, she found it good to be on her feet again and outside in the cool night air. Unsteady as she was, the touch of the night invigorated her. With the aid of Naya's medicine drink and salves, as long as Larani did not touch the burned portions of her body, pain remained a dull, persistent ache rather than the intense, mind-singeing agony.

"You must eat of the gland meat, Daughter!" insisted Eneela.

"Why?"

"So that you will shed moon blood and become a woman of the People. It is what you were born to be! To take a man! To bear children!"

"Daughter of the Sky has changed all that, Mother."

"No, Larani! You must not say it!"

"Why not? It is the truth." Her voice sounded strange to her. She formed the words slowly, being careful not to move her lips lest she loose the beast of pain from the burns that marred the left side of her face.

Eneela made an effort to lighten the moment. "Look! The other girls and women are dancing now. After the next hunt, you will join them. Why, the way you are healing is—"

"Is what, Mother?" Larani's heart ached so deeply that somehow the pain rivaled that of her burns. "Look at you! You stand downwind so that you cannot smell my ruined skin, and you avert your eyes lest you see what is left of my face."

Eneela's voice caught in her throat, but now she looked at her daughter eye to eye. "Yes! You are right! It hurts me to see you this way! But you will mend, Larani! You will again be as you were!"

"Will I?"

The question hung in the air.

"Yes!" insisted Eneela.

Too much time had passed between the answer and the query. Larani was suddenly tired. The night wind felt cold against her bare skin.

Now, staring off across the camp to where the men of the band were posturing and roaring with pride as they continued to reenact the hunt, she watched Manaravak whirling half-naked in the firelight and experienced another kind of pain, the pain of *wanting*. He would never again look at her with anything except revulsion . . . and he *had* looked, once . . . and she knew that he had, because she had looked back, and in that moment, when he had flashed a winning smile her way and loosed a howl of pure masculine pride, she had hoped that a day might come when Manaravak might be allowed two women. It would not have mattered to her that she would have been second at his fire. To have been his would have been enough—it would have been everything. But now it could never be.

"I will rest now," she said. "You join the others. I will watch you and share the gladness of this night."

"All right, my dear girl, if this is what you want. But at least eat some of the gland meat . . . to make your mother happy."

*   *   *

As the stars shifted their position across the night, the glow of contentment from every belly in the encampment of Torka reached every eye. All too soon, it seemed, the last of the dances were danced and the People settled happily into dreamy hours of storytelling. One by one they drifted into sleep until only Torka sat awake beside the warm, pulsing embers of the fire. He listened to the wind and to the call of wolves until the trumpet of a lone mammoth rose from the darkness at the eastern edge of the valley.

Hearing the call of his totem, Torka wondered why he could not rest content in the knowledge that he had found his luck at last.

2

Another day was beginning, and Naya felt drained just thinking about it because there was simply too much work to do. If only she were a stronger, bigger girl! Her back still ached after hours spent bending over freshly butchered caribou. The tips of her fingers and the heels of her hands were sore from the drudgery and meticulous tedium of lifting yards and yards of sinew from the bloodied back muscles of the kill. The labor was less palatable because autumn, the best time to prepare meat and hides for the coming winter, was also the time when arctic berries and tubers were ripe and most sweet.

"If we do not go in search of them now, it will be too late," she told Iana as they prepared to leave Grek's lean-to to greet the day.

Yona was also up and dressed. "Naya is right, Mother! And picking berries is more fun than making meat and working hides."

Iana frowned, disgusted with Naya. "You have already taken time from camp to gather willow stalks to ease Larani's pain. For now, that will have to be enough. The hides and meat must be prepared before they spoil."

"But Grek is leading the boys upland into good berry-picking country today to search out stone for spearheads and other tools. We could go with them."

"Stop wheedling, Naya! Grek and the boys will be too busy to look out for berry-gathering girls!"

"But—"

"Not another word, I say! What are a few berries and roots to us now? This is a meat-eating band above all else. We must set ourselves to prepare for winter in a camp in which everything—*everything*—must be made anew. New winter hut covers! New tools! New floor coverings and bed skins and clothes and moccasins."

Naya groaned as she went to look out into the morning. The other women and girls were already outside, working together, shooing the dogs away and enjoying gossip and laughter. While she watched, Swan, holding tight to one end of a length of sinew, battled with Snow Eater as the feisty bitch tried to make off with the other end in her teeth. The women and girls laughed at the tug-of-war.

Snow Eater growled with happy ferocity and wagged her upturned curl of a tail. Down on her front paws with her rump high in the air, the dog was so intent upon the game that she took no notice of Companion as he came up from behind and began to sniff her with interest.

"Good dog!" shouted Manaravak from the far side of the camp. The other men of the band, drawn by the promise of a good show, echoed him.

"Look to your rear, Snow Eater, before it is too late!" Honee laughed.

"Hurry, Companion, now's your chance!" prodded Umak.

"Hurry, dog!" called Torka. "We could use a litter of pups!"

Naya knew that Snow Eater had been in heat since early yesterday, and now her mate took full advantage of his opportunity. He mounted and began to pump while the men cheered. Naya's eyes widened; the big dog actually seemed to be smiling!

Not so with Snow Eater. She released the sinew and tried to free herself, but it was too late. Companion was in deep, gripping her with his forepaws. The big dog pumped hard toward climax. Snow Eater, dry and unready for penetration, yipped in protest and strained with all her might to be free of him. It was no use; although she whined and yipped pathetically, Snow Eater won nothing from Companion but snarls and continued ramming.

The men of the band were laughing now, still cheering Companion on. Naya felt sick. She did not know with whom she was angrier—the men of the band or the male dog. "He's hurting her!" she cried. "Make him stop!"

Now even the women laughed.

Naya could not understand what they found so funny. Desperate, ears back, Snow Eater was growling and showing her teeth. With yips of pain she began to claw frantically at the ground until her exhausted shoulder muscles collapsed and she went down hard on her lower jaw. Companion tightened his grip on her rear end and kept on pumping.

The men and boys of the band howled with amusement. The women urged Snow Eater to get up, and Eneela called out, "Don't make it easy for him, girl!"

With forepaws splayed and head down, Snow Eater began to whine pathetically as Companion rammed on until suddenly he came to shivering climax. Tongue lolling, he stared ahead as though in a daze. And yet he continued to hold on even though Snow Eater's cries continued.

Naya could bear it no more. "Get him off her! He is hurting her!" she screamed, and would have gone to Snow Eater's rescue had Iana not stopped her.

"Touch him now, and he'll take your arm off." Iana shook her head with mock disapproval and called out loud enough for all to hear, "Isn't that just like a man—to sneak up on a woman and slip it in before she's ready for it!"

Now the men of the band roared with mirth.

Sickened and so angry that tears were stinging her eyes, Naya looked at the dogs. Snow Eater was standing now, head down, ears tucked so close to her head that they seemed to have disappeared. Her posture was one of utter dejection as the big male continued to hold fast to her rump. When he tried to pull away, Snow Eater yowled in pain and snapped at him. He remained where he was—locked tight.

"I have seen this before," Iana said evenly. "Companion will stay on Snow Eater until his organ relaxes enough to withdraw. It might take hours."

"But we must help them! He is hurting her!"

"There's nothing we can do. If anyone were to force him out, she would be torn and bloodied. Time will ease them both. You will see." Iana turned away. "Come, Naya. The sinew awaits us! Time to put your back and hands to the task!"

Naya pouted. "Soon I will have no back or fingers left."

"Listen to me, Little Girl," Iana said angrily. "You cannot expect your old grandfather to care for you forever. It will be a good thing when you go to share the sleeping skins of Manaravak. But do you think that such a wild one as he will be lenient with his woman? You will have to learn to care for yourself and the babies that you will bear."

Babies? thought Naya. She had never really thought about that; after just witnessing the mating of the dogs, she did not find the thought pleasing. Having children was a bloody, violent, and painful experience; and once babies were born, they were a constant responsibility. And Naya was unused to responsibility.

"Ah . . ." said Iana. "That has made you think, eh? Yes. It *is* time that you learned to do your share. No more will this woman sew your clothes and scrape the skins that make up your shoes and your bedding! You had better get used to a sore back and fingers, for your work has only just begun!"

"We will see about that!" Naya declared defiantly, looking around for her grandfather.

Grek's request to the headman on his granddaughter's behalf was convincing. Torka listened to it, and to Iana's objections.

"What harm can there be in it?" Torka asked Iana, adding that tomorrow Naya would resume her work with the women.

The People watched as the small group left camp together—Grek, the boys, a smug Naya, and Manaravak, who had been assigned by Torka to go along as extra protection against predators.

"The girl is a troublemaker. . . ." Demmi hissed under her breath. "I, too, am sick of woman's work! I will gather berries! Let me pass, Dak."

"I will not. There is work to do, and you will stay to do it!"

Demmi glared across the encampment to where her father stood with the other men. She spoke loudly: "If Grek were not an old man who has found the soft place of pity within the heart of my father, would Naya be off picking berries?"

Torka's head went up immediately, and his features expanded into a mask of sudden anger. Demmi caught her breath. Rarely had she seen her father so furious.

"If Naya returns with healing plants and berries, this will be a good thing for all the band!" As Lonit reprimanded Demmi her eyes flashed with fury. "Torka's decision was one of wisdom and concern for us all!"

"I did not mean to imply otherwise," Demmi apologized. The last thing she wanted was to embarrass her father in the presence of his people. She wished that she could go to him now and tell him that there was no one in the world whom she loved more.

But there was. Manaravak. The entire band knew it, Dak most of all. She was aware of him standing close, watching her.

"Come, Demmi. I will help you to stretch out that doeskin that you said was ready for pegging," he volunteered, his tone strained.

She ignored him. She was sick of him, of being his woman, of being Kharn's mother, of the sameness of her life. She looked off to see that Naya was holding Manaravak's hand, as she herself used to hold it—when he was a boy and she was a young woman, a loving sister, sharing her life with him—teaching him, guiding him, setting aside everything for him until, one day, he had begun to look at Naya and had wanted his sister beside him no more. *Naya!* She ground the girl's name between her teeth.

Frustrated, she wheeled and stormed off toward her lean-to, cursing the taboos of her people for standing between her and the man she was born for. *Manaravak!* Their spirits were one! Their hearts leaped to the same drumbeat of life! In the land of her ancestors, had she been born into Simu's band instead of Torka's, she could have openly looked at her brother with a woman's eyes—and he could have looked back. They would have been one—man and his woman, brother and sister—and Father Above and Mother Below and all of the powers in this world and the next would have smiled upon their mating.

She nearly wept as she stalked by Swan, who was caring for Kharn.

"Is something wrong, Demmi?" asked her sister.

"They will never smile on *them!*" she proclaimed. Breathless with anger, she paused to stare after Manaravak and Naya.

Swan was puzzled. "Who?"

Demmi was so near to tears that she dared not speak. Ahead of her, at the edge of camp, Umak was gazing across the hills blank eyed and sad with longing for the granddaughter of Grek.

Suddenly furious, Demmi went to his side. "You can't be serious!" she asked him, her eyes following his. "You can't be looking moose eyed after *her*?"

He swallowed, embarrassed. "Naya . . . she . . . uh . . . is growing up."

"I wish that she would grow old and die tomorrow!" retorted Demmi.

And this time when a man struck her, it was not Dak. It was her brother Umak.

3

It was a fine day, the sort when the autumn land and sky were as sweet as the softest, longest day of summer. When Naya stopped to pick craneberry leaves along a sandy creek bed, Grek gave stern orders to Manaravak to watch over Little Girl and keep her safe; then the old man led Tankh, Chuk, and young Jhon and Sayanah to a place that he called Spear Mountain. Nantu had volunteered to guard Naya, too, but Grek said no, and the other boys teased him about his infatuation.

Naya, still angry with Iana, found immense pleasure in deliberately wearing her moccasins as she sloshed through the shallow creek and waded through a stand of willow to reach a luxuriant craneberry patch that greened the tundra just above the sandy streambed.

"Where are you going?" asked Manaravak, following and frowning as he noted that the buckskin sack that the girl carried slung over one shoulder was already bulging.

"There is more craneberry here! Oh, look, it is such a good, green clump!"

To Manaravak one clump of greenery was the same as the next unless he was hunting meat that might be hiding within it, but Naya was happier than ever as she chirped like a little bird about the curative properties of this evergreen. Manaravak found a spot well above her on the sunny embankment and watched her. Perching on a lichen-clad rock with his spear at his side, he thought that she was the prettiest girl in the band but wished that she didn't talk so much.

"This is called craneberry," Naya informed him loftily, "because when the flowers are new, they look like little long-legged birds."

Manaravak cocked his head thoughtfully. "So do you . . . under your clothes!"

Naya blushed, clucked her tongue, and frowned prettily. "It is as I suspected! There are plenty of leaves, but no berries left. I wish we could have come to this place earlier."

"In this place there have been no berries for a long time now," Manaravak told her. "Look at the leaves: Many are torn, and the branches are bent and cracked in places. The bear kind have chewed up all the berries in the last days of the long sun, long before we came out of the burned land."

Naya's face was suddenly pale. "Bear? Will they be angry that we have come to gather in this place?"

Manaravak saw her fear and answered in a deep, measured voice that intensified her dread. "Yes, the bear kind will be angry! They will come to drive us away . . . like *this*!"

Suddenly, with a boisterous laugh, he leaped from the rock and landed before her, hunkering low and doing the best and funniest imitation of a snarling bear that she had ever seen as he stripped leaves from the branches of the shrubbery and shoved them into his mouth.

"Manaravak!" She laughed with relief and delight in his unexpected antics.

He spat the leaves out. Seeing her lithe and lovely form moving with laughter beneath her heavy, ugly dress, he succumbed to the urge to reach out, grab her ankle, and pull her down.

She shrieked and, with a quick jump, avoided his grasp. Leaving her sack of leaves where she had placed it, she sped away, inviting chase. It was a game that they had played as children, and Naya felt giddy and giggly as she plunged into the willow shrub growth. He came crashing through the branches after her.

Laughing, she barely managed to escape him as he went diving past her. She scrambled to her knees and scooted farther into the cool shade of the nearly autumn-denuded willow grove. And then she froze.

There, in an instant, Naya recognized the small, blood-red, berrylike fruit that she had discovered growing in the far country beyond the burned land. She recalled her lost necklet and, with an exhalation of delight, realized that she would now have another. Her small hand shot out eagerly to pluck up a handful of little tough-skinned fruit that oozed warm juice as she closed her fingers around them. She raised her palm and licked between her fingers. Yes. It was as she remembered, except the juice was thicker, oilier. . . .

In this moment Manaravak tackled her and knocked her sideways. Her breath went out of her with a dizzying *whoosh*, and with her back pressed to his chest, she kicked and squirmed and laughed with joy in their game, fighting to be free of his enfolding arms.

But she suddenly felt the pounding of his heart and the heat of his breath at her neck, and a flurry of sensation broke loose within her . . . like the stroking wings of every kind of bird that she had ever seen, rising, falling, flying away and away within her body to some wonderful warm place of refuge. She relaxed, confused but loving the way she felt, loving the feel of Manaravak next to her and not wanting to be free of him at all.

She heard him exhale her name and did not know exactly when he shifted position. He was lying on his back now, moving his arms so that his hands were gripping her along her sides, lifting her, turning her so that she was facing down, being held above him as though she were a leaf or a feather and bore no weight at all.

And then, slowly, he drew her down until she was seated firmly astride him with her limbs folded on either side of his hips and her hands curled upon his chest. She was aware of the stickiness of her fingers and breathlessly apologized if she had soiled his new tunic.

His mouth moved with amusement at her concern. Like her own miserable excuse for a dress, it was only makeshift protection for his skin against the impetuosity of the insects and weather until better clothes could be made of decently cured skins.

"It is nothing," he told her huskily, fingering her dress. "This is nothing, too. Take it off."

It seemed an odd thing for him to suggest. "Then I would be naked."

"Yes. I will be naked, too."

The idea made her giggle. "Look," she said, and held out her palm to him. The berries that she had kept within her fist were a pulpy, seedy mash that plopped onto his chest. "Are these not strange?"

He was not looking at the pile of squashed berries that lay upon his chest. He was fingering the shoulder thongs that held her dress, then touching her braids, loosing the thongs that held them.

Naya did not mind; she knew that she would have to replait her hair anyway, and as he was fingering her hair she was alternately licking her fingers and rubbing the pulp into the rough skin of his tunic instead of whisking it away. It seemed a strange thing to do, but somehow she could not help herself.

"I found a bush of these berries in the burned land and made a necklet of them, you know, but the river . . ." Her voice had sounded so far away. She shook her head to clear it. "Here, taste the juice. It is sweet."

He took her hand and pressed her palm against his mouth.

She gasped as the most amazing sensation flooded her. His tongue was moving to trace the contours of her palm, slowly probing between her fingers. When he began to suck the juice from her skin, a sudden deep and most wonderful tickling warmth expanded within her loins and belly and breasts. She shivered and arched back as she gripped him with her thighs, pressed herself into him, and moved her hips, increasing the feeling in her loins and making the tickling worse and more wonderful than before. It expanded to fill her genitals with a fire that drove her to press him harder . . . faster. . . .

A throaty sigh came from his mouth. She felt the tension in his body. His hands were on her hips, holding her, moving her, then he raised his hips to meet the press of her body.

Naya trembled, amazed and delighted by this exquisite

experience. She found no cause to keep her feelings a secret from him.

"Good . . . so good . . . so *good* . . ." She sighed and moved and looked down at Manaravak, at beautiful, powerful Manaravak, who would be her man someday. The juice of the berries stained his mouth. His eyes met hers and held. How dark they were, how black and hot—and hungry.

Perplexed, she turned her head to one side. "If you are hungry, there is meat in my gathering sack—"

"This is the only meat I want from you!"

She gasped again, for he suddenly sat up and with a single motion jerked her dress down. The thongs that he had already loosened slipped away, and his hands were working hard at her tiny breasts.

Pain flared. "Don't!" she cried out.

He ignored her, and the look on his face frightened her. He leaned forward and mouthed her breasts, nipping and sucking. Beyond listening, he bent her back—hurting her as he ran his hands hard over her belly and downward . . . downward until his long fingers were invading her secret place, and shocked by the invasion, she screamed.

He snarled then and forced her back, gripping her thighs, and holding them wide while he bent to browse between them, scenting her, probing her with his tongue as a dog would do, and suddenly she thought of Companion and Snow Eater locked together and of the way that pups—and human babies—were born. In blood. In pain. And always after a mating.

"No! Stop! I do not want babies!"

If he heard her, he gave no sign of it. He was growling as, with one hand holding her down, he leaned back and freed himself.

Fighting him, she twisted sideways. For a moment she thought that she was free of him, but she was not. He had her by her leg, and then his hands were turning her, he was on top of her, straddling her, displaying himself for her as he roared his intent like a wolf. No! Not like a wolf!

"Wanawut!" she shrieked, and lost the battle against a sudden wave of terror as she stared at his organ and could not look away. Distended upward in full erection, it seemed enormous to her—a great, blue-veined spear that would surely pierce straight through to her heart when it entered her.

And now, although she screamed and screamed, he positioned himself for rape.

In that moment the boys and Grek came crashing through the trees, and the old man roared in anger as he dragged Manaravak off his granddaughter, and Nantu off Manaravak.

As Naya flew into the protection of Grek's arms, Nantu vowed to kill Manaravak. And in this way the moment passed, and although no one knew it, the world would never be the same for anyone in Torka's band again.

✦━━━━✦

4

✦━━━━✦

That night Naya sobbed as if her heart would break. The women and children were solemn, and the men engaged in low and troubled talk in the bone- and antler-walled council house of caribou skins.

Torka urged Manaravak to speak, but the young man did not know what he was expected to say. Everyone, it seemed, was angry with everyone else—and all the anger was directed at him as he sat solemnly staring into his lap. He was a man, not an animal, they reminded him as Torka sat in silence, waiting for a response from him.

He did not speak. He could not find the words. He did not understand their accusation. Of course he was a man! Had he not acted as a man? Did men not mate when roused by a ready and willing female?

Old Grek was sitting cross-legged on the fur-covered floor, yet he seemed to levitate as he reached out to stab the air in front of Manaravak's nose and roar at him like a bull bison set to charge. "Naya is a *child*! I warned you of this before! You shame us all!"

Manaravak looked up. *Shame?* He did not understand the concept any more than he understood why Naya had suddenly refused him when she had so eagerly led him into a physical state that had allowed him no retreat. Even now, when he thought of how she had pressed herself into his loins, he was not convinced that she had really wanted him to stop, and he could not comprehend why everyone was so angry because he had tried to force her to continue. It was understood by everyone that she would be his woman. What did it matter how or when he took her? The results would be the same. Besides, with the exception of Torka, they had all willingly shared their own women with him.

He thought about that. He had only used Honee, a bland and uninteresting partner, twice. Iana usually counseled "less wolfishness" on his part, and not enjoying a woman who criticized him through a mating, he usually turned to Eneela when the man need was on him. Although she never failed to look at him with disapproval by day, she would come whispering to him in the night without Simu's knowledge. She would slip into his lean-to, peel off her clothes, and lie naked beneath his bed skins, offering her great brown-nippled breasts to his mouth and opening herself wide to his explorations and release.

He frowned. Were the men angry because he shared their women? He did not know. He was the headman's son and the shaman's brother, but he felt like an outsider. It was a lonely feeling. He did not like it. He wanted to be one of them. He wanted to know why they all kept referring to Naya as a child. What kind of child led a man on through a willow grove to fall laughing in his arms, then worked herself on his groin in trembling anticipation of full sexual release? No child at all!

Perhaps he had missed some subtlety in the language of his people; he had not begun to learn their tongue until he was ten autumns old. Perplexed, he asked them: "Li, daughter of my brother Umak, she is a little girl, yes?"

"She is," affirmed his twin.

"And Uni, daughter of Simu, she is a little girl?"

Simu's head moved with begrudging assent.

Manaravak nodded. Up to this point his concept of what made a child seemed to be shared by the others. "Yona, the daughter of Grek, she is also a little girl?"

The old man's mouth turned down so far that the seams of his lips seemed to be gouging their way into his neck. "My Yona is a *baby!*"

Now Manaravak was more confused than ever. Babies cried and sucked milk from their mother's breasts and messed the hut floors of their parents. Yona, on the other hand, was six, and Uni and Li were five. He pictured their tubular little bodies, flat chests, and stick legs. He would hit *himself* in the head with a rock if he so much as thought of mating with any of them! Now anger stirred in him. Was this what they were accusing him of? "I do not understand!" he protested. "Naya, the granddaughter of Grek, she is *little*, but she is *not* a child. She has breast buds and round hips, and she smells like a woman, and she moves on a man like—"

Grek roared, "She has yet to bleed as a woman!"

Manaravak was still uncomprehending. "She will soon. And what difference does it make?"

"*All!*" Grek shot back and would have snapped to his feet and knocked down the low-ceilinged council hut had Simu and Dak not reached out and held him by his shoulders.

Seated at Torka's right, Umak rolled his eyes in disbelief of his brother's ignorance.

Torka's face was expressionless as he looked at his second son. "A man of the People may not mate with a girl who has yet to bleed as a woman, Manaravak. You have been told this."

Manaravak blinked and stared. "Yes." He remembered. At last he understood. He had broken some sort of prohibition; his people's lives were full of prohibitions. "In the willow grove with Naya, she made it easy for me to forget."

"She?" Grek leaned forward, trembling with rage, his old face contorted as he fought to control his temper. "You made Little Girl cry! If we had not heard Little Girl scream and if Nantu had not come running—"

Manaravak also leaned forward, and head to head with Grek over the small fire, he shouted at the old man. "Your Naya is no little girl! Ask Umak the way she danced before us naked on the day that Daughter of the Sky set fire to the earth. Your Little Girl was asking to be mated then, and she was asking to be mated when she led me into the grove! Speak, Umak, tell them!"

He waited. His eyes met Umak's and held. Why was his brother silent? Why did he look so distressed?

"Regardless, a man of the People must not forget the traditions of his ancestors, Manaravak!" Torka spoke with solemn emphasis.

Manaravak fell silent. He kept looking at his brother until Umak looked away. Loneliness and betrayal overwhelmed him. If Umak would not speak in his defense, who would?

Torka looked at Manaravak coldly, out of the eyes of a headman, not a father. "What has happened between Naya and you was wrong. There must be chastisement. You are no longer a wild boy whose ignorance of the ways of your people may be overlooked and forgiven."

Manaravak bent forward, cradled his head in his hands, and sighed. No matter how hard he tried, the ten long summers that he had lived as a solitary human being among beasts had made their mark upon him, and he could not free himself of it. The breast milk that had nourished him as an infant had not come from the breasts of a woman, it had come from the breasts of an animal. When he had been a child in need of warmth and comfort, no human mother had been there to draw the cold flap of a pit hut tight against the weather and hold him close, rocking him as she sang the songs and told him the wonderful myths that instructed a child in all that it meant to be a human being.

No. For Manaravak there had been a nest of bones, twigs, and bloodied feathers plucked from the breasts of screaming teratorns and eagles. And for Manaravak, all comfort had come in the massive, hairy, enfolding arms of the wanawut, in the cooing of the beast, and in the soft breath of a meat-eating animal blowing soothingly and lovingly upon his face and body to keep him warm. The memory touched him deeply. The motherly love of the beast had been enough for him. It had been everything.

He closed his eyes and pressed his lids with his fingers. The men of his band were arguing softly among themselves, coming to decisions. The sound was like a hum of blackflies droning in the heavy amber air of a windless summer day. Manaravak barely heard it. He was remembering his other life, his animal life, a life devoid of words or songs or abstract thoughts—a life of now, never of yesterday or tomorrow . . . a life in which the word *why* was never asked or even thought of . . . a life of pure, unthinking response to the drives of instinct and the need for self-gratification. He sighed. It had not been a bad existence.

"Manaravak?"

Torka's voice drew him from his reverie.

"It is now agreed among us." There was strength and remorse in Torka's eyes as he spoke. "Naya will not be for you. This is her wish, and it will be honored. When Naya becomes a woman, she will be free to go to Umak. He has asked for her. Honee is not well and could use help with the children at her fire circle."

Manaravak stalked from the council hut in a fury.

"Manaravak!" Umak followed him. "Brother, stop! Wait."

"Why? What kind of brother are you? Why did you keep silent when I had need of you to speak for me . . . unless it was because you knew that if you did not speak, you would soon be free to snap like a hungry wolf after my woman?"

"She is not your woman, Manaravak. She is not a woman at all." Umak stepped in front of Manaravak. "Listen to me, Brother. Naya has refused you. Grek has said that he will not allow her to go to you even when she does become a woman."

Manaravak's face was set and wary. "And meanwhile you do well for yourself, Brother Umak. You will take her to your fire circle, where already you have a female of your own. You are a clever shaman! You will have two women at your fire while Manaravak lives alone!"

"By your own choice, Manaravak. You could have chosen Honee."

"No, I could not. You are eldest. She was without a man. Tradition sent her to your bed skins. And now you will have my Naya, too! You are greedy, Umak."

Umak put a steadying hand upon his brother's forearm. "Right now she wants no man at all! You have frightened all desire to become a woman right out of her."

Manaravak's frown became a scowl. "I do not believe that."

"You had better believe it."

Manaravak's eyes grew hard. "You, firstborn twin, eldest son, and Shaman, you know everything. You *have* everything. The gift of the Seeing Wind is yours, but I am your twin. I am not blind to what is in your heart. I know what you want. Don't try to tell me that you do not."

They stood facing one another.

The other men were emerging from the council house.

"Let there be no bad feeling between us, Brother." Umak spoke strongly, with no attempt at deception or deceit. "If Naya looks at you again and smiles, if she changes her mind and decides to be your woman and not mine, I will be content if the council approves."

Manaravak nodded. "May it be so." It was no easy thing to remain angry with his brother.

"And if she smiles at me and consents to be my woman?" pressed Umak.

Manaravak raised a telling brow. He had always loved a

challenge, especially from Umak, who knew how to make a contest all that it could be. "I will be content if you will agree to share her!"

"Never!" replied Umak.

"We shall see," said Manaravak. "We shall see."

———◆———

5

———◆———

Autumn seemed to end in a single night. In the following cool, ever-shortening days of rising wind and occasional light snow, bad feelings were set aside at the headman's command and all worked together to make a strong camp against the long, endless night to come. The People could smell new snow in the high passes, and there was much talk of an early winter.

Larani was glad. Although she was still weak and in pain, her love for her mother had forced her to make concessions to Eneela's care. Nourished upon marrow broth, blood, and gland meat, she was beginning to feel stronger despite herself. The calling of loons had awakened her this morning, and for a long while she had lain still, listening, loving the sound of them. It had occurred to her in a rush of clarity that she had always loved the sound of loons, and even as the loons must soon rise from the waters and fly away before the first hard freeze, she, too, could rise from her lethargy and despair. In time, when she was healed, she could be of use to her people. What more could anyone ask of life?

And so she had risen and gone out to enjoy the bitter taste of the frigid morning air. For the first time since her injury, she looked forward to days of endless night in which she could sit at the back of the communal hut with her scars safely hidden in robes of gloom, close to the others again, listening to stories and conversing.

She looked across the valley toward the surrounding mountains. Under the leaden sky, they appeared as gray and forbidding as the scars of an old hunter . . . as gray and forbidding as her own ruined flesh would be when—and if— it ever healed.

Larani shuddered at the comparison, and her robe settled against her burns. Pain erupted. She shoved the wrap back and away, bearing her scars. She did not intend to cry out, but she did, and from all across the camp, people looked up from their tasks to stare her way.

Aware that Manaravak was among them, Larani pulled up her robe and, nearly fainting from the agony, ducked quickly into the privacy of her solitary shelter. She dropped to her knees. The robe crumpled around her. Her hands went to her face. When the door flap was brushed aside and the wind entered, she stiffened against her certainty that Manaravak had followed.

"Here, Larani. I've brought something for your pain."

Larani's spirit shriveled with disappointment at the sound of Naya's voice.

"Can I stay with you awhile?" asked the granddaughter of Grek.

"Go away, Naya. The hurt I feel cannot be taken away by any of your medicines."

Naya took a sip from the bladder flask that she had brought for Larani, then licked her lips. "Oh, Larani, may I stay with you? It's all I can think of to make the two of them leave me alone!"

Larani turned toward Naya. The girl looked pathetic— small and nervous and obviously preoccupied. The near rape had changed her, but not enough to allow her to realize how hurtful her words had been. "Poor Naya . . . what *are* you to do? It is truly a terrible thing to have *both* the headman's twins trying to win a smile from you."

Naya pouted. "Are you making fun of me, Larani?"

"No, Little Girl, I am envying you with all my heart."

Although the last of the migratory waterfowl had left the valley, the great mammoth totem Life Giver grazed with his kind in the spruce groves of the eastern foothills. When Torka led his fellow hunters on exploratory forays deep into the flanks of the surrounding mountains, they also found to their infinite pleasure and satisfaction that small herds of caribou and elk would indeed pass the winter in the wind-protected canyons.

"This *is* a good land, yes!" proclaimed Grek, grinning, as he wheezed from exhilaration and the overexertion brought on from the long overland walk.

Torka and Simu eyed the old hunter with ill-concealed concern until Dak pointed off and drew their attention to the hills to the south.

"Look!" he exclaimed. "The herd of horses that we saw when we first entered the valley is still there! And below, do you see the moose breaking up ice on the surface of that pond?"

Simu stared ahead; with a slow, reflective nod of his head, the corners of his mouth turned up as he spoke his thoughts aloud. "If our immediate supplies run out and our cache pits fail to provide us with enough to see us through the winter—and *if* the forces of Creation will allow it—there will be fresh meat to hunt and hot blood to drink in the depth of the long winter dark."

Our supplies will not run out, and our cache pits will not fail us, thought Torka with absolute resolve.

In the days that followed, his men, under his supervision, placed cache pits with infinite care so that whenever the hunters went out across the valley—or in the event of an emergency the camp had to be relocated—the People would always be near a ready source of food and supplies. Every pit was dug and lined with waterproof hides, then filled near to bursting with meat and fat, extra rolls of sinew and thong, bow drills and packets of kindling and extra wicks, spearheads and shafts, and spare new tools made of caribou bone and the fine stone that the men and boys had brought back from Spear Mountain.

Torka knew that never before had he stood at the edge of winter with a better-stocked encampment than the one into which he and his people had settled.

And yet, as the moon rose and fell and the days grew ever shorter, Torka refused to allow even the youngest members of the band to squander their time. The People speared fish and snared ptarmigan. The drying frames sagged beneath the weight of caribou meat, and the women had prepared hides to provide clothes, sleeping furs, and hut covers enough for three bands.

When Naya complained, Lonit told her to be still. "Stop wasting time, Naya. Even the little ones are helping to pluck feathers from the ptarmigan . . . even if they are making a mess of it!"

Naya looked off just in time to see Kharn throw pin feathers at Uni and Li. Swan—in charge of the boy, as always—tried to stop him, but it was too late. In seconds, Companion and Snow Eater had sighted on the game and were leaping, barking, and circling amid a blizzard of down. Everyone in camp was laughing as the wind scattered the feathers high and wide.

Kharn led the others in a wild, reaching, giggling pursuit of the blowing feathers. But Swan, deep in the cloud of flying feathers, captured the boy and tucked him under one arm. Leaping dogs and running children got under her feet, and she fell, tripped by an overexcited Companion. In a moment, Simu, Grek, Umak, and Torka rushed in to collect and scold their sons and daughters, while Dak was shooing the dogs away and helping Swan to her feet as he checked both Kharn and her for bruises.

"Fun!" guffawed the boy, spitting feathers.

"I am fine! Fine!" informed Swan, and although her blush was invisible in the snow of ptarmigan down, it colored her voice, so that when she placed Kharn into his father's arms and turned away, Demmi looked after her and mocked.

"Be careful, Swan! I'm watching you!"

"Good!" Swan replied under her breath, so low that only Torka heard her as she walked past him, her teeth clenched, eyes flashing, and cheeks blazing.

The next day Torka led the women out to dig the season's remaining sweet tubers. When this was done, he urged Naya to gather more healing herbs and berries. He sent her in the company of the other women and girls and watched over her himself, insisting that Manaravak accompany him so his son might see what is expected of an adult male when he is sent to guard the females of the band. Umak trailed along uninvited.

Manaravak comported himself well. Naya told him to stay away from her, and he did, but before the day was done, he had made her a necklet of odd-looking berries. In what was obviously an apology, he proffered them with awkward words and utmost deference.

"What sort of a present is that?" teased Umak. "I will make you a necklet, Naya, of the finest greenstone and blackest obsidian!"

The girl did not seem to hear him. She remained openly wary of Manaravak, but it was clear that the necklet pleased her, and as Torka observed in silence she accepted Manaravak's present.

*   *   *

That night the mammoth trumpeted in the eastern foothills and wolves sang a restless song that spoke to Torka and his people of changing weather. Soon the snow would come. The sun would slip away for another three moons, but Torka did not worry.

He slept well, and the next day when he walked alone outside the camp, an almost overwhelming feeling of contentment filled him. He looked back toward the newly established encampment of his people. Large and small, the conical winter pit huts stood against the sky. It made him feel good to look at them. Soon Torka and his people would endure their first winter in the Valley of the Great River. They would have shelter and warmth, and meat and fat upon which to feed. And over low fires of dung and bones and the dried gleanings of the autumn earth, or gathered around the light of Lonit's lamp, they would have stories of the ancients upon which to draw their strength. Soon the children of the new land would learn of how their ancestors had endured uncounted and uncountable winters in the far western country beyond the Sea of Ice. They would learn that they were descendants of First Man and First Woman, who walked together upon the yielding flesh of Mother Below beneath the vast, wrathful, star-freckled skin of Father Above while the beast wanawut prowled beyond the edge of the world learning how best to teach the People the meaning of the word *fear*.

6

It was the time of the long dark. It was the time when Father Above closed his yellow eye, wrapped himself in robes of storm darkness, and slept in the arms of his sister the moon.

Naya sat cross-legged and glum within the pit hut of Grek, sipping at a sour concoction of melted snow, melted fat, pulverized dry willow stalks, and all that remained of her family's supply of chopped adrenal glands.

"Drink!" Iana insisted.

Naya stared at her grandfather's woman. "I don't like it!"

"Too bad! You know that it is the gland meat that will do the trick! Larani has already come to her time of blood, and I want you to, also."

Naya made a face of revulsion. "I do not care if I *ever* become a woman!" she said rebelliously.

"*I* do!" Iana was openly angry. "Because then you shall leave this hut! Your poor old grandfather shouldn't be out in the winter dark hunting caribou so you might have fresh gland meat!"

The hostility in Iana's voice brought Naya near to tears; her chin quivered as she spoke in her own defense. "Swan has not bled yet, either. And I begged Grandfather not to go!"

Iana measured the girl with sudden thoughtfulness. "Naya, are you afraid to become a woman?"

The girl stared into her lap. "I am happy as I am, here in the hut of my grandfather." Then, suddenly, she shook her head violently. "I do not want a man—not Umak, not Manaravak, not any man at all!"

"You must not be afraid, girl. What happened in the grove was unfortunate, but Manaravak has tried to make amends and—"

Naya looked up. Her eyes flashed. "I tell you, I do not want a man! I am too young! Everyone can see that I am too young! Everyone still calls me Little Girl—everyone but *him*, and I do not want *him*, not ever again! Or Umak! I do not want Honee as a fire sister. I *have* a sister. Yes! Little Yona is like a sister to me." Her face gentled as she looked at the child. "Aren't you, Yona? Come. Let us play again with the new buckskin dolls that Iana has made for you! Come! I will let you wear my stone necklace!"

Yona took full advantage of the invitation. "I will play if you will make me my *own* necklace from the extra red berries in your big hide bag!"

In the cold blue light of the Arctic winter night, Torka, Manaravak, Grek, and Companion trotted out across the Valley of the Great River in search of caribou. The night was so cold that even the dog wore boots: paw bags of soft caribou hide bound, with the hair facing in, with sinew cords knotted midway up each furry leg.

The men needed more than just boots. Along with their pack frames of caribou antler, Torka, Manaravak, and Grek each wore undergarments, stockings, and mitten liners of the supplest skins of caribou calves, chewed to a consistency of velvet by the women and girls of the band. Their mittens were of caribou skins, tanned with the hair on and turned inward to form an insulating layer of fur between the liner and the actual mitten. Their boots were cross laced to the knee with strips of thong, lined with down and lichens, then triple-soled with hard-tanned hide. The bottoms were turned up well over the toes and heels, then crimped and stitched all around softer uppers made of short-haired caribou leg skins. Their tunics and trousers were of a double thickness of meticulously softened caribou hide worn with the hair facing in.

They rested for a few moments to cool off; even though the temperature was low enough to sear their lungs fatally had they not filtered each breath through the long guard hairs of their wolf-tail ruffs, the hunters were perspiring heavily. The warmth was not unwelcome. To be cold on this night was to die on this night. They all knew it as they went on.

At last they reached the deeper snow of the foothills. With Grek lagging behind, Torka and Manaravak paused and pointed ahead. Although no caribou could be seen, father and son nodded, knowing that they had found their prey; an extensive band of ice fog lay ahead—a frozen vapor created by the exhalations of living animals.

Torka and Manaravak hefted their spears. By asking Manaravak on this hunt, Torka had hoped to soften Grek's opinion of his second-born son.

"Remember now, three kills only," cautioned Torka. "One for the new woman, Larani, who must be honored; one for Swan, who needs gland meat if she is ever to become a woman; and one for Naya."

Grek's lips puckered peevishly. "Yes. Maybe someday."

"Then we are agreed," said Torka. "We come from a camp rich in dried meat and stored fat. It would be an offense to the forces of Creation and to the life spirits of the caribou if we were to kill more than we need."

The dog loped ahead and disappeared into the fog. Torka, Manaravak, and Grek had donned the new stalking cloaks that they had packed in their back frames, then moved forward, spears in hand.

Torka's spear struck true, and a cow fell. An adolescent calf turned its head to see the cause of the cow's *whoof* of surprise and pain. It, too, collapsed with Manaravak's spear in its lung, and death poured hot and red from its nostrils and gaping mouth. In that moment a second cow fell to Grek's spear, and the men and dogs howled together in triumph.

After endless days of confinement in the darkness of their winter camp, Manaravak was inspired to spear a fourth animal—a bull, a more fitting kill than a calf for a man—but Torka and Grek did not notice. They slew the fallen animals and ate of their raw flesh, feeding like lions until, sated on fresh, hot meat at last, Torka drew back, trembling.

Wolves were howling somewhere in the night, and for a frightening moment it seemed that something larger and more dangerous—and somehow almost human—was howling with them. *Wanawut?* He listened closely, but there was only the sound of the wind and of Grek and Manaravak feeding with the dogs.

He looked at them and noticed with a start that there were four dead caribou on the ground instead of three. Something that his long-dead grandfather had taught him so many years ago came to mind: Remember, Torka, only a thin caul of control separates the beast man from the beast animal, predator from prey. Ah, yes, Torka, you must never forget that only a fool fears the wanawut more than he fears the animal that lives within himself.

Suddenly impatient with the animalistic smacking, grunting, and sucking sounds coming not only from the dogs but from Grek and Manaravak, he commanded, "Enough! What are you trying to do? Eat all four caribou by yourselves?"

Grek put down the gore-slimed coils of intestine from which he had been squeezing the soft, undigested contents of the caribou's last meals into his mouth. He smacked his lips and drew back from his feast. Even in the darkness, it was apparent that the fur edges of his ruff were soaked in blood. "Sorry. Got carried away, yes! Four, you say?"

Manaravak remained as he was, straddling the rib cage of the caribou bull. He had tossed off his stalking cloak and thrown his hood back; he lay prone with his face buried in the throat of the animal, fiercely and loudly sucking blood from the wound that his dagger had made while life still pumped hot and hard out of the dying heart. The hind leg of the caribou jerked, and its forelimbs had begun to tremble spasmodically.

"Enough!" shouted Torka, because for the first time he saw that the animal upon which his son was feeding was still alive. "Manaravak!"

The young man looked up. There was blood on his face. "What is it?"

"Your spear in the side of that bull marks it as your kill—a *fourth* kill when I commanded only three. And you feed on it like a lion, not like a man!"

Manaravak took this as a compliment. "Had to kill better than just a calf to honor the new woman! We hunt like lions, the three of us! A lion knows the way to drink his fill before the blood freezes. Come, before this caribou dies and its blood stops flowing. Come, Father, and you, Grek, you old lion. There is life and strength here for men who must carry much meat back to their people!"

He was right, and Torka knew it. True, they had killed four animals instead of three, but what difference could it make now?

Grek was vain enough to gulp down the young man's compliment and grew visibly fat upon it as, strutting forward and searching out a place to draw blood from the neck of the caribou, he forgot his animosity toward Manaravak. "Old lion, yes?"

"Yes," replied Manaravak. "Old and strong and very dangerous to caribou!"

———◆———

7

———◆———

The hut of blood was a small, conical shelter not unlike the other pit huts except that it had been raised well away from the other shelters.

Peering from the entryway of the hut of blood, Larani stared across camp toward the large communal lodge. Her eyes fixed on the twelve-pointed double rack of antlers that spread wide over the entrance. Sheened with ice and dripping icicles, the antlers shimmered red, blue, and green in the cold, brazen light of a multicolored aurora. Larani cocked her head at the sight and listened to the sound of the shaman's chanting as it escaped, along with thick, gray smoke, from the vent hole high at the apex of the shaggy, curving roof. On any other night, Larani would have found beauty in the sights and sounds, but tonight they seemed rife with ominous portent.

"Umak sings for you," said Eneela proudly. "Come back inside, Daughter. The other women will be here soon, and there is much to do if you are to be ready for the celebration in your honor."

The words made Larani feel sick with apprehension. She found herself recalling the bleak but comforting acceptance of her condition to which the calling of loons had brought her less than a moon ago. But a moon ago she had been a girl who had yet to shed a woman's blood or to realize what would face her when she did. Now a new moon had risen and set, and the loons had left the Valley of the Great River. She closed her eyes, imagined herself winging her way southward with them, flying high and free and away from all that faced her now.

Her thoughts ran momentarily wild with hope. She could run from the hut and from the encampment. A few deep breaths would be enough to sear her lungs and make all future breaths impossible. She would die, but her spirit would soar with the loons, released from her ruined body and the pain of her burns, free of the shameful obligations that now lay ahead.

"Come away from the cold, Larani. Close the flap, Daughter, and kneel again before the fire. You need have no fear of it. I have plenty of water here if it grows too hot. Here now, you must breathe in the good smokes and sweat away the last of your childhood." Eneela added boughs of artemisia to the small fire. "Ah, my dear girl, since the day of your birth I have waited to share this joy with you! Oh, Larani, if only I could make you feel the sweetness of this moment as I feel it—to be a mother, to see one's eldest girl become a woman!"

Larani, suddenly furious, faced her mother. "Stop!" she cried, but when she saw Eneela's loving face fall, her anger bled away and her thoughts of death shattered. "I am sorry, but I do not want to be here and would *not* be here if Torka and Simu had not insisted upon it!"

Eneela clucked her tongue admonishingly. "You could not have stayed in your own hut, Larani! When a woman sheds moon blood, she must be secluded lest the spirits cause others to bleed, too! And would it not be something to have the men of the band begin to suffer cramps and—"

"I *was* away from everyone," Larani interrupted, in no mood for her mother's strained attempt at humor.

"Not far enough! What is the matter with you, Larani? Every girl dreams about coming to the hut of blood as a first-time woman."

"Look at me, Mother. See me as I am."

Eneela's head went defensively high. "You are healing nicely."

"I am scarred! Ugly!"

"You are a new woman who is capable of taking new life into her belly and creating the future of the band out of her own flesh! Nothing is more beautiful or wondrous!"

Larani hung her head and felt the new scar tissue at the side of her neck and head stretch and ache. She began to cry. Eneela would find her beautiful, no matter what. But what of the others? What of Manaravak? What would he see when the new woman was summoned forth to display herself? She reached for the bladder flask of medicine drink that Naya had left with her; Naya's brew had a way of dulling more than pain—it took the edge off reason. Larani drank deeply.

"Are you still feeling unwell?" asked Eneela with concern.

Larani pursed her lips against the unexpected sweetness of the liquid, immediately realizing that Naya had added something unfamiliar to this batch. A wave of nausea and light-headedness nearly overcame her. "I am feeling sick," she said, putting the flask aside. The wave was passing. She was sleepy now, and more than a little surly. "As sick as the People will be when they look at the new woman when she displays herself before the ceremonial fire!"

The hunters returned to the camp in the cold, brazen light of the aurora. The fresh caribou meat was portioned and prepared for the feast fire. It was a large blaze, fed with fat and bones and piled high with driftwood from along the riverbank.

"Ah!" exclaimed Naya, peeking out of Grek's pit hut. "If there will be a fire like this for me and presents and dancing and feasting, then I *want* to be a woman! I just do not want to take a man!"

Iana's keen eyes saw clearly that Naya was feeling much better for the first time in many days. Grek would have been glad to see this. He was out doing whatever males did in the council hut before a winter new-woman ceremony. Yona lay on her back, humming sleepily to one of her dolls.

Iana looked at her daughter out of narrowed eyes. Yona had been drowsy and irritable ever since Naya had given her a necklace of berries.

Iana had come close to examine the fruits. They were unfamiliar to her. "Wear them," she had advised Yona, "but do not eat them."

She still recalled how Naya had caressed the necklet and had smiled at it as though it were a friend that might smile back. "These berries are good. They have never made me sick," Naya had insisted.

Iana's frown settled into an expression of puzzlement because the berries seemed to make Naya feel well and happy. Even now, as the girl plopped herself cheerfully down onto her bed furs, she was chewing on yet another one.

"We must be careful of new foods, Naya."

"Yes, yes, of course." Naya was not in a mood to be careful. She was having a wonderful time combing her hair. "Look, Iana . . . do you see the way the tines work through the tangles? This comb Umak gave me works very well!"

"If you do not want to take a man, then you should not accept his gifts."

"Umak is different. He's my friend."

"And he is *still* a man—who desires you as much or even more than does Manaravak!"

Naya thought about this as she held the seedy little dried berry between her front teeth, moving her jaws to extract the last of its oils. "What is it like to be desirable?" Her voice almost a purr. "What is it like when Grek lies on you or when you are sent to ease the man need of Manaravak, and he lies naked on you and moves like a thrusting ram and howls like a wolf when his man bone enters? Is it pain or pleasure when you spread yourself wide for him, or are pain and pleasure the same thing when a man and a woman are joined and moving together and—"

"Naya!" Iana was startled not only by the girl's questions but by the look in her eyes. A change had come over the girl. She had dropped her comb and now sat rigidly upright on her folded knees, moving slowly on her heels. Her pupils were fixed and dilated. "What kind of questions are these to ask in front of Yona? And from one who proclaims that she has no desire for a man! Stop moving on your heels like that! Look at you—you are hot and ready for it!"

"It?" The question could not have been more guileless.

Iana was furious. Her slap came hard and fast. Incredibly, as though the blow had amused rather than hurt her, Naya smiled as she held her palm against her cheek. "You cannot hurt me," she said defiantly.

"Perhaps not," Iana allowed, "but I will tell your grandfather of your behavior. And he shall also know that I am again with child. Yes, girl, do not look so surprised! Soon Yona, Tankh, and Chuk will have a new brother or sister. And soon the hut of Grek will not be big enough for both of us!"

The people of Torka circled the ceremonial fire. In their hooded, heavy winter clothes they clapped their thickly mittened hands, sidestepped, feet sliding to the right.

Umak danced alone inside the circle until at last he stopped and, in the commanding, stentorian voice of a shaman, called out, "Larani!"

The dancing stopped. The people stared at their shaman, nodding in approval of his appearance and appropriately arrogant stance. Honee had designed his tunic and headdress, festooning every inch with the feathers of snowy owls and winter-white ptarmigan. Across his upper back and shoulders was a cloak fashioned of the feathered skin of a teratorn, its wings spread wide and fastened to his gauntlets so that when he spread his arms, he appeared about to soar into the night. The head of the teratorn crowned a thickly ruffed hood of fox skins that extended well out over his face with its beak agape and its eye sockets filled with two glinting flakes of shining obsidian.

Naya was watching. He stood taller and thought, *Soon a new-woman fire will burn for you! And then you will choose a man! You will choose me!*

Umak's contentment vanished when he saw that the old man was standing next to Manaravak. Grek's dour attitude toward Manaravak had changed since they had returned to camp. Everyone spoke of their gladness at seeing the newfound camaraderie, but Umak had been puzzled until he had heard Manaravak refer to the old man as "Old Lion."

Flattery. The wind congealed in Umak's mouth. *Two can*

play at that game! he thought, and knew that he, as shaman, already held the edge.

"Larani, daughter of Simu and Eneela! Larani, sister of Dak and Nantu and Uni! Larani, new woman, new sister to the daughters of this band, come forth now to the People!"

The women and girls of the band lifted bone flutes to pipe a high, atonal, cacophonous fanfare at the sound of the shaman's second summons to the new woman.

"Larani, new woman, come forth now to the sons of this band so that they may rejoice at the coming of the new woman! Come, new woman! This shaman calls you forth, as now the eldest of our people—*the bison-strong, lion-bold elder*—beats the drum of welcome as the new woman comes forth!"

With a flourish directly inspired by the unprecedented compliments, old Grek hefted the ceremonial drum, which had been made for this occasion. Tradition decreed that the eldest male must be the first to slap the drum with the flat of his hand before passing it on to the headman, who, after rousing the second beat of honor, then passed it on until each adult male in the band had completed his turn.

Simu was the last to accept it. As the father of the new woman, the drum was now his to keep until she took a man. When her virginity was a thing of the past, her mate would bring the drum before the headman and the assembled people. He would strike it one last time; then, as the new woman stood proudly by, her man would symbolically pierce the skin of the drum with his spear and return it to her parents, who would then burn it.

As Simu struck the drum now, he made the mandatory summoning shout, and the People cheered as the new woman was escorted from the hut of blood by her mother.

The resultant cloud that formed above the gathering glistened in the light of the star-jeweled aurora until it was consumed by the rising, tremulous waves of heat that rose out of the ceremonial fire.

Simu interpreted it as a bad omen. He was participating this night only because Torka had insisted upon it and because Eneela had sworn that if he did not, she would sleep with her back to him, as rigid and cold as a slab of ice . . . and if a need for woman's pleasure came over her, she would seek it with Manaravak.

Simu gritted his teeth. The latter was already a source of anger between them. True, he had Summer Moon to ease him, but she was at long last with child, and he would do nothing to jeopardize her long-hoped-for dream of having a baby of her own.

He stared ahead at his daughter. He had seen the fine new-woman clothes that Eneela had made, but instead Larani was shrouded in a tentlike covering of white caribou skins and fox fur that fell from the top of her head to the tips of her moccasins. The girl was wearing her new bed skins!

The bone flutes grew silent. An exhalation of dismay and pity went out of every mouth.

Simu struggled against disappointment. How he had looked forward to this moment! How he had imagined his fine, bright Larani striding regally to the ceremonial fire, folding back her hood, and allowing everyone in the band to see the radiance of her face as she announced proudly, "Yes! The new-woman Larani is here! Let the People celebrate as she walks away forever from the child who once answered to her name!"

Within his ruff, Simu could have wept for what might have been. He would never forgive Torka for refusing him her death or for insisting that she go through with this travesty of a ceremony. How could she be honored as a new potential giver of life when no man would ever want to lie with her . . . unless she were the last living woman in the band or kept that ridiculous tent of bedding over her! Or unless Torka rescinded his ruling about brothers and sisters not being allowed to mate; Dak would take his beloved sister to his fire circle no matter what she looked like.

"Larani, new woman of this band, come forth!"

Now it was Torka who summoned the new woman, but Larani did not respond. The People stared, waiting, then began to worry. To break with the tradition of their ancestors on a sacred night would not be a good thing.

Feeling the intense heat of the ceremonial fire at his back, Torka understood the young woman's fear of the flames. Ignoring the murmurings of his band, and without regard to tradition, he went to her and continued the ceremony away from the flames.

"Is this the new woman who stands before the headman of the People?"

Larani did not answer. Eneela held out the soiled skins upon which her daughter had shed first blood. "Here is the blood of my child Larani."

Torka accepted the soiled skins. Custom now demanded that the new woman take them from him and throw them into the fire as a symbolic offering up of the death of her childhood. He knew that she would balk, and she did not disappoint him. His heart ached for her.

"In this new land you are the first girl to come to her time of blood," he reminded quietly. "This is a great honor and a great gift."

"It is of no use to me."

"Like it or not, Larani, you *have* become a woman. In the Valley of the Great River the People will not dishonor the ways of their ancestors by ignoring the traditional ceremonies that must be made in honor of the new woman and of all that she represents."

"I represent nothing," she replied in absolute dejection. "Swan and Naya should have been first. That was what the forces of Creation wanted when they sent Daughter of the Sky after me. You should not have interfered. Forgive me, Torka, for speaking so, but the ancestors would have let me die at the hands of my father. By forcing him to let me live, you have dishonored them . . . and him and me."

Those words struck at him, as suddenly, with an upward movement, her uninjured arm raised the tent of fur and cast it away. Naked in the night and the cold, Larani stood boldly and defiantly in the golden, leaping glimmer of the ceremonial fire as her people cried out at the sight of her.

"You see?" she hissed at Torka. "This is a waste of good firewood! The child Larani has already been offered to the fire." Her words were slow, slurred, as though her tongue had grown too large for her mouth. "Do you all see what I have been hiding from your eyes these past moons? Yes, Torka has saved this life! Yes, it *has* lived on to bleed as a woman! But do not be fooled. Despite all of Naya's care of this woman's body, it is dead, killed long ago by Daughter of the Sky!"

Once again there was low, troubled talk in the council hut within the Valley of the Great River. The men sat in a solemn circle to decide how to deal with Larani.

"This man is ashamed," Simu said, anguished. "No female of this band has ever behaved so outrageously. Perhaps it is time to give Larani back to Daughter of the Sky." Simu's face was set, unforgiving, and yet his voice cracked when he spoke, and there was a half-wild look in his eyes that begged to be gentled, to be relieved, to be proved wrong.

"No!" Dak was furious with his father. "Death is no suitable chastisement for Larani. Her burns are healing, she is walking on her own, and soon she will have the full use of her arm. She is not a sickly child or a doddering elder who might, by tradition, be considered a burden and thus be put out of the band to die."

"You are right, old friend," said Umak. "It would be an offense to the forces of Creation to waste the life of a potential child bearer."

Beside him, Manaravak seemed perplexed. "She is not so bad ugly as I thought she would be—or as she thinks she is. Half a head burned, one arm and shoulder, and part of her upper back . . . but most of her face is still a face, and she has both eyes and ears and a fine, strong woman's body and breasts that—"

"Watch what you say of my sister!" Dak snapped with unbridled menace.

Manaravak shrugged affably. "No offense meant. Your sister is a fine new woman—even if she *is* burned around the edges."

"Why you—!" Dak lurched across the fire at Manaravak before anyone could intercept him.

Manaravak did not move from where he sat. He reached up and repelled Dak's attack by shoving his open hands hard upon Dak's shoulders. The son of Simu was propelled back across the fire into a seated position. He landed with a grunt of surprise.

As Grek hastily reassembled the scattered contents of the fire pit, Manaravak shook his head with calm disparagement and resumed speaking as though nothing had happened. "All the time you are too much angry, Dak. Talk does not come easy to me. You all know this. But Larani, I think that she is like a wounded animal that is just regaining strength, and fears that her life will not be all that it once was. I think that when she spoke bad words to her people, it was out of pain and uncertainty, as an injured animal cries out in fear when it is cornered."

"You should know!" Despite himself, Dak regretted his

nastiness. Lashing out at Manaravak had become instinctive with him; yet this time the man had shown a deeply insightful compassion. Was this the side of Manaravak that Demmi loved? The question loosed rage in him.

Torka saw it and raised a warning hand. "Stay where you are, Dak. If we cannot speak rationally among ourselves, how can we condemn the new woman for speaking irrationally against us?"

Silence settled. In the central fire pit, little clods of dung and sod slumped and sparked.

"We have heard no words of wisdom from our supreme elder," said Umak. "You must share your thoughts with us, Bison Man . . . Man Who Has Placed Two Spears in Three Paws . . . First Man to Test the River."

Grek stared at the shaman, and suspicion sparked in his little eyes. Then, beguiled by the oiling of his ego, he sat back and grunted with pleasure. "Grek says that the father of Larani must speak to his daughter, yes. Bring her back into your pit hut, Simu. It is not good for her to live alone. We males must overlook the crazy spirits that come into a female's head at certain times of the moon."

"There is no moon now, old man," reminded Simu blackly.

"Old man? Bah! This man hunts like a lion! This man charged Three Paws and drove the great bear away! This man found the way across the river. And this man would not turn his child out of the band to die!"

Simu eyed the old man with contempt. "You have shown us all how brave you are with the discipline of your granddaughter! It was her disobedience that caused Three Paws to attack the women at the lake! And it was her disobedience that called down Daughter of the Sky to turn upon my Larani in the first place."

Grek was clearly taken aback. "My little Naya is not being discussed here! It is a bad thing you ask, Simu—very bad. This old heart will not consent to abandoning Larani—or any member of this band—ever."

Torka felt suddenly tired. He felt suddenly cold. Grek was right. Simu was right. Somewhere within all of that conflicting rightness there had to be an answer to the terrible dilemma of the night. Torka's eyes moved to Simu. No one had ever doubted that Larani, who so resembled his beloved Eneela, had always been his favorite child. How could he now insist upon her death . . . unless he believed that for the good of all, it must come to pass?

Torka's brow came down. Might a time ever come when he, Torka, would be adamant in his insistence that one of his own children should be put out of the band to die?

"Never." The word came without the slightest hesitation. "No one—least of all that poor girl—will be put out of this band to die as long as I am headman."

Simu snapped to his feet. The entire hut shook as his head came in contact with the antler- and bone-braced ceiling. He cursed sharply against unexpected pain, and his hands flew upward to soothe his injury. "How can Larani live with the shame of such hideous scars and with the pain that they bring to her spirit and to her pride? Every day and night of her life she will know the agony of humiliation and be tortured by memories of what she once was!"

Torka measured Simu grimly. A new insight into the man made him scowl with revulsion. "I see. But tell me, who is more humiliated by your daughter's scars, Simu—Larani or you?"

Torka's question struck Simu like a spear hurled into his gut. He stared. "I . . ." And suddenly, shamed by the truth, he covered his face with his hands, seated himself heavily, and wept like a child.

Torka felt the eyes of Dak, Grek, and his sons upon him. He had had enough discussion. "The council is ended. Larani will stay with her people. If any of you question my decision, remember this: The forces of Creation sent Daughter of the Sky to burn Larani and throw her into the river like a flaming torch. We were led to a safe crossing because Grek went after the girl. We live in this good land because of Larani's pain. If she can endure it, then for her sake, so must we. For without Larani, not one of us would be alive to sit here in this hut discussing her fate!"

8

The dark days passed as one. Snow fell heavily within the Valley of the Great River and upon the surrounding hills and mountain ranges. Under Torka's leadership, the members of the band did their best to put aside their differences as they endured the endless cold and storms.

In the pit hut of Umak, Snow Eater went into labor and broke water on Honee's favorite sleeping skin. Honee carried the dog to the hut of blood "where all babies of the band must come forth!" The girls were allowed to watch as the young bitch strained and panted and the women did what they could do to soothe her . . . to no avail.

"A first baby is always the hardest," observed Lonit, kneeling close, rubbing the dog's back as Summer Moon looked on and, no doubt, thought of her own coming child.

Iana raised a knowing brow. "The pups must be born soon, or they will die."

Larani looked at Naya. "Have you a medicine drink that will hurry her labor?"

Naya nodded. "Thousand-leaf and bearberry boiled in water in which . . ."

"No!" Demmi peered in. Shaking snow from her head and shoulders and bare hands, she scooted forward on her knees. "There's no time to boil a brew, Naya! Stand aside everyone. I know what to do!"

"You are not a medicine woman," Naya protested.

"No? We will see!" Demmi looked at Swan with a telling wink. "I delivered you, Sister, when I was not much more than a baby myself. I just reached in with a slim arm, just as I will reach in now with a slim hand."

One by one, with Demmi's assistance, the pups came forth until there were ten little bloodied forms lying beside Snow Eater on the grass. Li cried because the first pup was stillborn, but soon she was smiling as Snow Eater nosed her new brood and licked them clean and dry as they rolled about, as blind and tiny as baby bears.

"Companion will be proud of his offspring!" said Demmi to Snow Eater.

The children ran off to bring fresh grasses from the nearest in-camp storage pit and shouted their news to the men and boys.

At Li's insistence, the body of the stillborn pup was taken out from camp and Umak spoke shaman's words over it as the People gathered around to watch Li reverently place the tiny body to look upon the sky forever.

That night wolves howled close to camp, and Li awoke trembling.

"They have come for Little Dog!" she cried.

"No, my little one," Umak assured her. "The life spirit of the pup is safe in the sky. No wolf can harm it."

But the next day, in the midmorning darkness, he went out from camp to check the site of the pup's abandonment. Because of the falling snow, it was with skill and patience that he uncovered the tracks of the wolves.

They are too close to camp, he thought. He found no sign of the pup. There was no doubt in his mind that the wolves had eaten it . . . until he discovered other tracks—big, deep. *Wanawut?*

His blood went cold at the thought of them. His gloved hand tried to define the tracks, but it seemed that they had been deliberately marred by heavy scuffing.

"You also come looking to see if wolves are too near camp?" Umak looked up, startled, to see Manaravak standing over him. "Wind speaks of storm, Umak. We should go back now."

An evasiveness in Manaravak's manner put Umak on edge. "Did you rub out the other tracks?"

"What other tracks?"

"These!"

Manaravak shrugged and leaned down. "Bear maybe. Or lion. Hard to say. I have not seen them before. Come, before weather closes in. We must advise Torka to tell the People to be on the lookout for wolves."

Under Torka's leadership, the men baited for wolves, and after three animals were caught and skinned, no more of their kind were seen or heard within the immediate proximity of the encampment.

Despite the hunters' success, the sound of howling beasts

entered Naya's dreams. She had been sleeping deeply, dreaming happily of suckling pups and dancing dolls until, awakened by a dull ache at the base of her neck, she lay still, listening to distant wolf song. Their song seemed strange, almost human, and Naya shivered, thinking of the wanawut. She tried to return to her dreams, but a sudden craving for berries sent her creeping from the sleeping furs that she shared with Yona.

Her movement woke Iana. "Naya? What are you doing, girl?"

"Nothing!" she replied, and wondered why she had felt the need to lie. It took only a moment to reach the sack of berries. She took out a handful, ate it, then scurried back into her bed furs.

Naya slept like the dead until, slowly, dreams unfolded within her mind: strange, disconnected dreams of wolves and men running wild across the land . . . of the wind, alive and breathing inside her—a warm wind that flowed within her veins and swelled within her breasts and loins until they throbbed with pleasure. She opened herself wide, moving, dancing, thrashing madly. The dream thickened. Wolves and men were running side by side, chasing her, but no matter how fast she ran, she could not escape. They were on her now, wolves with the faces of men—of Umak and Manaravak— and then, suddenly, no longer men or wolves at all.

"Wanawut!" she screamed as they straddled her and set themselves to consume her.

She fought them, but they had her on her back and were holding her by her wrists. The wind poured out of her, to leave her weak. The wanawut became one beast—a single, writhing, roaring, two-headed male organ that licked between her thighs, penetrated her, filled her. Screaming, she thrashed violently to be free of it, but like Snow Eater, she was trapped—mated—and the male thing was locked fast and swelling until it was choking her, suffocating her, lifting her as it extruded through her nose and eyes and ears as her body exploded. And in its place lay a mass of caul-slimed pups squirming in a mess of bloodred afterbirth.

"No!" she shrieked, flailing wildly against the hands that held her wrists pressed tight to her bed skins. . . .

"Naya! What is it, Little Girl?"

"By the forces of Creation, Yona, bring the shaman! Perhaps he can help!"

Staring up through plummeting blackness and horror, Naya saw Iana and Grek looking down at her with terror and confusion.

"Am I dead?" she asked, slowly realizing that it was Grek who was holding her down.

His hands released on her wrists, and with a convulsive sob of relief he pulled her into his arms and began to rock her and stroke her head. "No, my Little Girl! You were only dreaming."

She was suddenly ice-cold and shivering uncontrollably. "I have not had puppies?"

Iana's ragged sigh expressed her own relief. "No, girl! Of all the things to ask!"

Naya closed her eyes, leaned close to Grek, and held him tight.

"Grek! What is it?" Umak entered the pit hut after Yona. "Yona said that Naya is dying!"

Naya did not mean to scream, but when she looked up at Umak, she saw not the shaman but the leering face of the beast.

"No! Get away from me! Get away!" she cried, and buried her face in Grek's chest. "Don't let him touch me, Grandfather! Please, don't let him get me!"

Stunned, Umak drew back.

By now the hide door flap of Grek's hut was being held back as the headman peered in. Every member of the band pushed close at his back, trying to see inside.

"What has happened?" asked Torka.

Frowning, Iana shook her head. "Naya has had a bad dream."

Naya pressed closer to Grek. The dream was gone. She felt foolish. Carefully, she ventured a look toward Umak. "I am all right now," she whispered.

"Rest easily, girl." Iana's voice was tight with concern. "I will fix you something to drink. Or perhaps you would like one of your berries to—"

"No!" Naya was adamant. "No berries!" And she promised herself that in the future she would be more careful in her use of new foods and unfamiliar medicines.

Naya stood alone outside Grek's pit hut and watched the hunters and the dogs disappear into the distances of the winter dark. Snow Eater was hunting with Companion again.

Naya sighed and hugged herself within her furs. It was a very special morning! There had been blood on her undertunic this morning when she had awakened.

Since the night of her terrible dream, she had tried to do without eating the berries; but her breasts ached, her head hurt, and she found herself dreaming of the fruit by night and salivating for them by day. She was not certain when she had begun to find contentment in sucking on the berry-bead necklace that Manaravak had made for her. Iana had caught her at it and had told her to stop. She had tried, but soon the little dried fruits had been chewed flat. She missed their oily sweetness; she missed the lovely way the berries made her feel. Not wishing to rouse Iana's temper, Naya nibbled on her small supply of forbidden fruit when the woman wasn't looking.

When Iana had been out, Naya had rummaged through the woman's bag of sewing supplies and decorative trims and had taken all the berries that she could find. Good sense made her put back enough so that Iana would not notice the theft. The rest had gone into her own sewing pouch. Now the bag was almost always at her side. No one thought anything of it: Women and girls always kept their sewing supplies close by.

She stared off, chewing on a berry, waiting for the sun, wanting to see it on this most special of mornings—her first sunrise as a woman! Yes, let the sun rise in celebration of this momentous occasion! But the sun did not rise. The sun would not know Naya's secret. No one knew—not Umak, not even Iana. She had said nothing when she had discovered she was bleeding. She had risen quietly, pulled on her overdress and winter coat, and folded her sleeping skins over the stain that would forevermore mark the place where Little Girl had died. And then she had crept from the pit hut in triumph.

Now, as she stood with one of Yona's buckskin dolls secured between her thighs to absorb the truth of her condition, she chuckled low in her throat. Iana would be furious if she ever found out. Grek's woman had made such a fuss about what must and must not be done when her time of blood arrived. Iana had even prepared a special collection of woman skins and set them aside for Naya, but Naya would not use them. Her flow was very light; the doll would easily draw it in.

Little Yona was always misplacing her dolls. No one

would find it strange that one of them was missing again. Iana would scold Yona for being careless, Yona would cry, and Naya would make it up to the child by making her another doll . . . and another one after that . . . and in this way she would keep her secret, lest Iana drive her out of her grandfather's hut and into the bed skins of Umak or Manaravak.

She shivered, remembering the horrific nightmare. Trembling, she vowed that she would never be mated—never!

"Naya . . . ?"

Startled, Naya turned to see that Manaravak had come to stand beside her. He moved closer and lightly, tentatively rested a broad, ungloved hand upon her shoulder. It was apparent that he was afraid that she might scream or run away in horror at his touch. When she did neither, his hand relaxed. "I have a gift for you."

She did not know what motivated her, but she leaned toward him and told him a secret. "I have asked your brother Umak to bring back red berries for me from the cache pits. *Shhh*. Say nothing, or Iana will find out! My berries are almost gone. They are all I need, all I want. Look—see what has become of the fine necklet that you made for me?"

She reached up and opened her winter coat so that he might see her poor, chewed-up, dehydrated string of berry beads sagging against her bare throat.

"I have made you something better than this," he said as he reached out, ran a finger down her throat, and then reached around her neck and under her hair to loosen the thong and draw the adornment away.

"No!" Her hands closed around his wrists.

But the necklet came away in his left hand. She released her grip, and Manaravak fumbled in his surplice and came up with something that made her exclaim with delight.

"Helping Spirit!" she cried in instant recognition.

"I have carved an image of him out of antler bone."

Pleased, Naya slipped this extraordinary gift over her head. "Oh, Manaravak!" She sang out his name as, standing on tiptoe, she reached up to throw her arms around him with childlike delight. His smile was explosive as his hands went around her waist. He lifted her off the ground and held her high. "You like this gift I bring?"

"I like!"

He laughed and drew her down. He looked straight into her eyes until she moved unashamedly to kiss his closed, and when this was done, she kissed him on both sides of his unhooded face. She kissed him on his forehead, on his nose, and on his chin. She kissed him on his lips. And suddenly, after a sighing, yielding moment in which she pressed herself against him and opened her mouth in invitation to his tongue, she suddenly remembered her nightmare dream of mating and stiffened like a terrified little fish and wriggled ferociously to be free of the loving net of his fingers. He was forced to set her down, and with her hand curled protectively over her new talisman, she wheeled and disappeared into the shelter of old Grek.

He stood a moment, perplexed but not unhappy. His hand strayed to his mouth. She had kissed him! She had run away from him, but she had kept his gift, and she *had* kissed him. And *how* she had kissed him! He smiled as he turned to look off across the dark distances into which his brother had vanished with the others.

Bring her back berries if this is what she has asked of you, but your gift will mean nothing now that she has taken mine. Helping Spirit will turn her heart to Manaravak, and even without its magic, her kiss has told me a truth that she has yet to speak: that she is already mine!

"Do not assume too much."

He turned. "How long have you been standing there, Demmi?"

"Too long."

He heard the contempt in her voice and stood tall and defensive against it. "She will be mine. You will see. When she becomes a woman, Naya will choose Manaravak over Umak."

"Too bad for you."

He stared at her. Her look had a cutting edge, and he felt sliced by it. "My sister Demmi does not like the granddaughter of Grek."

"No, Demmi does not like the granddaughter of Grek."

"Why?"

"Except for Iana and me, I think that everyone likes Naya. And I think that Naya likes everyone . . . except Iana and me. That is one of many things that I do not like about her."

"You have become a sour-tongued, hard-eyed woman, Demmi."

"I am not like the granddaughter of Grek."

"No. You are not like my Naya."

"*Your* Naya? Is that what you think? Your sister Demmi is hard eyed and sour tongued, but what is Naya when she leaps into your arms all soft eyed as she opens her sweet mouth to your kiss? Hmmph! You must ask Umak when he returns to camp. Yes. You must ask our brother if he finds her as pleasing as you do when she flies into *his* arms like a happy little bird with her sweet mouth open and her soft tongue speaking his name and her eyes full of wanting."

A hollow opened in his gut. "Umak?"

She exhaled her annoyance through flared nostrils. "Open your eyes, Brother. I saw them together before Umak left with the other hunters. Poor Umak. Poor Manaravak. How can the headman's sons be so gullible? I wonder what our brother is thinking now as he does her bidding in the winter dark? Frankly, I do not think that she wants either of you, but she will have you at each other's throats nonetheless if this goes on much longer. And you ask me why I do not like her!"

9

The footprints of ravens overlay the tracks of the bear. No sign or omen could have been worse. The hunters stopped to stare in disbelief at the size of the blue depressions filled with starlight in the snow. They knew these tracks. They had all seen them before.

"Three Paws . . ." Torka exhaled the name. "I see no sign of her cubs, but she has come out of the burned land and now finds her meat by raiding the cache pits of the People!"

"Four ransacked cache pits," Dak grated. "If the greedy thief has done the same to the others—"

"Do not even think it!" Umak warned Dak to silence. Yet he thought it. If the bear had gotten to all their cache pits, the band had little chance of surviving the winter. When they found the fifth cache pit untouched, the men paused in a driving wind and heavy snow to thank the spirits of this world and the next. It was one of the largest caches of all.

"We will return with more sledges," said Torka, knowing that there was too much food in this pit for three men and a pair of dogs to transport.

"Let us check one more of the caches," the shaman suggested. "The one to the west of this one had good caribou filets and extra sinew and kindling and some dried fruits that might make our women smile."

Torka saw no reason to deny Umak's request. "If we find another of our cache pits intact, that will be reason enough to smile."

They found it in a driving snow . . . and there was cause to smile, as later the People ate the meat that was brought to them. Lest the women and children worry unnecessarily, the hunters made no mention of the great bear.

In the snow-driven night, Honee looked up from plaiting little Li's hair and smiled as Naya ducked into Umak's pit hut. "What brings you to the shelter of the shaman and his family?"

"I . . . have brought a healing marrow broth for the shaman's woman so that your body may drive away your coughing."

"How kind you are, Little Girl! Come, sit and talk with this woman awhile. Look at you! You are growing up so fast that it is hard to believe that you are not yet a woman! Umak, take the outercoat of our guest and bring a fresh fur from the stores for our Naya to sit on while we chat."

Umak obliged, piqued that Honee was blithely ordering him around in the presence of the girl, but Naya seemed not to notice. She was smiling at him out of her doelike face, and after handing her bladder flask of medicine drink to Honee, she slipped off her hooded coat and handed it to him with secrets in her eyes: secrets of a shared kiss, of soft arms around his neck, and of a promise that he had made to bring her a fresh supply of tiny red berries.

He smiled as he folded her furred coat and drew in the scent of it as he laid it alongside his own. Odd—it had the scent of woman . . . a woman in her time of blood! But that was impossible. The thought drifted as he left the coat, handed Honee the dry fur for Naya, and then seated himself with Jhon on the man side of the hut's central cooking fire. He had been teaching the boy how to secure a stone blade into the notched end of a long bone. Jhon had already picked up the way of it and wanted to finish the work by himself. Umak saw no cause to object; he would rather look at Naya.

The shaman smiled with bliss as he gazed at her. He imagined how it would be if she were a part of his family. The imagery increased his feeling of ecstasy. Umak grew warm with love—and lust—just looking at her, longing for the time when a moment like this would end with the girl naked and happy to be beside him beneath his bed furs. He closed his eyes, allowing himself the luxury of indulging his fantasy until Honee's voice startled him back into reality.

"Wake up, my man! Where are your manners? Our guest is leaving."

Umak was immediately on his feet and reaching for her coat.

Naya thanked Honee for her hospitality. "Drink deeply of the medicine when you wake, and then three times more until you are ready to sleep again. The thousand-leaf in the broth should ease the tightness of your breath."

"You *are* a sweet child, Naya! Just like your grandmother Wallah. Won't I be lucky if you choose Umak to be your man when the time comes for you to do so?"

"Will you come to live with us, Naya?" Li was over-joyed. "Would you be my big sister?"

"We are already band sisters," replied Naya. "So you may think of me as your big sister right now if it pleases you."

Evasiveness? Umak frowned, then castigated himself. He handed her coat back to her and, after shoving his feet into his moccasins, took up his own coat and escorted her out.

"That was thoughtful of you, Naya," he told her when they were outside. "Since the fire, Honee is often in great discomfort, but she would never complain of it."

She stood very still before him, very tense, as though waiting for something. Then: "Yes. It is good to have the healing way."

"Wallah would be proud of you."

"Yes."

"I often think of her, you know. Bold, brave old Wallah. Just like Grek. They were a pair, those two! I often—"

"Umak . . . I . . . have you brought my berries from the cache pits?"

He heard the impatience in her voice and felt foolish. "Yes. Here." He reached into his coat and withdrew a small skin sack that he had attached to the inner lining with a bone pin.

Her eager hand shot out and grabbed it.

"I hope there will be enough for your needs."

She froze. "Needs? What do you mean?" she asked defensively.

"Enough berries to trim the gift that you said you are making for Iana."

"Gift . . . Oh, yes, the baby carrier!" She was reaching eagerly into the sack, taking up several berries and popping them into her mouth. "Slowly now . . . not too many," she said, obviously to herself. Then: "Oh, Umak, what if there are not enough to last . . . I mean, for Iana's present."

"There are more in the other pits."

"And you would bring me more?"

"If you have need of them."

"I do! I mean, it is a very big baby carrier." She sighed. "Oh, Umak, how can I ever thank you for bringing my berries to me?"

"Be my woman when it is time."

She put a mittened hand to her mouth and made a vain attempt at composure. "Umak's woman . . ." She laughed.

He was confused and did not like the sound of her laughter; he sensed that it might be at his expense. Annoyed, he drew her close and, to his surprise, felt her go lax in his arms.

"Naya? Are you all right?"

Still holding the sack of berries, she put both hands against his chest and shoved back a little so that she could look directly into his face. "I am not afraid with you," she said, "not like with Manaravak."

Her hood had fallen back. Snow fell upon her face and blew into her hair to shine like white stars shivering against the blackness of a winter sky. "Naya . . ." He caught his breath at her beauty, too much in love even to think of kissing her. It was enough to hold her, to look at her, to know in his heart that she would soon be his. "Say it! Tell me that you will choose me. You will never regret it, my Naya. Never!"

Her head fell forward as she slumped against his chest. "Umak, my Umak." She seemed to sleep for a moment and then, with a giggle, she stood very straight and shivered. "It is cold. I am tired. I will go home."

* * *

Days of darkness passed. Storms swept across the valley. Then, under a new moon that was only occasionally visible through icy, wind-torn clouds, old Grek stirred his aching bones and sauntered out to join the other men in the council hut while little Yona began to cry for her doll.

"Another doll is lost!" she wept.

"But I see it there on your furs." Iana pointed out.

"Not the new one that Naya made me!" the child whined in exasperation. "One of the old ones. The big one with the stone-beaded eyes. It is lonely and lost in the snow!"

"Then you should not have taken it outside." Iana was clearly on edge.

"I did *not* take it outside."

"Then it is here in the hut somewhere."

"No, I have looked everywhere!"

Iana sighed and reached out to hug her daughter. "You must be more careful of your dolls, Yona, and then they will not be lost."

The girl looked grim and angry.

Naya, sitting cross-legged on her bed furs in the dull, foul-smelling light of Iana's tallow lamp, frowned as she secretly sucked a dehydrated berry and wondered how many of Yona's dolls would have to disappear before either the child or the woman caught on to her thefts. Her frown deepened as she watched Yona gather up all five of her dolls, set them firmly onto her bed furs, and then tie them together with a string of sinew.

"You will be safe now!" the child assured her dolls. "Yona is a good mother, isn't she, Naya!"

Naya exhaled a sigh, lay on her side, and curled up into a ball against the cramps that gripped her belly. One berry was no longer enough to relieve the pain that came with the rising of the moon and the gushing of her woman's blood. When she was certain that Iana was not watching, she took three more berries from her pouch and put them into her mouth.

"Oh, good!" cried Yona, scooting close in the shadowed gloom of the little hut. "You have taken out your sewing pouch! Are you going to make another doll for me?"

"Not now, Yona." Naya closed her eyes. The expected rush of light-headedness came almost instantly.

"Are you sick, Naya?" Yona asked.

The question caused Iana to turn her head. "Are you also feeling unwell, Naya?"

Naya did not reply. The dangerously meaningful *also* told her exactly where Iana's question would lead if she allowed it. Swan was not feeling well. All of the signs foretold that the headman's youngest daughter was about to shed new-woman's blood.

"Naya is asleep," said Yona.

Iana was silent for a moment. "*Hmmm* . . . it is not unusual for girls to come to their time of blood at the same time. No one knows why it is so, but often the new moon brings the blood of a woman and the birth of children." She yawned and lay down, settling herself into her furs.

Naya felt frightened. Did Iana suspect the truth? She would be furious! There must be some taboo broken when a girl kept her bleeding a secret from the band lest she be forced to make the choices among suitors and accept the responsibilities of a woman! But now the sweet residue of the berries oiled her mouth and seemed to be flowing thickly in her veins, taking all worry with it as she drifted into a dark and dreamless sleep.

For a long while the woman of Old Lion lay awake. Iana was troubled. Yona was obsessed with her missing dolls. Was it possible that she had actually *not* lost them? But what else could have happened to them?

She closed her eyes, and as she felt the child within her womb stir against her palm, she smiled with contentment and fell asleep knowing that when this baby was born it would be summer . . . and in the depth of the winter dark, under the cold light of a new moon with yet another storm building outside, there could be no sweeter thought than this.

10

"Soon the cache pits will all be empty." Torka whispered his fears to Lonit as another storm settled in over the Valley of the Great River and they lay bundled together in each other's arms within their sleeping skins. "It feels as though we have gone to ground . . . as though we were a band of squirrels or voles or bears."

She snuggled close. "I am glad that we are *not* bears. I would be sleeping with only my youngest cubs, then. I love my children, but it is much better to go to ground with you!"

He was too distracted by his worries to be amused. "The land around this once-good camp has been hunted clean of meat. There is animosity among our people, Lonit. Like a bad smoke, it stinks of singed feelings and burned pride and of dissension among the families."

"The time of the long dark cannot last forever, Man of My Heart. Everything will be better when the weather is warmer and the days of light return."

"And the mammoth . . . I have not heard its trumpetings in so long."

"Who can hear anything in all of this winter wind and driving snow? Our totem grazes with its kind in the wind-protected foothills. I am sure of it."

"How can you know unless you have seen it? I fear that it has gone east, into the great white mountains."

"You cannot be certain of that," she told him, then added with more than a hint of bemused contrariness, "unless *you* have seen it!"

"Fair enough," he conceded.

They lay very still, very quietly, listening to the wind hurling snow against the pit hut as Swan and Sayanah slept deeply within their own bed furs in the darkness of the unlighted hut.

Then Lonit, knowing the mind of her man by the tension that she felt in his body, propped herself onto an elbow and looked at him with grave concern. "There is still too much snow on the ground to think of breaking camp and following!"

"Yes," he agreed, "there is too much snow."

She sighed with relief. "I am glad. There are pregnant women in this camp. Honee is still not fully recovered from the fire, nor is Larani. And I worry about old Grek. Iana tells me that he sleeps for hours like a fevered child, and often when he is awake, he pretends to sleep so that he will not have to move and will not take so much as a sip of any of the pain-eating brew that Naya has offered to make for him. It would be a bad thing if he had to travel now, in this cold and darkness."

Torka knew that she was right. And yet so many compromises had been made on behalf of the old man—too many, perhaps. He exhaled restlessly. Wanting to change the subject, he spoke of mundane things—the new clothes that she was making for her family, of the baby carrier she was secretly constructing for Summer Moon, and the way that Sayanah was mastering the use of his new snow walkers.

She moved, laid her finger across his mouth. "You see? The time of the long dark is not all bad in this snug, warm camp that you have made for your people. We eat a little, sleep a lot, and there is also much time for this. . . ." She bent her head to kiss the worry lines from his brow, and then she kissed his mouth. It was a long, deep kiss of loving invitation to share warmth and pleasure. "Oh, yes, this woman finds it pleasing to go to ground with you."

"Even after all of this time together?"

She dimpled. "Old Grek says that many things improve with age. In your case, I would definitely agree."

"I am not certain that it is such a good idea to listen to old Grek. Do not forget that Bison Man prefers his meat soft and spoiled."

Lonit suppressed a teasing smile. Her hand strayed downward over Torka's belly. "As for this woman, I like mine hot and hard and *now*—that is, if you are able!"

Despite himself, he laughed at her challenge. "*If?*" Her hand was warm. It knew him well and worked him for his pleasure and her own as he drew her down and told her that he loved her.

"Always and forever?"

"Always and forever!"

"Show me . . . but show me quietly. This is no time to wake our cubs."

He found no difficulty in obliging. It was good love-making—it was always good with Lonit—and when her challenge was met and won, they slept contentedly in each other's arms.

Torka's dreams were of his youth and of only good things—until he heard the howling of the beast wanawut and woke with a start. Had it been real? *No.* He closed his eyes.

A nightmare vision rose beneath his lids. A vision of the wanawut walking with Manaravak across the land, hunting with Manaravak, bending beside Manaravak and then turning to stare at Torka for a moment before crouching to feed with Manaravak upon the bloodied body of . . . the *fourth* caribou. And somehow, in that moment, Manaravak and the beast were one.

Breathless, Torka felt sick as he willed the horror of the dream away. But it would not go. He rose, pulled on his outercoat and winter moccasins, and walked out into the night. He needed air. He needed the brutal cold to sear his face and lungs and make him know that he was awake and alive and not the hapless victim of a nightmare that had made his very spirit bleed.

But there was no peace to be found within the night. A beast *was* howling in the winter wind. He had not dreamed the sound. As Torka stared across the dark, snow-driven camp, he saw his son. Manaravak stood alone at the edge of camp. And Manaravak was howling.

Lonit wept with joy as her daughters Summer Moon and Demmi came to join her in escorting Swan to the hut of blood.

Summer Moon kissed her youngest sister. "May the watching spirits of all of our female ancestors smile on you as they have at last smiled upon me!"

Demmi came close and hugged Swan hard. "It is about time!" she teased with a wink. "But remember: Dak is mine!"

Swan looked at her sister thoughtfully. "Have you ever really wanted him?"

Demmi shrugged. "Not really. But who else was there for me? Besides, he is not so bad."

"He is wonderful," replied Swan, and blushed as red as

the throat of a loon when Demmi clucked her tongue, gave her a loving hug, and reminded her, "He is *mine.*"

Later, as he watched the other women and girls follow after his woman and daughters, Torka stood tall and tried not to grin like a fool when his sons and the men of the band came to congratulate him.

How proud he was! Three daughters, and all of them women now . . . one with a baby growing within her, and another with a three-year-old boy of her own. Where had the time gone? Away . . . away with his youth.

It was as though someone had just splashed him with icy water. He did not want to feel old. He did not want to feel the weight of his age hovering above him, mocking him out of the core of a man's pride, waiting to descend upon his mind and body and do to him what time was doing to poor old Grek.

"Come!" He raised his arm and summoned his sons to him. "We will go out to the cache pits and bring more meat, and maybe, if we find sign of the one who walks on three paws, the pelt of that great thief will honor the coming to womanhood of Swan."

Standing beside the hut of blood into which Swan had just disappeared, Lonit wheeled, still holding the edge of the cold flap in her hand. "No!" she cried.

He saw the fear in her eyes. Fear for her sons or for him? He knew her well enough to know that it was the latter. He glared at her. Did she think him too old for such a hunt?

"It will be a good thing," he replied in cool defiance. "If the forces of Creation smile upon us, we may even feast upon the flesh of Three Paws herself!"

He felt so bold, so filled with the vision of himself standing against the great bear, that it took him a moment before he realized that he had just broken one of the most ancient taboos of his ancestors: He had named his prey before he had set eyes upon it.

Everyone was staring at him aghast. Now, if he hunted the great three-pawed bear, the animal would know that he was coming.

His head went high. Let them stare. He had stood against more fearful things than a three-pawed bear in his time. He had faced wolves and rampaging mammoth, woolly rhinos, bears, lions, and the wrath of murderous magicians and marauding men . . . and most fearful of all, he had stood in the winter dark and had seen a son of his standing at the edge of the encampment and howling into the storm like a beast. The memory beat within his head like the hard, pounding, painful strike of a war drum.

He was sick to death of memories, sick of winter and somber faces and of bad dreams and ominous omens. His totem may well have vanished into the great white ranges to the east, but that didn't necessarily mean that Life Giver had taken his luck with it. For half a lifetime, all good things that had come to him had come in the wake of the great tusker, but before that, had there not been a time when he had been master of his own luck? Yes!

He had lived long enough to know that he could face whatever came on his own terms. Three Paws was out there somewhere. If she was raiding the cache pits of the band, he would see to it that she would become meat for his people. If he had inadvertently provoked her spirit and alerted it to his coming, what matter? She was an old lame bear. It was time for her to die.

He was Torka. He was not old! He was not lame! And he was not afraid to seek her out and kill her.

PART V

THE FOURTH CARIBOU

1

Luck. The word ran around and around in Umak's head
like a fish circling in shallow water within one of the stone
fish traps of the women. *Just what is luck anyway?*

The question bothered him as he walked behind the
other hunters. Breathless, he stopped and shook his head,
muttering to himself in a misery of conjecture. "Luck is an
invisible power that causes the forces of Creation to smile
upon a man. Yes, but if the power is invisible, is it possible
that a man might not know if he has lost it until it is too late
to win it back?"

He shook his head. A shaman should not have to ask
such questions; a shaman should know the answers. But he
did not know them. He cursed, but that did nothing to
relieve his frustration as he watched his father striding ahead
of him with Manaravak and Grek. They took turns dragging
the sledge, empty of all but a few provisions and the extra
spears that would be needed if the foray to the cache pit
turned into a hunt as Torka hoped it would.

Umak stopped. The others walked on, unaware that he
had fallen behind. As he watched his father, Umak saw that
the headman was walking across the snow as though his snow
prods and webbed snow walkers were a natural extension of
his arms and limbs. Umak felt a son's pride. Everything that
Torka did had power and grace to it. Why then was Umak so
troubled by doubt as he watched him now?

*Because he has allowed Grek to come along even though
he knows that the old one is unfit. Because he has broken an
ancient taboo by naming a specific prey before actually sighting it.*

"Wait!"

Dak's call caused him to turn around.

"We had all given up on you," the shaman said as the
son of Simu caught up with him.

"I had to go back to camp." Dak's face was a mass of

glowers within the confines of his ruff as he stopped and rammed his snow prods into the snow. "Demmi was following me. I practically had to tie her down to keep her from coming along."

"Why didn't you let her? She's as good a hunter as you and I."

"Because if the truth be told, this trek to the cache pits and challenging of the bear . . . it worries me, and I would not wish my woman to be in danger! And Grek—not my father, not the boys—should have stayed behind with the women and children. The old man will slow us down and hobble any action that we may be called upon to take against our prey—or in our own defense! Simu's not happy, Umak. He took being left behind as a personal insult. Torka seems set to challenge and demean him at every turn these days."

"Do you feel no pity for Grek's pride? And should Torka not have challenged your father when Simu wanted to kill Larani?"

Dak made a sound of despair and frustration. "I don't know, Umak. If I don't see the light of day soon, I don't know what I'm going to think or say about anything."

Umak released a spear pole and slung a brotherly arm around Dak's broad, blocky back. "We've both lived through long, bad winters before. Perhaps a hunt is just what we need to get us through it, eh?"

Dak was not in a mood to be cheered. "I've never been through a winter like this. What kind of a shaman are you, not to have known that the snow would grow so deep that even though we have found the place where the caribou pass the winter, we can't make it across the valley and into the canyons to hunt them?"

"The Seeing Wind comes as it will! Sometimes it blows true, sometimes it doesn't blow at all! I do my best. What more can you ask of me? Even Grek says he hasn't seen a winter like this one since he was a boy."

"Grek was a boy at the beginning of time!"

"And Grek has survived to recount his experiences to us. There is a very good chance that we will also survive the days of this long dark winter. You, on the other hand, may not, if you don't stop wheedling as though you were little Kharn reaching out for Demmi's arms!"

Dak's face twisted against the unfortunate comparison. "He's stopped crying for her," he said sadly. "It's Swan he wheedles for now. Your youngest sister is a better mother to my boy than Demmi. Why can't she be more like Swan, eh? And why can't Torka put his own daughter in her place?"

"If she had a place, it would be up to you to keep her in it! But Demmi has never been like anyone but herself. You knew that when you took her to your fire. And there was a time when you even liked it."

Dak's voice was flattened by his attempt to control it. "She has changed toward me. Nothing I do matters with her. But then everything seems to have changed around me lately. Look around you, Umak. Our people hunger in the winter dark. My sister Larani weeps in silence for all of her lost dreams . . . dreams of things that will never be for her in this 'fine, good' land to which your father has brought us. I ask you, old friend, has he brought us here to live or to die?"

Umak, refusing to hear another word, stalked on after the others.

They reached the cache pit to find bear sign everywhere. Nothing was left but a few tools and the makings for a fire.

The hunters piled what was left of their supplies on the sledge and knew that their last, good supply of meat was buried in the one remaining cache pit . . . if the three-pawed bear hadn't gotten to it, too.

On they walked. The wind was hard out of the north, and snow was falling heavily when they found the last cache pit. It was secure, untouched by the thieving bear.

"No way to track bear or anything else in this snow," said Manaravak.

Torka knew that Manaravak was right. A blizzard was closing in fast. With the wind rising, the air temperature plummeting, and the snow turning land and sky into a tumultuous sea of white, nothing was more important now than survival. The men tipped the sledge onto its side and, facing its solid bottom to the wind, used it as a frame over which they stretched a lean-to. Crawling inside, they were glad to rest and wait out the storm. The hunters ate their traveling rations and slept long and deeply. When they awoke, the storm was still raging. Lying close together, they spoke in low, easy tones.

Half daydreaming, Manaravak spoke his thoughts aloud. "The skin of the great three-pawed bear would make a fine gift for my Naya."

"She is not your Naya yet!" Umak reminded him. "She will be for me. She has told me."

Manaravak was instantly wide-awake. "She wears my talisman!"

"She couldn't. She told me that she is afraid of you!"

"Her lips spoke not of fear to me when she put her arms around me—"

"Stop!" Grek was furious. "You will not put the name of Little Girl in your mouths to chew up and spit out with your bad words! *I* will say to whose fire she goes when she becomes a woman, yes!"

Dak shook his head disparagingly. "*If* she ever becomes a woman."

"She will come to her time soon enough," said Torka. "And when she does, she will choose a man. You cannot keep her by your side forever, Grek. And I will not allow her to cause dissension between my sons."

"She has already done that," Dak remarked drolly.

"She has accepted a talisman from you? *When?*" pressed Umak.

Manaravak shrugged. "A carving of Helping Spirit. She wears it at her throat since the last moon."

"I, too, have brought her gifts. She has said that I am hers. Has she said as much to you?"

"No, but she has kissed me! A woman's kiss!"

Dak reached out and laid a hand firmly on Grek's forearm. "Make yourself useful, Old Lion. Tell them to stop arguing. You are supreme elder. Maybe they will listen to you."

They did. And soon they slept again. Grek snored, sucking on the ruin of his once-fine teeth as, hours later, Torka, Umak, Manaravak, and Dak awoke to howling.

"Wolves . . ." whispered Umak.

"No," Manaravak corrected his brother. "Wanawut. A band of them, far off. Many deep, male voices . . . no females . . . yes . . . maybe one or two . . . they were cold, seeking shelter."

"We do not need you to translate for us!"

Manaravak ignored Dak. He cocked his head, listening. "The wanawut are in the southern ranges across the river. They howl into the storm. They hunger. There is loneliness in their cries."

"Be careful, Manaravak," Dak drawled. "Or we will start thinking that you are longing to be one of them again."

"In a way I suppose I always *will* be one of them."

"Naya would not like to hear you say that," said Umak.

"The storm will be over soon," said Torka sharply, wanting to halt the conversation. "As soon as the weather permits, we'll start back for the encampment."

Beside him, old Grek smacked his lips and settled more deeply into sleep.

"This trek has been too much for Old Lion." Dak looked across the fur-covered mound of the sleeping man as he spoke directly to Torka.

Torka nodded in agreement. "It is time for Bison Man to become the woman watcher again. It is my hope that this trek will help him to see this for himself."

Dak was taken aback by this revelation. "Was this your intention when you brought him along and insisted that Simu stay behind to guard the camp?"

"It was," Torka spoke evenly, with a hint of a query in his voice, as though he could not imagine that the young man would have assumed anything else.

2

Swan raised her face to the sky as she was escorted from the hut of blood by her mother. Once the doeskins that were reddened by her first-time blood were ritually burned in the ceremonial fire, her people would rejoice and bring her gifts.

She stood very still. The snow fell straight and quietly as the headman spoke the official words of welcome to the new woman.

"Swan, new woman of this band, come forth!"

Swan obeyed proudly, and a little sadly as she thought of Larani and of how bitter this ceremony had been for her. Briefly, she remembered a night long ago when Naya, Larani, and she had clustered upon a single sleeping pad within the hut of the headman. They had talked all night about how it would be when they were grown and new women at last, beautiful and proud as they displayed themselves for all the band to see.

"All the men who look at me will be in love with me!" Naya had sighed with delight at the prospect of such universal admiration. "But I will choose only the best of all—and only after he has brought me many gifts and made me smile many times!"

Swan could still hear Larani asking: "And who might this man be?"

"I don't know yet! But he will have to hunt much, kill more, and risk himself many times before I will smile his way."

"I know who I want," Swan had confided softly, longingly. "He won't have to do a thing except hold out his hand and invite me to his fire—I will come gladly."

"Yes, so it is with the man I will have," Larani had agreed.

"Who is he?" Even in memory, Naya's voice was petulant and impatient.

Swan could still remember the way Larani had smiled and rolled onto her back and closed her eyes. "If you don't know who is best, there's no sense telling you anything."

"You aren't any fun, Larani! What about you, Swan? Who do you want for your man?"

"It's a secret," Swan had responded with a heart full of mirth. But there was no mirth in her heart now as she knew that she still wanted the same man and that he already had a woman and child at his fire.

Now, with a beaming Lonit at her side, she paused before her father and listened as her mother spoke the words that would end her childhood forever.

"Behold," said Lonit to Torka, holding out the soiled skins that had absorbed the blood of Swan's first menstruation. "Here is the blood of my child Swan. That child is no more. The new woman who stands before you now carries her name."

Torka accepted the skins and held them toward his youngest daughter. "Is this the new woman who answers to the name of Swan?"

"This new woman answers to the name of Swan," she replied, pushing her memories of the past behind her, glad for the happiness and pride that she saw in his eyes. She wanted this moment to be perfect for herself and the other members of the band, but especially for her father. There was tension in him these days that troubled her. If only the winter would end! If only the caribou would come out of the faraway hills and canyons! Perhaps, if this second ceremony in the new land would go forward with perfection, the forces of Creation would favor the People once more. With her head high, she took the skins and walked to the fire with them.

"New woman gives to the fire the blood of Swan. That child is no more. This woman now answers to her name."

As everyone waited with baited breath, she tossed her offering into the fire, then turned and, with outstretched arms, saluted her people and asked them to accept her as a new woman of the band.

As one they spoke her name.

"Swan! Daughter of Torka and Lonit, sister of Umak, Manaravak, Sayanah, Summer Moon, and Demmi, and aunt to Jhon and Li and Kharn! Come forth now to your people, Swan, so that the new woman may be welcomed into her band!"

There was much happiness in the encampment of Torka that night. Gifts were brought to the new woman, which were set aside for the time when she would accept a man and have a fire and pit hut of her own to tend. Grek gave her a cooking lamp, and Iana added a collection of finely made wicks. From Simu and Eneela came a new sleeping mattress wide enough for two. From Lonit came the traditional gift of kindling and an exquisitely made bow drill; a symbolic passing on of fire and warmth from one hearth to another. From her father came a woman's knife. From her brothers came gifts of awls and sewing needles. As with Lonit's gift of the bow drill, the gifts from a brother to a sister were also prescribed by custom and so, when Manaravak handed Swan a set of thimbles made of depilated caribou skin, she was surprised—as was everyone else—when Naya snickered as though the offering were somehow something that she would never have accepted from him.

The children of the band marched up to her with awkwardly fashioned strings of stone beads and gifts that made little sense to anyone but to them. Swan embraced each and every child in turn and thanked them. The gifts were not important; the gesture of concern and welcome behind the act of giving was all that mattered.

"What a fine circle the new woman Swan will someday make for a fortunate man of this band," said Honee as she placed her own gift of a beautiful matched pair of horn drinking cups before Swan.

Swan flushed. Pleasure dissolved into remorse within her. No man had spoken for her, nor was it likely that any would until one of the boys was eventually old enough. It would most likely be Nantu. He was the eldest, although she found him to be a single-minded, stubborn boy, and everyone knew that he was infatuated with Naya. Swan sighed. There was only one male in this band whom she truly desired—whom she had always desired. *Dak*.

She looked briefly across the fire at him. Was he waiting for a sign from her that would give him the courage to speak the words of invitation that would cause her to rise and say yes or no to him?

When Dak met Swan's eyes, it was with the warm expression of a caring friend, not of a lover. He was not going to ask for her. He would never ask for her. Swan stared quickly down into her lap lest he, or anyone else, see the tears of disappointment that stung beneath her lids.

The People ate, sang songs, and told stories. When no one was looking, Larani came out of Simu's pit hut to sit as far from the fire as possible while still being within earshot of the tales that old Grek was weaving as intricately as any woman could weave a snare net. In the darkness of the moonless night, Larani let her hood fall back. Starlight shimmered on her face until Manaravak noticed her sitting alone and, acting on a pang of pity, took it upon himself to bring meat to her.

"Go away!" she demanded, cowering and pulling her robe over her head.

He looked down at her for a moment before bending and setting the food at her feet. "Why do you hide away all the time, Larani?"

"Why?" The word curdled with bitterness.

"Yes. Why?" He repeated the question; it seemed simple enough to him.

With an exhalation of unexpected anger, she cast back her furs and glared at him defiantly. "Take a closer look, son of Torka! Do you still want to ask me why?"

He did not flinch. He stared. Her hair was growing back in patches. Her burns had an odd, shiny appearance—not like skin at all, but like some sort of slick, polished, dark stone. He cocked his head, lowered his brow, and reached out to touch the burned part of her head. She slapped his hand away so fast and hard that she hurt him and herself.

"Ouch!" they cried in unison.

Everyone turned to stare.

A small, pitiful, moan came out of Larani. "Well? Have you seen enough? Have you *all* seen enough?" She pulled the robe back over her head.

Manaravak shrugged. "You are not so bad ugly as you think, Larani."

"No? Would you take me to your fire? Would you name me woman?" She snapped to her feet. She cast the robe back again, allowing them all to look at her in the starlight. "Would any man of this band have the stomach to name me woman?"

The silence in the camp was total.

Manaravak was confused. Larani had changed; she used to be such a pleasant, friendly girl. Now she was nasty. And why was she displaying her burns with such defiance? Was she ashamed of them or proud? Her burns intrigued him. He thought that there must be great power within the body of Larani to have allowed her spirit to survive so much pain and wounding. Why was she so angry with him?

"Well!" she pressed him, once again hiding herself within the robe. "Go ahead, son of Torka! Tell me that you would name me woman!"

Not knowing how to react, Manaravak spoke the truth. "When I name a woman, the name I speak will be Naya's," he told Larani simply, and wondered why she shivered before she turned away to disappear into the confines of her father's pit hut as Umak called out a clear challenge from the far side of the fire.

"You will not be the only one to speak for Naya!"

Manaravak turned and looked at his brother. Now Umak was angry with him, too. And on the female side of the fire, Naya clasped her hands before her face as she failed to stifle the giggle of pure delight that bubbled through her fingers. Hearing it, Manaravak's bewilderment grew. Whom was the girl laughing at? And how could she laugh at all when her friend Larani was obviously so sad?

As he looked at Naya it struck him that although he grew hot in his loins whenever he thought of coupling with her, he did not like her very much. His brow settled into a troubled frown. Perhaps he would have done better to have given the Helping Spirit talisman to Larani.

But even as he thought this, Naya's hands lowered, and seeing his expression, the girl's smile vanished. She had the oddest look on her face—half-happy, half-sad, half-awake, half-asleep, as though she looked at him from a dream of complete befuddlement.

His heart went out to her across the flames. She was as confused by the moment as he was.

The night was ruined. Iana reprimanded Naya, who began to cry. Grek shouted at Iana for upsetting Little Girl. And Simu roared at Manaravak, accusing him of deliberately shaming his daughter.

Manaravak stared at Simu. "I only brought her something to eat!"

"That is for her man to do!" retorted Larani's father.

"But she has no man!" protested Manaravak. "And you always seem to forget that she is alive!"

"Better if she were not!" Simu rose, stalked to his pit hut, grabbed one of his spears, and stalked off into the night.

"*Aiy ee ay!*" wailed Eneela, and begged Dak to go after his father lest, in his state of temper, carelessness make Simu vulnerable to predators and cost him his life.

Dak obliged, and young Nantu scrambled for his spear and followed his brother with no word of protest from his mother.

"Wait!" Manaravak implored, calling Dak and the boy back. "If offense I have caused, it is I who should—"

"Offense!" Eneela commanded her sons to continue on after their father, then turned on Manaravak and called him stupid and callous. "When you bring meat to a woman, it is a statement of your willingness to care for her—to be her man and her mate! Surely you know this! How can you be so cruel? How long will you live among us before you learn our ways, or are you still an animal at heart?"

Manaravak, stunned by the venom in Eneela's outburst, stormed out of camp.

"You will be silent, Eneela!" commanded the headman.

"Yes, be silent, Eneela!" Lonit echoed him with a shout of outrage. "If an act of kindness to a member of this band is taken to be the act of a beast, perhaps we had all best behave as beasts instead of as people!"

"Frankly, Eneela," added Summer Moon, "we have all seen mammoth exhibit more concern for their injured young than our man Simu has shown to Larani!"

" 'Our' man?" Eneela was so angry that her voice sounded as though she were strangling on it. "Second woman! That is all you are to him! Second woman, taken as a favor to your father! Just because you are young—just because you carry his baby in your belly at last after all these years—"

"Eneela." Umak was on his feet. "Beware of words, woman. Once spoken, they cannot be recalled."

Demmi was standing tall and rigid beside Summer Moon as she glared at Eneela with eyes that flashed with dangerous intent. "It is my sister who has done a favor for your man, Eneela, and *not* the other way around. Yes—Summer Moon is young—but then you are growing old! And my brother Manaravak is a son of Torka. Do not ever forget that again, or I will personally take my dagger and—"

"Stop!" Swan was on her feet, a fringed, feathered, and beaded island of misery amid her assembled gifts. "You have spoiled it all! Oh, all of you, I wish that this night had never come!"

The light of the sun glowed gold along the high, white, serrated eastern edge of the world for the first time in longer than anyone could remember, but no one had much enthusiasm for the chants that were required of them when they assembled to observe Umak make the songs and magic smokes of greeting to the returning sun.

"My father and Dak are strong and wary hunters. They and Nantu will soon come back to camp with Manaravak. I am sure that he has gone after them. They will all be back soon. The return of the sun is a good omen," assured Larani as, covered from head to toe in her tentlike robe, she sought a moment alone with Swan.

"Is it?" responded the new woman with little enthusiasm. "After last night, I hope so. Now that the chants have been made to the sun, Torka and Umak are also preparing to go out after those who have not returned."

"I know. I am sorry about last night, Swan. I am sorry for selfishly casting my own shadow over what should have been a celebration of light for you."

"What is done cannot be undone."

"True enough. But can a friend still be a friend?"

Swan suddenly stepped forward and, being careful not to hurt her, embraced Larani. "Always! It seems that we are both new women in a band within which neither of us will ever have the man of our hearts."

Larani stiffened and pulled away. "No man has my heart."

"Friends do not lie to one another, Larani. Only Naya will have the man of her heart."

Larani exhaled softly. "Which of your brothers will she choose?"

Swan shook her head. "I don't know. Demmi says that whether Naya chooses Manaravak or Umak, she will find a way to make them both unhappy."

An anguished cry caused both girls to jump and turn in time to see Torka and Umak stop dead in their tracks as Eneela cried out again. By the time they saw what had made the woman of Simu scream, both Torka and Umak were striding across the encampment with their spears in hand, spear hurlers at ready.

Dak and Manaravak, returning to camp, moved slowly and in silence in the all-encompassing snow, like figures floating forward in a strange and misted dream. They walked side by side, which was startling enough, but it was the sight of Simu walking ahead of them that caused a wail to rise from the throat of every woman and the gut of every man to go hard with remorse and dread. Simu carried the limp, bloodied, headless remains of his son Nantu in his arms.

3

"Three Paws . . ." The name of the great bear bled out of Simu's mouth as he sat within the council of elders.

"You saw it?" Torka pressed him.

"We saw nothing," said Dak. "Only . . . what was left."

"Manaravak?" Torka looked to his son for an answer.

"I heard the screams of the boy, the shouts of Simu and Dak. There was fog where they were, thick fog, very cold. I ran . . . and found what . . . was left of the boy."

Simu wept. "When the fog closed in, I told Nantu to stay

close. That boy has never paid attention to me. I should have been stricter with him . . . should have—"

Dak looked across the dark interior at Manaravak. "You risked yourself for my brother. I thank you for what might have been."

Manaravak was staring into the dark well of his lap; his face was set, ashen even in the darkness. "In this band has it not been said that all are brothers?" His voice was very low. "I . . . wish . . . I . . ."

"We must hunt Nantu's killer." Grek spoke quietly and with great sense of purpose. "That animal has stolen the meat from our cache pits and now has begun to prey upon the People. It must be killed. Now. Yes!"

Simu seemed not to have heard the old man's words. "I told him to stay close . . . not to stray. But Nantu is always one to go his own way . . . everyone knows . . . but I told him, didn't I, Dak? 'Mind your father now, Nantu. Three Paws may be out there in the fog. Sit where you are. If you have need to relieve yourself, stay within sight. Yes, boy. Stay within sight,' I said. 'Fog is always thick along the river country this time of year. Hard to predict when it will form or when it will thin away to nothing. So stay close, boy. Listen to your father now and . . .' "

"Yes, Father, you warned him. You did all you could." Dak moved to sit closer to Simu.

"In which direction did the tracks lead?" Torka asked.

"I did not see," said Dak. "Manaravak brought Nantu through the fog. My father and I, we . . . we heard something moving off, north . . . northeast . . . hard to say."

Torka frowned. They said they had not seen it, yet Simu, in a state of shock, had named it, breaking the ancient taboo. Again he remembered the fourth caribou lying dead with his son feeding upon its blood. But he had broken the taboo himself when he had named the bear and boasted of killing it. The memory turned his heart to ice. "That which Simu has put name to, you *did* see it Manaravak? Was it the one with three paws that has raided our cache pits?"

Manaravak looked like a cornered animal. "What else would it have been? Yes, I saw it, but through the fog. It was *bear*! A big bear. What else could do to a boy what you have seen?"

Now it was Umak who was troubled. "Lion . . . wanawut

. . . a good-sized leaping cat or wolf. If you did not actually see the attack, how—"

"Wanawut do not rip the heads off boys!" Manaravak spoke so sharply that he startled himself. "I saw the attack! I saw the great bear! Come. I will show you. I will lead you to its tracks if you doubt me!"

The accusation hung in the air.

"There is too much snow now," said the headman, breaking the tension. "We will wait. We will allow the women to prepare the boy as best they can. We will keep a proper death watch—five days. Then we will go. Grek is right: That which feeds upon the People must be killed."

Nantu's mother and sisters and Simu's second woman cleansed his torn and broken body. When Larani counted all the claw marks in his skin, she left her mother and sister and Summer Moon and went to confront Torka. He sat outside his pit hut with Manaravak and Umak, preparing weapons for the hunt to come.

"I would speak for Nantu," she said.

"Speak," Torka bade her.

In her heavy robes nothing of her face was visible, but her posture was erect and rigid. "Without a head, my brother Nantu cannot hope to live again. Without a head, when my brother Nantu's body is placed to look upon the sky forever, he will not be able to see the sky. How will his spirit hope to find the world beyond this world if he cannot see his way? Bring this woman the head of Nantu, Torka. And for every claw mark that has been dug into his flesh, drive a spear deep. And as you do so, call out the name of Nantu and of Larani so that the great three-pawed killer will know that our spirits are with you as you claim its life."

"If the forces of Creation grant us the luck to find and kill our prey, this I will do," replied Torka, taken aback by the strength that emanated from the young woman.

"I thank you," she said and, without another word, turned and walked away, leaving the three men to stare after her in amazement.

Five days later, Nantu's body was carried out from camp on a clear, cold morning that made the senses sparkle even though the hearts of the people ached with grief over the death of a young boy.

His mother wailed. The women of the band wailed with her, to help her endure the impossible burden of her grief. Hearing them, the dogs howled and strained at their tethers within the encampment.

Custom mandated that the bereaved father sing the life song for a lost son, but Simu was so distraught that he could do little more than mumble. Hearing him, Dak looked imploringly to Umak, and understanding, the shaman began to sing in honor of Dak's brother, for young Nantu had been as brave as he had been bold. He deserved better at the end of his life than a stunned father's incomprehensible mutterings.

It was a sad and lonely ceremony. When at last the People trudged back to camp through the snow, no one spoke as the family groups separated and went to their own shelters.

Outside, the men were readying in earnest for the hunt.

The sun was up. Naya faced into it and smiled. Her head spun for a moment.

Umak was at her side. "Are you all right, my Naya?"

"Yes, all right." He steadied her with his rock-hard right arm. She liked the feeling and leaned closer.

"You must prepare your fleshers, awls, and scrapers, my little Naya, for if I am the one who is smiled upon by the forces of Creation, the skin of the great bear shall be yours. From its teeth I will make you a necklet that will put any talisman that Manaravak has given you to shame!"

It was a good-natured boast, but it had not been made in jest, and she knew it. Her hand drifted to her throat. How did Umak know about her talisman? It lay safely hidden within her winter tunic. But then, Umak was a shaman; the Seeing Wind told him its secrets.

She leaned more heavily into Umak's arm as, from where he stood with Dak and Torka, Manaravak stared at her. What a fine, handsome man he was! And Umak, too! How would she ever choose between them? And suddenly, on a wave of light-headedness that made her giggle, she had an idea. Looking up, she gestured for Umak to bend closer. When he did, although it was her intention to whisper, her voice sounded very loud.

"I think I will let the great bear decide by whose fire this girl will reside. Yes, in death Three Paws shall speak my heart and choose between the sons of Torka for me."

"Naya!" Lonit, kneeling over the assembled traveling

supplies of the hunters, was aghast. She looked up with incredulity. "Take back your words!"

Naya had never seen Lonit so angry. And wasn't it strange? She could not remember exactly what she had just said. "Words?"

"Yes! You have named the prey that our hunters seek! Would you have my sons contending against each other during the hunt instead of standing together for the good of all?"

Naya was flustered. Why was everyone staring at her with such fury? Surely they must know that she would never wish harm for Umak or Manaravak or any other man of the band. Her lips felt suddenly numb and dry and prickly, as though stinging insects walked within them. "I . . . take back . . . whatever I said."

Sitting cross-legged on the ground beside the headman's woman, Honee shook her head as she looked across the encampment and spoke directly to Umak. "Remember, to this woman and to your little ones, the skin of the great one who walks on three paws is nothing. The skin of the man is everything!"

4

"You will not accompany us on this trip, Old Lion. With Simu in the state he is in, I need a man I can trust to stay behind and serve the People as the woman watcher."

Grek's big, broad nostrils flared as though he was scenting the air for the stink of duplicity; certain that he had found it, he jabbed his wide chin out defiantly.

Torka extended a conciliatory hand and laid it upon the old man's shoulder. "Umak, Manaravak, Dak, and Tankh and Chuk will walk at my side. We will miss your strength, courage, and wisdom, but a man in possession of these qualities is needed here."

They left Grek standing at the edge of camp with his spears in hand and his pack frame on his back. As Torka walked on without looking back he wondered if he had ever done anything in his life as difficult as that.

"You had no choice." Umak came to walk beside him with Dak and Companion at his side. Manaravak and the two boys trotted on ahead.

Torka eyed Dak and Umak without slowing his step. "Do you two imagine that you will never be old?"

Dak replied with his usual curtness. "When I am old, I will have sense enough to know when it is time to step aside and let younger men take my place on the hunt."

"It would seem the best thing to do," Torka agreed. "But will you *know* when you are old? Or will your years sneak up on you like hunters tracking caribou . . . one after the other, each looking just the same until the stalking cloaks fall away and the spears of truth come out to wound you . . . until one day you are a young man trapped and rattling around in an old man's skin, still believing that your old bones can do all the things they once did in your youth and trying to prove it even if it kills you?"

Dak snorted in amusement. "Are you asking me to feel sorry for him?"

"Don't you?" asked Torka.

"No!" Dak responded without hesitation, then cast a quick glance ahead to make certain that neither Tankh nor Chuk was within earshot. Then: "Have you taken a good look at him lately? The past winter has been hard on Grek."

Umak looked at his father thoughtfully. "Grek should have volunteered to be woman watcher. It was wrong of him to allow you to walk from camp burdened by the weight of regret, for the guilt is his, Father, not yours. You did not shame Grek. He shamed himself."

There was no sign of blood or bear in the place where Nantu had died. Snow had fallen while they had kept death-watch for the boy. Afterward, air temperatures had risen drastically and then fallen fast, causing the snow to compact and then solidify into a thick, rock-hard veneer.

"Which way do we go now?" Dak asked, squinting across the distances.

"Our father would say that we must think like our prey to find our prey."

Who spoke? Tankh or Chuk? Torka did not take the time to care. One of the sons of Grek had just offered sound advice, but the headman expected as much from boys raised by Old Lion.

Torka scanned the horizon as he asked, "Which way did the killer of Nantu run when you saw it in the fog, Manaravak?"

Manaravak was silent.

"Well?" Dak pressed him irritably.

"In so much fog and at such a moment, it was impossible to tell!"

Dak snapped angrily, "You must be able to tell us more than that! After all, you lived with wanawut. The way of the beast we seek shouldn't be hard for you to understand."

Torka felt sick. "Enough! I will have no dissension on this hunt. There is danger enough awaiting us; we do not need to add to it by arguing among ourselves. We will walk to the east. If I were the prey we hunt, I would seek safety from wind and storms in the hills that flank the base of the mountains. There is southern exposure there as well as spruce groves in the canyons. It would seem good country for our prey."

"Or for a mammoth?" Umak asked.

"If Life Giver grazes there, yes, Umak, it will ease my heart to know it."

The hunters searched for bear sign across great distances but to no avail. They reached the last cache pit that Three Paws had raided and went on toward the east, closer and closer to the distant white mountains. Two sleeps from their encampment, a driving wind forced them to stop and set up camp. In silence they raised a single lean-to. Huddled around a small fire made of kindling and dried bones that they had packed along, they ate of their rations and shared them with the dog. With the wind rising and a wet, sloppy snow falling all around, they sought sleep.

And now, as Torka dreamed within his traveling robe of caribou skins, the cold, savage, unforgiving spirits of the dead rode the wind. Their forms were purely human.

Mother! Father! Grandfather Umak! Karana . . . Mahnie . . . Nantu . . . Navahk!

The last form shattered his dream, made it crack like old, thin ice as, beneath that ice, the face of the murderous, long-dead shaman looked at him and laughed. Other skeletal hauntings rose through the ice of his memories. They danced and whirled upon the shimmering blue rivers of the northern lights. They sang the songs of the past and of the wild, mountainous, compassionless Ice Age land that stretched wide all around.

Come! cried the spirits of the dead as suddenly a great spirit animal stood upright, towering out of cloud and snow, and high above, spears with enormous, lanceolate heads materialized in the fleshless hands of the dead.

Torka gasped as the ghost bear raised a mutilated forepaw to rip at the sky. A rain of spears fell from the clouds and the hands of the dead. The ghost bear roared, and its mutilated paw became a hand. The hand caught the spears and hurled them at Torka.

"No!" he cried, too late. He was struck, deep in his chest. He grabbed at the spears and tried to pull them out while the spirits mocked and beckoned.

Come! Why search for your lost totem and a luck that will never be yours again? Larani's burns have left scars that will never heal. Nantu's spirit is doomed to walk the wind forever without a head. The men of your band argue among themselves and challenge your decisions. The great bear eludes you. Because you are old. Old! It is time for you to walk the wind with us forever!

"No!" Torka raged back in defiance. He was not old! He was not ready to die!

"Father?"

He blinked. Umak was looking down at him.

"Are you all right? You cried out in your sleep."

He felt suddenly very tired but infinitely relieved. "A dream . . . only a dream."

Umak nodded, then lay down and went back to sleep.

Torka lay awake. Sleep eluded him now, as thoroughly as the great bear. He closed his eyes, cursing the bear and the deep, subtle aches in his bones that had not been there before the onset of winter. He thought of old Grek.

Will you know when you are old? He cursed the question and willed his thoughts away.

He must have slept then. When he woke, he felt very tired. The sound of wind and snow falling onto the lean-to had stopped. Umak, Manaravak, Dak, and the boys were breathing deeply and rhythmically on either side of him. Then, somewhere to the east, a lone mammoth trumpeted, and as Torka smiled, his tiredness fell away, and he knew that the ghostly apparitions of his dream had been nothing more than figments born out of his own fears. He was *not* old. He was *not* ready to die.

Life Giver walked the eastern ranges as he had somehow

known that it would. With the mammoth walking ahead of the hunters, Torka knew that they would soon find Three Paws, for surely they were on the trail of their luck at last!

And then Demmi walked into camp with Snow Eater at her side.

"May the dawn bring the favor of the spirits to these hunters!" Standing as bold as a snow-dusted lioness in her winter hunting clothes, Demmi offered the traditional morning greeting of her people. With Companion up and wagging his tail at her side, she kicked one of the stakes that held the lean-to in place and jumped back, laughing, as the tent collapsed and dropped its load of snow all over the men and boys within.

"Up now, men of the band! Take up your spears! This woman has found sign of the prey you seek to the south—wet and sloppy and stinking fresh!"

The men came up out of the snow, shaking themselves free of it.

"What are you doing here?" Dak demanded. "You have our son to care for!"

"Swan is looking after Kharn. He likes her better anyway."

"You were not asked to come on this hunt, Demmi!"

"Nor was I told to stay behind, Dak!" Her head went high. "Besides, after Naya's challenge, I had to make certain that my two 'baby' brothers were out hunting the prey that they are supposed to kill . . . and not each other!"

Torka stepped forward to put himself between Dak and Demmi. "Did I hear you correctly, Daughter? Did you find sign of our prey?"

"Great stinking globs of sign! And even bigger footprints of one that uses only one forepaw when it walks—a paw that is about this big!" Demmi held up her hands to indicate a bear paw that would be as broad as the head of the beast.

Tankh was looking up at the young woman with awe. "How brave you are for a female!"

Demmi reached down and cuffed the boy fondly on the head with a gloved hand. " 'For a female,' eh? Would *you* have come out across the land alone after what happened to Nantu?"

Dak flushed with sudden anger and gave his woman a hard, open-handed shove, then pulled her close, and when her hood fell back, he stared straight into her scowling face.

"Do not smile when you speak my poor dead brother's name! You are not so brave. Or have you forgotten that the last time you went out alone, I'm the one you threw your spear at and nearly brained with stones hurled from your bola when, in a perfectly female panic, you imagined that you saw wanawut lurking behind every boulder and within every puff of fog!"

Demmi shook free of his hold and raised her spears as she replied with anger that equaled his. "Is there a man or boy here who would say that I am not better suited to the spear than to sewing and changing baby swaddling? I am a woman, yes! But I am Demmi, daughter of Torka, and the forces of Creation have made me what I am!"

"Go back to the other women where you belong!" demanded Dak.

She shook her head vehemently. "I am where I belong. Simu cannot hunt with you because he is sick with grief. Grek cannot hunt with you because he is too old. So I will hunt with you. My spear arm is strong. My feet are quick. My heart is bold. And my spirit is willing to face this thieving, boy-killing prey. I do not fear it!"

But Dak was so furious with her that he pushed her down. "Once, just once, you are going to do as I say!" He stood over her, shouting his rage. "Get up! We will go back to camp together!"

"No!" Manaravak intervened. He was so angry that he was shaking as he reached out to pull Dak away from Demmi.

Torka saw Dak's arm rise. The headman took hold of Dak's sleeve before he could strike out at Manaravak. "Stop this. It is your right to discipline your woman, Dak. But you will not strike her! Stand back, Manaravak. You have no place in this. Get up, Demmi. Do as your man commands."

Mutely she obeyed and stood with her head down, staring at her boots.

The tension in the air was palpable. Torka was surprised when Manaravak spoke out to break it with words of conciliation. "Dak must stay. Dak has need to hunt the killer of his brother. This man will hunt another time." The words had not come easily to him, nor did the ones that followed as, with a sigh and shrug, he looked away from Dak to his brother. "Maybe you will make the final kill. If it is so, Umak, remember that I have walked away from this hunt. If Naya accepts you, it will be because I have made it possible.

You will have to share her. But that is for later talk. Now Manaravak will take Demmi back to camp."

"Get your filthy wanawut hands off my woman!" The low, deadly slur of command that growled out of Dak's throat was the sound that a lion makes when another member of its pride ventures too close to a hard-won kill.

Torka was appalled by what he saw in Dak's face at that moment—and in Manaravak's. Hatred, jealousy, malice, a willingness to kill. Quickly, he strode forward, took Demmi's hand, and jerked his daughter away from them both.

"Enough of this," he cautioned. "This prey that we seek will come to kill again. We must end its life, or no man, woman, or child will be safe." He leveled a warning look at Demmi. "You have found the sign for which we have looked. Lead us to it now. You may be a strong, bold woman, Demmi, but you are also thoughtless and immature. You will walk with us. No man will be turned from this kill for your sake."

◆――――――◆

5

◆――――――◆

"Mother, what is it?" Swan asked. She sat with the other women and children in the sun, working on small projects to distract them from worrying about the hunters. "You look so strange."

"I don't know." Lonit's words were soft and seeking. "Something disturbs me—a feeling that even as we stand here something is happening, that something has gone wrong."

"Everyone fears for the safety of the hunters," Swan told her. "And Demmi's absence makes it worse."

While she spoke, little Yona came screaming from the pit hut of Grek to fall weeping into Iana's lap as a highly flustered Naya burst from the hut.

"My doll is dead!" Yona screamed. "Look at all the blood!"

Iana stared at it in stunned silence. "Where did you find this doll, Yona?"

"Snow Eater brought her to me. Naya wants to take her out and bury her! Tell Naya not to bury my doll!"

Iana looked as though her skin were about to crack as she took the doll, brought it to her nose, scented the blood, and then rose to her feet slowly and with obviously dangerous intent. Her eyes were skewers of ill-contained rage as they fixed the girl.

"Bury it? Is that what you wanted to do?"

"I—" Naya had gone so pale that even her lips were white.

"Bury it with the other missing doll? One doll for each moon? You have hidden from the People the truth that you have become a woman!"

"No!" Naya's denial was too adamant to be anything but a lie.

While everyone stared at Naya, Iana stepped forward and slapped the girl so hard that Naya spun completely around before dropping to her knees.

Grek stalked forward in a rage. "What is this? You will not strike Little Girl!"

"Your Little Girl is a lying, deceitful *woman*! Look! She has stolen our Yona's dolls to use to stanch her flow! Four men, a woman, and our two sons are out on a hunt, needing all the luck that they can hope for, and in this camp your Little Girl has walked among her people as a woman for at least two moons, hiding the truth, deceiving us, teasing the sons of Torka, and making each of them believe that he is the object of her desire while, in truth, she obviously wants neither of them. She has broken every taboo concerning her gender . . . and we have wondered why the forces of Creation no longer smile upon this band!"

Grek was so stunned that he could not speak.

Slowly, regally, Lonit walked forward until she stood before the pit hut of Grek. Extending her right hand, she gestured for Iana to pass her the doll. She took the dog-tattered, moisture-stained little object, scented it, then let her arm fall to her side.

"I see," Lonit said coolly. Then, kneeling beside the distraught Naya, she raised the girl's face with her free hand. "Why have you done this, Naya?"

"I . . . w-want to stay w-with G-rek . . . to b-be a girl . . . n-not a woman. I . . . d-don't w-want . . . to ch-choose. . . ."

"Between my sons?"

The girl nodded pathetically.

"But you *must* choose, Naya." Lonit's voice was gentle,

full of empathy and concern. "All girls must become women. You will find it is not a thing to be feared."

Eneela had risen and come to pause beside Lonit. She stared down at Naya as though in shock.

"My Nantu, his heart was full of you," Eneela told the girl. "If you have bled and not gone to the hut of blood but have eaten and slept in the same hut with men, then you have contaminated the life spirit of every male in this band and have brought this calamity to my Nantu. Oh, and to think that my Dak is out there in the snow, with no luck, no—"

"No more accusations," Lonit interrupted. "Naya is of the People. She has healed Larani's burns and salved Manaravak's injuries. Nantu is dead because he disobeyed his father's command. Your own man has said this, Eneela."

Eneela trembled as she fought back tears of animosity toward Naya.

"I want Naya out of my pit hut." Iana's voice was unyielding as she glared at Grek with both hands laced defiantly across her distended belly. "For the sake of this child that I carry, for the sake of Yona and Tankh and Chuk, I do not want her near me or mine!"

"Grandfather!" Naya wailed.

But Grek was stricken. His face was as gray as ashes. "Naya, tell me that you have not done this terrible thing."

"She *has* done this thing," said Lonit. She rose, took Naya's hand, and drew the girl to her feet. Then the headman's woman gently tilted Naya's face upward again and said, "From this day, will Naya live by truth, and honor the traditions of her band?"

Naya gulped and stammered. "Y-yes."

Lonit nodded. "Then heed what this woman says to you now. When the hunters return to camp, this woman will ask Torka to call a council and choose a man for the new-woman Naya, who has forfeited her right to choose. Naya will go to her man—whoever he may be—without complaint; until then she will live in Torka's pit hut. Naya has forfeited her right to be honored by the feast fire that would have celebrated her life as a new woman. No gifts will be given to this new woman. The forces of Creation must see that the People do not honor those who risk ruining the luck of all in order to satisfy their own selfish whims."

* * *

There was a way for men to hunt bear. And there was a way for bear to hunt men. Midway across the hills, the paw prints led them across increasingly snowy terrain. When the trail dipped into a willow- and drift-choked defile, Torka called a halt.

"The great three-pawed one is leading us," said Dak.

His words were unnecessary; everyone knew the truth. But by then it was too late; they *had* been led. Before they could position themselves defensively, the bear charged downhill with snow exploding on either side of her. Her snout was up, her lips peeled back. Her teeth were bared, and sunlight flashed through a spume of slobber. No position could have been worse for them.

"Scatter!" Torka's command elicited an instant response. The hunters propelled themselves in all directions as hundreds of pounds of snarling flesh and blood and bone and fat came hurtling toward them.

Shoved hard by both Dak and Manaravak, Demmi lost her spears as she fell on her side, wrenching her back. Dak threw himself on top of her and grabbed her in his arms. The two of them rolled down the steep decline, gathering snow as they went.

Releasing a bloodcurdling howl, Manaravak scooped up his sister's spears and, arms up, went wading downhill after Demmi and Dak until his snow walkers tripped him. He fell directly in the path of the bear.

Safely to one side of the charging animal, Torka, Tankh, and Chuk fought to keep their footing on the slippery slope as they steadied their spears. They expected the bear to veer toward them, but her weight was propelling her forward, and she could not stop. As she went past, Torka cried: "Now!"

He and the boys loosed their spears. The bear was struck—three spears, three strikes. Not one was fatal. The bear kept on running downhill toward the felled Manaravak and, well below him, toward the stunned Dak and Demmi.

"*No!*" The roar came out of Umak. He and Companion and the sledge were well below the bear, in a position of relative safety since the momentum of the bear's charge would apparently take her past him—or would have if he had not elected to move.

"Manaravak!" Umak called down frantically to his twin. "Get up! Ready a spear if you can."

Then he turned, picked up the sledge, and found the

strength and balance to shove it into the bear's path. Umak jumped aside just as her bad paw came in contact with the sledge. She roared against pain and confusion while Companion leaped out and landed on her hideously scarred flank. Thrown off balance, she went heels over head as the dog fell into the snow. Umak rammed a spear deep above the bear's shoulder and downward with all his might into her lung.

Downslope, Manaravak stared up, saw what was happening, and fought to right himself, rolling hard to his left. And then, managing to loosen his snow walkers, he forced himself onto his knees and, with a spear braced, awaited the bear.

Torka shouted for joy. What magnificent sons Lonit had given to him!

The bear was spitting blood as she fell. Spears protruded from her body; they were broken by her fall and driven deep by her weight as she had landed on them. When she rolled to a stop before Manaravak, Torka released the second of his spears. Tankh and Chuk followed suit. From the bottom of the defile, Dak hurled the one weapon that he had left.

The bear was heaving, bleeding, and making gurgling sounds as she sucked for air from only one good lung. The great bear fought to rise. Now Manaravak would strike the final blow, and Three Paws would die. But Manaravak did not move. He stayed on his knees and held his spear at the ready, but he did not throw it.

A wave of horror rose within Torka, half choking him on despair as he realized that the burn-ravaged creature no longer looked like a bear at all. Standing upright, waving its forelimbs, the bear looked like neither man nor bear. It resembled another animal—the one creature he knew his son would never kill. *Wanawut*.

Demmi saw it, too. "Manaravak!" Her scream of terror rent the air.

Manaravak ignored her. Calmly, as though he feared no danger or threat of death, he laid his spear across his thighs.

Three Paws stood taller, extending blood-soaked forelimbs and head. A rain of blood and saliva fell upon Manaravak, and Torka knew that a part of him was about to die with his son.

Two spears flew from above. One went wide, the other struck true. Umak and Torka waded downward through the snow, brandishing their arms, yipping like wolves as they bravely attempted to draw the beast away.

It was too late. Manaravak's hesitation had cost him. The bear fell upon him with terrible ferocity as Umak leaped out and drove home the killing thrust.

The dead bear lay in a great sprawl across Manaravak. A frenzied Demmi sat astride its corpse, stabbing it and sobbing in anguish. Dak stood back, stunned by her savage display of grief. It took the combined efforts of all to pull the young woman away and roll the lifeless bear off Manaravak.

"He looks dead, but I think he is still breathing!" exclaimed Torka.

Barely daring to believe it, Torka knelt close and, trying not to recoil at the extent of his son's injuries, pressed his fingertips hard against Manaravak's throat. Yes! There was a pulse.

"Manaravak lives!" he declared.

Umak was at his side, his expression grim. "Not for long if we don't stop this bleeding. Tankh, Chuk, bring my medicine bag. It's strapped to the sledge. Hurry."

Demmi knelt beside Umak and her father. All color bled from her face. "Look at him, look at my brother, my beautiful brother!" she sobbed, and bent to hold on to Manaravak as though she would never let him go.

"Demmi, you cannot help him like this. Come away now, Daughter."

Torka tried to gentle her back, but she would not be gentled. It took the help of Dak and Umak to loosen her hold and force her away. Torka's temper was riled. For Manaravak's sake he calmed the storm of anger that he felt rising within him toward Demmi. Manaravak's breathing hinted at broken ribs, perhaps a pierced lung. He had been partially scalped and seriously raked across the back and arms and the left side of his face by the bear's claws. His appalling wounds would have to be stanched and packed and stitched, or he would surely bleed to death.

Dak, standing beside Demmi, noticed that Umak's right arm was bleeding badly. But the shaman, preoccupied with his brother, was oblivious to his own pain and bleeding. When Tankh and Chuk returned with the medicine bag, Dak snatched it, opened it, and retrieved a length of buckskin bandage. "I'll take care of the shaman," he offered.

Umak consented to be bandaged only when Torka saw the extent of his injury and insisted that he allow Dak to bind it.

"In days and nights to come, the People will speak of this hunt and of how Umak risked himself to save his brother," Torka told his firstborn son.

Umak accepted the praise in grim silence and endured Dak's ministrations. Then he and Torka set to the task of helping Demmi to put Manaravak into a condition in which he might be safely brought back to camp. Father, daughter, and son worked together wordlessly.

Unable to be of assistance, Dak led Tankh and Chuk to the carcass of the bear. "We have a bear to skin," he told them. "It must be ready to transport as soon as Manaravak has been prepared for traveling."

Umak was so preoccupied that later, when young Chuk came, he took no note of him.

"Look, Umak. Dak told me to show you this. It's one of your spearheads. Your spear made the killing blow. You'll be the one to have Naya now, won't you, Umak?"

Umak made no comment as he sutured his brother's brow. Manaravak's breathing was shallow. The color of his face indicated that he was in shock, perhaps near death. Naya was the last thing on his mind. Even if she had been standing beside him and asking him to take her, he would have told her to go away.

◆————◆

6

◆————◆

It had taken the hunting party two days and a night to bring Manaravak back to the encampment. Now he lay near death in his pit hut.

With Swan, Summer Moon, and Demmi assisting, Lonit cared for her unconscious son as she commanded Naya to bring her own bag of healing aids from the hut of her grandfather to ease Manaravak's fever and to eat the pain in Demmi's back.

Outside, in the center of the camp, the skin of the great bear was taken from the sledge and unfolded. The meat that lay within was portioned out, but none would be eaten until Manaravak recovered or died. The People prepared themselves to fast and pray to the forces of Creation.

Torka called no council. After he spoke privately with Lonit about Naya, he summoned his people and said, "Let no more traditions and taboos be ignored lest we all suffer for the carelessness and thoughtlessness of a few." He turned and pointed at Umak. "On the hunt yours was the killing thrust. All saw your valor. Let all the People know that the granddaughter of Grek is now the woman of Umak. There will be no ceremony and no gifts."

Umak was too stunned to speak. The girl must have become a woman in his absence, but how could she have gone into the hut of blood and come out again so quickly? What had she done to anger Iana and Torka and cause Grek to hang his head in shame? Suddenly Umak was furious. This was no time for a man to think of a woman—not even of Naya.

"I will take no woman until my twin's fate has been decided by the forces of Creation!" he proclaimed. "And this kill that I have made—I could not have made it unless my brother had put himself in the path of the bear. The kill belongs to us both!"

This said, he gave Torka no opportunity to challenge him as he cast off his robe and took up the skin of the bear. Wearing it as a cloak and blowing through a whistle made of hollowed bear bone, he beseeched the forces of Creation to spare his brother's life while he danced as he had never danced before.

Naya stared at Umak and fought against the shooting pains of a skull-squeezing headache. The shaman whirled before her. She did not like his dance or the way he looked in the horribly mutilated skin of the great bear. She hated the sight of the skin. She was sorry she had asked for it. If he tried to give it to her, she would tell him to take it away. She wanted no part of it or of him. He did not look like her Umak. He looked huge, menacing, terrifyingly male. She caught broad glimpses of the man beneath the skin—stark-naked except for his ceremonial paint and wristlets and anklets of feathers and bones.

How graceful he was. How magnificent. And how frightening! He was more powerful than she had realized, not as tall as Manaravak but broader of chest and back and just as lean of hip and belly, with an organ large enough to cause her to gasp at the sight of it. What must it be when it was distended?

Painted in the same red and black spirals that adorned
the rest of his body, Umak's penis seemed menacing—large
enough to become locked in a woman's body, causing pain,
tearing tender flesh, unable to withdraw. Wide-eyed and
terrified, she remembered the dogs—and the wanawut of her
nightmare of death. She felt sick with dread as she stared at
this never-before-seen portion of Umak. Unless Torka or
Umak changed his mind, the shaman could take her to his
hut and . . . She stared ahead, unable to think of it, but
unable to stop.

A day and a night passed in quick succession in the camp
above the river. And during all that time, as Manaravak lay in
his hut near death, Larani kept a silent vigil. Seated in her
furs outside her father's pit hut, she neither ate nor slept as
she beseeched the spirits to spare Manaravak. And all the
while Umak danced until at last he was as humpbacked as old
Grek and as heavy-footed as the mammoth that trumpeted in
the eastern ranges. His chanting droned on, broken only now
and then when Honee and Jhon brought water to ease his
parched throat. He would not eat. He would not rest until he
was certain that his brother's life spirit was safe within his
body once again.

Only the presence of the mammoth kept Torka's spirits
from falling, and only a basically forgiving heart allowed Lonit
to permit Naya to enter Manaravak's hut to administer what
healing she could. Naya's manner was one of supreme concern as she knelt beside Manaravak and took from her own
neck the exquisitely carved little talisman of bone.

"Our helping spirit," she whispered to him. "I have
brought Scorched Ears to help you. Look, do you see?"

Manaravak did not see. He was delirious as the young
woman gently slipped the carving around his neck. "It is very
special, but you need its magic more than I do now. Helping
Spirit will heal you and make you strong again."

As two nights and days passed, Naya's ministrations were
ceaseless. Her tonic of ground-up bits of red berries and
pulverized flowerets of dried thousand-leaf in a willow broth
began to eat Manaravak's fever and his pain; he began to
breathe more easily and sometimes, although still in a sweated
delirium, he would laugh out loud.

Her efforts allowed Lonit to sleep while a hollow-eyed,
resentful Demmi watched the girl closely. "It seems that

your old grandmother Wallah taught you well," Demmi said reluctantly. "You are not completely useless after all."

On the morning of the third day, Manaravak's fever broke. He asked for water. Naya brought it to him in an oiled bladder skin and held the smoothly polished bone spout to his lips just as Lonit came in through the cold flap. She scooted close to her son, touched his brow, and then bent to kiss it as she smiled and choked back happy tears. "Oh, Demmi, my girl, it looks as if the worst is over at last! And Naya, how can I thank you?"

The sound of Umak's rasping, weary chanting permeated the silence of the little hut. As Naya listened, she remembered the sight of the shaman dancing in the bearskin robe, whirling in his body paint and feathers, with his organ exposed—huge and dangerous to her eyes. She looked up at Lonit and did not hesitate. "Tell the headman that I am not ready to take Umak as my man. Ask him not to make me."

Lonit's smile faded. "Naya, you ask too much of me. Despite all of your help here, after what you have done, how can I ask Torka that?"

Manaravak's hand rose and closed weakly on his mother's wrist. He could have no idea to what Lonit was referring. Nevertheless, he spoke one word. It was all that he had strength for. It was a simple word—a grain of sand that would loose the boulder of fate and send it plummeting down upon them all. One word.

"Ask."

Torka was so tired that the request that his woman was making seemed trivial. "Return to Naya the right of choice. Manaravak still desires her."

"I cannot," he said. He had not forgotten the look of longing on Umak's face when he had said: *I want her. I want her more than I have ever wanted anything in my life.* "Umak has earned the girl. Although what he—or Manaravak—sees in her is beyond me."

"Manaravak would have died had it not been for the granddaughter of Grek. Surely she must deserve some consideration. After all, when you gave the girl to Umak, he was in no hurry to accept her."

"For good cause. I have already spoken on the matter, Lonit. Before the entire band I named her punishment."

"Is it against the traditions of our ancestors for a headman to change his mind?"

"I will not have my sons at each other's throats over Naya!"

"They need not be. Their love for one another is deep and strong. Let the girl choose. Truly, it is the only way that there will ever be true peace between them."

He closed his eyes, held her close, felt the warmth of her body soothe the weariness of his own. "A moon . . . I will give her that much time."

"With Manaravak as ill as he is, it is not enough. It should not be said later that if she chooses him over Umak, that her choice has been made out of pity for a sick man."

Sleep was closing in on him. "Then until the time of light returns fully to the Valley of the Great River. If the forces of Creation are with us, the one who lies wounded should be well and strong by then."

"Yes," she conceded, yawning now and snuggling close. "If the forces of Creation are with us. It will be a good thing, and I am sure that Umak will understand."

The shaman brooded. He felt betrayed by his parents and could not understand why Naya had lied about coming to her time of blood. Nor could he understand why, once her lie had been discovered, she had considered Torka's punishment to be anything but a fulfillment of her own wishes. He cursed under his breath. Torka had given her to him! But now the decision had been reversed, and if this were not humiliation enough, Naya was avoiding him.

Umak ground his teeth. Manaravak was alive only because Umak had willingly risked his life to save him. And while Umak had danced naked in the cold wind and gone without food for two days and a night appealing to the spirits to save his twin's life, Manaravak had asked Lonit to intercede for Naya on his behalf . . . and to give him a chance to win her favor again.

Umak trembled against frustration and rage. How could Lonit have agreed to speak for him? And how could Torka have consented? He could not understand. He was not certain that he wanted to understand.

7

The sun stayed longer in the sky each day. There was still snow upon the ground, and the wind still rose to drive storms across the land, but the storms seemed less intense, the snow had a different texture, and between storms the scent of spring was in the air. The People of Torka could smell it. They could feel it. Everyone knew that it would not be long before the Moon of River Ice Breaking. And after that the Moon of Green Grass Growing would rise above the Valley of the Great River. Summer would not be far behind. With the knowledge that their longing for endless days of light and warmth would soon be satisfied, the People's moods lightened, and gradually the tensions of the long winter seemed to be falling away.

In the hut of Simu, Eneela sat up, awakened by Summer Moon's song of welcome to the returning sun. The younger woman was outside, sitting with Uni in the gaunt but nourishing sunlight. The child was clapping her hands and humming happily along, doing her best to follow the words of the song.

"My Summer Moon sings like a bird," said Simu appreciatively, sitting up beside Eneela and nodding. The past days and nights had seen a gradual change in him—the madness of inconsolable grief had left his spirit. "The coming baby has made her happy."

"And you," said Eneela.

His face twisted with happiness, sadness, longing, regret. "Yes," he conceded. "It will be good to hold a baby again and to see the sun of summer and feel . . ."

His words went on, but Eneela did not hear them. She stared down at her hands: worn, callused, knotted at the joints, they looked like stalks of deadwood spread out upon the bed furs—an old woman's hands. But how could this be? At thirty-six, she and Lonit were close in age. And yet she did not need the calm, reflecting waters of a tundral pool to tell her that she looked older. Her hands told her that, and

the weight of her breasts as they sagged against her belly.
They had been her pride once. Fine, firm, bounteous breasts,
filled with milk for her babies and occasionally for the babies
of other women who had not enough to sustain their own
sucklings. Beautiful breasts made for the pleasure of her man.

But now Simu sat listening to his second woman, lovely
Summer Moon, whose slender body was ripe with new life.
Listening to the light, joyous song of the much younger
woman, Eneela was filled with sadness and longing for her
own lost youth and for her dead children.

"Eneela! Why are you crying?" Simu asked with concern.

She was startled to discover that tears were coursing
downward over her cheeks. Flustered, she wiped the tears
away, but in doing so she looked at her hands again and
began to sob. "Oh, Simu, Nantu is dead, and Larani is
burned, and I am an old, dry woman!"

He pulled her into a rough embrace. "You? You are my
first woman, Eneela. Many years will pass before we will
grow old together. In the end, Summer Moon and the babies
that I will get on her will take care of the two of us!" He
laughed, a first since the death of Nantu. Smiling, he eased
her back onto the furs. "But what kind of talk is this from my
Eneela, eh? Who is to say that I cannot put a baby into your
belly again?"

There was a young man's fire in his eyes. It warmed
Eneela, and she blushed. "I do not want to be old, Simu."

"But you are not old, Eneela. And you are with me now.
Let us be young together for a while."

On a clear day bearing the promise of spring, Umak
intercepted Naya on her way to the place where the women
went to relieve themselves. He stood in silence, deliberately
blocking her way until her chin went up and her lower lip
quivered.

"How is my brother?" he asked.

She heard the unspoken censure in his voice and stammered. "B-better. Every day he is better."

"And how is my Naya?"

Her eyes went wide. "I . . ."

"Will you ever be 'my' Naya?"

"I . . ." She stared at him. The dark center of her eyes
seemed to float amid the white . . . large black moons drifting, filling with shadows, black on black. It was like looking

into the eyes of a blind woman. He was suddenly worried about her.

"Are you all right, Naya?"

"Yes! Why would I not be all right!"

It occurred to Umak that in her concern for his brother, she was not taking care of herself, not keeping her lips moist with fat; a woman who did not lubricate her skin soon dried up and withered like an ill-tended hide left to cure in the sun too long. It also occurred to him that he would love her even then.

"Let me pass, Umak," she demanded.

He did not want to yield but knew that he must. He stepped aside. As she hurried by him he asked once more; "Naya, why have you refused me?"

Without slowing her pace, she looked back over her shoulder and, with a sudden giggle, smiled at him and spoke the words that brought the sun back into his heart. "I have not refused you at all!"

Now, when the weather allowed, the children played outside, the women brought their sewing out of their pit huts, and the men of the band began to make new spears in the light of day.

Still weak, in pain, and beset by a lingering low-grade fever, Manaravak, longing for the warmth of the sun, forced himself outside to sit out of the wind before his pit hut. Naya and Demmi hovered near, making certain that he had bed furs around his shoulders and over his limbs. Now that Manaravak was out of danger, he returned the Scorched Ears talisman to Naya with his thanks. Lonit smiled as she brought him a new backrest, and Sayanah led the other boys close to admire his brother's wounds.

"Look! He will have many scars!" Sayanah proclaimed with awe and envy, for among the hunting people, a man without scars was a coward who had never risked himself.

Larani happened by at that moment. She stopped and looked closer, then smiled a little. "Scars, eh? So you like scars do you, Sayanah?"

Larani had long since stopped hiding under her new-woman sleeping skins, but she still kept a drape of hide over her head, wearing it like a hood. Sayanah looked up at her as though afraid that she was about to take it off.

She made an exhalation of indifference, then appraised

Manaravak coolly. *"Hmm*, yes, Sayanah is right. You will have many scars, but perhaps you will not be 'too bad ugly' when you are finally healed!"

Manaravak glared up at Larani. He could see all but the burned side of her face smiling at him from within her hood. Merriment sparkled in her eyes. Memories suddenly flared within him, and he realized that she had deliberately taunted him with his own words. Was it possible that he had been so callous toward her? He had not intended to be.

Now, despite the bravado of her posture and tone, compassion settled on her face, and she laughed—not *at* him but somehow *with* him and at herself, as though the two of them had been the butt of some terrible joke. "Don't be so glum! You're alive and all in one piece, aren't you?"

Suddenly, the wind turned without warning, baring Larani's head before she could grasp at her hood and pull it up again.

In the clear light of day her scars had been terrible to behold. Most of the great, dark, clotted scabs had fallen away; her new skin had an opaque pinkish-purplish sheen to it. It looked rather like the tiny petals of rhododendrons that grew high in the mountain valleys. Her hair, once singed to near baldness, was growing back on the unburned side of her head; it was a thick, black stubble that shone with bluish tints in the light of day. As he looked at it, it made him think of the mane of a young horse, for where length allowed, she had combed it sideways, encouraging it to fall over the curve of her damaged scalp where hair would never grow again. In time the length would hide her disfigurement.

"At what do you stare? Did you see enough? Am I not beautiful?" The young woman's head went high. Her eyes flashed, and her nostrils flared defensively, daring Manaravak to voice his thoughts of revulsion.

He had none. He was thinking that in a strange way she *was* beautiful—reshaped and redefined by fire—and he was also thinking how much she reminded him of a horse—yes, of that wondrous, burning horse that had come leaping over the abyss, raining flesh and fire upon him as it died. Had its spirit sought a new life within the daughter of Simu and Eneela? The thought amazed and entranced him as much as the sight of the strong, defiant young woman inspired him. What were his pain and scarring when compared to Larani's courageous heart?

"Well?" she pressed haughtily. "Did the sight of me make you so sick that you can't even speak?"

He shook his head. It hurt. He did not care. He kept on staring unflinchingly up at Larani. "You are beautiful."

She stiffened. Searching his eyes for mockery and finding none, she could not believe it. Her mouth set itself into a straight, hard line. "You are a liar . . . or a blind man!" she said, and without another word, she turned on her heels and walked away.

Clouds moved in from the northwest to cover the sun. By dusk it began to rain, a thin, cold rain that smelled vaguely of salt and of strange, unrecognizable essences.

Umak stood in the rain, allowing it to fall upon his face and into his mouth. Ever since Naya had spoken up to encourage his continued affection, he had been in a fine mood. He was even speaking to Manaravak again. After all, he could afford to be forgiving. With his own eyes he had seen that Naya had returned Manaravak's talisman. The granddaughter of Grek *was* going to be his woman, after all. He was certain of it!

Night was coming down. Now, as he called upon the Seeing Wind to help him understand the meaning of this rain that smelled like watered blood, the wind turned and the scent disappeared. Umak could find no threat in it.

The rain fell off and on for most of the night. Sometime before dawn it turned to sleet. And then, just when they were all certain that winter was over, the cold returned with a vengeance. The pit huts were glazed, and icicles glinted in the light of a sun that shone brightly but withheld its warmth.

Then at last, under intermittent clouds, caribou were sighted coming out of the distant mountains and into the far side of the Valley of the Great River. The men readied themselves for the hunt, and the women prepared to butcher the kills of their men. The headman said that the cold was a gift from the spirits, enabling the hunters to cross the still-frozen river to the caribou on the other side.

Torka led the men of the band toward the distant herd. Umak was glad that Manaravak was not well enough to accompany them. With the big dog Companion loping easily at his side, he was confident that this time he *would* bring gifts to Naya. Manaravak could do nothing that would stop him.

In stalking cloaks and with spears launched out of spear

hurlers, they killed caribou. This was the first hunt of the year. There was no limit on the number of animals that were to be killed. No one knew when wolves and dogs emerged from the snow-covered hills, but soon man and beast were hunting together, killing together, and feasting together. A thread of oneness connected them, predator and prey, land and sky, and all the unseen but strongly perceived elements of mystic savagery that united man and animal with their environment.

When at last the kill was done, the exhausted men drew lots. Simu was selected to go back to bring the women across the river. As was customary, when a kill was as large as this, the women joined the hunters at the killing site to make a temporary butchering camp. Here they would cursorily dress the hides and prepare the meat before transporting their treasure home on sledges. Given the extent of this kill, many trips would be required before the People were settled back into the camp above the river and the last of the bones and unwanted portions of meat and hides were left behind for carrion.

As the hunters watched Simu go they rejoiced in their extraordinary success and praised the forces of Creation. A hard wind was blowing out of the west, driving forward what promised to be a nasty storm, but they were not concerned. Simu would be back with the women before it struck. Soon there would be warm fires and fresh meat as the band celebrated under capacious lean-tos that the hunters set themselves to erecting.

With Umak working beside him, Torka felt better than he had in many moons. He had performed well on the hunt. All had seen his strength and daring. Umak had also done himself proud, bringing down a particularly fine bull. The pelt was unusually pale; even along the back and sides it was almost as white as the belly and underlegs.

"For Naya?" Torka asked.

"For *my* Naya!" Umak affirmed.

"She will smile upon such a fine skin."

"And upon the man who brings it to her!"

They worked ceaselessly until night settled over the Valley of the Great River. The hunters were too tired to raise a fire. Within the protection of their lean-tos, they slept with bellies full of meat and dreams aflame with memories of the hunt.

The women reached the killing site toward dusk of the next day. Dragging sledges loaded with all of the necessary supplies to assist them in the work to come, they happily sang the appropriate songs as they followed Simu into what was to be the butchering camp.

The hunters greeted them enthusiastically: Lonit and Swan and Summer Moon, Eneela and Larani, Iana and Honee. The older children followed.

"Where is Demmi?" Dak asked his father.

Simu measured his son with pity. "You want Demmi? *You* go get her."

"But all of the women have come out to assist their men. The only female who has cause to stay behind is Naya. She watches over Manaravak and his fever."

Simu looked impatient. "Why do you waste yourself worrying over a woman like that, eh, Dak? Look over there to her sister Swan. Now there's a fine young woman for you. Make her an offering of a few of these fine hides, a bit of fat and feathers, and she'd be happy to say yes to you. Torka and Lonit would be pleased."

"Enough, Father! Demmi is my woman. I will not be shamed!" He eyed the lowering sky. "When the weather breaks, I will go back to camp and bring her here, if I have to blacken her eyes and drag her, kicking and screaming, all the way!"

"Dak?"

The shaman came to stand beside Simu and was dressed for traveling. Companion sat at his side, harnessed to a well-loaded sledge.

"Come on, old friend. Between the two of us we ought to be able to talk some sense into Demmi. A butchering camp is supposed to be a camp of celebration! If we hurry, we can be back in the camp above the river before the storm breaks. And I don't want to wait to show my kill to Naya. Have you ever seen a more beautiful caribou skin in your life? Since she couldn't come out with the others, I want to give it to her as a surprise!"

In the camp above the river, the storm swept across the land like a great white tide, wailing and whispering. Within Manaravak's pit hut, the fire guttered and went out. Demmi fell asleep beside her brother after drinking Naya's brew to ease the pain in her back. He lay awake, however, listening to the wind and the snow and to the howling of wolves. At last, Naya came to him. He watched her through the darkness—so small, so light on her feet, so lovely.

She stood above him, bending low, allowing her braids to fall forward over her snow-dusted, fur-clad shoulders. "I have brought you more of my healing drink to ease you through the night." She knelt. Her palm was cold against his brow. She smelled of the snow and the storm and of all good things. "Let me check your brow for fever."

He smiled at her. "It is not so bad to be a man with fever when the granddaughter of Grek comes to tend me with her healing ways."

She knelt back from him and looked at the sleeping Demmi. Surprise registered in her posture; Demmi was always awake for the final check each day.

"I am glad you have come," he said to Naya, accepting the new supply of brew from her, and as she held the bladder skin to his mouth he sucked greedily at the bone spout and gradually relaxed as he felt the heat of the liquid expand within his belly and veins until he was helpless to do anything but relax.

The girl bid him good night, but he held her hand.

"Stay with me while I sleep, Naya. The storm grows wild outside. There is no need for you to go out into the cold."

Naya could not sleep. The storm raged outside the hut, and now and again she thought she heard something howling. She shivered, pulled her coat up around her shoulders, and sat still, determining to wait until the wind dropped before she went back to Grek's hut.

Naya looked closer at Demmi, and then pulled back in amazement. The woman was smiling in her sleep and actually looked happy.

Manaravak, on the other hand, was tossing and moaning against troubling dreams. Concerned, Naya soothed him with soft words and offered occasional sips of her tonic. After each swallow he slept more easily. With a sigh, Naya took a draw on the bladder skin herself.

She sat very still, thinking about her medicine. She could not sleep without it, and often in the middle of the day, she would find herself thinking about it so intensely that if she did not take a drink, her head would ache and her hands tremble.

She sighed, took another pull on the bladder skin and then another and another until, remembering that her berries could sometimes bring bad dreams, she stopped. But her thirst was so deep, she could not refrain from drinking again. She doubted if she had ever drunk so much of her medicine before. How good it was! How warming. All at once she was maddeningly warm and irresistibly sleepy. She pulled off her coat and tunic. The fireless hut was cold. The air caused her to shiver violently. Her breath formed a mist before her face. Suddenly cold and needing warmth in the same driving, mindless way that she had needed her medicine a few moments before, she pulled back the bed furs that covered Manaravak, crawled onto his mattress, and cuddled close.

Manaravak turned slightly. As she drew the bed furs over them, Naya suppressed a giggle, wondering what Demmi would say if she awoke to find her brother and Naya naked beneath his bed furs.

Manaravak awoke with a start as cool, questing fingertips tentatively traced his mouth. He stared into the face of Naya and realized that he was not alone. She lay naked beside him, propped on an elbow, one slender limb casually thrown across his thigh as she looked at him in the most curious way, almost as though she were weighing the merits of a stranger and finding them to her complete satisfaction.

"Man . . . ara . . . vak . . ."

He stared, entranced. She seemed to be speaking out of a dream. Her eyes were open, and yet he was not certain if she was awake. His fingertips touched her lips even as hers lingered upon his. When the tip of her tongue touched the backs of his fingers, the contact was so purely, provocatively sensual that he gasped.

She smiled and continued to move her tongue and slowly slid her bare limb up and down over his.

Perhaps if she had not sighed so dreamily and moved closer to him in that moment . . . perhaps if she had not allowed him to inhale the sweet scent of her breath and to feel the hot, peaking tips of her nipples against his chest . . . perhaps if she had not whispered low that she was glad that the spirit of life had decided to remain within him . . . perhaps he would not have kissed her.

Soon she might be his brother's woman, but now she was here. Although she had made no formal statement of choice, she was accepting his kiss, encouraging the slow trespass of his tongue, arching her tiny body forward to ease the exploration of his hands, allowing him to feel her eagerness and readiness as she began to work her round, soft hips and press herself against his thigh.

As in the willow grove so long ago, she allowed him to position her with ease . . . only this time when she straddled him, she observed his distended organ, and giggling like a child, she fondled it. When she felt it move and swell, she looked at him guilelessly and asked him if it had a life of its own.

The question made him laugh. "Yes," he affirmed. "Oh, yes, Naya. Here, let me show you. Let me share that life with you."

Naya had no fear of him—only fascination. Her body felt light and heavy all at once. There was no thought; there was only sensation. Manaravak was browsing, licking, encouraging her to do the same. His body was warm. He tasted of salt. She wondered dreamily how she could ever refuse him anything. Her loins were throbbing, moist, empty, as though in need of filling. But with *what*? Somehow she knew that Manaravak was about to give her the answer.

Her skin was afire with his fondling, his stroking, his wondrous invasions. She yielded, opened herself wide, and offered no resistance when at last his powerful hands slowly lifted her. He brought her down slowly, so slowly, upon that part of him that roused surprise and ecstasy. It seemed to Naya that Manaravak caused the sun to explode within her body. Its heat, its radiance—*this* was the need she had sought! And now, as he held her hips and rammed deep, where once she might have screamed in terror of her memory of the savage mating of the dogs, now she screamed with rapture. Only reciprocal movement could satisfy her need for more of him as ever-expanding waves of pleasure shook her to her very soul.

She screamed again. There was no pain in the sound, only pleasure as Manaravak released into her. But still she moved on him until a cold and terrible gust of wind and a wave of snow entered the hut along with Dak and Umak. Manaravak withdrew and, with a moan and an exhalation of shock, set her roughly away from him.

"No!" cried Naya, staring at the intruders and seeing

them as nothing more than faceless, unwelcome figures taking shape within a dream. Her loins were throbbing, not yet fulfilled. She did not like the way the intruders were ruining her dream. "Go away!" she demanded, and got to her knees and moved to Manaravak, whimpering softly. "Fill me . . . again. . . ."

And suddenly a man who looked very much like Umak was glaring at her and Manaravak with unspeakable disappointment and bitterness.

"She is yours, then. Behind my back and without honor, she has chosen. Here. Take these skins. A gift from Umak to the new woman and her new man!"

———◆———◆———

8

———◆———◆———

Leaving Naya in a befuddled heap, Manaravak stumbled to his feet and followed Umak out of the hut.

"Brother! Wait!" Manaravak called, his heart chilled by his twin's anguish.

Umak kept walking into the wind and snow.

Naked, barefoot, and still dizzy from his fever and Naya's medicine, Manaravak took off after him. His mind was in panic. He could not free himself of the image of his brother's tormented face. He had not realized the depth of Umak's love for Naya until now—indeed, he could not understand that kind of love. If only Umak would face him, perhaps he could explain that what had transpired between Naya and him had not been intended. A lustful mating on a snow-filled night . . . was it so important? Why was Umak so upset? If Naya meant so much to Umak, they could share her.

The snowfall was intensifying. A deep, thick layer of white was beginning to drift high around the pit huts. At the edge of the encampment, Manaravak tripped. He lay sprawled on his belly, staring ahead into the wind and snow and darkness.

"Wait! Umak, I . . . she . . ."

Umak stopped, turned, and waited.

Distressed and in pain, Manaravak was still not thinking

clearly. Meeting his brother's glance, he found that he did not know what to say to make things right, so he said nothing.

Umak turned in disgust and walked away more rapidly, angrier than before.

Confusion struck at Manaravak's mind. He rose. "Umak!"

Only the wind answered him. He knew that his brother would seek solitude at the edge of the camp to the lee of his pit hut; there would be no talking to him now, no reasoning, no hope of understanding or forgiveness. The feelings of desolation that assaulted him were absolute. Among those of his own kind he was a stranger—an alien. Someone in the band was always angry with him. Everything he said or did seemed to rain havoc upon others. He did what he had always done when feelings of confusion and loneliness overwhelmed him: He threw back his head and howled.

And from somewhere across the river to the southeast, from within the stormy vastness of the tumultuous, mountainous land that lay beyond the Valley of the Great River, a voice answered his cry.

He stiffened. He fell to silence and listened to the voice of his own kind.

"Wanawut!" Demmi cried in dismay.

Dak did not listen. He yanked her to her feet by her hair, then grabbed her shoulders and shook her until her teeth rattled.

"How could you have slept through that!" he raged at her. Then he turned to Naya. "And you . . . put your clothes on. Maybe Manaravak and Umak cannot have enough of the sight of you, but if it were up to me, I'd have you skinned!"

Suddenly the entire pit hut shook as Grek threw aside the cold flap and demanded to know what all the yelling was about. Dak recounted every detail.

"No, no!" Naya was crying from beneath the bed furs now. "I . . . don't remember. I feel so . . . sick!"

"Impossible!" The old man's face expanded into a mask of horror.

"Umak sits alone outside camp, not far from his own hut. Manaravak is no longer in camp at all. He ran toward the southeast, toward the howling of the wanawut. From the way he was running, I do not think he will come back!"

*   *   *

Dak, Umak, and Demmi went out in search of Manaravak. They walked and called as the storm enclosed the world in howling white.

Umak was silent and somber. Regardless of Manaravak's actions, a brother was a brother—and a twin was more than that. "We must go on," he said. "In his weakened state he cannot long survive."

"Perhaps, for all concerned, that would be best," said Dak.

Umak wheeled and struck him down.

No one spoke. Then Umak extended his hand to the son of Simu.

For a long while Dak stared at it. Then, without apology or thanks, he took it, got to his feet, and started off again, leading the search with Demmi at his side. But even the most resolute hunters could not conduct a search in a white-out. Dak turned back to stand with Umak. He shouted to be heard above the storm, his face invisible within his icicle- and snow-encrusted ruff. "Do we tie ourselves together and go on?"

Umak's head swung from side to side. "We'll have to take shelter here. Even roped together, we would probably walk in circles. The snow fills our tracks practically before we lift a boot to make others." He turned, seeking to offer words of comfort to Demmi. "Do not worry. We will find him when the weather—"

His words stopped in midflow. Demmi was gone.

Across the river in the temporary butchering camp, the People had waited out the storm, feasting on caribou and listening to stories. No one noticed the sudden change in the wind's direction. Now, a fierce gust struck the communal lean-to in which Torka and Lonit were sleeping. Much of the night had passed since she had drifted into sleep within his arms. He had fallen into deep, untroubled dreams beside her, but now he lay awake, listening to the wind, dozing intermittently, until suddenly he rose and, pulling on his winter parka, stood into the storm.

The wind was no longer from the north, and it was no longer freezing. It was driving sleet and rain before it, and from all around the butchering site came the sound of water running off melting snow.

How long had the temperature been rising? Long enough

to melt the newest snowfall, but surely not long enough to loose the fury of the spring thaw! No. There was nothing sure about it.

"Up! Everyone! Awake now! We must take whatever caribou meat we can pack onto the sledges and hurry back to our camp above the river!"

Faces peered out of the lean-tos. Everyone was staring at the rain. No one had to tell them that if the snow in their encampment was melting, the ice on the great river would be melting, too. If it began to break up, they would be caught on the far side, and there would be no way for them to cross the river again until summer had come and gone and the time of the long dark had returned to freeze the water solid once again.

Lonit was on her feet. "Have you not heard your head-man? We have work to do, and quickly! If the river ice breaks before we are across, only the forces of Creation will know how long it will be before we are reunited with those whom we have left behind!"

PART VI

---◆---

THE GREAT MAD RIVER

1

Demmi tracked Manaravak toward the river. She did not look back or concern herself with the others. *Let them worry!* She would not walk with them if all they talked about was turning back and abandoning the search for Manaravak.

Her steps were aided by the force of the gale that pounded at her back. On and on she went, ignoring Dak's imperative calls. The wind carried his voice to her across the considerable distance that now lay between them. He sounded distraught, and it briefly occurred to Demmi that she had been wrong to leave his side without a word. But if he caught up with her now, he would probably show his relief by striking her.

Instinct guided her. She stood in a world where land and sky were one. There was no horizon; the world disappeared into wind-driven white. She turned and became disoriented.

Tired and frustrated, Demmi called out, "Manaravak! For once in your life, behave as a man, not as a wanawut-raised fool who runs away every time he makes a mistake! Come back, and we will work it out! Umak has forgiven you!"

Alone and afraid, Demmi visualized bestial forms moving through the whiteness that surrounded her. She gripped her spears tightly. Whatever she had seen was gone. There was nothing there—not wanawut and not Manaravak. Demmi fought against tears and, winning, settled down to spend the worst of the storm curled up in her traveling clothes within a hollow that she hacked out of the snowpack with her spear and dagger. She could not sleep as she thought of her wound-weakened brother walking the world alone, barefoot and weaponless.

Well before dawn, a shift in the wind alerted her to a change in the storm. She crawled from her burrow and hurried on in a snow that was turning to sleet. Even as she jogged on, sleet was becoming rain, and the rain was turning into a downpour. With her heart in her throat, Demmi lengthened her stride. If the previous days of warmth had loosened winter's last hold on the river, then the ice could crack wide at any moment, catching Manaravak if he was not safely across or marooning him on the other side if he was!

Fear for her brother's life kept her going. The river lay ahead. Desperate, Demmi forced herself on until, at last, she dropped to her knees in the water-soaked, icy slush of a broad, sloping embankment. She saw his tracks and knew that she was too late. Manaravak had crossed the river.

She could see him on the other side, heading southeast, into unknown country out of which the wanawut had called to him.

"Wait!" she screamed at the top of her lungs.

He paused, turned, and stared across the river.

She was on her feet, waving, beckoning, her heart pounding with relief and joy to see him. She had found him. She had found him alive at last. "Come back!"

For a long moment he stared at her.

She knew that he was not going to come back. And she knew that she could not let him go.

"Wait!" she cried again, and this time she was running forward, stumbling toward the river, and then moving across it, slipping, falling, rising again, running on and on until a horrendous cracking roar seemed to split the very sky. But it was not the sky that had been rent asunder; it was the river. A vast, black gash of open water appeared in the ice ahead of Demmi.

On the far side of the river, Manaravak turned and without a moment's hesitation raced for the river's edge.

"No!" Demmi warned him back.

But Manaravak had committed himself to the river. It was a mistake. The ice was already breaking up beneath his feet.

Torka led his people in a desperate race across the river. Convinced that panic was a greater threat than the river, he kept them moving, straining against the weight of their hastily loaded sledges, certain that if they could keep up a steady pace, they would soon stand triumphant on the far shore.

His will to survive gave him strength. He leaned more resolutely into his load and moved doggedly westward. Suddenly the air was split by a terrible, explosive crack, and the ice beneath him rose, shifted hard to the right, and then fell. He fell to his knees with it but not through it. It was still solid, capable of supporting his weight. Beside him, Lonit and Swan and Sayanah were down. His sledge had yawed sideways, its leeward runners lodging into a narrow channel of water that had suddenly appeared in the ice ahead . . . and all around him.

A thin, bitter drizzle was driven at a slant by the wind. The headman cursed himself for wasting precious time in trying to save the meat. The time that they had spent loading the sledges would have seen them safely across the river by now. On his feet again, he scanned the river's surface, which had broken into vast white wedges, each bobbing on the water.

"Abandon the sledges! Boys, help your mothers and sisters! Now!"

"But there is so much meat!" Simu protested.

"Stop arguing and do as I say, Simu! The meat of the caribou will feed this river. The flesh of the people of Torka will not!"

The Seeing Wind came to Umak in a vision of death . . . of warm, pale flesh going down into roaring water. He stopped in his tracks. "We must go back!"

"Not until we find Demmi," Dak said.

Umak was adamant. "If Demmi crossed the river before the wind turned, then she is safely on the far shore by now. If not . . ." He did not wish to complete the thought. "Either way, there is nothing that we can do for her now. But if we hurry, we may be able to help the others before it is too late."

"*Move!*" Torka roared at his people. All of them except Eneela leaped to obey. Paralyzed with fear, she was unable to call for help when Simu moved ahead to lift a heavy-footed, fear-benumbed Summer Moon to her feet.

"Come on, Eneela!" Simu's command hung in the air before the rain pummeled it into the ice. He kept walking, holding up Summer Moon.

"Stay close to me, woman of Simu! I will protect you!" Tankh moved past her with Larani at his side.

"Hurry, Mother! We're over halfway there!" Larani urged, moving on. Balancing herself and helping to steady Tankh, she and Grek's son leaped from one bobbing wedge of ice to another across ever-widening narrow openings of dark water.

Blinking rain out of her eyes, Eneela stared across the distance to the faraway shore, then looked down. The ice beneath her feet was moving up and down, up and down. The force of the river caused the frozen surface to heave and swell as though some great, gasping beast were moving beneath it.

Try as she might, Eneela could not force herself to move, even though the rest of the band was nearly across now. Voices were calling her name through the rain and the sounds of the river. She heard Torka, Lonit, Summer Moon, and Simu.

"Eneela! Where are you, my woman?"

"Come to us, quickly!"

"No, stay where you are! I will come for you!"

As the wind thinned the clouds Eneela saw the others gathered on the far shore. Simu was coming toward her, striding out across the ice, leaping from one floe to another, with Torka in pursuit.

Eneela's eyes went wide; they were putting their lives in jeopardy for her sake.

"Stop, Simu! Wait, Torka! I am coming!" she cried just as the ice broke wide beneath her feet.

"Eneela!" Simu cried.

The ice shifted, surged, and dropped the men to their knees as Eneela staggered and fought valiantly for balance. The river was changing so fast, adjustment to it was impossible.

On shore, Summer Moon wept, and Lonit needed the help of Iana, Honee, Swan, and the boys to keep Larani from hurling herself into the river—and it was a river now, no longer a frozen pathway. The broad, flat plates of ice that only moments before had allowed the people to pass over them were now beginning to override one another, to twist, to eddy, to roll in response to the river, which was flowing fast and free.

Torka and Simu fought from being swept off the ice as the current began to carry them downstream. Open water lay between them and Eneela, who was trapped in the middle of the river on a flat island of ice that was disintegrating even as they watched.

With a choking sob of despair, Simu reached out for her, forced himself to one foot and then to another only to lose his balance and sprawl forward. Torka, now prone upon the single slab of ice that supported them both, dug the toe edges of his ice walkers into the ice and grabbed Simu by the fringes of his boots just in time to keep him from going headfirst into the ice-choked waters.

In a moment they lay side by side, breathless, sickened by the ever-increasing circular motion of the slab of ice that was spinning them farther and farther downriver and by the horror of their impotence to save Eneela.

"Father Above!" Torka cursed all the malevolent spirits of this world and the next as he watched Simu's woman growing smaller and smaller, trapped on her island of ice. Then, without warning, the surface beneath her feet was lifted straight into the air as a mountainous iceberg exploded upward into the light of day from the fast-flowing deeps, shattering the surface ice into fragments and hurling Eneela high into the rain clouds.

Torka and Simu saw her fall . . . and fall . . . turning in the air until she hit solid ice and lay as limp and motionless as a sodden buckskin doll.

Torka heard a low moan go out of Simu—and out of himself—and then, as Simu spoke his woman's name again and again, suddenly the ice beneath them hit something. The impact caused Torka to roll sideways toward the water. This time it was Simu who saved him. But for what? The slab of ice was listing hard to the right, sinking at one end and rising at the other until it stood poised straight up in the air with the two hunters clinging frantically to the upper edge.

When it fell, it plunged so rapidly that Torka and Simu had no time to release their grip. With the river roaring all around them, they were thrown into the water. Stunned, with the air knocked from their lungs, they found themselves on their backs in the river with the full weight of the ice on top of them, pressing them down . . . down . . . deeper into freezing depths that allowed them no escape.

Umak, followed by Dak, charged into the water to drag Torka and Simu from the ice-choked shallows where the raging river had left them to die. Half-drowned and stiff with cold, the shaman sat shivering on the embankment, rubbing the warmth of life back into his father while Dak did the same for Simu as he sobbed out the details of the death of Eneela.

Grief struck Umak. *Eneela, friend, it was your death I saw, your death that I could not prevent.*

The Seeing Wind was a low, poisonous whisper at the back of his mind. Eneela was gone. They would never find her lifeless form except in their memories. Could he tell his father that Demmi and Manaravak were also missing?

Later. He would tell Torka later. Now the Seeing Wind was a tide that rent his soul with vision, and he knew that he must advise his father of another devastating truth. "The flood that will soon be upon us shall be like none we have ever seen. We must get back to the winter camp to move it to higher ground!"

"And Demmi and Manaravak? Are we to turn our backs upon them, too?" Dak's question was acidic with rebuke.

Dumbstruck, Torka stared at Umak, waiting for an answer.

Umak spoke with the voice of reason. "Father, what has been done cannot be undone. The river will rise to fill the lowlands and sweep us all away if you do not heed me. Those that are lost—may the forces of Creation be with them. But if you are to save the band, you must walk with me now and not look back."

"I will not leave my woman!" Dak was emphatic.

Torka was more so. "Demmi is my daughter, and Manaravak is my son. But Umak speaks the truth. The future of the People lies with the band. The lives of the women and children depend upon us. We cannot risk them—not even for those we love."

Clinging to one another, Demmi and Manaravak were swept downstream, and only their combined strength and will to live allowed them to keep their heads above water until a turn in the river cast them hard upon a spit of icy gravel that extended far out from the shore. Stunned and shaking violently against the cold, they sat numbly together in the rain.

"Tired . . ." Manaravak exhaled. "So c-cold . . ." His eyes rolled back in his head.

Demmi was certain that he was dead. Terrified, she knelt close. Manaravak was naked in the cold rain, yet his skin was hot. His effort to save her life had cost him dearly. His fever was back, and his breathing was erratic. Kneeling close, she pulled him up against her and held him in her arms and rocked him as though he were a child again.

Manaravak's head fell onto her shoulder. He slept in her embrace. In the rain and wind, he slept like a mindless, exhausted animal beside the raging river.

Something flowed by the gravel spit: a furry mound

upon a whirling floe of ice. Demmi began to tremble with dread. The river was running so fast and wild that the form on the ice was almost lost to view before she could fully focus upon it. Almost.

It was enough to allow her to glimpse a human hand lying motionless upon the ice, a fall of hair, and a face staring open-eyed in death as blood darkened the ice beneath the gaping mouth.

"Eneela?"

The floe was gone. Stunned, Demmi waited in horror for other familiar corpses to float by her on the ice. When none did, she tried to convince herself that she had imagined the first one.

Now, as she focused upon the ice-thick waves, she realized the water level had gone up substantially since she and Manaravak had crawled onto the gravel bar only moments before. The river was rising! And the thaw had only just begun.

"We cannot stay here!" She tried in vain to rouse her delirious brother and pull him to his feet. The effort exhausted her. She dropped to her knees again. Manaravak's strength had been destroyed by weakness and fever. He could not get up. His life was in her hands. And although she was alone with him at last, she could not rejoice, for they were isolated from their people on the wrong side of the river, on a spit of land that was even now disappearing underwater.

◆————————◆

2

◆————————◆

As Umak had predicted, the river overflowed its banks with a vengeance, drowning or driving all living things before it. There was no time to mourn for Eneela nor to wonder what may have happened to Manaravak and Demmi.

It was a silent, desolate band of travelers that walked away from the raging river toward the high hills that flanked the eastern ranges. They carried only bare essentials and dragged no sledges at all. When a family of hares bounded ahead of them, Naya assured everyone that the animals would lead them to Manaravak. Her reward for speaking out was a sharp clout to the side of the head from Iana. Grek ignored her protest. And when Naya sought to walk with Umak, he sent her shrinking back with a warning to stay out of his way.

Lonit found no reason to pity the girl. Although Naya swore that she had no idea why Umak was angry with her or why Manaravak had run off into the storm with Demmi in pursuit, Grek had shamefacedly revealed enough of his granddaughter's inexcusable behavior to cause Lonit great distress. She had trusted the girl, and Naya had brought trouble down onto her own head again—a trouble that would be dealt with later in an official council . . . if the river allowed a later to any of them.

On and on they walked, with the river at their backs. When the little ones began to lag behind, Torka commanded their elders to carry them; when the footsteps of their elders faltered, Lonit commanded them to focus their hopes upon Torka—he would not fail to lead them all safely to high ground. And yet, for the first time in her life, doubt lay beneath her words.

Two of her children were missing. Nantu was dead. Larani was scarred for life. There was little hope of Eneela's being found alive. The Valley of the Great River was driving the People away as viciously as Daughter of the Sky had done. If the great mammoth totem, Life Giver, still walked ahead of them, there was no sign of it. Perhaps Torka had lost his luck after all.

Demmi would never be certain how she was able to find the strength to bring Manaravak out of the river. It was already pouring across the gravel spit when she got him up and dragged him onto solid ground.

"Leave me," Manaravak whispered. "Save yourself."

"You *are* myself! Get up. Help me. I cannot do this alone!"

"You will have to."

"Never! Since we were children, have I not always cared for you? Since we were children, it was always Demmi and Manaravak together."

They clung to each other as they sloshed forward, always moving away from the river and toward the hills. But the river was following them, spreading across the land like a vast and terrible roaring shadow. Chunks of ice slammed up against their legs, knocked them off balance, and sent them sprawling into cold, turbulent currents that were increasingly difficult to overcome.

From the sky and from the hills, water was running madly, racing through old, familiar stream channels, cutting new courses onto the outwash plains and across the vast alluvial fans that girded the loins of the great mountains. Out of every canyon and glacier and snowfield that stood at the perimeters of the great valley—as well as from every drop of water that fell from the sky and from the substance of every piece of ice, large and small, that was breaking apart upon its surface—the river was calling upon its kindred spirits cloud, rain, ice, and water to join it in its mad run across the drowning land.

Overwhelmed by the magnitude of the catastrophe that was engulfing her, Demmi tightened her grip on Manaravak. When he fell, she fell with him and felt his weakness as he sagged against her with a moan of surrender.

"Don't give up on me now!" she screamed at him. She slapped his shoulder and pulled him up, nearly expending the last of her strength in the effort. "We're almost to high ground," she lied. "Come on. I need you as much as you need me!"

He looked at her sideways, nodded, and for her sake, he fought his way to his feet.

Together they stumbled on. The water was up to their knees and rising fast. Terrified, Demmi locked her arms ferociously around her brother. A block of ice struck her hard from behind. The land beneath her feet disappeared. There was no bottom now. Demmi and Manaravak were being swept away.

"Hold on to me!" she implored, and then cried out in anguish because before she could stop him, Manaravak deliberately twisted sharply in her grasp and shoved her away.

"Swim, Demmi! *Live!* For Dak and Kharn, you *must* live! Without me to hold you back, you have a chance!"

"No!" she screamed as she saw him go under. The water closed over him and refused to yield him up again even though she reached for him and dove under the black, raging surface. She could not see him; she could not see anything.

Her senses were battered by the force of the current, the bruising, buffeting, mind-stunning contact with floating ice, and the horrendous roaring of the river itself. Underwater the sound was alive, invasive. It entered her body to beat and to hammer within her eyes and ears and chest until she felt certain that it was going to explode outward through her skull and skin and tear her to shreds. She felt herself succumbing, yielding, relaxing in the current as it carried her away and away to . . . to . . .

Suddenly her forward motion was sharply arrested by something massive and solid and immovable. The force of the river began to pull Demmi past it. With all that was left of her strength, she grabbed for it and found her fingers clinging to some grassy shrubbery that held her fast against the icy torrent. She closed her eyes and longed for her lost brother. *May he be alive, swept onto dry land!* She was too weak to give voice to her hope. It was all she could do to keep herself from being carried off by the river. With half her body awash in the floodwaters and weakness overcoming her, she climbed higher, entwining her fingers more tightly into the long, hairlike strands of shrubbery, twisting it around her arms so that if she should drift into unconsciousness, the river would not be able to pull her away to certain death.

Moments passed. Incredibly, she slept. . . .

She awoke with a start. She was moving again, being carried off by the river . . . ? No. The river was flowing around her, past her. And yet she was moving forward, at a slower, heavier pace. Her body was lifted up, out, and down, up, out, and down, again and again until slowly it dawned on her that the object to which she clung was carrying her.

In the rain and darkness it took her a moment to realize that the object to which she clung was the massive, towering forelimb of a living beast. And when she looked to the side as she was lifted forward, she could see others of its kind plodding steadfastly through the rising waters.

"Mammoth!"

The river had sent her colliding into the leg of a mammoth! Startled and suddenly too numb to hold on, she fell. When she hit the water, she was on her back, staring up at the greatest tusker of them all—Life Giver. *Totem*.

With what seemed a huff of annoyance, the mammoth extended its trunk, and as Demmi screamed in horror it hefted her from the river, lifted her high above its massive tusks and the twin domes of a head that towered twenty-two feet above the river bottom, and swung her back to deposit her with an unceremonious, sodden plop upon its sloping shoulders.

I am dead and in the spirit world, for only there can such things happen! she thought. Demmi grabbed handfuls of the mammoth's hair for leverage as she clambered high upon the back of the beast. Slumping into a seated position at the base of its neck, she wrapped its hair around her thighs lest she slip again or be knocked into the river by the mammoth's jolting, swaying gait.

Exhaustion struck at her. Again she told herself that this could not be happening, for she saw Life Giver's trunk reach out and pluck a limp figure from the water.

"Manaravak?" She was weeping when the mammoth placed her brother's naked, semiconscious body across its neck in front of her.

"Demmi . . ." he whispered her name. "Am I dreaming, Demmi?"

"You are dead," she told him. "We are both dead. For not even in dreams can such things happen!"

———◆———◆———

3

———◆———◆———

When the flood abated, Torka and his fellow hunters searched a devasted land for signs of Demmi and Manaravak and for Eneela's body. Their efforts were in vain.

Although they found the corpses of many an animal, bloating and beginning to rot in the sun, they found no sign of the ones who were lost.

"They say it is your fault."

Bereft and red-eyed from hours of crying, Naya looked up as Yona came toward her. She sat alone at the edge of a desolate temporary camp. Beyond the miserable lean-tos, the men were gathered within a sagging tent, where they had been talking since dusk.

"The men and older boys are angry at you, Naya! Even Grek. Simu says that the forces of Creation have turned against the People because of all the bad things you have done!"

Naya held her aching head. They were right, of course. It was all her fault. They said that she had lain with Manaravak. They said that she had shamed Umak. How could she have behaved as they said and not remember it?

"Are you listening to me, Naya?"

"I do not want to listen." She felt sick with remorse as she drew a berry from the few that remained within her pouch and, not caring whether Yona observed her or not, stuck it into her mouth.

"Iana will be angry if she knows that you are eating those berries," said Yona.

"She is already angry," reminded Naya. "No one but you will speak with me."

"You are in big trouble, Naya." Yona's expression of smug vindictiveness was puzzling and hurtful.

"You are not being very nice, Yona. Why are you so pleased by our people's anger toward me?"

"You killed my dolls!"

Naya sighed. "No one can kill a doll. Besides, I made you another and—"

"You killed my dolls! I saw the blood! I hope they listen to Simu and put you out of the band."

Naya suddenly felt cold with dread. To be put out of the band was a certain sentence of death. "They would not do that. It is a punishment of the old ways, of the ancients. Torka would never—"

"Torka is very sad and is listening more than talking. Simu says that the time has come to remember the old ways." The little girl's face was radiant. "When they send you away to walk the wind forever, Grek will love me best! When they send you away, I will not have to watch over my dolls, because nobody in this band wants to kill them but you."

"I will hear no more of death."

The grim finality in Torka's voice told all who heard it that no challenge would be welcome . . . or wise.

Only Simu dared to look at the headman eye to eye. "I do not accept your decision! The girl has brought these calamities upon us. My son Nantu is dead! My daughter Larani is scarred for life! My Eneela has been lost to the river. The dog pack has been reduced to two animals and a litter of pups. We have been driven from one hunting camp to another by fire and rain and river and ice!"

Grek's eyes blazed. "Daughter of the Sky is no stranger to the People under the Moon When the Grass Goes Yellow! You cannot blame my Naya for that! And your Nantu, he disobeyed you and walked off alone to feed himself to Three Paws. You cannot blame Little Girl for that! And when we crossed the ice, if Eneela had kept up, she would still be with us! My Naya did not force her to fall behind. And Demmi, woman of your son Dak, she has been as much trouble to this people as my Naya! Why not blame her for the burning of Larani and the death of Nantu and—"

"Demmi may well have already answered to the spirits for her ways," Umak said. His voice held an odd, twisted edge.

Simu met the shaman's gaze. "Well, our shaman speaks at last!" he snapped. "Are you forgetting the shame that Naya has heaped on you—with your own brother? Are you over-looking the fact that her actions drove Manaravak and Demmi out of camp and into the storm? If anyone has a right to speak against Naya, it is you!"

"Yes. All that you have just said is true, Simu. But emotion is the enemy of wisdom. That is a truth that would serve you well if you would take the time to learn it."

The shaman's reference to Simu's behavior embarrassed the hunter. "Bah! A man without feelings is no man at all. Are you going to sit here and allow this issue to remain unresolved?"

"It *has* been resolved," Umak replied coolly. "The head-man has resolved it. Only you have contested his decision."

"But there has been no punishment!" Simu shouted in frustration.

"Enough!" Torka's open palms came down hard onto his thighs. "I have said that there has been enough talk of death. I have *not* failed to come to a decision."

All eyes were upon the headman.

"The granddaughter of Grek has been trouble to us all," he conceded. "Nevertheless she is young and may yet learn new and better ways. She was given to Umak once. Now she *will* go to his fire circle. He is Shaman. He will deal with her as he will. This is his right."

Umak's face went blank with shock. "I . . . do not . . . want her anymore."

Torka shook his head. "Then would you have her abide by Simu's will and walk the wind forever?"

"I . . ." Umak looked as if he was going to be sick.

"She cannot go back to the fire circle of Grek," Torka told him. "Old Lion has shown that he cannot control her."

Grek hung his head.

"That leaves only Dak," Torka continued. "Would you take Naya to your fire?"

Dak winced. "I have a woman!"

"Too much talk leads nowhere and accomplishes nothing. I am headman. The talk must end with me. I say that Umak, as Shaman, is the best man for Naya. Umak, you *will* take the granddaughter of Grek to your fire circle—if not for your own pleasure, then to ease the burden of Honee."

"And if Manaravak returns?" Simu's voice was congested with anger.

"She will be Umak's woman," Torka repeated. "There will be no contention."

"Where Naya walks, contention follows like a shadow!" Simu was livid. "What if she flaunts the ways of our ancestors again and causes the luck of the band to turn bad again?"

The question hung black and foul in the air like the smoke of a burning brand that has been dipped in rancid fat. Torka drew it in and then solemnly exhaled his reply: "Then, for the good of the band, I will be forced to command her death. Does that satisfy you, Simu? Does that satisfy *all* of you?"

"No." The shaman's eyes were black and desolate with terrible resolve as he spoke to his father and fellow hunters in a low, weary tone. "If I must be Naya's man, then I will claim my rights and my responsibilities as her man. If she offends the forces of Creation and puts the band at risk again, it will be my obligation to kill her."

4

Demmi awoke and looked toward the sun. Life Giver had plucked Manaravak and her from its back with its trunk and deposited them on the lip of a wide, deep, sun-warmed cave as though they were no larger or heavier than the tiny, sparrowlike longspur that sought shelter upon Demmi's shoulder. It all seemed like a dream to her: Manaravak at her side . . . the sun on her face . . . the deep, shadowed interior of the cave at her back . . . the mammoth moving slowly away below, and the little bird nesting at the base of her neck . . . all were strange, mystical elements in a wondrous tale. Her body was bruised, and her feet were battered; nevertheless, she felt so good, so full of life. When the longspur opened its wings and flew off toward the northeast, she smiled and knew that it would be seeking its own kind.

Standing with his weight on one leg, Manaravak was stoop shouldered and drooping with fatigue beside her as he looked out of the cave. "They will all be dead on the other side of the river. We will never see the People again. I can smell their death. Yes, I can smell their decay."

He slumped onto the stony floor of the cave and, moaning softly, shook his head as though to clear it. Concerned, she knelt beside him. For the first time since awakening, Demmi looked closely at her brother. The mammoth had saved him from the river, but he was still terribly ill. She touched his shoulder. His skin was afire with fever.

"Stay here and rest," she commanded. "I will bring you water and try to find something to keep you warm."

"Do not worry about me."

Shaking her head with loving admonition, she slipped her hunting tunic over her head and placed it firmly around his shoulders. "How could I not worry about you, Manaravak, when I have always done so?"

"You should not have followed me."

"You should not have run off into the storm!"

"Dak should have beaten you more!"

Dak! What did she care about Dak now? Demmi was glad to be free of the unwanted responsibilities he represented. She was glad to be alone with Manaravak. But now she must make him well! She rose. Naked to the waist, she shivered in a draft from the depths of the cave. It was cold, turgid, moist. For the first time, she heard the sound of water dripping and pooling within the cave. Since there was water inside, she need not trouble herself with how she was going to transport it to the cave for her brother to drink. Catching the stench of rotting meat, she wrinkled her nose. Was it a creature that had denned within the cliff and died there, or was it meat dragged into the cave by a living animal that was feeding off it even now or likely to return to feed upon it soon? Lions did this, and so did bears.

Demmi swallowed hard. In the state that she and Manaravak were in, they would not have a chance against a predator's attack.

"We cannot stay here!" she said to him.

But even as she spoke she realized that he could not hear her. He had slumped to the cave's floor and was delirious. She actually hefted him and made a few faltering, back-wrenching steps until she realized the futility of her effort—the mammoth had lifted them high into the cliff face, and in order to descend, she would have to climb down a hefty portion of mountain wall. With Manaravak, it would be impossible. She lowered him onto his back, then knelt beside him, touched his face, kissed his brow and mouth, and touched the scars with which the great bear Three Paws had marked him. Then she kissed him on the mouth again, a woman's kiss. Dak would not have approved. But Dak was not here to see her as she drew back from her brother and wished him strength and life if she failed in what she was about to do.

Slowly, with her heart pounding and her mouth dry, Demmi rose and walked into the interior of the cave with her skinning dagger in her hand.

Still seated at the edge of camp where she had been dozing alone, Naya stared up at Umak as he came toward her with his back to the morning light. His face was set. His eyes troubled Naya as he stopped in front of her. They were dark and fixed and hostile. They were not the warm brown eyes that she knew so well.

"Get your things and come with me."

"No!" Naya shouted in dismay and disbelief. "Umak, tell me that you're not going to send me away!"

"Collect your things and come with me, Naya. Do not make me say it again."

Naya was too frightened to move. From where she sat, she could see faces peering toward her from the various family lean-tos. The hunters had emerged from the council tent at last. They were standing still, all staring toward her. Grek turned his eyes away when hers made contact with his.

"Come, I say!"

She winced. Umak's command had been as sharply placed as an angrily hurled spear. She grew cold with fear. The man who stood before her was not her Umak. He was Shaman. He was aloof and openly threatening.

Naya's heart froze as she remembered the way he had danced before the forces of Creation on behalf of his wounded brother—painted, feathered, his powerful naked body displayed for all to see, his male part as big and bold and potentially dangerous as the rest of him.

"No!" she cried, cowering. "I will not go anywhere with you!" Tears burned and welled within her eyes. She gritted her teeth to keep from screaming.

He reached down, grabbed her by her hair, and jerked her to her feet with such force that she nearly dropped her sewing bag.

"Do not say no to me again," he warned as, without another word, he began to drag her across camp toward his lean-to.

Umak was all at once ferociously angry and sad and ecstatically happy. Naya was his and would do as he said or die. His power over her pleased him as much as it aroused him. He had never wanted her more—and yet, perversely, he did not want her at all.

He dragged her across the encampment toward his lean-to. He felt no pity. When she tripped, he kept on dragging her until she managed to get to her feet. He shoved her into his lean-to, past a gaping Honee. Li and young Jhon jumped aside as she went stumbling forward onto his neatly piled bed furs.

Stunned, she scrambled into a seated position, clutched her sewing bag, pulled her knees up to her chin, and wrapped her arms around her lower legs, shivering.

Umak stood glaring at her. Anger could make a man hard with need. He was both.

Honee ordered the children outside. "Your father will be alone with his new woman for a while."

The woman's words fell upon Naya like an avalanche. She burst into tears. She sobbed for her grandfather and made to rise, but Umak pushed her down.

"Grek will not come," he told her coldly. "This is your fire circle from now on. The council has commanded it. The sooner you get used to the idea, the better off we will all be. You have shamed me, Naya. You have shamed yourself and your people. The least you can do now is accept the will of the headman and of the forces of Creation. You are my woman. If you value your life, you will remember that and be obedient to everything that I say."

Naya's head dropped onto her knees. Her entire body convulsed with sobs.

Honee swept Jhon and Li from the lean-to, then paused a moment and looked at her man out of a face that was contorted by concern. "She *is* just a girl, Umak. Be kind to her."

The softly spoken plea roused irritation instead of compassion. "If I were not kind, Simu would have had his way in the council. He was right about her: She *is* trouble."

Honee stood very still. Her face was grave as, without another word, she took up her warm robe and said that she would return when he called for her.

"You need not leave."

She appraised him and the sobbing girl with knowing eyes. "I would rather not stay."

He watched her go. He knew Honee well enough to be certain that she would take the children to the lean-to of Grek and offer comfort and assurance of Naya's welfare to the old man.

Naya's sobbing drew his attention back to the small, vulnerable young woman. He did not understand her fear of him; he would not tolerate it.

"You did not weep when you spread yourself for Manaravak. You did not sob when you worked yourself for him and begged him to fill you . . . again."

She looked up. Her face was colorless, haggard. "I don't remember."

"No?" Umak was untouched by her piteous tone. Her guileless expression enraged him. A woman could not behave as she had behaved with Manaravak and not remember. "Well," he said, and reached down to pull her to her feet. "You will remember this!"

Even as he reached to kiss her she cried out that she was going to be ill. She was violently sick. After sobbing and vomiting, she then collapsed into a pathetic heap at his feet and wept and said that she was sorry.

He did not know when the anger bled out of him. He only knew that he was on his knees, holding her, rocking her in his arms as though she were a small child. "Don't, Naya. I did not mean to make you cry."

She sobbed until exhaustion took her, and she sagged against him. He rose, brought moist skins to wipe her face, then picked her up and carried her to a clean pile of bed furs. He felt her watching him as he returned to gather up her mess, and after wrapping up his ruined sleeping skins, he tossed it all out of the lean-to. When he returned to her, she was sitting slumped and weary, red-eyed and shame-faced. He knelt before her and asked her if she still felt sick.

"My berries . . ." she whispered. "In my sewing bag over there. They will make me better."

He brought the bag to her and saw her frown with great concern as, with shaking, eager hands, she brought out several wrinkled orbs the color of dried blood.

"They are almost gone," she told him, sighing regretfully, allowing all but one of the berries to slide back into her pouch. "I must not waste them. I must make them last." She ate the dehydrated fruit.

He watched as her face relaxed. Color returned to her lips and cheeks. All of his old feelings for her were back as she smiled wanly at him.

"Good medicine," she said, closing her eyes. And then suddenly she flung her arms around his neck and clung to him. "Oh, Umak, why is everyone so angry with me?"

He was devastated by the depths of his love. He stroked her arms and her back, found his fingers straying absently along a single length of thong that lay about her neck. "You must learn to think before you act, lest others continue to carry the weight of your mistakes and thoughtlessness."

She trembled a little as she buried her face more deeply into his shoulder. "Sometimes I do things but do not know why or remember afterward what I have done. This is not a good thing."

"No. It is not a good thing." He held her, kissed the top of her head, and continued to stroke her neck, absently slipping her thong necklet between his thumb and index finger. "You must remember that you are a woman now. I will help you to be more careful. You will not regret that you have become my woman."

"I do not want to spread myself for your man bone. It is very big." There was no mistaking the repugnance and trepidation in her voice.

"You spread yourself for Manaravak."

She drew in a troubled breath, then: "I do not remember. He must have *made* me! And afterward I hurt inside and bled. His man bone was very big, too! It was not a good thing for me." She stiffened in his arms a little, then deliberately changed the subject. "When the time of endless light comes, will my Umak help me to find more of my good medicine berries?"

"If this will please you."

"It will please me very much. But we must not tell Iana."

"You are my woman now. You need not worry about Iana."

Again she sighed, happily, sleepily. "Good." She yawned. "I do not like Iana."

The warmth of her breath against his throat was as sweet and welcome as a summer wind. He closed his eyes and held her close. She made no attempt to move away. She was his now, safe and content in his arms. Whatever would be between them as man and woman would come as it would, when it would. He would not force it as Manaravak had done. He would lead her gently, guide her tenderly, open her to his need so gradually that her body would soon fit his like a fine and yielding glove.

His brow came down. So Manaravak had taken her against her will! When he had burst in upon them out of the storm, jealousy must have caused him to imagine the worst, and so that was what he had seen and heard. Naya had not been a willing mate to his brother. She had no wish to lie with him ever again. Manaravak had forced her, hurt her. No wonder he had run away!

Umak smiled a sad and bitter smile. Poor Manaravak. Always the wanawut howled at the back of his spirit, loosing an animal nature that was never quite able to conform to the ways and restrictions of his fellowmen. Perhaps if the forces of Creation would bring him safely home again, he might yet learn; in any event, Umak would forgive him. After all, they were brothers, twins, and Naya was his now. Nothing that Manaravak could do—in this world or the next—could ever change that.

Demmi did not look back. She walked steadily on into ever-diminishing light toward the appalling stench of putrifying meat. The cave was deep and wide and filled with cold drafts that gusted like errant ghosts through unseen breaks in the mountain wall. Demmi shivered, not liking the cave—she thought, to calm herself, that bears preferred a tighter den, and lions sought drier, sunnier aeries in which to shelter.

She paused, in deep shadow now. She drew in a breath, and a few more steps brought her through the thickening dark to find what she was looking for. The dead animal that lay at the back of this cave had not normally denned within it; there was no evidence of meat being dragged in, no fecal matter, and only a few stones were disturbed here and there as the great bear had found its way into the cave to die.

Demmi laid her hand across her mouth and nose to filter the stink of rotting flesh. The carcass was big and female. Its hide was bison brown. Its claws were the size of small horns, and the paws from which they had grown were as wide as the heads of two men standing close together. She knelt and wondered what had caused its death until she saw the terrible gaping gashes that slit its belly. What could have made them? Lions? A pack of wolves? A giant sloth? Or wanawut? She shook the thought away. It did not matter what had killed the bear and the half-formed cubs that now lay shriveled in its exposed womb.

Demmi's gorge rose. She downed it, but barely. She hung her head and fought off a wave of light-headedness. Clenching her teeth, Demmi wondered if she was pregnant. She had missed her last time of blood, and the two previous times had been scant and spotty; but in stressful and hungry times, it was not unusual for women not to bleed at all.

She had hated being pregnant. She had hated being sick and slow moving and unable to hunt with the men. But there was no time to worry about this now. Manaravak needed her. And there was much work to do if the hide and flesh and marrow of the dead bear were to provide warmth and food for her brother and her.

5

It was said by the ancients that time heals all wounds. Even wounds that proved fatal brought a respite from pain through death. Yet as Torka led his people out of the devastated Valley of the Great Mad River in search of better hunting grounds, he knew that the ancients were wrong. There were wounds that would not heal, wounds that kept on hurting, that killed the spirit yet left the flesh alive to ache and bleed for want of precious things that were lost and could never be found again. The entire band seemed to feel the weight of sorrow. Even the children and dogs were subdued.

The need to find fresh meat beyond the flood-ravaged valley pushed the band on. The hunters had searched for Demmi and Manaravak, but aside from Companion's discovery of Demmi's moccasin, which convinced everyone that the woman was dead, no sign was found of the siblings. Nor had they found Eneela's body.

Dak, having lost his woman, his mother, and his younger brother, could not eat and was in deep despair. "The river has taken Demmi and Manaravak," he had told Umak. "My woman has won her way at last. She will be with her brother forever. We will never see them again . . . in this world or in the world beyond."

When the People reached the wide, rolling hill country at the northern edge of the valley, they paused to put the Great Mad River behind them. But first they enacted a solemn ritual of farewell to those who could not follow them.

It was late in the day. The sun was low. The wind was

sweet from the west as they walked somberly to the river's edge and consigned Demmi's moccasin and Manaravak's bear-skin of Three Paws to the river in which their life spirits would now dwell forever. As the skin and the moccasin washed away on the current, the band released all hope that those who were lost would ever be found alive.

At that moment Dak's broken cries of anguish rent the assembly, and Umak, Torka, Simu, and Grek ran forward to prevent him from plunging a dagger into his own breast.

"No!" Larani screamed as she raced to her brother's side.

But to everyone's amazement, Swan was swiftest of all. Leaving Kharn behind, she was at Dak's side in an instant, gripping his arm. She hung on, pulling his hand down as hard as she could, grimacing with her effort as she raged at him through gritted teeth. "Selfish! Thoughtless! What a terrible man you are! Let go of that knife! Can't you see that Kharn is watching? He has lost his mother and grandmother! Must he lose his father, too?"

Her words cut as sharply as any blade, but it was the violent kick that she managed to bring against his shin that caused him to lower his arm and stare down at her in a daze. When she slapped him so hard that his head snapped to one side, the sound of her blow stung the very air.

No one moved. Larani saw Torka's eyes narrow and heard Honee gasp in amazement just as her own mouth fell open. Never had she imagined that gentle, mild-tempered Swan could display such fury.

"You ungrateful, miserable excuse for a man!" Swan's eyes flashed as she shouted at Dak. Tears rolled down her cheeks, but she made no attempt to wipe them away. "Coward! Weakling! How unworthy of Demmi, for whom you say you mourn! Her spirit must be withering with shame to see you like this . . . as does mine!"

Dak blinked, incredulous.

"Look at me!" she demanded. "I weep like the woman I am, for my lost sister, for my brother, and for your mother, too. But most of all I weep for you, for the shame that you would bring upon us all!"

Dak stared down at Swan as though at a stranger.

She glared up at him, fiery eyed, tear streaked, red cheeked, and sneering with contempt. "Why do I waste my words on you? Go ahead! End your life if you cannot find the courage to face your loss and your grief like a man!"

She turned on her heels and stalked off to seat herself on her traveling pack, staring off across the river until Kharn came walking up to pull at her sleeve. Without hesitation, Swan pulled him onto her lap and cuddled him as she said loudly, "What a big, brave boy you are, Kharn—as brave as your *mother*!"

Dak's head went high, and his jaw clenched. His knife arm rose slowly, and when Larani, Torka, and Umak moved to stop him, he warned them back with a growl.

"What I do now I do for Demmi, so that from this day forth all may see the mark that she has made upon my life . . . and so that never again will anyone—especially a woman— have cause to name me Coward!"

Larani saw Swan stare at him out of widening eyes, then quickly turned Kharn's face away as Larani cried out in dismay. "Don't, Brother! Please!"

With infinite slowness and without a sound, Dak stoically drew his dagger across each temple, downward over each arm, and then across his chest. The leather of his sleeves and shirt opened, and blood welled to stain his garments.

In silence the people of the band watched as Dak raised the bloodied knife and hurled it into the river.

In silence they passed the night, and in silence they awoke at dawn, took up their packs, and walked on without looking back.

Late in the day the People rested. Teratorns were seen circling once again to the south. Lonit stared wanly off and urged Torka to lead the band in that direction in the hope of discovering the final resting place of the bones of their loved ones.

"If they lie dead under the shadows of the great carrion-eating birds, at least we may set their bones to look upon the sky forever."

Torka's brow came down. "We have consigned their spirits to the river. Your hope must lie in the future now. You must look ahead, not back. Our luck has always lain to the east. If we are to find it again, it will lie in the track of the great mammoth, Life Giver."

Disconsolate, Lonit sighed, but she gave no argument.

Faraway across the river, Manaravak dreamed of a galloping horse racing across the face of the sun with Daughter of the Sky, crying out his name as she rode burning upon its back.

"Manaravak!" Demmi pushed his shoulder to rouse him from his dreams. He came up out of them blinking, half expecting to see Larani, who reminded him of the blazing horse and of fire.

"Listen!" Demmi's voice was imperative.

He propped himself onto an elbow, disappointed to see that it was only his sister hunkering beside him on the lip of the cave. How long had she been there, holding the two crudely made staves that she had fashioned of bear bone, watching, waiting, ready to protect him with her life? Days. Nights. He had lost track of time, but he felt stronger now than he had in days and was hungry for the first time.

"Do you hear them?" she asked.

He heard. "Wanawut!" he said, smiling.

"Don't look so happy!" She looked at Manaravak's face. The wounds there and on his arms were festering despite her best efforts to keep them clean and slathered with healing fat taken from the body of the bear. Her hand strayed across his face, his throat, his shoulders and chest. "Even though you will be scarred, you are still the best of all men for me to be with and to look upon."

"Let me rest, Demmi."

"Are you still sorry that we are together?"

"Yes . . ." He was drifting back into his dreams. "Better if you had not followed."

Demmi set aside her spears and crawled beneath the sheltering warmth of the bearskin to cuddle beside Manaravak.

Her hand moved across his belly, and then downward until, after only a moment's hesitation, at last she did what she had longed to do for all too many moons. She touched his loins, stroked and fingered until his penis stirred and swelled beneath the gentle pressure of her palm and the slow, purposeful curling of her fingers. "Your body does not echo the words of your mouth, Manaravak."

Not without effort, he turned away from her. "Let me sleep, Sister!" he growled, his voice full of pain and irritation. "It is forbidden between us!"

Her hands were moving along his back. "Only because we are of Torka's band. In the far land of our ancestors, among Simu's people, it would not have been forbidden."

"Leave this man alone! I do not want you!"

She lay still for a long while, trembling with her desire as he relaxed into sleep beside her. She did not move, allowing him his dreams, until, at dawn, she heard the sound of rain. She stayed beside him—warm and full of a woman's need for a man.

He was on his back now. His skin was hot and dry with fever. From the occasional low exhalations that escaped his lips, she knew that he was in pain. Once again she sought to ease him with gentle strokings and whisperings of affection. Her hands strayed to his loins. He was asleep, but he was not dead—he was as hard as she was moist and ready for him.

Slowly, with her heart pounding, she moved to kneel over him, to handle him until he was erect and throbbing. Only then did she position him and gasp with rapture even before she lowered herself. How big he was! How perfectly he fit her as she moved to take him deep. Her body was aflame. Had it ever been like this with Dak? *No!* She had never yearned for the son of Simu as she yearned for Manaravak . . . never lusted for him . . . never burned for him as she was burning now. Breathless, she leaned down, balancing above him upon splayed hands, and worked herself to completion as she sobbed his name.

Eyes closed, he reached for her hips, arched up, and with a low, husky exhalation of release, came into her and held her fast as he shivered with pleasure and probed upward with his organ for more.

"Manaravak!" she cried. "At last! I knew it would be like this for us!"

With a growl, he opened his eyes, stared up at her resentfully, and then pulled out of her to cast her roughly aside. "Between us this is forbidden!" He shouted at her, with revulsion burning in his eyes. "Never again, Demmi. Go away. You shame us both!"

She did not go away. She knelt beside him. She told him that she loved him and that their people were far away and need never know what transpired between them.

He pulled the bearskin over his head and refused to speak to her for the rest of the day. When night came down, he made her sleep alone.

And so another night passed for them, and then another day. The wounds on his face and arms festered.

"The spirits are angry that a brother and sister have been man and woman together," he said.

"Then let them take out their anger upon *me*, for you were not a willing party to our mating."

One black brow arched. "I do not sleep as deeply as all that, Demmi."

Their eyes met and held.

"It is growing dark again," he said. "Can the spirits see into caves to know what this man and his sister have done together?"

"I cannot speak for the spirits, Manaravak, but I do not fear them when I am with you. Here, let me soothe your wounds again with fat from the bear."

But it was not the fat of the bear that soothed him; it was the touch of his sister as he lay back and allowed her to love him as she had loved him before. Weak and hurting as he was, Manaravak saw no reason to resist. They were far from the People now—far from watching eyes that might betray the breaking of the ancient prohibition that had kept them from coupling until now.

———◆———

6

———◆———

Far to the northeast, Torka and his band continued traveling into the face of the rising sun. The trek was long, but they had known longer. The hunting was poor, but they had known worse. The weather was fitful and sometimes treacherous, but they had never known any other kind.

The tundral barrens seemed endless. On and on they walked, ever closer to the still-distant mountains. Umak, carrying his daughter on his shoulders, found his mind drifting, remembering, as he listened to the wind moving across the barrens . . . whispering . . . sighing . . . until suddenly he stopped dead. It was not the wind that was whispering around him; it was the voice of Eneela.

"Remember me, Shaman. Remember me, and I will live forever."

He gasped.

"Father! What is it, Father?" asked Li, leaning down and trying to see his face.

The wind sighed around him. He could not move. At his right, Honee did not question his reason for coming to a halt. She was always glad to rest, as was Naya, who trudged along at his left.

"Listen," he urged them now. "There are voices in the wind."

They listened but heard nothing and said so.

Their reply was ignored by the shaman. Eneela was with him, and she was not alone. He felt the cool breath of the wind on his face, but somehow he knew it was not the wind— it was the passage of spirits moving in the air around him.

"Do not grieve for those who are lost, Shaman. And tell my Simu not to mourn. I walk the wind with all those who have gone before. I am not alone. Karana and Mahnie are with me. Old Umak—for whom you are named—walks the wind at my side with the great dog Aar, and my Nantu is with me. Together we search for his lost head. You are Shaman, Umak. The People have need of your wisdom now more than ever before. Be strong. Listen to the Seeing Wind. Trust in your power. Remember me, and do not look back."

The wind dropped.

"Wait!" Umak cried to the ghost of Eneela, listening for other voices, for a sister, for a twin brother . . . but if the life spirits of Demmi and Manaravak walked the wind forever with Eneela, she had not named them, nor did they speak to him now. Perhaps they never would. His anger and possessiveness of Naya had driven them out of camp.

Umak's wisdom gave heart to his people. Ever watchful for signs of Life Giver, Torka led the band through the bog lands and around the tussock "forests," always seeking areas that might offer potential browse to mammoth. He found antelope instead.

The men hunted and killed. They made camp and rested from their long trek.

Still mourning the ones who were lost, they made no feast, but they thanked the life spirits of the animals that they had slain as they ate well for the first time in many days. They cracked the bones and scooped out the nourishing marrow until all of it was gone. They prepared the skins and sinew. They cut the meat that could not be consumed at one sitting into filets and laid the steaks across frames of bone to dry in the wind and feeble light of spring.

It was a good camp, close to a shallow stream, with

budding willows growing tall enough to break the wind. The women seared ptarmigan and set traps for ground squirrels and hares. All prepared to stuff themselves with this sweet, pink meat except Dak, whose brooding still robbed him of appetite.

Not far away, Larani knelt by her catch. After selecting two of the plumpest of the squirrels that she had trapped, she gutted them and stuffed fragrant gray sprigs of wormwood into their body cavities. Now, using lengths of freshly removed gut, she spitted and trussed the squirrels on long bone skewers, then walked toward the cooking fire that Summer Moon had raised outside Simu's pit hut.

"May I roast these animals at the fire of my father even though they will not be for him?"

Summer Moon cocked her pretty head. "The heat of this fire is yours as well as mine, Larani. We will chat while the squirrels roast."

Larani stared at the flames, wondering if she would ever be able to approach even the smallest fire without fear. As she extended her skewers and felt the strong, vibrant heat emanating from the well-tended coals, she doubted it. Nevertheless, she held the meat steady and low. "I have captured these rodents for my brother and for Kharn. The boy loves the way I cook squirrel, and Dak has never been able to resist fresh squirrel stuffed with wormwood leaves. I am so worried about him, Summer Moon."

"You are not the only one who worries about Dak, Larani," the older woman said just as Swan came to stand beside her, holding a bladder of marrow broth.

"Mother has made this for you, Summer Moon. She says that it will be good for you and for the baby."

Summer Moon accepted the bladder flask. "Larani is fixing one of Dak's favorite foods. Perhaps she might allow you to bring it to him?"

Larani looked up in time to see Swan blush bright pink. She understood at once. "Of course. Here. The meat is done just the way he likes it—charred almost black on the outside, soft and juicy inside with the meat still as pink as your cheeks!"

Swan's blush deepened, but when Larani handed up the meat, she did not hesitate to take it.

"Dak?"

He sat unmoving before his sloppily erected lean-to. He did not answer.

"Dak, may I speak with you?" Swan came closer, measuring her steps, fearful that he might suddenly rise and strike out at her for her earlier impertinence. He had yet to talk to her after the way she had admonished him the day they had left the valley of the Great Mad River.

He did not move. With Kharn sitting between his boots, playing in the mud—and covered from head to foot with it—Dak sat glaring at the ground.

Swan observed his disheveled appearance and the careless way that he had erected his shelter and scattered his belongings before it. She cleared her throat, took a few steps closer, and kept her face turned down with utmost deference as she stopped before him, just out of striking range. "You have hunted. You have brought meat into the camp, but you have barely eaten. Here. I have brought these from Larani."

"I am not hungry."

"Your sister worries about you, Dak."

"Go away, Swan. But you can leave the meat for Kharn."

She did not go away. "The boy needs more than meat," she suggested softly, handing the skewers down to him. "A clean face and hands would do no harm, and he is soaked. Look, the mud has soaked through his—"

Dak looked up at her. His face was set, and his eyes were black and hard. "Take him, then. No doubt that is what your mother and my sister have sent you here to do. Why did they not come themselves?"

"Because you have disdained their concern and sent them away several times. And no one 'sent' me, Dak. I have come because I care . . . about Kharn."

"Bah! You need not trouble yourself over my son. As you see, he is happy enough as long as his belly is full."

"You forget—Kharn's mother was my sister, and a child needs more than a full belly to be happy."

"Demmi would not have agreed."

Swan tilted her head to one side. His words had been so sharp, so contemptuous, but he averted his eyes when he spoke them, and now he glared down at the ground again with a muscle throbbing hard at his jawline. When he gestured her away, she remained motionless.

"I miss Demmi, too," she whispered after a moment, then knelt beside him. "And I miss Eneela. And I am sorry for the things that I said to you before. I would make them up to you. I—"

"Go away, Swan. Take the boy with you if it will make you happy, but leave me alone."

She was suddenly annoyed and impatient with him. "I will *not* go away! I will stay at your side until you are so sick of me that you will *have* to eat. I will not go away until you do!"

He looked at her again. "You *are* Demmi's sister, aren't you?"

"I am!" she affirmed proudly.

He shook his head. "Who would have thought that you would turn out to be such a nasty girl!"

"I am not nasty—you are! Sitting here glowering, refusing to eat, making everyone worry about you. Have we not all endured enough worry, enough pain? Your suffering will not bring Demmi back. And now that she is gone, how can you dishonor her memory by treating her son as though he is of no more concern to you than one of the dogs!"

"She cared no more about him than that," he reminded her with a resentful snarl.

She snarled back at him. "Well, *I* do. Come, Kharn." She reached for the boy and smiled radiantly at him as, still gnawing on the spitted squirrels, he came eagerly to her outstretched hands. "Good boy! Come to Swan. Look at this mess of a camp that your father has made for you. Here, my sister's big, brave boy. With you to help Swan, we will have it—and *you*—cleaned up in no time!"

In the shadows that lay before the lean-to of Simu, Larani looked wistfully across camp to where Swan had just scooped up Kharn.

"Dak is irked, but he does not send her away," she told Summer Moon. "Perhaps my brother will have a new woman soon."

Summer Moon thought for a moment. "Simu is planning to ask Torka to allow you to be Dak's new woman."

Larani was appalled. "Dak is my brother! It is forbidden by the headman!"

"Among Torka's people, not among yours."

"Torka's people *are* my people. I have never known any other!"

"Yes, but your father was from another band. And increasingly he finds that the customs of my father's people chafe against his own traditions, his own needs. He is so unhappy, Larani. Since your mother died, all he thinks of is the past—of Nantu, of Eneela, of how it might have been for you if—"

"I will not lie with my own brother to ease my father's grief!"

Summer Moon looked miserable. "I know, I know. I have been wanting to tell you the things he has been saying, but I have not known how! He means well for you, Larani. He only wants to—"

"I do not need you to speak for me!" Simu, who had gone off to relieve himself, now stomped forward and came to an angry halt before his fire pit. He fixed his woman and his daughter with measuring, censorial eyes, then turned his gaze completely upon Larani. "So you will not have your brother, eh?"

"I will not!"

"In the far country of your ancestors you would not have had a choice!"

"I am not in the far country of my ancestors. I am here—a woman of Torka's band!"

He exhaled a snorted deprecation. "You're no woman at all as far as I am concerned—not until you're mated, not until a man speaks for you and takes you from your father's hut."

Summer Moon paled. "Simu, please, don't!"

"Be still! She must hear the truth!"

Larani stood and faced him across the embers of the fire circle. "If you do not want to be responsible for me, I will—"

He snorted again; this time the sound held impatience, and a hint of repentance as well as censure. "Bah, girl, be silent. Your face is not what it used to be, and your upper back and burned arm are not a pretty sight, but you are strong. Your burned arm works as well as the one that is unburned, and in the shadows of my hut, I have seen that your breasts and backside and flanks are still as they once were. A man could take you to his fire and, in the dark at least, find pleasure in releasing into you, making new life in you—new sons to lighten his load when his years begin to tell upon him. I will talk to Dak before he and Swan become too—"

Aghast, Larani shook her head. "I will not go to Dak!" she shouted at him.

"A man is a man. You know that Dak would always hold a special affection for you. It could be a very good thing. I have been discussing the possibilities with Summer Moon. She is right when she says that I worry about you, Larani. I will talk to Torka about it soon. After all, it is the headman who insisted that you be allowed to live, so he is responsible for you. He *must* see to it that you find a man. Torka will have to break the traditions of his ancestors and allow you to live as a woman with your brother, or it will be his obligation to take you to his own fire!"

Larani went cold. "If you still feel the need to challenge the ways and the decisions of the headman, then do so. But you will not use me as your excuse! I am not fit to be the headman's woman. And I want no man's pity! Am I not of help to you now that Summer Moon is with child and Eneela is gone from this fire circle? Can my father no longer bear to look at me, even though I earn my meat as a useful drudge in his camp?"

"Even if you disagree with me, you must be an obedient daughter. Too much do you challenge me these days. You must do as I say."

Larani's heart bled. "What else can I do? I am only a female. But whatever you say to Torka, no man—not even a brother and most certainly not a headman—will have a woman with a face and body as scarred as mine. You are not the only one who looks away when I come near, my father. They all look away, all of them except—" She paused. She could not bring herself to speak his name.

Manaravak! He had never turned away. He was the one she could never have . . . unless she died and walked with him in the spirit world.

That night Naya's head ached, and not even two of her rapidly diminishing supply of red berries could fully ease her pain. Honee gave her a mash of fat and willow oil, which helped, but not enough. Umak came to offer comfort, but when he lay down behind her and gently drew her against him, she felt his heartbeat quicken against her back and his man bone move and swell and emanate heat against the curve of her bare buttocks until, frightened, she screamed and sent him away to Honee's bed furs. He was not happy with Naya for that, and Honee was not happy with him for making demands of "her" Naya.

"She is not 'your' Naya, woman, she is mine! And I made no demands on her at all!" Wanting no part of his women, he snatched up his robe and went to the far corner of the hut to sleep alone.

Naya lay still, glad that Umak was not beside her. Nevertheless, she remained troubled, wondering why she was suffering from so many headaches. They were a thin, bright, constant pain that sometimes became so intense that she was nearly blinded by it. The gradual withdrawal of the red berries from her diet seemed to coincide with their onset.

She puzzled over this. Was it possible that the same berries that took away pain when eaten could cause pain when *not* eaten? It did not seem logical to her. Two or three berries no longer eradicated her pain. She had to have five or six, and soon they would all be gone. She moaned with longing and experienced a twinge of regret as she remembered Iana's warning:

Wear them. But do not eat them. We must be wary of new foods.

Now, with her head so tight and hot with pain that she was close to vomiting, Naya had no patience with warnings or with memories, or with any thoughts at all. She rose. Desperate for relief, she sought out her medicine bag, fumbled deeply for the few remaining fruits, and shivering with need, chewed them greedily.

Long waves of light poured through her. In seconds the pain was gone. Back in her bed furs again, Naya fell fast asleep.

Her dreams were of tall, green bushes sagging from the weight of endless red berries growing round and fat in the light of the sun . . . and of a young girl dancing naked, running wild and careless amid the shrubs, plucking the berries and squeezing them between her fingers. She rubbed the juices over her body, staining her breasts and belly and thighs, and laughed as she ran wild across the golden plain, displaying her body for the two gray wolves who lay watching . . . waiting . . . hungry eyed and ravenous for . . .

She turned in her sleep. She felt warm, so warm. Deep within her loins was the need for filling . . . for the heat of a man. Although she slept alone, a faceless, formless man was with her. A warm wind rose, sweeping over her skin, caressing her breasts and licking between her thighs.

She touched herself, arched her hips, opened her limbs wide, and cried "Yes!" to the wind and invited it to enter her until, groggy and light-headed, she sat up to find Umak sitting beside her, stroking her brow.

"Are you all right?" he asked.

"All . . . right?"

"You have changed your mind?" His voice was deep, husky with desire as he joined her beneath her bed furs. "It will be good between us. You will see."

What was he saying? She held up the fur as a wall between them. She was still asleep, dreaming, hallucinating. Umak was not Umak; he was a stranger—not even a man but a black-haired, featureless buckskin doll that leaned forward to kiss her. And out of the face that had no eyes or ears or nose or lips, an aperture gaped wide and closed upon her mouth as he took her down.

His kiss was suffocating her, sucking the life out of her body. She was a limp, lifeless vessel through which the wind was filling her, killing her as it extruded through her. Suddenly the dreaded nightmare was back. The beasts were on her—wolves, wanawut, the terrible, faceless doll, the killing wind . . . and she was dying in a tide of blood and horror until—

"Naya! By all the forces of Creation, stop it!"

She blinked. The dream ebbed. Umak was kneeling beside her, holding her by her shoulders.

"Go away," she whispered. "I am so afraid. Please, Umak, go away and take my dream with you."

The look on his face was one of utter confusion—then dejection, then disgust. He snatched up his clothes and moccasins and left the hut.

Honee spoke from out of the shadows. "Naya, to invite a man and then to turn him away is not a good thing."

"I did not invite him!"

"But you did, my dear girl. You called his name and begged him to fill you. I heard you quite clearly."

"No!" sobbed Naya, and pulled her bed furs completely up over her head.

Toward dawn, the ululation of dire wolves woke the band. Only Umak had been awake for hours. Restless and frustrated, he had left his lean-to and had stalked the peripheries of the encampment with Companion.

"You have more luck with your woman that I do with mine!" he told the dog. "If only I knew what it is that frightens her so." He paused, aware that Torka was standing alone in the fading starlight, staring eastward, awaiting the rising of the sun.

Glad to be distracted from his thoughts of Naya, Umak joined him, and for a long while they stood together in silence. Companion yawned, seated himself, and sagged a little against the shaman's leg.

"What troubles you, my father?" Umak asked, idly fondling the top of the big dog's head and ears.

"Too many things these days, my son." Torka's voice was low, thoughtful, heavily weighted by worry.

"We have known bad times before. Things will be better soon."

"Do you speak as Shaman or as a son who longs to ease his father's heart?"

"As both," replied Umak, and wished that he were as certain of the last part of his statement as the first.

Torka continued to look eastward. The sun was rising beyond the serrated ice peaks of the eastern ranges, leaching away the night, turning the bottom edge of the sky into soft pinks and golds and throwing the mountains into starkly black, intimidating silhouette.

"This band is so small. . . ." Torka said the words as a lament. "This land is so big, and the mountains that lie ahead of us are so high and wide and white."

Even as his father spoke Umak saw that thousands of tiny dark V's had begun to swarm like blackflies above the mountains. Wonder and delight filled him as the V's suddenly began to sparkle. He realized that what he was seeing was the light of the as-yet-unrisen sun striking the breasts and wing tips of distant, migrating waterfowl.

"Look!" he exclaimed, pointing off. "The birds return to the tundra from out of the rising sun! And have you ever seen so many? Could we ask for a better omen, my father?"

Torka looked but was not heartened. "The birds, at least, seem to know where they are going. Each year at the same time they fly out of the east, and each year at the same time they fly back. Where do they go, Umak? And why, if not to a warmer land—the same land toward which the great herds turn at the ending of summer—a place where the time of the long dark never comes and where the Starving Moon never rises because there is always game! Think of it, Umak: a land in which our people would never know cold or hunger again! For a lifetime I have been seeking it, but no matter how far I walk, the time of the long dark always catches up with me, and my people are left in the cold and dark while the birds disappear and the herds follow them."

As Umak watched in dismay, Torka allowed his words to settle into an inner well of bitterness and frustration. After a moment, the headman shook his head and exhaled harshly through his teeth.

"With the return of the birds, it is certain that we will not go hungry in the days ahead. But will we have enough meat to get us through another winter? I worry. Your mother worries. There is dissension among my people, Umak. Somewhere along the way Simu has become my enemy. I feel him watching me these days, waiting for me to miscalculate again, to—"

"You? You are Torka! You are headman! Let Simu think what he will. He has been silenced in the council."

Torka drew in a deep, steadying breath. "*Because* I am headman, Umak, it hurts me to know that I have lost the confidence of one who once turned his back upon his own people and chose to walk at my side. Simu was once my friend. I know his heart. He blames me for Larani's burning, for Nantu's death, and for his and Dak's bereavement . . . as though I am not also bereaved! As though I do not mourn the loss of my own children! As though I do not stand here in the dawn—*every* dawn—asking the forces of Creation: Are they *truly* dead—and if it is so, is it because of me?"

Umak was taken aback. Never before had Torka shared so much of himself with him. The shaman was honored and deeply moved, but the son was disconcerted by the realization that for all of his father's strength and wisdom, Torka was nevertheless a man who had been ripped and savaged by grief.

"We must let them go, my father. Demmi and Manaravak . . . all of them . . . we must let them go. Unless we release their spirits, we will never regain our own. I have heard the voice of the Seeing Wind. The ghosts of the past have come to me from the world beyond this world. They have said that we must walk on, and we must not look back."

7

Many days had passed since Demmi had left the cave to hunt and had returned safely with fresh meat for herself and her brother. Now she awoke with a start and lay very still, staring up into the predawn darkness of the cave. The sounds that had awakened her were unmistakable: wanawut. One moment they were full of growling threats and anger; the next they were high-pitched, ear-stinging screams such as a woman might make if she were being disemboweled. Now they were settling into a long, ululating series of moans and hoots and terrible, cacophonous wailings. This was not the first time she had heard them since discovering their tracks, but the howl that had awakened her was from inside the cave.

Now, though, the sound was far away and growing very faint. Afraid, she stared off, listening, until the rising of the sun. The wanawut were silent at last, and Manaravak spoke. He was sitting cross-legged in the gloom at the far edge of the cave, with his half of the rough bearskin around his shoulders.

"They have hunted well."

"How long have you been awake?" she asked him.

"Long . . . listening and sounding to my brothers and sisters as they hunt at the far side of the world."

"You woke me with your sounding. Don't do it again. One of these nights your howling is going to draw them right into the cave, Manaravak. When they attack us and try to make a meal of us, you will see that they are *not* your brothers or your sisters!"

The light of dawn was beginning to flood into the cave in a thin, colorless tide. It shone upon the face of her brother, defining his scars, his strong, handsome features, and long, introspectively narrowed black eyes.

"They have brought down moose," he said. "Big and old but strong enough to bring pain to one of them as they killed it. Perhaps one of them is dead."

She shivered. "You think too much of the wanawut, my brother. You cannot possibly know what they are hunting!"

"I know. They have told me . . . as they have told me that they are lonely. There are so few of them left in all of this world. If they do not find more females soon, there will be none of them left at all."

A strange, skin-prickling coldness within Demmi's body intensified. Manaravak had changed since he had fled into the storm. Since they had come to the cave, nothing that she said or did had been able to stanch the flow of his brooding or drive the word *wanawut* from his mind.

She observed him from beneath a furrowed brow. "Torka has taught all his children to tell the difference between animals' sounds of stress or hunger or pain. But animals have not the gift of words, my brother. I cannot believe that they can tell you what they hunt or why they are lonely."

He looked at her with sad eyes. "Unlike men and women, Demmi, the wanawut have no need of words with which to confuse one another."

"You are *not* a wanawut!"

"No?" A bitter smile played at the corners of his mouth. "I have spoken the words of man, but you do not understand or believe me when I speak. The language of the wild and the ways of the wanawut are better. And until now, between Demmi and Manaravak there has never been a need for words."

The truth stung, and she replied defensively. "Until now Manaravak has tried to be a man, not a beast. You have been hurt by Three Paws and weakened by the Great Mad River. But you will be completely well soon, strong enough to—"

"No, Demmi." His face was set. "Can you still not understand, my sister? You have always come closest to knowing my heart. Can you not see into it now? The bear and the river have not weakened me; my people have done that. They say that I am a man—but everything I have ever done as a man has offended them and tormented my heart. My spirit is one with the wild and with the beast wanawut. Perhaps the time has come for me to walk with them again."

Horror-stricken, Demmi was on her feet in an instant. The morning wind sent shivers into her naked body as she crossed the cave and dropped to her knees before him. Gripping his shoulders hard with both hands, she forced him to face her as she shook him ferociously.

"Never!" she cried. "I have not turned my back upon my people to follow you into the storm so that I might stand by and watch you walk off with beasts. And if you imagine that I will walk at your side as one of them, then truly we do not understand each other!"

"You should not have followed me, Demmi."

"Should, should not, what matter? We are together now. I will not give you up to the wanawut!"

Still kneeling naked before him with her hands gripping his shoulders and her breasts pressing warm against his chest, she kissed him on his brow, at each temple, and along the line of the scar that ran to the edge of his mouth. And then she kissed him on the mouth.

When she drew back, a look of triumph crossed her face, and then an expression that betrayed mixed and tumultuous emotions. She knelt back, rested her palms upon her thighs, and stared at him out of narrowed eyes. "Are you a man of the People or a wanawut? Which, Manaravak? Or is Dak right when he says that you are both?"

He stared back at her, confused. He snarled at his sister.

"Do not be angry with me, Manaravak. We must nurture and look out for one another." She pressed her body against his and wrapped her arms tenderly about his head. She held him gently, made of him a consenting captive as she moved slowly back and forth, swaying on her knees like a supple, sun-warmed tree in the soft wind of the rising dawn.

How could he be angry? Her body was speaking to him of her love and repentance, of her need for his forgiveness and affection. He gave both with strong, sure, upward strokes of his hands along her flanks and sides and firm, full buttocks. She sighed and moved closer. The scent of her was pure woman. The texture of her breasts against his cheek was like that of the warm, silken belly of a lactating animal. Instinctively, he moved his face, mouthed them, and heard her gasp and felt her nipples peak and harden against the movement of his tongue and the sure, steady draw of his mouth.

"I could not love a beast," she whispered as she bent to kiss the top of his head. "You *are* a man, Manaravak! A man of the People! Never doubt that! I want you so much, Manaravak . . . over so many years I have wanted you."

Far to the east, Umak stopped midway in the conversation that he was having with the other men of the band and turned to the south. A feeling in his gut told him that Manaravak and Demmi were still alive. Was it premonition or false hope? He shook his head. Would he never be resigned to their death? Even if by some wondrous magic they were to return, their presence would complicate things, for Swan had made herself a part of Dak's fire circle, and his own relationship with Naya was bound to improve. Perhaps, in the end, things had worked out best for all concerned?

The thought disconcerted him. His brother and sister and the first woman of Simu were dead. How could that be "best" for anyone? He shrugged the question away and turned back to the others.

Torka was speaking sternly. "Swan has taken her sleeping furs to the fire circle of Dak without the consent of the headman or of—"

"Of Dak!" the son of Simu defended himself hotly.

"You have not sent her away," reminded Torka.

"I have! More than once. She always comes back! She sneaks up on me when I am not looking, builds up a fire, and cooks a meal—for love of my boy, she says."

Umak appraised his friend knowingly. "Not for you, eh?"

"I haven't laid a hand on her."

Torka let the statement settle a moment before asking: "Why not?"

Umak was taken aback by his father's completely unexpected question. So were the others.

Dak was openly amazed. "I . . . she . . . I mean . . . your daughter Swan is a good new woman, Torka, but I mourn for Demmi. My sister looks after me. Larani is enough."

"Larani!" Simu interrupted vehemently. "Do you hear that, Torka? Larani's a better choice for my Dak in a band that might otherwise be burdened by a poor, scarred, ugly woman. Swan, now, she is strong and pretty and sound of flesh. No use wasting a new woman like her on my Dak when he does not want her!"

Umak saw Torka's face work against ill-contained anger as the headman cautioned, "I have warned you before, Simu. It is forbidden for brothers and sisters to be man and woman with one another."

"Among *your* people! Not among mine."

Dak eyed Simu with disgust and disbelief. "Is Larani such a burden to you, my father? As long as I am able to lift a spear, I will hunt for her and see to it that she is kept warm in the winter dark, even if you will not! I do not have to take her as my woman in order to assure her place in this band."

Torka's eyes narrowed. "Bold words, Dak, from one who has been all but useless in this camp! I have watched you, waiting for you to behave as a man again—to hunt with enthusiasm, to show interest in your son, to join with your people in the fellowship of camp life—but to no avail. Your behavior is an offense to me and to the spirits of your ancestors! You must look to the future again, son of Simu. Demmi is the past, and Swan has looked at you as a man."

"And I have not looked back!"

Umak winced. He knew that Dak had intended no insult to Swan. Nevertheless, he had given it.

Torka sat motionlessly, seemingly unperturbed as he turned his gaze to Grek's older son. "Tankh, perhaps it is time for you to think of taking a woman. You are young, but Swan is not so much older. In a band as small as this, our women *must* be mated! Since you now hunt as a man and sit in council as a man, Tankh, perhaps it is time for you to—"

"Wait!" Dak protested. From the look on his face it was apparent that he had never thought of the possibility of Swan's going to another man. It was a possibility that he did not like at all.

Tankh, meanwhile, had shrunk visibly within his furs, and a *whoof* of pure relief went out of him.

Insight stabbed the shaman, and he understood that Torka was not only acting on Swan's behalf but had seen into Dak's heart and guessed a truth that was only now beginning to dawn upon the son of Simu. Demmi would live forever within Dak's heart, but she was beginning to share that space with the infinitely more caring and attentive Swan.

Torka nodded solemnly. "Swan has taken her bed furs to your fire circle, Dak. Whether this has been to look after Kharn or to lie with you, only the two of you can say. What matters is that she acts of her own will and honors you with her concern. By your failure to reciprocate, you dishonor her, me, and your people. After all that our people have endured, it would be a good thing to celebrate the joining of a new woman to a man of the band."

Simu looked up at the headman and snapped like a riled dog, "Bah! Had it not been for the granddaughter of Grek, we *would* have had cause to celebrate! We *would* have had cause to prepare a ceremony that joined a new woman to a man of the band!"

"Be silent, Simu!" Torka demanded. "The matter of Naya has been settled by this council. Do not bring it up again." The headman turned to Dak. "As the custom of our ancestors decrees, Dak will hunt. He will bring back new-woman gifts of meat and skins to honor Swan. When he has returned with these gifts, he will formally accept responsibility for her before an assembly of the People, or I will give her to Tankh *now*!"

As Dak caught his breath Tankh's face went pale with dread.

Dak remained silent. What Torka was proposing meant Dak's acknowledgment and acceptance of Demmi's death.

"Well?" Torka prodded. "What is your decision?"

At last Dak conceded without the slightest trace of emotion: "For Kharn's sake I will hunt. For Kharn's sake I will bring the bride gifts. I would not dishonor or bring shame to the sister of my Demmi. I will take Swan as my woman."

Simu was still growling to himself. His eyes were glinting like black embers. "And what of my Larani? Who will mate with her, eh? Who will bring new-woman gifts to honor *my* daughter? Whose babies will take life from her belly in a camp where the headman says that all women must be mated?"

Tankh shrank within his furs again until Torka spoke.

"Mine . . . if she will have me."

"If?" Simu was grinning like a happy wolf. "You are the headman of the band! Of course she will have you!"

Far away beneath the wide, windswept vault of the Arctic sky, ravens flew across the face of the sun and the animals of the tundral world looked toward the hills. A wolf howled within the cave to which the great mammoth had brought the son and daughter of Torka. But it was not a wolf; it was a man. It was Manaravak.

And as he rode his sister to sexual completion he took her from behind, like a wolf.

Demmi whispered, "Wait! Manaravak, not like this! You go too deep, too fast, and I think I am with child. Stop, please stop."

He heard, but her words were a distraction to him. He would not waste his time with them now! Demmi had roused man need in him, and now his need was driving him—pure, mindless, male-animal need that swelled and throbbed and took him deeper and deeper into her.

Demmi cried out in pain. "No! No . . . too soon . . . wait . . ." Release came as it always did with him, violently and quickly. The molten force of his life burst through his loins like magma searing through fissures in the flesh of the earth itself.

Still ejaculating, he gripped her breasts when she tried to crawl away, and gripping them tightly, he pulled her back and forced her to take him deeper still. When she tensed and twisted and tried to pull away, he would not allow it. No woman had ever told him to wait, although Iana had always tried to gentle his "wolfish ways," and Naya had screamed in terror of them.

Naya. His heartbeat quickened at the memory of her—so small and pretty, so soft of flesh, so moist of mouth and sweet between the thighs. Umak would be her man now—perhaps even riding her now.

Incredibly, Manaravak's organ was swelling again. He was salivating, growling with prolonged ecstasy as he began to thrust again deeper, harder, hotter, until Demmi fell forward begging him to stop. He could not have stopped if he had wanted to. He stayed on her, pumping until she screamed in protest and flailed her arms back at him. He kept on moving, thrusting, exhaling a single name again and again in rhythm with the jabbing of his hips.

"Naya. Naya. Naya!" Her name came through his clenched teeth. He saw no reason not to speak it. Demmi had always known his heart. Why then did she go suddenly limp?

"Why am I not enough for you?"

The question angered him. *Not enough?* What did she mean? His organ filled her, burned and pulsed with sensation as it was encompassed by the moist, throbbing warmth of her body. What more could she want? What more could *he* want?

Naya. He wanted Naya. But the granddaughter of Grek was far away. Demmi was here. Demmi had offered herself to him. Why was she now trying to pull away?

He was suddenly furious. He did not understand the females of his kind. He had seen the matings of wild animals. Never had he seen a female animal try to run away once the male was up and buried deep inside her.

His thoughts confirmed his actions. As Demmi tried to separate, his organ was leading him forward. He followed ferociously. Still gripping her, he thrust harder. He was a wolf! He was a lion! He was a wanawut! Once mounted on a female, he would not be driven off. Once aroused, the sensory excitement that was to be found upon a female, any female, could not be denied. All that mattered was the moment, and the pleasure and satisfaction that he found within it.

As the last of his fire extruded into her, he threw back his head and howled again and again in the pure bestial ecstasy of an orgasm that shook him to his very soul.

Wolves and lions responded to his cry, and far away to the south, the wanawut knew the sound that he made and, recognizing it as belonging to one of their own, howled in response.

And as the power went out of his arms and limbs, he fell sideways, with a stunned, hurting, unfulfilled, and disappointed Demmi still in his arms. Sated at last, he relaxed and, still joined to his sister, slept like a contented beast and dreamed of Naya and of Larani and never heard the words that left Demmi's mouth or saw the tears that fell from her eyes.

"You *are* an animal!" she sobbed, and as she listened to the sounds of hunting beasts howling in the world below the cave, she thought of Dak—of her strong, steady Dak and of their many lovemakings during which he had spoken her name again and again, as Manaravak had spoken Naya's.

She wept from disappointment. Her brother had coupled with her out of man need, not for love or even a specific desire for her. He might have been pounding an orifice in a rock for all that she meant to him. The realization struck her to her heart. She closed her eyes, and as she laid her hand across her belly and felt the movement of Dak's unborn child, her spirit ached for want of him and for all the wrongs that she had done to him, and she knew at last that he had been right about her brother all along: Manaravak had lived too long among beasts not to have become one of them.

"Oh, Dak . . ." She trembled as she spoke his name. "How I long to see you again and to lie beside you and Kharn as I tell you of our child that is to come. Oh, Dak, do not forget your Demmi, who will now live only for the day when she will walk at your side as your woman once more . . . a woman who will never want to lie with her brother again!"

8

"You shame me," Lonit whispered as she knelt before her tallow lamp in the center of the headman's hut and looked across its glow at Torka.

He met her eyes—soft, antelope eyes that he had loved for nearly all of his lifetime—and explained again, "You must understand me, Woman of My Heart! It is what I must do. Simu set his trap, and I walked into it. For Larani's sake, what else can I do? You are my always-and-forever woman, but—"

"But!" She cut him short with an impatient snap to her voice. "There is no room for 'but' in this conversation. I am not shamed because you have asked for Larani. You shame me by actually believing that I would not understand! Seeing what Simu has been up to, I can't imagine why you have not asked for the girl before now. Poor child! How her pride must be aching. We must make her welcome, Torka. We must make up to her for all the pain that she has suffered."

"We?"

"Of course! You will have a new woman in Larani, and I will have a new daughter to sit beside our fire again now that Summer Moon and Swan have men of their own, and Demmi is—" She paused. "I dream of her so often . . . of my lost girl . . . and my lost son. I know the Seeing Wind has brought a vision of their death, but I still cannot believe that they are—"

"Speak of it no more, Woman of My Heart. I, too, still grieve for them. I grieve also for what I must do now, for although I will speak for Larani, my spirit belongs to you alone."

"You shame me." For the second time a woman spoke these words within the encampment of Torka. Larani's accusation stung the air of her father's pit hut.

"Shame?" Simu was incredulous. "You—who in any other

band would never have a man at all—will now have the best of all men!"

"The best of all . . ." Larani turned the words softly as her thoughts went running back across the years. She saw herself as a child lying close beside the headman's fire, with Naya and Swan on either side of her. The secret yearnings of three young girls echoed out of the past to mock her now. They had all longed for the best of men—and now Naya had Umak, and Swan had Dak, and Larani had . . . dreams of Manaravak. She sighed. They were enough. She wanted no more.

Simu laughed triumphantly and slapped his thighs. "This old hunter has laid his snares well. Just look what I have won for my girl, eh?"

Larani winced. "You are not so old," she told her father honestly and then, with an equal measure of truth added, "I have no wish to become Torka's woman."

Simu's smile dissolved.

"As a new woman who has never been with a man, the right of choice is mine. I will not have him. Nor will I take a boy like Tankh to my bed furs."

"But you must be mated! Don't you *want* to be mated?"

"Once, yes. Long ago. No more. What you ask of me, Father . . . the shame would be worse than the pain of my burns."

"Shame? What are you talking about? Imagine it, Larani! Even now Torka prepares to go out from camp with Dak to hunt for new-woman gifts. No one in our family has ever been so honored!"

"I am not honored. I am pitied. It is not the same thing."

"And what about me?" he shouted. "Have you no pity for me? What about my shame, eh? To look at you each day, to see what you have become! Torka has brought this misery on you by allowing you to live! He is responsible for you! He *must* honor you! It is his obligation. And as my daughter, it is your obligation to accept him!"

"I would rather die," she said coolly.

"Then do it!" he roared. "Refuse Torka, and from this day you will receive no meat or shelter from me!"

Larani's head went up. "So be it, then," she said evenly, and with a great, hot lump in her throat that would not be swallowed down, she rose, turned, and began to gather up her things.

"Larani . . ." Simu's voice broke; he, too, had a lump in his throat, it seemed. "I do not want this."

She did not move. "Nor do I."

"Then when Torka comes to speak for you, say yes to him."

She sighed and closed her eyes lest tears spill onto her cheeks. "Torka wants no female other than Lonit. What he has conceded to you has been done out of kindness and pity. To accept gifts from him, to go to his hut, to know that Torka will force himself to be a man with me . . . these things I will not allow. Truly, my father, he *is* the best of men. And although you mean well for me, I *would* rather die than say yes to him."

And so it was that when Torka came to the hut of Simu, Larani came out to greet him with words of refusal.

"I have spread myself for no man," informed Larani. "According to the ancient customs of Torka's people, a virgin may claim the right of first choice. This woman will *not* take a man . . . any man . . . until she is ready."

Torka was completely taken aback. He had not expected to be turned down, and he most certainly did not expect to feel disappointment now that he had been. Indeed, the girl had bruised his ego soundly. His brow curved downward as he looked at her strong, marred face, her straight back, and the way her fine, high breasts swelled the fabric of her tunic. Even with scars, Larani's character made her beautiful to Torka. How could Simu not see this? And how had his sons been blind to it and turned their attention to Naya when a girl of Larani's worth had been there for the taking?

"This woman will not offend the headman of her band!" Simu was seething. "And no longer will this man feed or clothe her."

Torka's brow came down. "I am not offended," he informed the hunter. "Larani will choose a mate. Soon. Won't you, Larani? But now she is right. After all she has endured, she has earned the right to choose her first man. There are already two pregnant women in this camp. Dak is about to hunt new-women gifts for Swan. If the Father Above and Mother Below smile upon their union, perhaps yet another belly will swell like a full moon in this camp. It is good. If your father will not feed or shelter you, Larani, you will be welcome within the circle of my protection—as my daughter or sister or woman, whichever you prefer."

He could feel Lonit's eyes upon him and was glad that she stood behind him—he was blushing like a callow youth.

Larani's eyes softened.

"I thank you," she said sincerely, and would have added more had Dak not spoken up with obvious antagonism toward his sire.

"As I have said in council, there is always a place for Larani at my fire circle!"

"Good." Simu's head was down, his eyes were narrowed, and as he whirled away and sought the privacy of his pit hut he had the look of a cornered wolf about him. "She will need it, because she is no longer welcome at mine!"

Dak took up his spears and hefted his pack frame of caribou antlers. Swan came to him and asked him if he had everything he needed. "I do not really want gifts. You are enough for me. I will be a good woman, Dak. You will not be sorry that I have come to share your fire."

"I am sorry now!" he told her, and went his way, but even as he spoke he knew that he was lying. He was not sorry, he was guilty. Demmi was dead and her younger sister shared his fire and his hut . . . and he was much too glad. So glad that he was delighted when Umak called out to him and redirected his thoughts.

"Hold! Wait for me!" The shaman and the big dog, Companion, were at his side in a moment. "Tradition demands that your spear brother accompany you on this hunt."

Dak eyed Umak. He appeared to be ready for a long trek. "What tradition is that, old friend? I've never heard of it."

Umak winked. "Neither have I, but if I don't get away from Naya and Honee for a while . . . I need a hunt, old friend. It will make me a new man again! Come on. The sooner we have the camp behind us and are off across open country, the better I am going to feel!"

Demmi sat at the mouth of the cave and watched the sun rise over the eastern mountains. Caribou were already cropping lichens on the plain that bisected the southern ranges, and she had no doubt that when the grass greened with the rising of the next moon, big game would follow.

She rose and stretched, contented with the knowledge that she and Manaravak would soon prepare traveling packs and set out to find the People.

Demmi turned to scan the face of the cliff and was not surprised when she saw no sign of her brother. She had been nasty since their last coupling. He was understandably avoiding her.

The baby moved within her. It was the slightest of swimming sensations, and as often happened since she had coupled with Manaravak, it was accompanied by nausea and dizziness, and sometimes, afterward, there were traces of blood on her tunic. Worried, she talked to the unborn child as though it could understand every word.

"It is my fault, you know, not Manaravak's. He is what he is, and I have expected far too much of him. And now I am short-tempered with him because of you. I have been selfish and have broken with the ways of our ancestors and have not cared about you until now. I am sorry that I let Manaravak hurt you. He did not mean to. He knows about females and mating and cubs, but he does not understand about women and loving and babies. There is a difference, you see. I will try to make him understand. It will make things easier for him when we at last return to the band."

She paused, distracted by movement in the canyon. She stood and peered down onto the canopy of spruce and budding hardwoods as she tried to see what walked there. Whatever it was was lost to view beneath the trees. Her curiosity almost prompted her to climb down to investigate, but before she went hunting, she wanted to make things right with her brother.

"Manaravak! Manaravak! I want to talk to you. I am sorry for behaving so badly! Manaravak!"

She paused, waiting for a reply. None came. She did not blame him. Had he treated her as she had treated him, she would not be speaking to him, either.

The lake was not wide, but it seemed endless. For the last five days Dak, Umak, and Companion had been following the shoreline into increasingly bleak country, until the lake separated itself into many streams. It was as inhospitable a landscape as they had ever seen. Apart from lichens, mosses, and severely weather-stunted scrub growth, there was no vegetation. The few trees that they literally stumbled over grew laterally, with miniature branches and trunks pressed flat to the tundral earth, veining their way around rocks and through crevices to stay out of the wind and to absorb as much sunlight as the cold, clouded sky would allow.

"I do not like this place," said Dak. "We should go back."

"If you are ever to find gifts for Swan and if I am ever going to find a fresh source of berries for Naya, we will have to keep going until we come into better country than this."

"Berries? Is that all that the granddaughter of Grek wants you to bring her? Not furs or rare feathers?"

"Naya has used up the last of those odd little dried fruits. She longs for more."

They slogged on. It had been raining off and on since their second day out from camp—not a hard, driving rain, but a soft, whispering, wind-tattered drizzle that seemed to be no more than an afterthought of the clouds. Their waterproof rain capes and overboots of oiled intestine kept them dry. A square of the same material was laced across the back of the dog to protect Companion and the side packs that he carried. They snared and ate a few ground squirrels, and using portions of leftover squirrel livers as lures, they stoned several raucous, raven-sized, hook-beaked birds of a species that was unknown to them. The meat of the birds was disappointing—red and stringy—but they took the skins with care, agreeing that the gray-blue feathers would make a start on the bride gifts that they were supposed to be collecting for Swan.

"You don't really want to take her as your woman at all, do you, Dak?"

"Demmi is my woman."

"Will you never accept that Demmi is dead?"

Their eyes met and held. "Demmi is a part of me, Umak. I cannot just put her out of my mind and heart." He made a rude snort of derision and crushed one of the feathered skins in his hand. "Swan is a fine woman, Umak, and I have come to care for her . . . perhaps too much. But sometimes, even though I am not a shaman, I know that Demmi lives—she and your wild fool of a wanawut brother. I feel them both. *Here.*" He let the feathered skin drop as he splayed his hand across his heart. "Do you ever feel them?

Do you never fight against the need to go in search of them just one more time?"

"No." The word was clipped and tight. Umak wondered if Dak could sense it was a lie. He reached down and picked up the crumbled skin of the strange bird. "Come," he urged. "We must flesh and dry these skins and prepare them for packing before we can go on. They will make Swan smile, and if Demmi watches from the spirit world, I am sure that she will smile, too."

Demmi was not smiling. Manaravak was gone. She was standing in the cave with her back to the wall, her bola armed and ready in one hand and her spear in the other. It did not matter. The wanawut kept on coming.

There were seven of them—all adult males except two, and one of these, although female, was a creature of massive and dangerously powerful proportions. Only the leader of the pack, a big silver-backed male, was larger and more menacing.

Demmi's breath caught in her throat. Terror and incredulity flared simultaneously within her and numbed her senses. She did not throw her spear. She did not whirl her bola. She *knew* this beast! It stared at her like a huge, stump-legged, slouch-shouldered man out of small gray eyes that glinted dangerously above its long cylindrical snout. When it leaned forward, swaying slowly as it balanced its weight upon the huge knuckles of its clawed and hairy hands, she knew exactly where and when she had seen it before.

"You!" The word was a barely audible whisper of recognition of the nightmare image that she had seen in the fog so long ago and so far away. Dak had mocked her, had assured her that she had been imagining it, but there *had* been something in the fog—something big and male and threatening.

She recognized the massive musculature of its furred body, the shaggy, grizzled mane bristling along its upper back and shoulders, the short, thick neck, and its face. . . . She felt sick at the sight of its face.

There was no fog to confuse her vision now. She saw the projecting brow ridge humping up out of the sloping, flattened cranium, the pointed, yet grotesquely manlike ears set low at the side of its head, the broad-lipped mouth that was pulled back to reveal stabbing teeth as long and deadly as a lion's, and the flaring, hairless nostrils that expanded as it smelled her fear.

Excited by her scent, it exhaled a series of deep, quick huffs and swayed more quickly on its hind limbs. At its back, the other wanawut were clearly agitated, salivating as they moved forward.

"No!" Demmi stood her ground. Spear in hand, bola at ready, she had nowhere to run. Only her knowledge of Manaravak's love for these creatures stayed her hands. Perhaps he was right? Perhaps they only *looked* dangerous? "Get back! Get away from me!"

They stopped. Their eyes were fixed upon her—curious, not cruel—the steady, unblinking, compassionless eyes of carnivores appraising a prey animal that was about to become meat.

Demmi felt sick. Where was Manaravak? When and if he ever returned to the cave, he would be lucky if he could recognize any of the fragments that his beloved beasts might leave of her bones . . . and the bones of her unborn child. *The child!*

"Get back!" she commanded the wanawut with a newfound ferocity and courage. "For the sake of my brother who, by some magic that I will never understand, was raised to be one of you, I give you one last chance!"

The wanawut reacted to her threat. The silver back stood erect. He pounded his chest in outrage as the big female screeched and charged.

Demmi hurled her spear and then, whirling her bola, she sent the stones flying.

A single scream rode the north wind. It was the sound of someone dying.

Manaravak stopped and stood absolutely still. Again he heard a scream. It was from far away and thinned by distance, clinging to the wind like a dying spirit. His breath rasped in his throat, and his heart leaped in his chest. High, raging screeches of agony were followed by a terrible silence that spoke to him of pain and blood and death.

"Wanawut!" The word escaped his lips in longing and with empathy.

Silence settled over the world again. It was broken only by the mocking slur of the wind and the long, pain-filled, desolate wails of a faraway woman.

"Demmi! Have you killed them, Demmi? Or—" A devastating possibility nearly dropped him where he stood. "Or have they killed you?"

He could not bear the thought. He had abandoned her, his fine new clothes, and his new spears, to rejoin the world of beasts. He had been certain that Demmi would come to no harm, but she was alone!

"Sister!" He sped back toward the cave and tried not to think of what he would find when he reached it, because now, for the first time, he knew in his heart that he had been lying to himself. The ghost of Nantu told him so . . . the ghost of the long-dead boy who had walked into the fog one night to lose his head—not to Three Paws but to the beast that Manaravak had seen running off with it into the mists— the beast that he had not wanted to see . . . the beast that had been trailing his People all along . . . the beast wanawut!

Umak, Dak, and Companion followed growing numbers of wheeling, screaming seabirds northward across the delta of the Great Mad River. Joined by yet another north-flowing river, it had struck out across the barrens until now, broken, gentled, and divided into many lesser streams, it poured on and on. Umak and Dak paused where no men had ever stood before—on the shores of the Arctic Ocean. They stood amazed. Never had they seen so large a "lake." Slowly, Umak walked forward to become the first human to stand upon this shore and make a cup of his palm so that, as he knelt, he might drink of this strange and wondrous body of water. His taste buds sparked with the pleasurable sting of salt. He had no word for it—any more than he had a name for the aggressive, hook-billed, ferret-eyed gulls that wheeled overhead, or for the many large, unusually lean and long-legged white bears that were fishing and feeding not far away on a wide sandbar that lay within one of the innumerable streams of the delta.

He and Dak marveled at the uncountable legless beasts that barked like dogs and yet had the tails and fins of fish. The largest among these possessed tusks like mammoth and bellowed like moose, while others were whiskered like lions and made odd *ork*ing sounds as they lazed in huge herds along the beach or oozed their way on and off the offshore rocks and icebergs to swim in the lake with ease.

"This water tastes of blood," Dak shouted as he knelt beside Umak. The sound of the sea and the many rivers and streams and vast herds of bellowing, *ork*ing animals was deafening. "And of tears and sweat."

"Yes, as though it were a living thing."

Umak rose and scanned the shoreline. A slow, deep excitement was rising to fill him. "So *many* . . ." he said with reverence.

"Yes, but so many *what*? Are you sure that they are real and not bad spirit animals? They are ugly enough."

"Do not insult them when we have only just met their kind for the first time! They are real enough, if we are to judge from the stink of their droppings and the sight of their many newborn. Look: The birds are feeding upon the afterbirths—a sure sign that these creatures are living animals and not spirits. And to a hunter of the People, no animal is ugly unless it is not edible or if its skin proves useless."

"You aren't suggesting that we hunt these . . . things?"

"Why not?" Umak answered. "We have come to hunt. Would the spirits of these animals not be offended if we did not think enough of their worth to lift a spear to them so that we might see what they are made of?"

Dak mulled over the shaman's reasoning. After a moment, he found it sound enough.

And so, with Companion running ahead and doing his best to herd the creatures that men of another epoch would call walrus, Umak and Dak were soon baffled by the creatures' behavior. Having never seen a human being before, the animals made no move to flee. Umak and Dak waded into the herd, avoiding nips and occasional charges that twice overran newborn animals and crushed the life out of them. Perplexed and disgusted by the stupidity and passivity of the big animals, Umak and Dak moved away, reticent to kill such unworthy prey. But then Companion roused a male that was as big as a long-horned bull bison. Its tusks were nearly as long as Dak and Umak were tall.

While its harem looked on, the beach master was baited by Umak and Dak. Despite a lack of legs, the courageous animal moved with disconcerting speed when provoked into a charge. At length their spears struck deep and true, and soon they were hunkering at the edge of the herd, feasting at their kill site and sharing the eyes and rich, odd-tasting meat and fat with the dog.

"It isn't bad," Dak conceded.

"A man could develop a liking for it!" Umak remarked.

"Yes, and many lamps could burn all winter long if fed with the fat from only one of these creatures. Have you ever seen more fat on an animal in all your life?"

Umak shook his head. "I have not found any berry bushes for Naya, but I will bring fat for her lamp and fat enough for old Grek, too! This will make her look kindly at me when we return."

Dak looked at him askance. "Does she not look kindly at you now? How does Honee react when all you do is speak of Naya?"

"I will bring fat for Honee's lamp, too!" His appetite sated, Umak wiped the grease of his meal on his face to keep his skin oiled and stared off to where the white bears were fishing—bears that he and Dak had taken care to keep at a distance and on the right side of the wind. His mood shifted instantly. "Look: *white*, all of them. Including the cubs!"

Dak looked but did not seem impressed. "Given all that has happened, I have had enough of hunting the bear kind."

"But what a bride gift one of their pelts would be for Swan! And for Naya—I mean for *both* my women—and for my little Li."

Dak eyed the bears thoughtfully. "I would not like to return to camp without something worth showing. We might manage to bring back a pelt or two and still come away with our own skins and scalps . . . if the forces of Creation will smile upon our effort."

Umak nodded, full of enthusiasm. The sound of the sea, the smell of the air, and the lay of this land appealed to him. Excitement was stirring deep within him again. "Beside this Lake of Watered Blood is enough meat to feed the People for endless moons! And bone and tusks and sinew and skins! Indeed, everything we need to live is here! Perhaps the forces of Creation are smiling upon us! Do you see it, Dak?"

Dak looked around dubiously. "I see open country. I see many rivers running to a cold lake with mountains of ice in it."

"And I see high ground over there upon which a good, dry camp could be made. And I see mountains of meat for the People!"

"But what kind of meat? Not caribou. Not bison. Not elk. Not horse or moose or—"

"If these animals stay by this lake all winter—or even if they migrate into these waters to bear their young on this shore during the spring—then perhaps, after all that we have endured, the Seeing Wind has led us north to show us that we need not always search for the big game of the open steppe. Perhaps we have found a new kind of meat upon which to nourish ourselves! Look around, Dak. What better omen could there be for any of us? Perhaps the bad times are behind us at last! Perhaps the Seeing Wind has led us north to discover the luck that Torka has been seeking!"

Watching the feeding bears, Dak remained thoughtful. "Maybe. We will rest, sharpen our spears, and make chants to the life spirits of our intended prey. Next we will hunt. Then we will see."

Although Umak's blood was already rising for the hunt, he knew that Dak was not thinking of killing bears or of the fine white pelts that he would bring to Swan. As Dak scanned the beauty of this strange northern land it did not take a shaman to know from the mournful look on his face that he was still thinking of Demmi.

It was dark within the cave. Manaravak could smell blood everywhere. Gore slipped beneath his bare feet. He paused and tried to stop shaking. It was unnaturally, almost hideously quiet. He did not speak. Words—even the name of his sister—refused to form upon his tongue. What matter? Words were his enemies. He would know the truth of what had happened soon enough without them.

He took a bold step forward only to draw back in fear and revulsion. Something lay dead at his feet. He could just make out the body. It was gray in the darkness—drained of blood even as the interior of the cave was drained of light. He saw the long, familiar lines of the torso and arms and limbs . . . the breasts . . . the head turned sideways in death, blood running from a ruined eye . . . spears protruding from several killing wounds: Demmi's spear and three of his own.

Manaravak fell to his knees. He mewed and sounded like a bereft animal as he touched the body, drew out the stone that was embedded in the shattered, jellied eye socket, and then took the furred and lifeless body of the female wanawut into his arms and held it close, rocking it, cooing to it as though it were not a beast but a lifeless member of his own family.

From the deep dark at the back of the cave, Demmi watched him and could not bring herself to speak or to look away. How long had she been sitting in the dark with her back pressed to the cave wall? The fire that she had kindled at her feet had gone out long ago.

Slowly, without a word, she rose shakily to her feet. She stood in the darkness, watching Manaravak, trying to remember if she had ever felt so tired before. Not even the Great Mad River had exhausted her so completely. This day she had faced and overcome more dangerous adversaries. She had stood alone against the wanawut! She had wounded two, killed one, and driven off the entire ravening pack of them. But what she was feeling now was a weariness that had nothing to do with physical exhaustion—it was the cold, numbing, spirit-killing weariness that could only come to a devastated soul.

Her eyes had long since grown used to the night. Indeed, after the attack, she had actually welcomed it, for she had known that if the wanawut tried to storm the cave again, they would be silhouetted against the stars and vulnerable to her spears. Maybe they knew it, too. Perhaps this was why they had not come. Manaravak had come instead! She had *known* that he would come. Over all the long, terror-ridden hours in which she had lived in fear of the return of the beasts, she had known that Manaravak would have second thoughts and come back to her. She was his sister! He could not possibly abandon her!

And yet now, as she watched him and heard the low animal sounds that were pouring out of him, the night seemed to be inside her. It was a night without stars. It was a night without a moon. And in its darkness she saw the expression of grief upon his face and knew that his love for the dead thing that lay limp and hideous within his embrace was absolute. The hope that had welled so joyously within her only moments ago, when she had recognized his silhouette against the starlight, faded and twisted back upon itself into the most profound disappointment she had ever known.

Not once had he called her name or asked the night and the silence of the cave if she was alive or dead!

Steadying herself against her stave, she walked forward, crossed the cave, and stopped before him.

He looked up. "Demmi, did you do this . . . and with my spears as well as your own?"

"I did."

"How? Look at her! She could be Mother."

Demmi felt as though something within her had died. He was not speaking of Lonit but of the long-dead animal that had raised him. The years that he had spent as an animal living among animals had marked him forever. She understood, and she pitied him. And yet she was sickened and angered and hurt as she cried: "It could have been *me*, Manaravak!"

"No, never. I would not have left you if I thought they would hurt you. They would not! I would not! They—" He stopped.

She was appalled by the look of horror that tore his features and completely shattered his composure. His face twisted with sadness, regret, and bewilderment. Slowly he laid the body of the beast down, stared at it long and hard, and then, as in a dream, he rose and came to draw her into an embrace that had all of his heart in it. "Forgive, me, Sister, if you can. I nearly killed you."

With her heart wrenching and her spirit bleeding, there were tears in her eyes as she put her arms around him and held him close. "Not you. They. The wanawut."

"It is the same."

His statement shook her. She stood back from him. "No. It is not the same!" She took his hands, placed them on her belly, and pressed until he felt the baby move within her.

"My life lies here, Manaravak—a *new* life, a continuing of the generations of the People. Dak's child. And yet in a way it is your child, too—not because we have been lovers but because you are my brother. The blood of our family flows in us both, and it will flow in this child when it is born . . . *if* it is born. I cannot stop you if your heart tells you that you must turn your back upon your blood and walk with beasts. But can you truly look at that dead animal upon the floor of the cave and say that you are one if its kind? It is *not* the beast that raised you, Brother! It would have killed and eaten me had I not stood against it. And if I had failed and you had returned to the cave alone to face it and its pack, they would have killed you, too!"

She paused, expecting him to dispute her. He did not. His silence heartened her. She went on in a rush of words: "Do you not long for our people, Manaravak? For our father and mother, for our brothers and sisters, as I long for them and for my man and son? The mammoth has led us into this good country. Despite the presence of wanawut, luck has been with us! Let us find our band and bring them here! Together we could drive the wanawut from this good land and force them to seek other hunting grounds as we claim these for our own. Never have I seen a better or more game-rich land than that which lies beyond the southern ranges. As Torka has always assured, the spirits smile upon those who walk in the shadow of Life Giver. And if this is the truth, perhaps this is why the great mammoth saved us—not for our sake, but for our people's! Of what real worth are you and I beneath the vast skin of the sky? We are but two; the People are *many*. It is because of them that we still live. I must go back to them, Manaravak! I must tell them of this good land where the great mammoth totem lives with our luck and theirs! Come *with* me, Manaravak! You can learn to live as a man among men. I *know* you can! And so I ask you now—I *beg* you—as I have stayed at your side when you were weak and sick, stay at my side now. Be my strength and my courage as I carry my baby-to-be back across the drowned lands in search of our people. I must go back to them, Manaravak! With you or without you, I must go home!"

PART VII

WALKERS OF THE WIND

1

There was joy once more in the encampment of Torka. Umak and Dak had come home with a sledge laden with gifts: meat and fat and hides of glistening white, feathers and tusks, and tales of hope and wonder for all to hear.

After a gathering of the elders, the shaman sang and danced, and the hearts of the men of the band were light as their headman announced that tomorrow they would break camp and travel north.

The women and children sang in anticipation of better times, and the People gathered with the dogs around a high, hot fire to feast upon steaks of bear and walrus meat as they waited in great excitement for the formal dispersal of the gifts that Umak and Dak had brought back from the far north.

Old Grek sucked on pounded blubber through the ruin of his teeth, and Iana smiled to hear him say that although not rancid enough for his tastes, the fat had an odd, fishy taste that pleased him greatly.

When the fire was its hottest and the tales of the Land of Many Waters were their boldest, Torka stopped the good and boisterous talk and reminded his people that before any gifts could be given he must ask the son of Simu if Dak had not forgotten something.

Silence fell upon the encampment. Only the wind whispered. Only the fire dared to spit sparks and embers noisily into the sky. Grek went wide-eyed as he elbowed Tankh meaningfully and hard, which caused the boy to gag on the bear meat that he had been about to swallow.

Annoyed with his son for his lack of decorum at such a potentially auspicious moment, the old man struck him forcefully upon the back. Tankh coughed, and along with a wretching, choking explosion of sound, bits and pieces of the meat went flying.

Everyone looked at Tankh with disapproval.

Then Dak spoke, his expression fixed and unreadable.

"The son of Simu has not forgotten." He rose and walked away.

Swan hung her head in shame and disappointment while Lonit sucked in her breath with disbelief.

Umak appeared to be more shocked than anyone else when his spear brother disappeared into his hut.

The lines in Torka's face cut deep as he rose in anger. But before the stunned muttering of the People could form into words, Dak emerged from his pit hut wearing a necklace of bear claws interspersed with blue-gray feathers and carrying the pelt of a great white bear across his arms.

Swan looked up cautiously as he stopped before the headman and held the bearskin outward on his extended arms.

"For the new-woman Swan, bride gifts from one who would be her man."

Even in the light of the fire the people saw Swan blush. Lonit smiled with relief, and Torka nodded in approval.

Everyone waited. Although not a single member of the band doubted for a moment that she would accept Dak as her man, a rousing shout of approval nevertheless went out of every mouth—except Grek's—as she stood her ground and nodded in approval of the gifts. With her head held high, Swan allowed Dak to transfer the heavy necklace of feathers and claws from his neck to hers, and when she smiled, Larani, standing alone and well away from the fire, smiled with her.

Later, while others still sang praise songs for the presents that Dak and Umak had brought to them, Dak took Swan's hand and led her to his pit hut. This night, Kharn would sleep in the arms of Larani so that his father and new mother might lie together undisturbed upon the skin of the great white bear.

Although Dak lay beside Swan for the first time, he did not join with her. Instead, as on all the other nights when she had shared his hut without his permission, he turned his back and pretended to sleep. "I know your heart in this matter, Dak," she told him quietly, "but I want you to know that it does not matter to me if you still love Demmi or still want her and no other woman. I love my sister, too. There will always be room in this woman's heart and in her pit hut for the spirit of Demmi . . . as long as I can hope that someday there will be some small place in your heart for me."

Her words touched him more than he could say. He turned toward her and drew her close. "You deserve better of life than the son of Simu, Swan. I am—"

"You are all I have ever wanted," she interrupted. "I would have shared you with Demmi. And I would not have minded being second woman to her. I do not mind even now when her spirit lies with us here upon this wondrous white fur that you have brought to me . . . if you will give me only one more gift."

He frowned. "More? The skin, the necklace, the meat, and the fat are not enough for you?"

"No. I want a better gift."

He would have shoved her away, but she held him by his shoulders and looked him straight in his eyes. "Do not let Demmi be *between* us! On this night when our people sing for us, give me something to sing for, too. Here in the dark, while the feast fire still burns outside, give me a bride gift to burn here, *within*, for us. Love me, Dak. Love me only a little. It is all that I will ever ask of you."

And so it was that when the feast fire died and Torka's band dozed in its lingering warmth or walked arm in arm back to their pit huts, Dak and Swan lay joined as man and woman for the first time. And for the first time in all too many moons, Dak smiled in his sleep and did not suffer tortured dreams of Demmi.

While Umak took off his shaman's raiment, Honee settled the small, sleeping form of Li onto the bed furs that mother and daughter so often shared. Jhon hurried to take his father's sacred garments and arrange them upon the back ledge of the hut with infinite and reverential care, and Umak went to his own bed skins and invited Naya to come to him.

She stared at him, and the blood drained from her face. Apart from his body paint, he was naked. "My head aches," she lied.

Honee looked at Naya with a worried frown. "Your time of blood is over, Naya. Your head should not ache. It has not ached all day."

"It aches now!" she insisted.

Jhon turned. His eyes were narrowed with dislike as he

looked at Naya over his shoulder. "Your head always aches when my father asks you to share his sleeping skins!"

Naya glared at him. She was beginning to hate Jhon. Then she looked down and stroked the thick, silken fur of the magnificent bearskin that Umak had divided into thirds so that each female at his fire circle would have a piece to sleep on. Naya pouted. She would have preferred to keep the skin all to herself. Her portion was not enough to enfold her completely. In its entirety it had been almost as large as the one that Dak had presented to Swan.

Envy turned Naya's pout into a scowl. What a fine gift it had been for the new woman—especially when, as far as Naya was concerned, Swan should have received no new-woman gift at all. The daughter of Torka had gone to Dak without his consent and against the traditions of her people. And while Swan's taboo-breaking behavior had been over-looked, Naya had been severely punished, given to Umak without choice or ceremony or gifts or songs or feast fires—just given, as though she were valueless. Irritated, she pushed the bearskin away.

"Where are my berries?" she demanded of Umak. "You said that you would bring me some!"

Jhon stared at her with disbelief. "My father has brought you the best portion of the skin of a great white bear and you ask him for berries?"

"It is *not* the best portion! It is only one of three, and Honee's is bigger! Why should I not ask for my berries? I put them in my medicines. I *am* a medicine woman, am I not? How can I make medicine without them? Where *are* my berries?"

It was clear from Umak's expression and his tone of voice that he was not happy with her. "If you want berries, you are going to have to wait until the end of the time of endless light when the fruits of summer are ripe and ready for picking."

"I know only that you promised to bring me berries!"

"I promised to see if I could find any of the *shrubs* upon which they grow."

"Well? Did you?"

"No, I did not."

She pouted again. She had not missed the resentment in his voice. It occurred to her that she was being stubborn. It did not seem important. She glared at Umak. "If you were a great and powerful shaman like Karana, my poor dead father,

or my grandfather Navahk, or a true spirit master like old
Umak, for whom you are named, you could *make* me berries!"

It was suddenly very quiet within the pit hut.

"Naya . . ." Honee spoke with a lowered voice. "Where
are your manners? Go to your man when he asks you to come
to him and speak no more of berries!"

"Naya."

She blinked. Umak had spoken her name. She looked at
him as he spoke again.

"Come to me. Dak and I have been gone too long from
camp. I have missed you. I have missed all of you! Rest
beside me. I *am* Shaman. The least I can do is to try to find
the magic to drive away your headache."

Honee made a broad pretense of a yawn, then asked her
man if he would like her to extinguish the tallow lamp.

Naya flinched.

Umak rose and moved toward Naya.

"Oh," she wailed. "I am going to be sick!"

He took a step toward her, and as she shrieked he
reached over and pinched out the flame that burned in the
centrally placed tallow lamp. Darkness filled the hut.

Naya waited. Terrified, she closed her eyes. She clenched
her teeth and her thighs, and with her arms folded across her
chest, she pressed the little bone talisman tightly within her
fist. "Go away! Go away! Go away!"

She began to cry. This was the night that Umak would
not be turned back! The nightmare would come true at last,
and all she feared would come to pass. She would be like
poor Snow Eater, locked to her mate, hurting, crying to be
free of him while everyone laughed and mocked her.

But to her amazement and infinite relief, Umak turned
and went back to his own sleeping furs. She heard him
settling himself, exhaling with disgust. "Go to sleep, Naya.
You talk too much. You are not the only one who is sick!"

The darkness thickened. The stars walked slowly across
the skin of the night, and as Lonit crept from her bed skins to
seek out her man she found him standing alone, staring
toward the east and the glistening wall of ice that shimmered
blue in the starlight.

"The Mountains That Walk are beautiful, but they are
cold and desolate." She threaded her arm through his and,
sighing with contentment, leaned close and rested her head

upon his shoulder. "I am glad that we are to turn north and away from them at last."

"Are you?" There was sadness in his question, and regret.

Disturbed, she raised her head and looked at him. "The closer we come to the eastern ranges, the more impassable and lifeless they seem. Umak has found good hunting to the north."

"But no sign of Life Giver."

"He has found much meat! I do not understand, Torka. If you have second thoughts, you must call another meeting of the elders."

"I must see to it that my people are no longer hungry. I must lead them to meat. For now I will be content to find my luck in that."

She put her head upon his shoulder again, and he put his arm around her and held her close. "As I am content," she told him. "Always and forever, for I have found my luck in you."

Toward dawn a star fell out of the southern skies. Only Larani was awake to see it. She sat alone by the remains of the feast fire. The flames were dead, but there was still warmth to be found in the embers. She had watched Torka and Lonit disappear into their pit hut. How long ago had that been? Half the night ago, now. And how long had they stood together beneath the sky, silent, arms entwined, lovers still after how many years together?

Larani's·heart ached. There would never be a love like that for her. *Never*.

Bundled in her furs, she closed her eyes and thought of what it must be like to be loved and to be mated. *A good thing,* she thought fervently, and for a moment she imagined the sweetness of it and smiled until she felt the chill of the dying night upon her face and was aware of the cold, stiff puckering of her scars.

She shivered in revulsion and opened her eyes to stare up at the vast, star-strewn skin of the night. Father Above was up there somewhere—Father Above, who had sent his lightning-bolt penis into the earth to give birth to Daughter of the Sky. Did he know what that mating had done to one young girl? Did he care?

Tomorrow the band would head north. But what did tomorrow matter? It would only be another day, and after that there would be another day and another, until the time of endless light was upon the world. And then, slowly, the dark days would return, and the endless cycle of dark and light would begin again and again, until she was old and her spirit walked the wind forever.

Her eyes remained fixed on the southern sky. The falling star had left a trace of light in its wake, like the imprint of a flame when it has burned high and then subsided to leave a temporary shadow of itself upon the night.

"Manaravak. Is that you, Manaravak? Are you there, watching from the world beyond this world? Do you know that I love you? Are you offended? Do not be. My love is nothing. It matters no more than I."

◆━━━◆

2

◆━━━◆

Demmi trekked homeward. A sober and contrite Manaravak journeyed at her side.

The land was wide. The sun grew higher in the sky every day. At last they reached the Great Mad River and stopped. In silence, they stared ahead.

"It is wider than I remembered."

Manaravak was moved by the despondency in Demmi's voice. "We crossed before."

"In winter and on the back of a mammoth, and we were still nearly drowned!"

"That is not the same as completely drowned. Besides, there may be shallows ahead of us."

She laughed. There was no merriment in the sound.

He felt her mood and wished to ease it. "Soon the time of endless light will come, and the sun will drink of this big river. The level of the water will drop. We will cross then. In the meantime we will follow this big river back to the place of our people's last encampment . . . and maybe, if we are lucky, the mammoth will see us longing to be on the other side and come to help us once again!"

Demmi laughed again, and there was no more merriment in the sound than before. For many days and nights they walked along the course of the Great Mad River. Although travel was tedious and slow, there was neither sign nor sound of the wanawut, and so they took their time, pausing to hunt for fresh meat and to revel in the increasing warmth and astounding beauty of the land as they sang praises to the sun and to the new Moon of Green Grass Growing.

A new moon was rising over the Land of Many Waters when the people of Torka's band made camp on high ground above the Lake of Watered Blood. All the omens were good.

Only Torka stood back and with grim foreboding appraised the hunting grounds to which he had consented to lead his people. He hated the look of this place. He despised its smell. Every animal except the white bears revolted him, and in the bears he saw only potential danger—there were too many of them. With the exception of the cubs, each one was bigger and whiter and more menacing than Three Paws had ever been. How could Umak and Dak not have seen the hazard in this? He was puzzled and worried. Umak was Shaman, but what had happened to his common sense?

Nothing good can come to my people in this place, thought Torka. But he kept his thoughts to himself. His people were hungry. They must eat. He must encourage them to take meat and hides until winter rations were assured. By then the pups would be large and strong enough to pull fully loaded sledges. By then Iana's baby would be born, as would the child of Summer Moon. The women would be ready to travel back to the tundral steppelands, where the luck of the band would be found in the shadow of Life Giver and where the spirits of their ancestors walked the wind forever in the face of the rising sun!

In the days that followed, Torka led the men of his band to hunt, and the women worked hides and set up bone frames upon which to dry the meat of seals and walruses and of many a fine, fat, thick-skinned fish. The cloud cover finally lifted over the Lake of Watered Blood. Under the watchful eyes of all, with Torka's assistance, the children gathered seabird eggs and made a game of trying to ride the pups as they taught them not to bolt against the traces of a heavily loaded sledge.

"If I did not know better, I would think that you were readying to leave this camp!" Umak teased his father.

Torka was not amused. "And if I did not know better, I would think that you were still a shaman."

Naya could not say what had made her feel so much better. Perhaps it was something in the air. The smell of salt in the wind heightened her senses and cleared her head, and the rich, oily taste of fish and walrus drove away the recurring images of her red berries. Even Jhon was more agreeable now that he was spending most of his time hunting with the men of the band, Sayanah, and the other boys. Simu was still surly, but killing seemed to curb his nastiness, although the sight of Dak and Swan walking openly together, holding hands and kissing, sometimes made him growl.

"I never thought I'd see the day when Dak would be so happy!" Umak said to Naya as he came to stand beside her. She knelt opposite Honee over a sealskin that the two of them were fleshing.

"It is good to see Dak smiling again," she replied in earnest.

"A good and loving woman can do that for a man."

The subtle undercurrent of dissatisfaction in his voice made Naya uneasy.

"Do I not make you smile, Umak?" asked Honee in a light and teasing tone.

He looked at her thoughtfully. "Always, dear one. But Naya could do more."

Honee suddenly and uncharacteristically exploded at Umak. "Shame! Our little Naya is trying as hard as she can! Who would have believed her capable of such usefulness when you first dragged her, kicking and screaming, to our fire circle? Shame, I say, whenever I think of that! Poor child! A good, hardworking woman has my little band sister Naya turned out to be—as good and hardworking as your sister Swan! But for Naya there have been no feast fires or new-woman gifts, or even looks of approval from the headman! Shame, I say! Shame! What woman could do more . . . when she has been so badly used!"

Naya was so taken aback by Honee's outburst that she could not speak or look at Umak.

He was silent. "Is that what turns you against me, Naya? The way in which you were given?"

Naya stared into her lap. "I . . . no . . . It is not that."

He did not believe her. "I will talk to Torka. You are right, Honee. Time has passed. Naya has been an obedient woman to me . . . in all ways but one. But perhaps that will change now. Yes. We will see. We will soon see."

"No!" Torka was adamant. "No feast fire! No songs! Because of Naya, Manaravak and Demmi are dead, and for all I know, Simu is right when he says that Naya is to blame for the maiming of Larani and the death of Eneela and Nantu as well! I took pity on the girl for your sake, Umak, and for old Grek and for the good of the band! I will not do it again. If you want to give her gifts because she pleases you, do so. She is yours to do with as you will. That is enough! Do not ask more of me. Simu still believes that she is bad luck. He points to her flat belly and says that she will bear no life and so deserves no life among us. Prove him wrong, Umak, and you will make us both happy men. Put a baby in her belly. Make sons on her and assure the future of the People. But if you are still the shaman you once were, look into my heart and know this: Where Naya is concerned there can be neither sympathy nor mercy."

The full glory of the time of light returned to the tundra. As Demmi and Manaravak continued to seek their people, the once drowned and devastated land burst into bloom around them.

"Like you!" said Manaravak, smiling as he patted Demmi's expanding belly. "Dak will smile to see you so!"

She shook her head as she scanned the distances ahead. "I may have this baby at my breast by the time we find our people . . . *if* we ever find them."

"We will find them, my sister. The land is big, and the river is long, but we *will* find them."

Demmi paused to look back. "Before the wanawut find us?"

"We have seen or heard no sign of them."

"In my dreams I see them." She shuddered. "Will our people remember us, Manaravak? Will Dak be glad to see me or even care about this child?"

He frowned. "Of course they will remember us. Naya has my talisman. Helping Spirit will not let her forget me."

Umak was angry with Torka, Honee, Jhon, and Naya. And he was furious with himself. Was he not the headman's eldest son? Was he not the grandson of a spirit master, and a shaman himself? Had he not led his people to this amazing land of endless meat? *Yes!* But still Naya would not lie with him! And Honee continued to huff at him and told him angrily that he was behaving shamefully when he pressed the granddaughter of Grek to perform the most basic and—to any other woman—pleasurable of duties!

Umak wanted to make love to Naya . . . not rape her. Rape was too easy. Besides, according to Naya, Manaravak had already done that, and it was for this reason the girl feared the very thing that Umak wanted most of her . . . besides the commitment of her affection.

Even though he had tried to explain all this to Torka, the headman would not reconsider a decision that Simu had coerced him into making in the first place. Umak's temper boiled to think of it. If *he* could forgive Naya her transgressions, why could Torka not do the same? She had been punished and humiliated. Yes, she had been a thoughtless, foolish young woman who had inadvertently led a good man to rape, but the tragedy that had resulted had not been intended. Naya had suffered over it and had learned from it. Now all she wanted—aside from a handful of her red berries—was to be accepted by her people once again, to be accorded the same respect that was given to every other new woman when she went to her man's fire circle.

Was it asking too much of Torka to allow his son—and the shaman of the band—to give Naya her new-woman celebration? Umak's knuckles went white with frustration as his hand closed upon the haft of his spear. *No.* It was not asking too much.

A memory flared. In his mind's eye, he saw Naya and Manaravak rutting like wolves, and Naya screaming in ecstasy—no vanquished virgin, but a well-broken-in woman begging for more.

Umak's anger focused inward. Manaravak was dead and gone. In the long, bitter, and tormented days and nights that had passed since his disappearance, Umak had come to realize that jealousy had twisted his vision. He had not witnessed a passionate mating; he had witnessed his brother's rape of the woman he, Umak, loved. If he still had doubts about that, surely Naya's irrational terror of coupling proved the truth.

He drew in a deep and steadying breath. Manaravak was dead. Naya was his woman now.

Torka might forbid her the joy of a new-woman's celebration of honor, but he had not forbidden his son to bring her gifts. Now that Umak thought about it, Naya was right to complain about receiving only a portion of a bearskin. He owed her better than that.

Now, he stared out of camp, to where the great white bears had last been seen fishing. His hand tightened on his spear. He would bring Naya a new-woman gift that would make her proud. And when she smiled at him in gratitude, he would take her down upon it, and although she might weep and cry at first, he would have her on it, and he would make certain that she would have no cause for tears . . . and no reason to speak the name of Manaravak or to ask him for help ever again!

* * *

3

* * *

It was never completely dark now. From their little camp above the river, Demmi and Manaravak heard mammoth trumpeting in the thin blue gauze of night, and in the full light of the Arctic day, the siblings saw the herd of shaggy cows and calves browsing in the foothills not far away.

"A good sign!" proclaimed Manaravak. "And look! There is Life Giver! I think that maybe he and his mammoth band follow us, to make sure we are safe."

Demmi could find no cause to argue with him.

For the first time the land seemed familiar. The river was growing wider and shallowing noticeably. Demmi felt her senses quicken. Perhaps they would find a place to cross before winter.

A herd of horses ultimately showed them the way—fine, tawny, shaggy horses with striped backs and black manes and tails and eyes afire with sunlight. Led by a mare with a belly as spotted as a fawn's, they raced along the river's edge in an explosion of power, ferocious neighing, and flying water that turned into fragmented rainbows as it caught the light of the sun, and then plunged across. They galloped on until, suddenly in deeper water, they lost their footing briefly and were swept downstream. After swimming strongly, they regained their footing and disappeared into the green grass and flaming stands of fireweed that grew along the far shore.

"They have found a way across!" Manaravak let off a series of triumphant hoots. Entranced by the sight of so much power and beauty and meat on the hoof, he raced after them.

Demmi called him back. "Manaravak, wait! We cannot follow them!"

"Why not?"

His question seemed absurd. "Because we are not horses!" she replied.

Ignoring her, he raced headlong into the shallows. He kept on running until, like the horses before him, he plunged into deep water and was swept downstream.

She cried out in fear for his life. Racing along the shore in a vain attempt to keep up with him, she saw that his arms were up and waving as he screeched and yipped with joy.

With her heart in her throat, she saw that he still had his spears and that the current was carrying him safely across to the far shore. Once on dry ground, he waved again and shook himself in the way of a wet dog.

"It is good!" he called across to her. "Come!"

She hesitated only for a moment. The water was cold. The crossing was frightening at first, and then exhilarating.

He was waiting for her on the far shore with outstretched arms, beaming and dripping like a giddy child. She stopped before him and dropped him where he stood with a hard right to his jaw.

He stared up at her, testing his jawbone with careful fingers. It made a cracking noise beneath his questing fingertips.

She knelt down. "I am not a horse, Manaravak! I am a pregnant woman who is not feeling as strong as she once did. I do not want to lose this baby, Manaravak. And I do not want to lose you."

Her words had their intended effect. He was sobered. His hand moved from his jaw to her face. "You will not lose me. Together Demmi and Manaravak must take Dak's new baby home!"

"Umak, wait!"

Umak heard Dak's imperative call, but he paid no heed to it. At his side Companion was taking one slow, measured step at a time—head down, tail tucked, snout out and sniffing at the wind.

A lone bear had come down to the shore to feast upon the carcass of a seal that lay stinking in the wind. It was a big bear and still too far away for Umak to tell if it was *the* bear that he wanted for Naya—white overall, with no serious scars to mar the pelt. From here it looked very promising indeed!

He had three of his best spears with him. His spear hurler would allow him to increase the power and range of his thrust. He walked toward the animal very slowly, taking full advantage of the angle of the sun and the fact that he was downwind of the creature. He could see its ears twitching and was close enough now to see that the pelt of the animal was of good quality, not snow white but cream, with only the softest washes of yellow at the belly, elbows, and the tips of the ears, like dawn sunlight on new snow.

He wanted this bear for Naya. He could feel her eyes on his back—hers and the eyes of everyone in the band! Let them watch! Let them see what he could do! Let Torka see just how much Umak was willing to risk in order to make his new woman smile!

"Hold now and steady, old friend," he commanded the dog in a whisper. "You and I have faced this kind of death before and come away alive. Let us do this right, Companion, and let us do it now!"

There was no missing the challenge in Umak's raging cry as he ran forward and hurled first one spear, and then another and another at the bear. But the challenge was not only to the animal; Torka knew that the challenge was also for him. It had to do with the heated words they had recently exchanged about Naya. Umak's aggression was a deliberate and direct assault on the headman's judgment against her.

He was not angry; he was proud to have such a son. When the other men and boys made to run to Umak's assistance, Torka ordered them back. This kill would be Umak's alone. He had the right to it, and if he made it, Torka's heart would sing for him.

Nevertheless, Torka had his weapons ready and gestured the others into defensive positions. If Umak failed to make his kill and the bear charged past the hunters into the hastily assembled members of the band, someone was likely to be hurt, perhaps even killed. And all because the granddaughter of Grek still twisted the heart of his son and made it bleed for her. The realization darkened his spirit.

Naya was not even there to appreciate her man's valor; she was in the hut of blood with Iana, whose baby was about to be born.

A terrible cold expanded within Grek and prickled at the backs of his hands, along his shoulders, and up his neck into his scalp. He wished that his teeth would stop hurting. The pain was in his jaw now. It throbbed at his temples. It pulsed deep inside his ears. And then it was gone completely; Lonit had come out of the hut of blood to raise a shout of joy.

He wheeled around and saw the woman of the headman standing tall and serene with Honee, Larani, Swan, and Naya peering happily from the hut behind her.

"Come forth, Grek!" cried Lonit.

Grek ran like a youth, oblivious to his pain and to the protests of every twisted, creaking, groaning, and hurting bone in his old body.

Lonit held a square of white caribou skin in her outstretched hands. He could see that the skin lay over a mound that was supported at each end by her upturned palms. The mound moved, and the headman's woman smiled as Grek paused before her. Although he was breathless, his heart sang.

Lonit's face was radiant. "Iana has made a male child for Old Lion," she announced loudly enough so that all might share the joy and pride. "Iana has asked Lonit to bring this male child to Grek. Iana has asked if Grek will accept this child of the People?"

Grek drew back the caribou skin and looked at his son. The baby was small and pale but perfect. His little hands were clenched into fists, and his tiny feet kicked, and as Grek took the squirming infant into his big, steady hands and held him high for all to see, the baby's tiny penis erected and a stream of hot, steaming urine fountained high and hit Grek in the face. He laughed. Everyone laughed. No omen could have been better!

"The son of Grek *lives*!" he announced to all. "Woman of Torka, tell Iana that Old Lion accepts this son and rejoices in this *third* hunter that she has made for this 'old' man!"

He had watched the headman's son kill the huge white bear, then turned to see Lonit carry the new boy forward.

Perhaps these happinesses would finally set Simu's mind to rest about Naya's being a bad-luck bringer. When Grek placed the infant back into Lonit's hands so that she might bring it to its mother's waiting breast, the headman's woman spoke the sweetest words of all:

"You must give special thanks to Naya. This little one was backward inside his mother. It was Naya who turned him, who remembered Demmi's example with the pups and, because her arm is as slender as a child's, reached in to coax him out. And so now, because of Naya, you have another son, and the band will have a new hunter, and the people of Torka have good cause to smile upon the granddaughter of Grek once again!"

Under the ever-lengthening sun, Manaravak and Demmi continued to follow the mammoth eastward away from the Great Mad River. On an afternoon in which high clouds created rainbow-colored halos around the sun, they picked up the trail of the band. It was not long before they were able to tell by the number of footprints that a woman was missing.

"Naya!" Manaravak, bereft, fell to all fours, his nose to the earth like a scenting beast as he repeatedly whispered her name.

"No!" Demmi frowned, disgusted. "Get up, Brother! It is Eneela who is missing, not Naya. I told you: On the night that we were swept away, I saw her lying dead upon the ice."

He rose, his face alight with infinite relief. "You are sure?"

She was suddenly fiercely angry with him. "A woman of the People is dead, I say! Why do you smile?"

He was instantly contrite. "I am not glad for her death, Demmi. I am only glad that Naya is not dead, too."

"You must forget her, Manaravak. By now she is probably growing big with Umak's child."

"She accepted my talisman. She should have been mine."

"Manaravak, have you forgotten why she was given to Umak? Have you forgotten why you ran off into the storm? If Naya kept your talisman, she is indeed foolish!" Her face worked against anger. "Whatever magic may have been between you is over forever! When we return to our people, you will have no right to speak to Naya or even look directly into her face without Umak's consent."

Manaravak stared at his feet. It was obvious that he

found her words unpalatable, yet he said quietly, "I have shamed him once. I do not wish to do so again."

For five days Naya would not leave Iana's side in the hut of blood as the other women came and went with food and water and changes of bedding for the new mother and child. For five days Naya did not see the sun except when she left the hut to relieve herself and to breathe in the pungent smell of the sea while she thanked the forces of Creation for having allowed her to be the one to save the life of Iana and her baby—and for having kept Umak from putting a baby in her belly and subjecting her to the bloodied horror of a birth such as Iana had barely survived. She shivered with dread every time she thought of it. Naya cleaned and cooked and cared for the baby. She fussed and smoothed bedding and plumped backrests. She told stories and sang songs of such sweetness that she gave Iana cause to regret every harsh word that she had ever spoken . . . and for five nights, although she fought against sleep, she lost the battle and fell victim to her recurring nightmare. She woke sweated and dry mouthed and barely able to stifle her screams.

At dawn on the morning of the sixth day, Umak broke the spears and shattered the stone spearheads that had ended the white bear's life. With the remains of the projectile points in his bare hands—and all the members of the band following except Naya, Iana, and the baby—he went naked from camp to the place where he had killed the animal. He shouted away ravens and carrion-eating birds that were still feeding upon the skull of the great carnivore that now lay brainless and staring at the sky out of empty eye sockets.

Umak stood facing the rising sun. With arms upraised, he spoke to honor the life of the bear, then threw the shattered spearheads in all directions and asked the forces of Creation to release the bear's spirit to join its ancestors.

This done, without another word, he walked back to the encampment and strode to the hut of blood.

"Come!" he called. "Iana, woman of Grek, the spirit of the great white bear has gone to walk with its ancestors. It is time for you to bring the new son of Old Lion into the light of day!"

She came, blinking proudly, with her tiny boy in her arms, and her body clothed in new garments that the women and girls had sewn for her.

Grek beamed. His head was held high, and his grizzled hair was combed for a change. With Tankh, Chuk, and Yona at his side, his expression was one of love and pride.

A soft, gentle wind was rising with the new day. All things seemed to Torka at equilibrium with the People. He and Lonit stood close. Dak and Swan held hands. Larani smiled, holding Kharn, and did not flinch when the boy touched her scars; they fascinated him. Even Simu was not glowering as he stood with Summer Moon. Soon he, too, might have a new son.

Umak remained standing before the hut of blood. "Naya!" he called. "Woman of Umak, come forth and receive this gift of honor, not only from your man but from the shaman, who would praise the healing ways of one who has brought forth new life from another!"

A murmuring of appreciation rippled through the band. Torka nodded in approval. Not even Simu could possibly argue against Naya's being rewarded now. The girl had proved her worth and deserved her moment of recognition.

"Naya! Come out, my Naya!" Umak called again.

But the moments passed, and only silence came from the hut of blood until, at last, Umak called for his woman to come out again and a single word rang through the encampment.

"No!"

Iana reentered the hut of blood with her newborn son in her arms and worry on her face. "Naya, you must come out!"

The granddaughter of Grek sat with her knees drawn up to her chin and her arms wrapped about her knees. "I have a headache."

"Umak is Shaman. He will rid you of your headache."

"No. He will make it worse. Just looking at him makes it worse!"

"What are you saying? Umak is no stranger to you. He has risked his life to kill the bear. This is a great honor."

"I never asked him to kill it," Naya responded. "I do not want his gift! Tell him to give it to Honee! She is fat! She needs a whole bearskin for herself!"

Iana's mouth tightened over her teeth. "Honee has been as a mother to you since you came to the fire circle of Umak. That is no way to talk about her!" She stopped as insight flared. Honee *had* been behaving toward Naya as a mother.

It was beginning to make sense to Iana now. "Naya, you and Umak *have* joined as man and woman, haven't you?"

The girl's silence was answer enough.

Iana went to Naya and knelt beside her. "This cannot be. You must go to him. You must accept his gift. You must accept *him*! He loves you, Naya. You must not shame him before the band. If not for his sake, for your own!"

Naya's eyes were enormous. Even in the gloom of the hut, her face was deathly white. "He will hurt me! He will make me bleed! He will fill me and fill me, and I will explode and die! Like in the dream! Like you almost died, with your baby stuck inside you! I do not want to die, Iana! I do not want him inside me!"

As Iana held her newborn in the curl of one arm, she encircled Naya in the other, listening with revulsion and pity as the girl slowly told her about the nightmare—of the horror and blood, of death and endless pain.

"Dream or no dream, Naya, you cannot avoid Umak forever," Iana said gently.

"Why not? Larani has not been forced to take a man!"

"Only because Torka has a gentle heart."

Naya scowled. "Not toward me he hasn't!"

"Were it not for Torka, you would not be here talking to me now. And as for your fear of mating and childbirth, your nightmare is only that, Naya. Look at me: I have been with many men in my time—some have been cruel and have brought me pain, while others, like Grek, have been tender and caring. I have given birth to many children. As with the men who have lain with me, some births have been better than others. But I have never exploded, except in passion . . . and despite the pain and blood of childbirth, I have lived a very long time!" She looked down lovingly at the infant as it suckled fitfully at her heated breast. "Long enough to give life to this little one. It will make Grek feel strong and young again."

"And what of you?" Naya asked irritably. "Has this baby made you feel strong and young again? You look sick to me, Iana! And your milk smells odd—no doubt from your fever! This baby would have killed you had I not been able to turn it and guide it out!"

Iana sighed and shook her head. "Something will kill us all sooner or later, Naya. That is the one thing in our lives that *is* certain."

4

When the horses broke through tall stands of budding fireweed, Manaravak took after them. Briefly—so briefly that the thought was gone before he was even half aware of it—he thought of Larani: of long, lean limbs and fine, firm breasts, of hair as black and shining as the thick bristling mane of a healthy mare. Larani, like the fireweed, was a wonder to behold, despite her scars . . . or because of them?

He sent his spear flying after the horses. It was only a matter of time before one of the striped mares fell back. Wheezing, she circled and fought for life and breath, only to go to her knees several times before he was able to wade across a narrow stream and walk right up to her.

He drew his skinning dagger and slit her throat. She died quietly, almost gratefully, while he knelt beside her, stroking her flank and sucking blood from an open vein as he thanked her for her life.

When the vein collapsed, he leaned back, absently wiping blood from his face with the backs of his fingers. He looked around and recognized the old, stony hills and gravel-bottomed little stream along which he and Naya had once frolicked like children . . . and then not like children at all. A strange mix of emotions swept through him: happiness, sadness, nostalgia, and loss. He was actually glad when Demmi came across the stream and angrily kicked water at him.

"What is the matter with you? What will we do with so much meat? We are traveling, Manaravak, not settling into a winter camp."

Manaravak eyed the dead horse thoughtfully. "We have been traveling long. We have hunted little and eaten less. I am hungry. I could eat this horse myself! Besides, my sister looks tired. Rest your muscles and bones for a few days, eat. Maybe then Demmi will not be as quick to snap as a badger being taken from a snare!"

Demmi knew that he was worried about her, and she appreciated his concern. Although she did not want to admit to being tired, she knew he was right. They had been living off the light, almost bloodless meat of ptarmigan and squirrels. The rich, sweet meat of the horse was welcome.

"All right, but we will not stay in this place too long," she said.

He shrugged and looked at her through lowered lids. "There has been neither sign nor sound of wanawut, Demmi."

She shivered at the hated name. "No. Still . . . we will not linger here any longer than necessary to appease the life spirit of your kill and the traditions of our ancestors."

Together they feasted upon the eyes, tongue, and liver before Demmi lay down to sleep.

When she awoke, Manaravak was busy butchering the mare's carcass.

"A fine hide this horse has," he said, smoothing the skin appreciatively with his palms. It was a soft, tawny brown, with pale, smoky-looking black stripes running through it. "I will flesh this hide and bring it to Umak, to show him that I would be his brother once more!"

The words soothed Demmi. She closed her eyes and went back to sleep, only to dream of Naya walking sulkily across the tundra in a horsehide dress. With a start, she was awake again, staring ahead at Manaravak as he busied himself scraping the flesh from the skin. "Naya had a dress of horsehide," she reminded him.

He kept on working. "No, coltskin. It was ruined by Daughter of the Sky. With this fine, good hide she can make another. She will smile at this man when she sees it, I think."

Demmi propped herself onto an elbow. "Manaravak! You said the hide was for Umak!"

He looked at her with a spark of humor in his eyes. "For Umak, yes! But if Naya smiles at this hide that I will give to my brother, Umak will give it to her. Then Manaravak will smile, too!"

She shook her head with open disapproval. "You have lived with wanawut, and you have lived with men, Manaravak. Why, then, are you thinking like a fox?"

Demmi and Manaravak slept the sleep of the exhausted and the well fed. Sometime after dawn, the wind carried sounds that should have roused their sense of danger, but it was the nickering of a colt that finally awakened them. To their mutual distress, they watched the confused, frightened adolescent nuzzling the mutilated remains of its mother. Demmi slowly reached for her spear.

Manaravak stayed her hand. "What are you doing?"

"It will starve and become prey for wolves if we don't kill it."

"Better wolves than us. Wolves will be hungry. We have enough meat. Besides, it looks to be well past the age of suckling. The herd will return for it." He cocked his head and appraised the colt. Memories made him smile. "When I was a boy, I once rode a caribou. Did I ever tell you about that, Demmi? It was long ago, when I was a wanawut."

She made a face of revulsion. "You were never a wanawut!"

"I was, long ago."

"And why would a wanawut ride a caribou?"

"To kill it! To leap upon its back as the lion leaps. I have never forgotten the way it felt. To feel the caribou between my thighs, warm, moving, carrying me forward. To sit so high and hold tight to an antler and race into the wind . . . imagine riding on the back of a horse!"

"Impossible!"

"No! If men can walk with dogs and train them to carry loads, why could men not ride horses or train them to carry loads, too? Horses could carry more!"

The colt skittered off. Manaravak stared after it. It would not be a good thing to kill the colt. Demmi always was too fast to reach for her weapons. She should not have raised her staves to the wanawut in the cave. Just as poor Nantu's scream of terror had cost him his head, it was Demmi's irrational fear of the wanawut that had provoked their attack.

He ground his teeth. By now they would be finished mourning their slain female and would be hunting again. But would they be hunting beast or man, food or vengeance? He knew the answer. The wanawut had long and unforgiving memories. He would not mention this to Demmi. And he resolved not to tell her that she was right to believe that the wanawut might be following.

"Stand aside!" demanded Umak.

"I tell you, Umak," Swan said, blocking her brother's passage into the hut of blood as nearly everyone in the band gathered to watch. "Naya is still not feeling well enough to come out."

"Then I will go in and get her!" the shaman threatened. "She's been in there for three days!"

Honee gasped. "No man may enter the hut of blood! It has always been forbidden!"

Simu growled, "Honee is right. It has been said among my people that when a man enters the hut of blood, the woman spirits that live inside attack him. They take hold of his man sacks and squeeze them until they shrivel. They grab his man bone and suck the juice right out of it, then they break it and twist it so that it remains limp forever! I would not go in there if I were you, Umak. And most certainly I would not go in for *her*."

"One time too many has Old Lion heard Simu speak against Little Girl! Now I will—"

"Be still, Grek." Torka's voice framed a clear warning. "I am headman. I will deal with this."

"No need, Father," Umak said. "If Simu quakes in fear of woman spirits, we must be sympathetic. As he keeps reminding us, the ways of his ancestors are different from ours. As for me, I have no fear of woman spirits. If Naya is so sick that she cannot come to me, then I will go to her."

Lonit's voice, soft and caring, quivered a little with dread: "Wait, my son. There is no need for risk! And there is no need for hostility between you and Simu. Iana has assured us all that in a day or so Naya will be well again. It is just that without a full supply of her healing leaves and roots and berries, she is at a disadvantage to offer cures to any of us, including herself."

"Don't tell me. . . ." Umak addressed his mother in a tone acidic with sarcasm. "My Naya has a *headache*?"

"Why, yes," replied Lonit, surprised. "She does."

With a snarl the shaman stalked forward to the small hut and swept the door skin aside. Making a small compromise lest he offend the traditions of Simu, he stood poised in the entranceway, looking at Naya.

"Well, I see that Medicine Woman is still alive," he said with unmistakable irritation. "How is your headache . . . after all these many days?"

Umak did not miss the fact that Iana had to force Naya to get to her feet.

"Go to him!" the woman hissed, and for a moment Umak was taken aback by Iana's pallor and by the gray-blue shadows beneath her eyes.

He stared at her with concern. "Your fever is still with you."

"It will pass." She smiled to assuage his worry. "Do not look so concerned, Shaman. It is not as though this were the first infant that ever came out of my body! Here, take Naya away. She has given too much of herself to me. It is time for her to do the same for you."

His face flushed red with shame. How could Naya have told the woman of Grek that he had yet to take her? What must Iana think of him! What would everyone in the band think of him! What would Simu have to say if he knew?

Suddenly furious, he exhaled a wordless curse at Naya. "Come!" he demanded with a shout, and as Iana gently shoved the girl forward he took her roughly by the hand.

"Umak . . ." Iana's tone was soft, entreating. "Ask Naya to tell you of her dream."

"Dream?" He could not think through his anger. "I am Shaman! In the hut of Umak, it is I who have the dreams!"

Without giving her a chance to comb her hair, straighten her garments, or put on her moccasins, he jerked Naya into the light of day.

She did not speak. She walked with her head down, her hair falling in unplaited disarray over her back to below her hips, and her bare feet scuffing dejectedly.

The people of the band had the courtesy to look away. Only Grek stared a moment too long, frowning and mumbling to himself with worry.

Umak lengthened his stride. When Naya balked, he pulled her on, and in a moment he was escorting her small, rigid figure inside.

Across the hide-covered floor was the skin of the great white bear.

She stared at it, head down, her hands folded at her throat. Even in the dull shadows of the unlighted interior, the white fur glistened like snow with the radiance of dawn sheening upon it.

They were alone in the hut. Honee had arranged to be away with the children. She had aired the bed furs and laid the bearskin over them, hair-side up.

Umak stood close at Naya's back and placed his hands lightly upon her shoulders. "Behold Umak's gift for his new woman! Umak has killed this great white bear so that Naya might take pleasure in its life . . . and so that Umak and Naya might take pleasure on it together. It has been waiting for you, Naya, as has *this*."

He turned her around with one strong hand, and with one deft movement of the other, he freed his second gift and displayed it proudly. He stood tall and bold. He was big and growing bigger.

Her eyes went wide. Her expression was fearful, incredulous, her face unnaturally pale amid the wild black fall of her hair. It occurred to Umak that he had rarely seen her hair unplaited. Somehow it was more beautiful unadorned. He touched it. His fingers entwined themselves in it, combed downward to where the strands ended upon her thighs.

"The time has come for you to stop fearing me, Naya. I am a man. I have the needs of a man. You are my woman. I *will* have you. *Now!*" His hands took hers, drew them forward, and placed them around his organ. He swelled with pleasure and moved for her until her back went as straight as a spear shaft. Her fingers stiffened and practically curled backward to her wrists to be away from him. Her eyes rolled up, and then she collapsed onto the bearskin in a dead faint.

Anger flared within Umak, then concern. He knelt beside her. "Naya! I did not mean to frighten you! You must know that I would never hurt you!"

Her breathing was fast and shallow. He brushed aside her hair and loosed the shoulder ties that secured her dress. In a moment she was naked. He caught his breath at so much beauty, and then he snarled, for there, lying between her breasts, was Manaravak's talisman, Manaravak's helping spirit! In a sudden fury he snatched it into his fist and ripped the thong from her neck. He knew that he had hurt her. He did not care.

She cried out as pain roused consciousness. Her eyes were wide with terror as he held the talisman before her face.

"Is this why your thighs are closed to me and your head aches whenever I come near? Because you wait for him? He is *dead*, Naya! You are *my* woman now. *Mine!* And yet you wear his talisman! It was not rape, was it? No! I see that now, as I *did* see it then. The two of you together, behind my back—and not only once I'd wager. And you loving it every time, and wanting it, like *this!*"

He hurled the talisman and broken thong across the hut. All feelings of compassion gone, he smothered her scream with a kiss that cut her mouth. He tasted blood and liked it. Engorged with rage and lust, he was huge now, larger than he had ever been or ever thought he could be. Her hands beat at his shoulders. He felt the sting of her scratches. She arched upward in a vain attempt to free herself of him. He caught her wrists and pressed them down and kept on kissing her until she could not breathe. He felt her yielding, sobbing, losing strength as he forced her wide, positioned himself, and then rammed deep and hard, even though he knew that she was not ready to accept him. He wanted to hurt her, to make her pay for his shame, for all the times that she had professed fear of him when, in fact, she was rejecting him out of desire for his brother.

He knew he was raping her. She deserved no more from him. He thrust once, twice. She was very small, very tight for one who had opened herself to his brother only the forces of Creation knew how many times! He was buried deep, still swelling, throbbing, filling every portion of her until release came—wrenching him to his very spirit, burning, driving him deeper and deeper until he collapsed upon her . . . still ejaculating and, impossibly, still swelling . . . locked tightly within her as though, somehow, her body had melded to his organ and would not—or could not—release him.

The nightmare! For Naya it was the nightmare come true—the pain, the horror of her body being twisted, pulled, sundered, and smashed and filled until she could no longer breathe. And all the time the monster was at her, the doll, the hideous faceless doll, hurting her, becoming one with her.

And now, still joined to her, he slept. She wept at the betrayal of it.

With his arms locked tightly around her, she cried herself to sleep.

A golden aurora was pulsing against the thin caul of the early-summer night when Umak was at last awakened by Naya's moaning.

Reason and regret walked his mind now . . . and more shame than he had ever felt from her denial of him. He withdrew from her slowly, knowing from her reaction that he had hurt her badly even before he caught the scent of blood on the bearskin beneath him.

He drew her close. Even if she had lain willingly with Manaravak, she had not deserved this from him. "Forgive me, Naya," he whispered as he tenderly stroked her into wakefulness.

She began to shiver—against the cold, in fear of him, and with revulsion of what he had done to her. He drew the bearskin over them. There was a welt on her neck now where he had ripped away the talisman, encircling her throat like a necklet. His fingers traced it.

She winced and began to cry. "He is dead now, truly dead. You broke the thong! You have thrown his helping spirit away! I would have worn an amulet for you, had you been lost. I would have worn it even if you were not my man. I would have worn a talisman for you and for poor Nantu and for Eneela, too, if someone had made one for them!"

He lay still, not knowing what to say, and then decided that truth was best. He spoke of his jealousy and of his love for his twin. He told her that he did not know how, but that it was possible to ache for the return of a beloved brother and to yearn for his death at the same time. He spoke to her quietly of gentle things that had nothing to do with a man and a woman lying together on a bearskin—but of life within the band, of childhood memories, of times of endless light and of endless dark, of star showers that flamed across the sky like embers thrown to earth out of the spirit world, of auroras that seemed to catch the stars in the vast black net of the night, of sunrises and sunsets . . . and of his love for her, regardless of what had happened between them upon this skin of the great white bear.

"It will never be like this again between us, Naya. No matter what has happened before, from this moment we begin our lives. The next time that we join together, it will be for the first time—only when you are unafraid and willing in my arms, and then, for both of us it will be magic. It *will*—I swear it!"

She seemed to relax a little. He drew her closer, and this time when she shivered, he rocked her, holding her more gently than before. He spoke on, and gradually his words took them both into the shallows of sleep as, on the skin of the great white bear, they lay close in each other's arms, and wrapped in the magic of Umak's tender words, although their bodies were not joined, they were one at last.

5

Manaravak, laughing, trotted back and forth. Hidden within the scent of the mare, he was nickering and snorting, whinnying and stomping his legs, and to Demmi's amazement, the colt was following him—walking when he walked, circling when he circled, stopping when he stopped.

"I realize that the herd has not returned for this colt, Manaravak," she said, "but you will never make a mother for a horse!"

"No?" He laughed again, deeply, good-naturedly. "The time spent in this camp has restored your sense of humor. You look strong and ready to travel. It is time for us to move on, Sister! You watch! This colt will follow. Three sleeps from now this colt will name me Brother just as you do!"

"But there is still so much meat left uneaten!"

"We *must* leave it, Demmi!" All traces of humor were suddenly gone from his voice. "The horses have not returned for good reason, and this colt stays near in fear of more dangerous carnivores than the son and daughter of Torka."

She sat very straight. "Wanawut!"

"I have not wanted to speak of it until I was sure, but I feel them behind us. After what you have done, it would be best if we set our feet in the tracks of our people. The mammoth walks ahead of us. It is time for us to follow."

Torka sat beside the Lake of Watered Blood with his bludgeon across his thighs and his carving blade loose in his right hand as he tried to decide how best to cut the image of this awesome body of water onto the timeworn piece of whalebone. There was hardly a space that was not incised with pictographs . . . soon there would not be room enough to make another mark. His brow settled into an introspective frown. He did not like the implications of this and could not help but wonder if his life or the life of the People might come to an end when there was no space for future inscriptions upon the bludgeon.

He scanned the northern waters. He had seen many a

lake in his time, but never one like this. There were fish as big as mammoth—fish that blew water into the sky. No fish should be that big. Staring at his bludgeon, Torka recalled that it was carved out of the broken rib of just such a fish, whose carcass he had discovered upon the vast steppelands beyond the Sea of Ice. He had never been able to understand how so huge a fish had come to die upon the land or how its bones had turned to stone. It had all seemed like magic, so he had taken up the piece of rib and had carried it across a lifetime, to the shores of this great heaving lake.

He liked the lake less now than when he had first seen it. Even now, when the sun never left the sky, there were huge, drifting plates of ice and bergs as big as mountains. The water surged over the rocky shore and headlands, and the ice was strange and restless. He did not like the ever-present smell of salt. The salt formed a residue of white upon the huts of the People and everything else that was left outside for any length of time.

Nevertheless, he had to admit that hunting was good and his people seemed happy. Whatever had happened between Naya and Umak seemed to have settled something between them. The girl was deferential to the shaman now, and although more quiet than usual, she seemed relaxed and comfortable in the presence of her man. The women worked fine, albeit unfamiliar skins, prepared sinew, pounded blubber, and rendered fat into oil for their lamps. The drying frames sagged under the weight of gutted water birds, fine filets of Arctic char, and walrus steaks. It *was* a good camp.

His only real regret was Larani. What a proud, valiant woman she was! He should have forced her to accept his offer. Short of that, he could at least have insisted that young Tankh begin to gather new-woman gifts for her. But that had seemed a travesty—too much good woman for a boy, even if Tankh had been willing.

Troubled again, Torka stared out to sea. The meat of the animals that abounded here was strange to his taste and so easy to obtain that it made him edgy. The walrus bellowed and bawled but rarely moved away when the hunters strode in to make their kills.

Torka watched a gyrfalcon as it shrieked above him on wings that cut through the air as silently as feathered blades. The bird led Torka's eyes across the open ocean to an eternally clouded horizon. What lay beneath those clouds? he wondered with deep trepidation. If there was a far shore, he could not see it. When the wind blew from the north, it carried the scent of ice—*only* ice. Even now, in the time of endless light, the north wind remained cold, as though it blew out of the land where the world of men ended and the world of spirits began. The thought made him restless. What would winter be like here?

His hand tightened on his bludgeon. It was time to leave this camp! Umak and Dak would not approve, but Simu openly hungered for big game that did not taste of fish. Grek had enough supplies of pounded fat to keep his gums soothed and content. The pups were big now, and growing fat; a long haul inland into more wind-protected country would do them good. But what of Iana and the baby? The woman of Grek remained feverish. The infant was too sickly to be subjected to a long trek across the camp, let alone across the country.

Torka exhaled his frustration. How he loathed this north country! And where was the mammoth? His luck had always lain in the shadow of Life Giver! If the mammoth did not live in the land, how long could he or his people hope to survive in it?

"Torka!" He turned at Yona's summons. "Come quickly!" sobbed the child. "Please! Iana's new baby is dead!"

The People kept a deathwatch over Iana's baby for five days. Umak danced the dances that might summon its spirit back from the spirit world, implored it to return to its people, and assured it that it was loved and wanted, that its mother's breasts would ache without its little mouth to suckle them.

But Iana's breasts already ached. Delirious, she was mercifully unaware that they had swelled to three times their normal size or that her nipples had cracked and now produced bloodied pus in place of milk, or that the flow that came from her grotesquely distended womb was no longer clotted but free flowing and as foul to the nostrils as the milk upon which she had been trying to nourish her newborn child.

The woman drifted in and out of consciousness. In her delirium she relived her youth, speaking to her first man, her children. When she woke, she asked for Tankh and Chuk and told them to look after Grek and Yona.

Iana also spoke softly to Naya, exhorting her to be a

woman of courage and to bear children lest she find herself
old, unloved, and childless.

When Grek came to his woman's side, Iana tried to talk,
but her weariness was absolute. Spirit Sucker was with her,
and her spirit became enmeshed with his.

And so the shaman danced for Iana, too. He raised magic
smokes on behalf of the wandering life spirits of Iana and her
newborn son while Naya wept and Grek sat alone, refusing to
be comforted. He rocked himself and mumbled like an old
man whose spirit wished to leave this world and follow his
woman and infant into the realm of the dead, where they
might walk the wind together forever.

On a bleak, windy day Iana and her newborn son were
placed upon a low, rocky headland to look upon the sky
forever. When the last of the ceremonial songs were sung,
the People made their way in solemn procession back to
camp. Only old Grek hung back to sit beside the fur-covered
mounds of his woman and child while the restless waters of
the Lake of Watered Blood surged in and out and lapped
higher and higher at the shore.

All day Grek stayed with the bodies, and his people
mourned in silence. The wind rose and wailed, whisking
gravel into the air and sending it flying across the land like
singing insects. That night the old man sat by his woman and
child in the bitter wind and the light of the midnight sun.
Tankh, Chuk, and Yona went out to him, but only Yona came
back, and she was screaming.

"The water has risen to take our mother and brother!"

Disbelieving, the People rushed from their encampment
in time to see Grek and his boys wading against the pull of a
wind-driven tidal surge that would have swept the old man
away along with the bodies of his woman and newborn son
had Tankh and Chuk not held him fast. Never before had the
People witnessed such a thing.

"Let me go!" bellowed Bison Man. "Let me follow!"

But his sons would not let go, and in the end, Grek,
Lion no more, was an ancient, exhausted, grief-stricken hunter
who no longer had the strength to resist the pull of the sea or
the strong arms of his sons.

"The time of mourning is over. We must leave this
camp," said Torka. "We will go back across the barrens,

south and then east to the edge of the drowned land in search of big game, our totem, and our luck."

Simu's face split in a broad, expansive smile. "I hear good sense from your mouth again at last, Torka!" he proclaimed, then commanded Summer Moon and Larani to prepare for traveling at once.

"Wait!" Umak said. "I do not understand. There has been sadness here, yes, but this camp has been a good one. We have meat and provisions enough to see us through the worst of winters. Why leave it?"

"I can see nothing good in this country, Umak," replied Torka.

Umak's brows came together across the bridge of his nose. His father's words struck him as a personal insult. "I am Shaman, and I can see nothing bad in it! There is meat for the taking, and fine pelts, and fat and—"

"Two of our number have died in this place, my son. The lake has risen to take them into itself. This is bad enough for me."

"And now we know why these waters taste and smell like blood!" injected Simu with a shudder. "I haven't liked the looks or the stink of this place from the start."

Umak felt the stirrings of anger. "You haven't liked anything in so many moons that I've lost track of when you started your eternal complaining!"

Torka raised a hand. "We must go to the east, in search of game fit for men of the open steppe."

"Yes!" Simu cried jubilantly. "Meat with hair and hooves! Meat with legs, not fins! Man meat! Not meat that barks at us like our dogs!"

Standing close by, Dak placed an arm protectively around Swan's shoulder as he looked at Simu dubiously. "There was little enough meat in the barrens before, Father. Why lead our women and children out of a camp full of meat on the assumption that we will find it now?"

"Where we find Life Giver, we will find meat," said Torka coolly. "It has always been so. It will be so again. We should not have come so far north. But now the sun is high. Like Larani, the land that lies behind us has had a chance to heal. Like Larani, it will be new again."

The unscarred half of Larani's face flushed at the unexpected compliment.

Umak was too upset to notice. "And if it is not?" he pressed.

"Bah!" declared Simu. "We will leave caches of food and supplies behind us. If things do not work out for us, we can always come back!"

"No," said Torka. "We will never come back. A land that is not fit for mammoth is not fit for men. We will disband this camp and make ready to walk to the east."

Umak was trembling in his effort to control his anger as he stood his ground and said in a hostile voice, "Be careful, Father. Someday you may lead us all off the edge of the world in your quest for the sun!"

◆━━━━━━◆

6

◆━━━━━━◆

The People broke camp and moved on. No one looked back except Umak. In this far land by the Lake of Watered Blood, his prophecy had come to pass: Hunting had been good, there was food for all, and Naya had truly become his at last. Thus was he loath to leave. Again and again he called upon the Seeing Wind to grant him visions of what lay ahead, but the only wind that touched him was the north wind. He turned back to linger along the shore of the great lake. As the barking animals of the sea watched him, he placed offerings of gratitude to the spirits of this special place and beseeched the forces of Creation and the Seeing Wind to grant him a sign that would convince Torka to stay. But there was nothing. The north wind blew hard at his back, as though driving him on. Unhappily, Umak was forced to concede that perhaps this was the only sign he was going to get. And if this was the case, then Torka was right: Maybe it was time to move on.

The dogs dragged fully loaded sledges, and the children wore back rolls packed tight with their belongings. The women walked in silence, bent almost double under fully loaded pack frames, and the heavy leather brow band that helped to keep the weight of Naya's pack from shifting forward cut into her skin.

Plodding along beside her, Honee noted her discomfort.

"You didn't line your brow strap with buckskin padding! Did you never have to carry a fully loaded pack frame when you walked with Grek?"

Naya sighed. "Never."

Honee clucked her tongue. "It is a woman's pride to know that she can ease the burdens of her man. Grek has not done well to spare you this pride, Naya. Your brow would have been callused by now, and your load would have seemed lighter to you."

Naya turned to see her grandfather trudging along with Yona and his boys beside him. He looked so old! So bent! He was an ancient, humpbacked, grizzle-haired bull, who would live only as long as his teeth. And Naya knew that his teeth had begun to die long ago. Tears stung her eyes, and her heart ached for him and for herself. What a silly, self-centered child she had been! How could she have assumed that she was the center of Grek's life? Her grandfather had loved and spoiled her, yes, but without Iana, Grek had lost all will to live. Nothing that Naya had been able to say or do had given it back to him. Now that Iana and the infant were dead, Naya was not convinced that it was not her fault. What had gone wrong? She had done no more or less than Demmi had done on that snowy day when she had come stalking into the hut of blood, shaking snow from her ruff and cleansing her hands before starting to deliver Snow Eater's pups.

If only she had been more careful about maintaining the contents of her medicine bag, she would have had the necessary leaves, roots, and dried thousand-leaf to stop Iana's bleeding and cool the heat of her fever. But instead of searching these things out, she had been more concerned about her dwindling supply of red berries. Sadly, because she had selfishly kept most of them for her own use, there had not even been one of them left for Iana. She had failed miserably in her responsibilities as a medicine woman.

"Iana was right in all of the things she used to say about me," Naya admitted quietly to Honee. "If Iana were here, I would tell her that I will try to be a better woman from now on—a caring and thoughtful and obedient woman."

Honee paused and looked at her. "You do not have to tell her that, dear one. She knows."

"How can she know?"

Honee turned back to her rummaging. "Her spirit walks the wind, doesn't it? And the wind is following us. Even as we speak I am sure that she is with us! And she is smiling at you, Naya. You did your best for her. And in the last few days you have been all that you say you wish to be." Honee reached into a pouch at her waist and smiled at Naya. "I almost forgot. I found it underneath the bed skins when I was straightening up the pit hut a few sleeps ago. I meant to give it to you long before now. It is yours, isn't it?"

Naya stared as her fire sister rose and handed her Manaravak's talisman. Deep within her heart a voice cried out to her: *Throw it away! Throw it away!* But she did not. Her fingers curled around it. "Why, yes! It *is* mine. Thank you, Honee. But do not mention it to Umak. Manaravak made it for me a very long time ago, and I have chosen not to wear it lest it remind Umak of his brother and make him sad."

Endless days of light spread out before the travelers as they trekked inland across the barrens. Under a bright sun and in a strong steady wind, Summer Moon went into labor. A temporary camp was made, but the baby was born so easily and quickly that not even half the lean-tos were up before its cries of life were heard.

Naya stood by in silence, her healing skills uncalled for and unneeded as Honee nudged her meaningfully.

"You see?" asked the big woman. "Birth is not always a terrible thing. When you become a mother, you may deliver with no trouble at all!"

Three days later, at Summer Moon's insistence, the band made ready to move on. But Grek sat down upon his traveling pack and would not get up.

"This man is tired, old, and useless. This man will walk the world of men no more."

"No!" Chuk was clearly devastated by his father's words.

"Get up, Old Lion!" demanded Tankh. "Who will hunt for Yona if you set aside your spears forever?"

Grek looked up briefly, then stared at his feet again. "You will hunt for Yona. You are man enough. I am tired . . . tired of being a man at all."

Silence fell upon the travelers.

Then the daughter of Simu walked to the old man, slung off her pack, and seated herself beside him.

"I will stay with this old man," Larani proclaimed.

"Go away," Grek said through the wind-wafted tangles of his hair.

"I will not go away!" she insisted, looking unflinchingly at the incredulous faces of her people. "I, too, am tired. I, too, am of little use to this people. Go. Leave us. Grek and Larani will walk the wind forever."

An exhalation of shock and dismay went out of every mouth.

Torka, understanding her motives, liked and admired what he saw.

Simu appraised his daughter suspiciously. "What is this, Larani?"

"You are eager for me to be mated, aren't you? Well, the moment has finally come! As Swan was allowed to name the man of her choice, I will now do the same. I choose Grek."

The old man raised his head. "I do not choose you!"

"But you must. You have no woman. In this band, Torka has said that every woman must be mated, and every man must do his share to increase the number of the People. Torka has been kind and patient with me, but now I am well enough to see that I have been selfish. I cannot allow the men of this band to covet my 'beauty' forever, and I will not allow myself to remain a burden to my brother when it is not necessary. I *must* take a man or forfeit my right to live within this band."

Grek stared at her as though she had lost her mind. "Torka offered to take you to his fire circle. Take *him*."

Larani shrugged. "Torka has a woman."

Lonit was clearly distraught. "For the good of the band, I would—"

Torka elbowed her to silence. "I do not ask for a woman twice! Larani has missed her chance with me!" he said sternly, doing his best not to smile, while ignoring the befuddled expression upon his beloved Lonit's face.

"Then take my son Tankh!" insisted Grek angrily. "He has no woman!"

Larani looked at Grek and smiled sweetly. "This I would do, but Tankh has no appreciation for older women . . . or for 'interesting'-looking women like me. In time the eldest son of Grek will smile upon one of the younger girls—Li, Uni, or Yona—won't you, Tankh?"

The youth said nothing, but he looked at Larani with a tremulous smile of relief.

"Stay as you will," the old man snarled, "but this man will not be your man! Grek is not the fool you think he is, girl. Grek will not walk on with the band out of concern for you!"

Larani folded her hands upon her lap. "Nevertheless, I will stay."

"So be it, then," said Torka, and led his people on. He refused to listen to the weeping of the women and children or to Dak's arguments against the abandonment.

The headman walked with Umak, gradually drawing him away from the others as he spoke quietly, glad to have a mutual concern that would bring them close again. Umak was in a sullen and unforgiving mood, but as Torka continued to speak, Umak raised a telling brow and listened approvingly for the first time in many days. But then Lonit came up, took hold of Torka's arm, and actually shouted at him.

"Torka, we cannot do this! We must go back for them!"

"Father, you can't just leave them!" Swan was devastated as she walked with Dak. Kharn trudged along beside his father, proudly carrying his own pack frame.

"Larani is a woman with no man to speak for her," Torka explained evenly. "She has the right to speak for herself—unless, of course, her father were to forbid it." He stopped abruptly, and all of his people and the dogs of the band stopped with him. "Do you forbid it, Simu?"

Simu looked like a cornered animal as Summer Moon and Uni gazed at him hopefully. "I . . . no . . . I cannot forbid it! Larani was right. If no man will mate her, what good is she to the band? None, I say! Bah! It is a clever game that you and Larani play, Torka. I am onto both of you. She will follow soon enough with that toothless Old Lion ambling along at her side, growling to himself."

"But what if she does not? What if *he* does not?" exclaimed a tearful Naya.

Simu's face twisted with pain and then with anger and hatred. He was glaring at Naya now, causing her to shrivel with fear of him. "Your grandfather is useless. What he does is no concern of mine! As long as we put the Lake of Watered Blood and the barrens far behind us, I will walk easy! If Larani wishes to stake her own worthless life on the virtue of what is left of an old man's pride, what do you expect me to do? She's been as good as dead since Daughter of the Sky picked her up and threw her in the river—and all because of you!"

Tears stung Naya's eyes. "I did not mean to—"

"Bah! What's done is done. There's no use slobbering about it!"

"You might at least *pretend* to care about Larani." Dak's voice was heavy with disgust, his eyes hard with accusation. "But no matter. If there is no sign of my sister and the old man by the time we settle in for sleep, I will go back for them. I am sorry to go against your will, Torka."

"And I will go with you!" Swan proclaimed as she took a step closer to Dak. She looked at her father with a touching mixture of indignation and apology. "Larani has been as a sister to me since we were babies. I am sorry, Father, but I cannot just walk off and leave her."

Torka shook his head at them. "How righteous you are. But what about them? Is Simu the only man who can dare to face an unpleasant situation with honesty?"

Thinking himself vindicated, Simu stood taller. "It is no easy thing," he agreed.

"No . . ." said Torka. "It is no easy thing, but Larani saw it at once. Grek is broken and near the end of his days. For want of the very pride of which Simu speaks, he must be given cause to want to live again and follow on his own, or we might as well leave him behind."

"But if he has truly lost the will to live, Larani's life is at risk as long as she stays with him," said Dak.

"Yes," Torka affirmed. "It is."

Lonit was indignant. "I do not understand you, Torka. Grek may refuse to eat or drink until he grows too weak to lift a spear. If danger threatens, even if he wanted to help Larani, he will not have the strength."

"Danger *will* threaten," Umak predicted. "It will threaten soon, before the old man has a chance to lose what vigor he has left. Of this you can be sure."

"How?" asked Jhon with awe. "Has the Seeing Wind spoken to you again?"

A conspiratorial look passed between Torka and Umak. "Something even better has spoken to me," replied the shaman, and for the first time since leaving the Lake of Watered Blood, he laughed with pure delight. "Torka has told me of his plan!"

In the skins of fur seals and walrus, Torka led Umak, Dak, and the boys in a wide circle until they began to close on Grek and Larani.

With Simu back in camp guarding the women, children, and dogs, the other hunters advanced on Grek with infinite caution, crawling, keeping their distance—close enough to be seen but not identified. Their movement was guaranteed to drive the old hunter mad with curiosity. They watched him: His head was up, scanning the area. Larani was on her feet, looking tense and nervous.

On Torka's signal—a fine imitation of a frightened ground squirrel—the hunters responded with the snarls and growls that would bespeak a brief, savage feeding frenzy. Then they were silent, absolutely silent.

Grek stiffened, alert to danger but evidently still telling himself that he did not care enough about life to be threatened by its alternative.

Torka did another ground-squirrel imitation. Umak answered with the menacing howl of a hungry wolf.

Larani froze, hands at her sides, turning lightly on her feet, her head raised. She was speaking to Grek, imploring, then clearly berating. His posture was stiffer than before, and something about the way he held his shoulders told the hunters that he was listening to the young woman.

No one moved. Then Umak loosed another howl. Torka, Dak, and the boys set up an impressive chorus of snarls and growls that had Grek leaping to his feet just as Larani, despairing of protection, made a grab for one of his spears. The old man roared at her in protest and shook the fist that held the spear in her face.

Torka smiled. His ruse had worked. He was so filled with satisfaction that he did not notice the howls that came from too far away to have originated with Umak and Dak or any of the boys.

Umak and Dak were lounging and catching their breath on hastily rolled seal and walrus skins, and the boys hurriedly assumed positions of feigned ease. Not long after, old Grek came stalking into camp with Larani trailing at a respectful distance.

"Why do you all stare?" he demanded. "Old I am, yes! And tired, yes! But there are many hungry wolves waiting to feed upon my bones out there . . . wolves that would also eat of the flesh of this stubborn girl of Simu's. For Larani's sake I have returned—not for my own. Maybe tomorrow I will walk the wind with Wallah and Iana. But now I have walked a long way and am hungry. Since I am not to *be* eaten, I see no reason why I should not eat!"

The rest of the band prepared to eat with him. No one said a word about the true identity of the wolves that had driven the old man back into the company of the living, nor did he show the slightest suspicion that he was sharing a meal with them. Naya and Swan both came eagerly forward to bring meat and drink to him, but Larani stepped forward.

"A hunter who has a woman to tend his fire circle needs no charity from the women of other men," said the daughter of Simu.

"Go away, Larani!" commanded the old man. "My woman is dead! I no longer have a fire circle! Tomorrow I will walk the wind."

"Tomorrow will see to itself," she countered softly. "Now the daughter of Simu walks in the shadow of one who has saved her from wolves and from drowning. The honor of this woman's ancestors demands that she look to his needs."

The old man growled impatiently at her deference, but Larani would not be growled away. She brought pounded fat to him and knelt quietly before him as she awaited any command that he might choose to give her.

Grek chose to give her none, but it had become apparent to the old man that Larani was his only source for food. He begrudgingly condescended to accept the fat from her, even though he turned his back as he ate. When he lay down to sleep, he did so without a word in her direction and not before dragging his pack roll away from Larani's.

Dak took his sister by her arm and tried to escort her to the comfort of his own fire circle. "You will always be welcome," he told her.

Larani thanked him and sent him away.

Swan and Naya came close and whispered low lest the old man hear and be offended. "You are like my sister, Larani!" Naya said. "Thank you for being so brave for my grandfather's sake! What would I do if he walks the wind? You do not think he still will, do you?"

Larani's face hardened as she looked at the two of them and whispered back: "You have Umak to look after you, Naya. And Swan, you have Dak. Now I will have Grek. It is what we always wanted, isn't it? To have our own men to fuss and worry over us? Go now. Fuss and worry over your own and leave mine to me!"

Swan's hand came out and stayed Larani's movements as she fumbled with the thongs of her pack roll. "Larani, he is *old*. He is *not* the one you want."

"The one I want is dead! And even if he were not, he would not want me now. No man wants me now! I will stay with Grek. He *needs* me! It is enough!"

Without ceremony she picked up her traveling pack and, ignoring Swan and Naya, trudged back to Grek and lay down beside him.

Later, when Grek awoke, Larani was already up, kneeling beside a small fire over which she was roasting skewered cubes of walrus blubber. The scent of seared, heat-softened, dripping fat was more than he could resist. He did not refuse it when she held it out to him, and although he did not say as much, he knew what the making of even the smallest of fires must have cost her.

When the band moved on, Larani walked beside him. The old man did not send her away, nor did he choose to walk the wind that day . . . or the next.

"You are a stubborn lion of a girl," he said at length. "A young, scarred lion who growls back at the forces of Creation, no matter what they bring against you, yes?"

"They have brought me to you, Grek. Why should I growl against that?"

He heard the bitterness in her voice and, understanding, held no rancor. "Because you are young and I am old . . . very old."

She eyed him sadly. "I think I am older."

"Life has hurt you, Larani, but you still have your youth. It is this that makes you brave and as kind as the clever wolves who flushed me from the cover of my sadness and made me want to live again."

The unscarred half of her face paled with amazement. "You *knew*! But how? When I first heard their howling, I was not certain that it was not wolves."

"Too many years has this man hunted in the way of wolves not to understand them! Such noisy wolves! And how breathy were the men of my band as they pretended to be at ease when you and I walked into camp."

"It was not done to rob you of your pride but to make you see that there was still need of it—and of you."

"Yes, this I know. But what would you have done had I not been frightened back into the world of the living?"

She did not hesitate. "I would have stayed with you."

"And died? Torka would never have allowed it."

She thought a moment. "I would have stayed."

He saw the earnestness in her poor, ruined face and knew that she meant what she said. He was the best hope of a man that she could ever have . . . and still maintain some dignity.

"I *will* be your man, Larani," he told her. "I will hunt for you. I will protect you. I will share with you the best portions of my kills, for in truth—as you may already know—pounded fat and prechewed meat are all that is left to me! Do not expect much of me, young woman, for my teeth are not the only part of me that has grown weak . . . and in my heart I will always grieve for my Iana."

Shyly but firmly, she reached out and threaded her arm through his. "You are not the only one who misses Iana, Grek. Tankh and Chuk are nearly men now, and there is much you may yet teach them as they assume more responsibility on future hunts. And Yona is still a little girl who needs her father. Iana would smile to know that you have not forgotten her children. They are a part of her, and as long as they live, Iana will live in them and in the little ones who will come after them."

He stopped and looked down at her for a long time. Then: "You are a good and caring woman, daughter of Simu. Together we will be strong—a pair of lions. Grek and Larani . . . each supporting the other. It will be a good thing."

❖━━━━◆━━━━❖

7

❖━━━━◆━━━━❖

And it was so. As Torka led his people across the barrens, through the tussock forests, and back into the country that lay in the high, blue shadow of the Mountains That Walk, Larani stayed resolutely at Grek's side. She cooked, carried, pounded fat, and saw to it that the old man's pack was not as heavily loaded as it appeared to be. She made certain that Tankh and Chuk, although they occupied a separate lean-to, paid the proper attention and respect to their father. She was diligent in her care of Yona, seeing to it that the girl was well fed and properly clothed and that the tender skin of her sullen, resentful little face was slathered with fat against the clouds of biting flies that swarmed upon the summer tundra whenever the wind was down.

"You are a good mother to my girl," Grek told her with approval.

She nodded deferentially and did not tell him that whenever he was not looking, Yona resisted her ministrations.

"I do not need a mother!" Yona told her. "Especially not a sickening-to-look-at woman!"

Larani appraised the child without visible reaction. "Good," she replied. "I do not need a daughter, either— especially a sickening-to-be-with girl! What I do for you, Yona, I do for your father . . . and in memory of your mother. You are going to have to put up with me and do as I tell you, because I am not going away."

Yona's mouth worked into a clump of hateful puckers. "I made Naya go away!"

Larani frowned. "Be that as it may, I am here to stay at your father's fire circle. You will not make me go away, Yona. Only Grek can do that."

As the days wore on, Yona came to a grudging realization that Grek had no intention of sending Larani away. With the young woman ever at his side, Grek walked with new purpose. He was always finding little things in his path to make Yona smile—flowers, seed heads, and stalks of lichen that looked like caribou antler. His voice was strong when he spoke to his sons, urging them to learn from their father as he pointed out the subtleties of the land and the ever-changing summer sky. When their interest waned, Larani reinforced his purpose.

She suggested that all the youths would benefit from walking close to her man and listening to his words. "The wisdom of Grek has been born out of a lifetime of experience. It is a gift to the People! Accept this gift! Cherish it!"

She saw Torka watching her with open surprise and then with admiration. He insisted that she be obeyed. Later, while the old man slept and she sat mending a snag in the sole of one of his moccasins and stuffing extra mosses and lichens into the padded innersole, Torka and Lonit came to her.

The headman's woman knelt and handed her a bracelet

of braided sinew onto which a single shell-shaped stone had been stitched. "Here, I have taken a stone from my necklet and made a gift for you."

Larani stared at it in disbelief. It was a rare and unprecedented offering. Lonit often told the story of how she had gathered the shell-like stones in that strange land beyond the Sea of Ice. Over the years, all the shells had been lost except for the few that remained interwoven with wolf claws onto the one necklet that she took off only when she slept.

As Larani stared up at the necklace, she saw that a bead was missing. "I cannot accept this," she murmured, handing up the twist of sinew with its single precious bead. "It is too fine for me."

"Not fine enough!" Torka contradicted brusquely and, with his arm about his woman, turned and escorted Lonit away without another word.

Larani sat in silence, holding their gift in her cupped hands. How fine Lonit and Torka were, how perfectly matched and beautiful to behold as the wind gusted fitfully in the fringes of their garments and in their obsidian-black hair—like a pair of rare dark swans, serene and confident in their love for one another.

Soon after, when the rest of the band lay bundled beneath their traveling robes lest the marauding blackflies attack them while they slept in the light of the midnight sun, Grek drew Larani close and held her in his arms.

His touch was caring, solicitous of her scars. His passion was brief—exhausted almost before it was begun—and he told her that he was sorry. She assured him that she did not mind, that being with him was enough for her. She nestled close and stroked his big, crooked back until he relaxed beneath her touch. She listened to him begin to snore and suck the remaining stubs of his teeth. With a sigh, she wondered what that big, broad back of his must have been like when it was young and straight and rippling with the power of a hunter in his prime. He would have been a man for other men to envy . . . and the best of men for any woman. But it was so long ago, it did not matter. She sighed and, trying to decide if she cared or not, drifted off to sleep. With the bracelet that had been a gift from the headman and his woman knotted about her unmaimed wrist, she dreamed of another lion . . . the black-eyed, black-maned Manaravak . . . son of Torka . . . tall, lean, magnificent, and as wild as the wolves that were calling to one another in the dark, tumbled ranges of the south.

Torka also dreamed, of yesterday, today, and tomorrow . . . of the living and the dead, of laughter and tears . . . of his band trudging across the endless landscapes into the face of the rising sun . . . and of the wind blowing at their back, blowing them on and on as though they were of no more importance than seed filaments cast upon the tides of time at summer's end.

He sat up. Wolves called across the lean and hungry land. He listened to their song. The wind distorted it; it sounded almost human.

The wind had turned. It was cold and made him think of Iana and her infant, of Nantu and Eneela, and of Demmi and Manaravak. The pain of loss was a spear in his heart. Too many ghosts rode this wind. He sighed, wondering why his spirit felt as desolate as the land across which he was leading his band.

He pulled his sleeping robe higher around his shoulders and tried to think of the way that Dak and Swan walked hand in hand these days, of how Naya was becoming a reasonable young woman at last, of how Umak beamed with lovesick delight every time he looked at her, and of how the fine, bold heart of Larani had overcome the inconsolable grief of old Grek and given him the will to live.

Good things, thought Torka. And yet, although his sleeping robe kept the bite of the wind away, the coldness invaded him again—an inner coldness, of doubt and misgiving. Larani had given Grek the heart to live—but what of her own heart? Naya obeyed Umak—but with downcast eyes. And Demmi and Manaravak were dead.

Scowling and suddenly fiercely irritated, he got to his feet and walked restlessly about the traveling camp. He thought of caribou and bison and vast herds of migrating, grazing animals moving ever eastward into the face of the rising sun. Since his boyhood he had seen them do this, and since his youth he had followed until now, at last, the herds were gone and he had reached a land where there was no sign that they had ever passed this way at all.

Where did they go? How did they get through the mountains?

Wolves were howling to the south again. He stopped;

they were the strangest sounding wolves that he had ever heard. The wind turned, and he turned with it, toward the wolf sound. A mammoth trumpeted. Suddenly every dog in camp was on its feet and barking. The wolves were howling again—close now, very close. Even as Torka watched in disbelief and Lonit began to weep with gladness beside him, the great mammoth totem, Life Giver, emerged at the crest of the far hills.

And then Torka was not the only man to be standing in his sleeping robes staring toward the south, for the "wolf sounds" were at last recognizable as the jubilant cries of a man and a woman.

The mammoth was not alone. Two human figures walked in its shadow, with a horse following close behind.

And as Torka cried out with joy all his earlier misgivings fell away. He had been right to lead his people away from the Lake of Watered Blood! For here at the base of the cold, blue vastnesses of the Mountains That Walk, he stood with his face to the rising sun and turned to find his luck in the shadow of a mammoth. Demmi and Manaravak had returned. He *had* found his luck at last!

Sayanah, with the dogs at his heels, led the children and youths of the band out to greet Manaravak, waving and shouting jubilant welcome. Grek followed his boys, and Honee, gushing with happiness, waved Umak on as she hurried forward after Jhon and Li. But Umak could not move. Stunned, he stood with Naya and stared ahead in disbelief.

Naya's eyes were very wide and round as she whispered, "I knew they would come back! I *knew*!"

"Manaravak! Demmi! My *children*!" Lonit was laughing and weeping all at once as Manaravak, in a robe of striped horse skin, loosed the tether of the colt and, with Demmi at his side, ran to greet their mother and lift her high into the air with a shout of pure joy.

Umak watched Torka follow the others out of camp. The headman walked slowly, regally, as though wishing to prolong the moment. Dak and Swan walked with him, with Kharn riding on his father's shoulder. It took no shaman's magic for Umak to see the hesitancy in their steps or to tell from their set expressions that Dak and Swan were ill at ease. Swan paused and turned back while Dak and Torka continued on ahead. Umak was not surprised; he knew that she would come to stand beside him, and she did.

Manaravak had put Lonit down, and Torka wrapped his powerful arms around his woman and his returning children and held them as though he would never let them go.

Swan's face was pale, her features set, her eyes dulled by shock and disappointment. "Some shaman you have turned out to be, Brother. You swore to Dak that you had seen them dead. What will our sister say when she finds out that I took her place at Dak's fire circle? Oh, Umak, how can I face her? How can Dak face her? What can either of us possibly say to make her understand?"

"The truth," said Larani solemnly as she and Simu stopped next to Swan. "Kharn needed a mother, and Dak needed care. You have done no wrong, Swan. Umak may be a shaman, but he cannot know everything! Demmi will understand and be grateful."

"Will she?" Swan's voice was tremulous with uncertainty.

Simu shook his head. "Look at that, would you?" he asked, with awe and admiration. "I've never thought much of your twin, Umak, but only Manaravak would dare to return to his people from the world beyond this world and bring a pregnant Demmi back with him! He may have been raised by beasts, but he *is* a son equal in daring to his father!"

Umak winced. "Demmi was with child before she left this camp!"

Simu raised a telling brow. "Was she?"

"All the women suspected it!"

Simu smirked. "Perhaps, but whose baby is it, Umak? Dak's or your brother's? Come, Shaman. Are you trying to tell me that you can see the truth of this more clearly than you saw the death of your own brother and sister?"

Swan caught her breath, aghast. "Tell him, Umak. Demmi and Manaravak would never—! It is forbidden!"

"Enough!" Umak's emotions were in turmoil. "My brother and sister have returned from the world beyond this world, and that is enough for me . . . and for you, too, Simu, if you know what is best for you!"

"Do you threaten me, Umak?" Simu appeared hopeful.

Umak measured the man. "By your union with Summer Moon, you are also my brother, Simu. Why must you always make yourself the burr under every man's pack frame?"

Simu raised his hands in mocking affability. "You are the

shaman, Umak. You should be able to tell me. After all, I am only thinking of the ways of your ancestors and of the good of the band. If your sister is pregnant by your brother, it is no offense to me or to the customs of my people . . . only to my son if he has not consented to—"

"The People are one!" Umak interrupted hotly.

"So Torka always says," Simu agreed contemptuously. Then, shaking his head, he went to pay what respects he would to the returning pair.

"Dak will never forgive you for this, Brother," Swan said mournfully to Umak. "I can only hope that he will forgive me."

"He loves you," Larani said, staring forward with the saddest expression that Umak had ever seen.

"He loves Demmi more!" Without another word lest she burst into tears, Swan followed Simu.

Umak took Naya's hand. "Come, Naya. We must greet Manaravak and Demmi. And Naya, remember that you are *my* woman now. Whatever was between you and my brother is finished. Let this be the last time that we have cause to speak of it."

Naya walked beside him, her thoughts and emotions in as much turmoil as Umak's. The others cleared a way for the shaman, so suddenly she was standing before Manaravak and Demmi with her right hand held tightly in the curl of Umak's fingers. At a loss as to what to do, she stared down at her toes.

Manaravak pulled his brother into an embrace that broke the shaman's reserve. Naya felt the change in Umak as he threw his arms around his long-lost brother and sister.

"Manaravak! Demmi! I am not the shaman I thought I was," he admitted as he stepped back to beam at them. "The only vision I could see of you was a vision of my fear of your death! But look at the two of you!"

Naya ventured an upward peek and caught her breath. Demmi did not look well at all. Her eyes were on Dak and Kharn—such warm eyes, so full of love for her man and son. Naya was startled. Demmi had changed!

But Manaravak had not. Now that he had finished hugging Umak, his eyes were devouring her. She wanted to look away but could not. A broad, purplish gash ran from the corner of his mouth upward across his cheek to his temple. It looked like a striping of ceremonial paint, and yet, coupled with smaller scars on his brow, it enhanced his looks. In his roughly fashioned but well-made garments, with his hair hanging loose over his horsehide cloak and a garland of thickly strung leaves adorning his shoulders, he was magnificent.

She looked back down at her feet and took a step closer to Umak as he possessively put his arm around her.

"Naya is my woman now," Umak informed Manaravak.

"We knew it would be so," Demmi said quickly. "Didn't we, Manaravak?"

Manaravak did not speak.

Demmi broke the silence. "Remember your promise, Manaravak . . . and our gift."

"Gift! Yes!" Manaravak's affirmation was explosive. "For Naya, granddaughter of Grek!"

Naya looked up. "A gift? For me?" She felt Umak's arm tighten about her as Manaravak lifted the garland from his neck and laid it around her shoulders. She was instantly engulfed in the rich fragrance of wormwood and willow, of thousand-leaf and bearberry, of sorrel and angelica, and of so many of the healing leaves that she had shown him long ago on that day in the gorge below Spear Mountain when he had made her laugh and they had frolicked like happy children until, in the end, he had made her cry. The memory disturbed her, as did his closeness. Sooner or later, all men made her cry.

Her free hand touched the leaves, as if she were not certain that they were real. There were so many that her fingers could not penetrate the varying textures of gray and green; nevertheless she probed deep enough to discover a sprig of dried berries. She plucked one.

An exclamation of delight escaped her lips as she looked at the familiar, wrinkled orb. "Oh, Manaravak, thank you! This is the best of gifts! There is nothing I have wanted more!"

Beside her, Umak went rigid. She could feel the anger in him as he commanded in a voice that was tight with control, "Give the garland back, Naya. You may accept gifts from no man unless I consent to the giving."

Naya pouted. "But Manaravak has brought me berries."

"Give them back."

The tension in the air was palpable until Manaravak broke it with a conciliatory outward gesturing of his hands.

"This gift I bring is not for my brother's woman, Umak! This gift is for Medicine Woman! This gift is for all the People! To make them live long and to take away the bad spirits of fever and pain whenever they are sick!"

"Oh!" cried Naya, suddenly so distraught that her hands flew to her face lest others see her tears as she thought of her failure to heal Iana and the baby.

"What have I said wrong?" asked Manaravak. "The gift I bring . . . it is a bad gift?"

"No," replied Umak. "It is not a bad gift."

Naya was grateful when he held her close. He was relaxed now. She knew that he would let her keep the garland. "It is a wonderful gift," she said, then hung her head and snuffled through her tears. "It is just that it comes t-too l-late."

"For what?" pressed Demmi.

Torka spoke. His voice was low and solemn as he explained how Naya had saved Iana and her baby, only to lose them for want of the very healing leaves that Manaravak had just placed around her neck. "We have suffered much sadness since the night that the two of you disappeared into the storm. It is a good thing that you have come home. It is a good thing to have something to smile about!"

Demmi's head went high as, in a gesture of goodwill that startled Naya, she reached out and laid her hand on the younger woman's shoulder. "You need weep no longer, Little Girl. The great mammoth totem saved our lives. Life Giver led us to a good land that lies to the south—a land of much meat . . . a land where the People will grow strong again and smile all the time and where Medicine Woman will never want for the healing leaves and roots that she seeks." She paused and looked at Torka. "This is the gift that we bring to you, my father."

"No." He shook his head. "*You* are the gift—you and Manaravak. Come now. We will raise a feast fire and sing songs of gladness. Demmi and Manaravak have been reunited with their band. That is the greatest gift of all!"

Larani smiled. She had ventured close enough to hear but not close enough to be seen or drawn into the conversation. Grek had accepted her excuses and had, at her insistence, gone on ahead while she lingered near their lean-to, ostensibly to comb her hair and arrange her garments so that an undue exposure of her scars would not put a shadow upon the happy events of the day.

She had not combed her hair or rearranged her clothing. Instead she had remained close to the lean-to, staring spellbound at Manaravak, drinking in the sight of him, fighting against the tears of gladness that threatened to overwhelm her.

After all of these long months of thinking him dead, he was alive! *Alive!* And now she continued to stare at him, loving him so much that her throat burned against the need to call his name, and her hands clenched against her desire to reach out to him until, suddenly aware of her glance, he looked in her direction. She caught her breath and turned away lest he set eyes upon her when her heart was open and vulnerable.

It took her only a few moments to return to the shelter that she shared with Grek. By then she was weeping. Manaravak was back among his people! Why had she turned away from him? Because she was Grek's woman! Grek's scarred, ugly, pitiable woman! By what right did she allow herself to be overcome by her love for a man who could never be hers, who would never look at her without revulsion? Grek was her man now. Grek needed her.

"Larani!"

She heard the old man call her name. By the time he peered in and smiled at her and asked her to come out to join the others, she had regained her composure. She wiped her eyes and combed her hair, sweeping the shafts sideways, grateful that the new growth was at last long enough to allow her to bind the ends together with a single length of braided sinew at her jawline. It was an odd hairstyle, but it effectively covered that portion of her scalp that would forever remain a shining purplish cap of rumpled scars. When she emerged into the light of day, she was red-eyed but no longer tearful. She stood before Manaravak and welcomed him and Demmi back into the ranks of their people in a manner that was aloof enough to give the impression that she did not really care whether they had lived or died.

8

There were singing and dancing in the encampment that day, and although Manaravak and Demmi were saddened by news of the death of Iana and Eneela, their joy in being reunited with their people assuaged their sorrow.

Surrounded by well-wishers, the brother and sister were escorted to places of honor before a hastily assembled feast fire. Manaravak knew that he was grinning like a man who had drunk too deeply of the juice of fermented blood and berries and pounded roots. He did not care. He wondered if he had ever been happier than he was at this moment—Naya had smiled at his gift; he and Umak were close once more.

The barking of the dogs had him on his feet again. They had surrounded the colt. "No! Back! Away!" he shouted as, wading through the confused but obedient dogs, he took up the colt's tether and led it into camp.

"Meat! At last! Good, red meat from an animal fit for men to eat!" Simu exclaimed as he reached for his butchering knife.

"No!" Manaravak raised a hand to stay the intent of the other man. "This colt is better than meat to this people."

Simu drew out his knife. "What is better than the sweet meat of a young horse?"

Manaravak wound the end of the colt's tether around the stake of the headman's lean-to, then returned to the fire to stand proudly. "I bring this colt as a gift for my people. It will grow strong and be all that the dogs have become, only better because it will carry what twenty dogs could not carry!"

This said, he seated himself between Torka and Umak and, with a wide smile of brotherly affection at Sayanah, asked, "What meat did you eat at the Lake of Watered Blood?"

Sayanah grimaced. "You will taste it soon enough!"

And it was so. Manaravak and Demmi marveled over the

strange but pleasant taste of the meat and fat that their people had carried away from the lake.

"The herds of these animals are enormous, and there is enough fat on them to keep the lamps of our women burning through a lifetime of winters!" Umak exclaimed, his face alight. He then asked Honee to bring out a sampling of the unusual skins that she and the other women had been working on. "Look at these pelts! Have you ever seen finer?"

Manaravak and Demmi were impressed as they handled the unusual furs and hides of seals and walrus and listened in amazement to the shaman's tales of the animals that swam like fish, barked like dogs, and had fins in place of feet.

"It is everything and more than your brother says," added Torka, shaking his head and scowling. "I have no wish to set eyes upon it again!"

"You will not have to!" Manaravak assured him, focusing his gaze so completely upon Torka that he failed to see Umak's glum expression. "The land to the south is also full of meat and fat."

"And wanawut," added Demmi.

Silence fell.

Manaravak wondered why everyone was staring with horror upon their faces. "We have never hunted in a land that was free of wanawut," he reminded them.

"Except in the country around the Lake of Watered Blood!" injected Umak with resentment.

Demmi was tired and happy. She had not meant to cast a pall upon the festivities, but it seemed less than honest not to speak of the wanawut or of the incident in the cave.

"Then why would you and Manaravak lead us back into the country where you have seen the beasts?" pressed Umak.

Simu cracked the marrow bone that he had been gnawing on. "Why not? I would like a chance at them."

When Manaravak glared at Simu, a ripple of sadness went through Demmi. Despite everything, a part of him would always empathize with the wanawut. She shook away the disturbing thought as she spoke to her people: "Now that I have confronted the wanawut, I can tell you that we have no cause to fear their kind more than we fear any other carnivore. Pierce their flesh with a spear, and they bleed and die as we would bleed and die. Life Giver will protect us as we venture to the south."

Manaravak was nodding enthusiastically, but Umak, shaking his head, apparently still longed to return to the Lake of Watered Blood. Everyone else seemed mollified, with the exception of Swan and Dak. Neither had said more than a perfunctory word to Demmi since she had returned to camp. Swan was more quiet than usual, and Dak had not touched Demmi or commented on her pregnancy.

Her eyes strayed to her son, who sat stiffly beside his father on the man's side of the fire. How much he had grown! She was so thrilled to see him, she was neither annoyed nor angry with his refusal to display any affection toward her.

"I will be a better mother to you from now on, Kharn," she had assured him.

He had looked at her through hostile eyes. "Swan is my mother now!"

Regret touched her.

Later, Demmi told herself. *Later Dak and I will be one! It will be as it was when we were first together. I will tell him that I have been foolish and inconsiderate. I will give him cause to be glad that I have come home to him at last!*

"I have heard enough of wanawut and new hunting grounds and the Lake of Watered Blood," said Dak, rising. "This day has been long. I will rest now. Come, Kharn. It is time for us to sleep."

And so it was that "later" came for Demmi.

She kissed her mother and her sisters, and like an obedient woman, she followed her man to his lean-to, suppressing a smile when she thought of how shocked everyone must be by her behavior.

When she paused before the shelter, Kharn was already inside. Dak was looking past her. She turned. Swan stood behind her.

"I am back from the far country, Sister," Demmi said kindly. "I will care for my son and for my man. There is no longer a need for you to help them."

Swan did not reply, nor did she walk away. The look that passed between Swan and Dak struck Demmi even more cruelly than Dak's words:

"I have grieved for you, Demmi," he said. "I could not eat or sleep or care for our son because my spirit bled for want of you. But time has passed since you turned your back upon me and our son and chose to follow Manaravak. Now I, too, have made a choice. I welcome you back to your people and to my fire circle, but no longer are you the center of my life. Swan is my woman now—my caring and loving woman, a mother to Kharn, a gracious maker of meat and fur and all the things that make a man and a family strong."

Demmi did not speak. She stood tall and silent before his every word. She wondered if he could hear her heart breaking; the sound of its shattering was so terrible to her own ears. At last he was finished. At last a tearful Swan moved to stand close at his side and offer apologies until Demmi could not bear to hear another word. With an exhalation of remorse that shook her to her spirit and beyond, she turned and would have walked away, but Swan reached out and clutched her arm.

"Demmi, please try to understand!" Swan begged. "I would never do anything to hurt you. You are still the first woman of my man and the mother of his son! Tell her, Dak!"

Dak hesitated, then he said coolly, "There will always be a place for you in the light of my fire, Demmi. Long ago, before our people, I named you my woman. I have not forgotten my obligation."

Demmi shivered. "Obligation? Is this all that you feel toward me?" She waited. In a moment he would recant his statements and speak about the good times they had shared.

But Dak said nothing.

"Dak, I am sorry for the way I behaved toward you and Kharn. Something perverse in my nature blinded me to everyone and everything but Manaravak. I have changed. My heart is full of you, our son, and our coming child—" Insight flared so brutally bright that she nearly fainted as she whirled to face him.

"It is *yours!*" she declared. "Do you imagine that I would come back into this encampment to shame you with my brother's baby in me? Look at me, Dak! The passing of the moons speaks to name this child yours!"

His eyes were distant, filled with hurt. "It would not be the first time that you have shamed me with him."

Guilt twisted in her gut. She remembered the cave, the savage coupling, the wolf and the man both in the skin of her brother. Manaravak, both riding her and hurting her, howling like an animal. The memory sickened her. "Never again," she vowed. "You are the only man I want. I love you, Dak. I have always loved you. I just haven't known how much until now."

Swan hung her head in abject misery.

Dak stiffened. The ragged suck of air that hissed inward through his teeth was the same sound that a man makes when he has been dashed with ice water. The exhalation that followed was just as cold. "Too late . . . too late." He looked at Demmi out of eyes that seemed more tired than before. "You do not look well, Demmi. You should rest now. I think that we have all had enough of words for one day."

Later, under the soft, dusky glow of a midnight sun, Torka walked from camp alone. Lonit watched him go. She had felt him rise but had not said a word when he left. Only when his footfall grew as soft as the midnight wind did she get up, pull her sleeping furs around herself, and go outside. Standing before the lean-to, she watched his figure grow smaller and smaller as he walked across the hills beneath the pale blues and pinks of a night that held both sun and stars within it.

She knew where he was going. She knew what he would do when he stopped. In silhouette against the southwestern sky, he stood facing the mammoth—a man and his totem etched against the infinite.

Her heart seemed to be beating in her throat as she saw Torka raise his arms. Life Giver lifted its trunk. Slowly, as though in a strange and wondrous dream, man and mammoth advanced toward one another until both paused. Torka's arms lowered slightly. The trunk of the mammoth reached out and touched the hands of the man.

A sob of joyful wonder escaped Lonit's lips. She turned and reluctantly reentered the lean-to. This moment belonged to Torka.

My man has found his luck again! The mammoth walks with the People once more. My children have come back to me from the world beyond this world! What more could this woman ask for? She praised the forces of Creation for their goodness and mercy, then with a contented sigh, she lay down and sought sleep. Soon Torka returned and joined her, and they slept deeply in the comforting embrace of one another's arms.

*   *   *

No one in camp except the dogs and the colt heard the sound that woke Manaravak and had him up, staring toward the south. The wanawut were out there somewhere! For a long time he listened to their calls, then he smiled. Demmi would be pleased to know that for the first time in his life, he felt no need to answer.

9

Naya, outside her man's lean-to, knelt on her haunches before a square of sealskin, busily sorting her newly acquired leaves and roots and precious berries. This was the first time since Manaravak had placed the garland around her neck that she had been able to look closely at all the treasures he had brought her.

Umak watched, unable to remember the last time he had seen her so happy; his gift of the bearskin had not pleased her half as much as Manaravak's garland.

With Honee and Li bending close, Naya babbled on to them about the medicines that she would make and about the many uses to which they would be put. She tasted a berry, swallowed it, and then took up another and another, chewing until she raised her smiling face toward the pale light of the evening sun and closed her eyes.

For a long while she remained motionless, oblivious to Honee's rambling conversation and to Li's imperative tugging at her sleeve.

"Will you let me help to make medicine, Naya?" asked Li.

Naya did not move.

Li made a face of impatience. "Naya! Did you hear me, Naya?"

Naya remained perfectly still.

Disappointed, Li turned away, took her doll from her pack roll, and not bothering to stifle a yawn, plopped down and began to smooth the doll's musk-ox hair.

Honee's chatter ceased as she appraised Naya with motherly speculation. "Those berries always did make her sleepy.

Come to think of it, I am sleepy myself. The day *has* been long. I think I will get some rest."

Umak ignored her. His thoughts were far away, back to the Lake of Watered Blood, where Naya had been his, and Manaravak had not been around to distract her with presents that overshadowed the gifts of her own man.

Frustration nagged him. His eyes took in Naya's child-like beauty, the graceful arch of her back, the pulsebeat at her throat, the curves of her diminutive breasts as they rose and fell beneath her lightweight traveling tunic, the way her hands were stroking the curve of her thighs. He swallowed. Something was infinitely sensual about the movement of her hands and about the way she was now swaying slowly.

Umak looked to his back. Someone was watching him. He was not surprised to see Manaravak, but his lips tightened over his teeth when he realized that Manaravak was not watching him, he was watching Naya. The look on his face made Umak think of a sexually alert stallion scenting the air for a mare in heat.

Furious, Umak snapped to his feet, stared at his twin, and shouted across the camp to warn him loudly and aggressively. "Do not look at my woman like that, Brother, or I will forget that I had rejoiced at your return!"

The reaction in camp was instantaneous. The People stopped what they were doing to stare at what promised to be a confrontation.

Manaravak was startled. His eyes darted away from Naya to settle upon his brother. There was no apology in his expression; if anything, he looked hurt and saddened. He frowned, shook his head, then offered a wide, friendly, guileless grin that might not have driven Umak to distraction had he not chosen to look back at Naya and lick his lips like a hungry wolf.

"I meant no offense, Brother," said Manaravak earnestly.

A single breath of relief seemed to go out of the entire band.

Umak commanded Naya to come with him. When she did not react to his command, he stepped across Honee's well-made cooking fire, reached down, and hauled the granddaughter of Grek into his arms.

She gasped with surprise when he lifted her, then giggled, burrowed her face into the hollow of his shoulder, and seemed to fall asleep.

Holding his woman, he stood to his full height and glared across the encampment. "It is a good thing that you have returned to your people, Manaravak, but do not forget the circumstances under which you left us! Naya is my woman now! Do not look at her with hungry eyes again!"

The strangest expression crossed Manaravak's face—as though water rippled beneath his skin and clouds rose within his spirit to shadow his eyes. But he said nothing as Umak whirled around, ordered Honee to occupy herself outside for a while, and then disappeared with Naya into the shadowed privacy of their lean-to.

The People did their best to resume whatever they had been doing before Umak's outburst. Torka saw Demmi cast a disapproving glance at Manaravak as he walked past her to seat himself glumly beside the colt outside camp.

The old worry was back in Torka's gut—the all-too-familiar frustration with decisions badly made and difficult to live with. Nothing had changed between Umak and Manaravak. Naya would be a cause of enmity between them as long as she lived. He ground his teeth. If only he had given her to Manaravak, as had been originally intended! If only he had listened to Simu and put her out of the band!

If. The word riled him, as did the realization that it was not in his nature to condemn a young girl to certain death as punishment for stupidity and flirtatiousness. Besides, he was beginning to suspect that the problem lay less with Naya than with his own sons. They were a stubborn pair, and Naya was capable of sucking reason right out of their heads. She had done nothing this day to spark antagonism between them.

Uneasiness rippled through him. He had to admit that there had been a certain sensuality to the arch of her back and the way her hands had moved over her thighs, which had drawn his own glance across the encampment. Perhaps Simu had been right about her being a bringer of trouble. She was, after all, Navahk's granddaughter as well as Grek's. Perhaps, when all was said and done, she could not be anything else. If this proved to be the case . . .

"Who will be Manaravak's woman in this camp now that Eneela and Iana walk the wind forever?" Lonit inquired, worrying aloud.

"Women!" Torka snapped at her, causing her to wince. "Do you imagine that men have nothing on their minds except who will couple with whom? Until the younger girls mature, Umak will share Honee with his brother. And there is always Larani if Manaravak's need is intense enough. Besides, she is a good woman. Were it not for her burns, he could ask for no better mate."

Sadness touched Lonit's face. "Larani loves him, you know. But I do not think Manaravak will want her now, even if Grek would consent to share her."

Something ominous twisted deep within Torka as he looked off toward Umak's shelter. "His feelings toward Naya have become unnaturally possessive. It is not a good thing. He has two women. Manaravak has none. Like it or not, for the good of the band, Umak may have to share Naya with his brother."

Lonit's eyes grew large and watchful. "You were never willing to share *me*."

"It is not the same!" he said, but he knew that she had spoken truly.

Memories settled. He chewed them resentfully, wanting to spit them out and have done with them. How many times had he fought for Lonit? Many times. And lost only once—to Navahk.

The recollection of the man was disconcerting. Navahk the Slaughterer . . . Navahk the Beautiful . . . Navahk, Magic Man, father of Karana . . . paternal grandfather of Naya . . . and raper of Lonit. The ghost of that evil shaman haunted him, whirling and mocking, dancing maniacally in the white skins of winter-killed caribou with his black hair whipping in the winds of time, his mouth set into a leering smile that displayed the teeth of a wolf . . . small, deadly sharp, serrate-edged teeth—not unlike Naya's or Umak's.

No!

He opened his eyes and stared straight ahead. He would not acknowledge the possibility of that ever again. Umak was his son, not Navahk's. When he had given Naya to Umak, it had not only been to punish Manaravak for his animalistic behavior—it had also been in the hope of silencing all doubts of Umak's paternity forever. Had he believed that Umak and Naya shared the same grandfather, any union between them would have been strictly forbidden. And yet when Umak took on the raiment of a shaman, sang a shaman's songs, and danced a shaman's dances, even though Torka told himself a thousand times that the young man had inherited the ways of the spirit master through his own line and through his own grandfather, he could not help but think of Navahk and wonder if, through some dark magic, Navahk had found a way to have the last laugh.

"Torka?" Lonit was at his side, her hand on his forearm, her head resting against the side of his shoulder. "Talk to Manaravak. He looks so unhappy."

"What shall I tell him? That he must be content with Honee and Larani while his brother keeps Naya to himself?"

"You have given Naya to Umak, Torka. You must make Manaravak understand. You are his father, the headman. You will know the right words."

Torka shook his head. He would not allow the ghost of Navahk to shadow his thoughts again, nor would he allow a descendant of that hated man to come between his twins. Naya would do as she was told or be put out of the band, and once and for all his sons must be made to see reason where she was concerned. "Manaravak has come back to his people. He has brought Demmi with him. The great mammoth has shown him its favor. I cannot overlook these things. Nor can Umak. He must be willing to yield on this matter of Naya now that his brother has returned."

She looked at him in dismay. "Umak will not share her, Torka!"

"No, not now, but in days to come, he will see that his love is better placed in loyalty to a brother than to such a silly, thin-brained creature as Naya."

Lonit's expression changed as she chided gently, "Torka, we have lived as man and woman for nearly all our lives, but I tell you now that you are not the man I think you are if you believe that either of our twins has any interest in Naya's brains!"

"You are *my* woman. *Mine,* not his!" proclaimed Umak.

Naya stared up at him through the gloom of the lean-to. "Yours," she echoed dully.

She was reaching up to him, moving sensually on the fur and making soft purring sounds. If she was afraid of him, she showed no sign of it at all as she wrapped her arms around his neck and kissed him as she had never kissed him before.

Never before had she been eager to make love. She was eager now. She took his breath away. With impatient fingers she helped him undo the lacing of her tunic, and with equally impatient fingers she helped to free him of the hindrance of his own clothes. She moaned when she felt him naked against her, then gripped his shoulders and pulled him close, moving her breasts back and forth against his chest until her nipples peaked and hardened. With a gasp of delight, she opened her mouth to his, sought his tongue with her own even as she fought against the weight of his body, not to be free of him but so she might open her limbs wide.

Breathless and amazed, he responded to her kiss and moved to accommodate her readiness. It was all he could do to hold himself back lest he explode. The last thing he wanted now was to inadvertently hurt her and rouse fear in place of passion.

Her hands had found his organ. Such warm, moist, little hands, stroking, working, leading him, placing him. He could not keep himself from entering, slowly. The sensation was so overwhelming that his eyes rolled back in his head and he shivered with ecstasy. He would have preferred to withdraw and slow the pace, but she sensed his intention and would not allow it. With a ferocity that stunned him, she curled her limbs around him, locking her ankles tight across his lower back, taking him deep. There was no holding back. When climax came, it was so exquisite that he nearly wept.

Pleasure swept Naya away on waves of ecstasy until, as she trembled violently, release came. Still the pleasure lingered. She was too weak to sustain it. Her head was spinning. Her body went limp as he slumped onto her.

"Naya . . . my Naya . . ."

She frowned. Who was speaking? It did not matter. His voice was deep, gentle, affectionate, and satisfied with her. She felt so strange, so light-headed and completely wonderful.

Slowly, her head began to clear. Strength was returning to her body now, tingling beneath her skin and within her loins.

"Umak?" Yes, it *was* Umak. His eyes were half closed.

He slipped his arms beneath her back and rolled over, so she lay on top of him. With her hands on his shoulders, she levered up and looked down at him curiously out of the tangled, sweated masses of her now unplaited hair. She cocked her head. This was not at all like the dream. She liked this feeling and wondered why she had ever feared him . . . or *this*.

"I love you, Naya," he told her. "We *are* one, you and I, as Torka and Lonit are one. So it is with Umak and Naya, always and forever."

She was feeling very sleepy, infinitely content, and so pleasantly warm. His hands were stroking her back. She liked the sensation. It occurred to her that she liked Umak. She closed her eyes, snuggled close, and laid the side of her face against his chest.

"Naya?"

"Yes?"

"Do you love me? Now, at last, do you love me?"

Sleep was taking her, warm, black, dreamless sleep. She yielded to it. But first she yawned and sighed a single word of acquiescence—to him or to the welcoming oblivion of sleep, she was not sure. "Yes," she said, and knew no more until hours later, when a headache woke her.

From where he sat dozing beside the colt on the peripheries of the temporary camp, Manaravak could not have said what it was that woke him. He had not been sleeping deeply. His father had come out to talk to him after Umak's hot-tempered display. Torka's well-meant advice had disturbed him. Bitterness turned his mouth down. Once again he was a man without a woman, and there was as much tension between Umak and him as there had ever been.

"Only now it is *worse*! Umak flies into a rage when I even *look* at Naya." Manaravak scowled, annoyed with the situation and with himself for having spoken out so loudly.

The colt moved closer, nudging his shoulder. He glanced up and raised his hand to fondle the animal's muzzle. A bond of affection and trust had developed between them over their long journey. "It is so among your kind, I know—always one stallion must have all the mares. But, I ask you, are the People horses? No. I do not want all my people's women, just one—and not even all the time."

The colt blew moist, warm air through Manaravak's fingers and shook its head as if in admonishment. Manaravak looked up, met the large round eyes, and nodded as his fingers rubbed the short hairs of the colt's muzzle. "Yes, you know my heart. Umak knows it, too. Perhaps better than I know it myself! I did bring her a gift, and I did make her smile, but I would not join with my brother's woman unless he offered her to me. I would not shame him or break with

the ways of my people again. I have learned to be a man, not
an animal. Sorry. I meant no insult. You and your kind show
more self-control in your herds than I have ever shown in
mine."

The colt nickered softly.

"Demmi warned me not to look at her," Manaravak told
the young horse. "But how can a man *not* look at Naya? The
way she was sitting—it was as if she was asking every man in
the band to look and to want!"

The colt shook its head, took a step forward, and nearly
knocked Manaravak over.

"All right! I will do as my father has commanded. Until
Umak offers to share Naya with me, I will not even think of
her—or of any woman! I have had enough of them, anyway!
Females twist a man's head until he does not know which
way it should be facing!"

At that moment, across the encampment, Honee rolled
over just as Naya tried to step over her.

With a startled cry, the granddaughter of Grek went
stumbling forward. Naya was naked.

Manaravak stared. There was no way in this world or the
next that he could stop himself from looking at her . . . even
when Umak emerged from the lean-to and demanded that he
turn his eyes away.

◆━━━━━◆

10

◆━━━━━◆

The mammoth led them on slowly, ponderously, day
after day, until at last the barrens lay behind them . . . as did
the endless days of summer. The sun rose and set over the
mountains once again.

Now, in the soft glow of dawn, inner shadows made the
moment cold as Torka turned to face the bleak, blue ice
peaks of the eastern ranges and to survey the camp in which
he and his people had spent the night: Everyone was up and
preparing to travel on. The men and boys were assembling
sledges out of the same hides, thongs, and long bones that
had served to brace the shelters of the night before. The

women and girls were preparing traveling packs and meticulously picking through their fire pits for leftover bone fragments, heating stones, and unburned dung and tundral sod, which could be carried to sustain a new fire at day's end. In front of Umak's downed lean-to, while the shaman worked with his son to assemble the family sledge, Naya was busily helping Honee and Li load the pack frames.

Torka appraised the young woman. Despite his misgivings, Naya had been behaving—although she occasionally giggled at inappropriate times and now and then swung her hips in a way that invariably earned an admonishing but loving slap on the rump from Umak.

As for Manaravak, Torka was gratified to see that he appeared to be going out of his way to make up to Umak for past offenses. He avoided even the most incidental contact with Naya. Now, as Torka scanned the camp, he saw that Manaravak was securing side packs to the colt. While traveling, he spent most of his waking hours with the young horse. When resting or in camp, he occupied himself flaking and reflaking stone blanks into innovative, elongated, bifacial-fluted spearheads, which he had designed while in the far country to the south.

Grek, his sons, and Simu were impressed with this new style of projectile point. It pleased Torka to see his old friend set aside his earlier dislike of Manaravak. Torka's son appeared to have left all wild, undisciplined behavior behind him. For the first time in his life, Manaravak was succeeding in his efforts to be one with his fellow hunters. He was rarely alone. When Larani brought food to Grek, she lingered to watch the stone working. Torka's brow expanded as he remembered Lonit's words: *"Larani loves him, you know. She always has."*

He frowned, wondering if Grek were observant enough to notice. For all the good it would do her! Torka's frown deepened. He felt terrible whenever he looked at her; he still held himself responsible for her burns.

Now his eyes strayed toward Dak's fire circle. The son of Simu had gone off to round up his dogs while his women and Kharn loaded the family sledge.

Demmi looked wan, and Torka worried about her. She had changed so much since her return: She avoided Manaravak and was quiet and obedient to Dak's every command. Although the son of Simu was civil to her, nothing cut through his aloofness. Nevertheless she did her best to accept a situation that she—and everyone else—knew that she had brought upon herself. She showed no animosity toward Swan. She assumed the role of the less favored woman with calm dignity.

Torka shook his head. As her father, it hurt him to see her in this situation.

"Dak, toss me that tether, and I'll give you a hand. Snow Eater is leading the pups off again!"

Torka turned at the sound of Umak's voice. The headman was not certain if Dak would respond to Umak's offer; there had been a definite cooling between them since Demmi and Manaravak's return. Dak hesitated, but only for a moment. Before Dak tossed Umak the tether and trotted off to give his boyhood friend much-needed help, Torka saw Dak staring toward Demmi with a pained longing that spoke of a love that had never completely died.

Torka smiled. Soon his wild, willful, and unpredictable second daughter was going to have another chance at happiness! Torka felt wonderful. The dawn was suddenly bright again, new again, and his spirit was free of shadows again as he loped off to help Umak and Dak round up the dogs.

The people walked on until they reached the Great Mad River. They would have made camp in familiar country, but Simu argued against it. "There are too many memories in this country. Nantu died here. And there we crossed the ice, and all but Eneela lived to tell the tale." His eyes closed. He stood awash in grief. "I say we walk just a little farther south, to a part of the valley that does not have so many ghosts."

Everyone agreed that Simu was right.

"I don't like ghosts," said Yona, falling into step beside Larani as the band moved on.

"Nor do I," replied the daughter of Simu. "But walk as we will, the kind of ghosts of whom Simu speaks always follow. We carry them with us in our heads . . . memories of all the things that we have ever loved and lost."

Yona frowned. "I lost my mother and my dolls. Naya killed my dolls, you know, just as she killed my mother."

Larani stopped in her tracks. "You must not say such a thing! Naya tried to save Iana. If she had possessed the right medicines, your mother might still be alive. We cannot know. All of us must die someday of something, Yona. There is no blame to be fixed. It is simply the way things are."

"What other ghosts do you think about, Larani?"

"I think of my mother, Eneela, and of a pretty girl whom the rest of the band left behind in the land that was consumed by Daughter of the Sky. She would have had a fine life. I liked her, and I miss her. I am glad that her ghost fills my memories. And I wish that she walked here with you now instead of me."

Yona looked puzzled. "We left no one behind in the burned land."

"Yes, we did."

"What was her name?"

"Larani."

The next day, at an assembly of the men and youths, Grek drew the single long bone that elected him to keep watch over the camp while Manaravak led the rest of the band to the gorge at the base of Spear Mountain.

"This is where I made my gift of many leaves for Medicine Woman," declared Manaravak. "Plenty of healing things are still here to keep the People strong!"

"It was so," Demmi affirmed with an edge of weariness to her voice. The day had just begun, but the previous night's rest had done little to soften the dark shadows under her eyes or ease the pensive set of her mouth. .

Simu turned his gaze to Umak, raised a derogatory brow, and said loudly, "You disappoint me, Shaman. If you hadn't been in such a hurry to move off to the north, perhaps our women would not have run out of healing leaves. Your Naya might have been able to save Iana, and we would have been reunited with your brother and sister long before now."

Naya flushed, as did Umak, but it was Honee who replied—and so furiously that her face turned purple. "What is it, Simu, that twists your spirit so? Before Manaravak was lost across the river, he could do nothing right in your eyes! Now that he is back, he can do no wrong! It is not enough for you to pick on him and on Naya. You must pick on Umak as well! But you go too far! I am Honee, daughter of the great chief Cheanah and of generations of headmen before him. No man insults *my* man!"

Umak grabbed Honee by the straps of her gathering pack just in time to abort what might have proved to be an effective charge against Simu. "I do not need you to defend me!" he scolded sharply.

Honee's eyes and mouth appeared to explode outward as though about to fly right off her face. "No! You do not! You are the shaman! Simu would be well-advised to remember that . . . lest the spirits who speak to Umak in the Seeing Wind decide to make Simu pay!"

Something ugly contorted Simu's face. "Oh, I *will* remember," he replied with bitterly mocking deference. "And I will tremble every time I think of it! After all, with a shaman like Umak to intercede for a man on behalf of the spirits, and a luck-bringing girl like Naya to make the forces of Creation smile, how can anything go wrong, eh? Unless we want to start counting the dead and the injured and—"

"Simu!" Torka's warning was as dark and dangerous as the deep-water currents that ran in the Great Mad River at flood tide. "Let it rest! And before you speak against Umak again, remember that *I* led you eastward out of the valley. Honee says that she does not know what twists your spirit, but I know. Too long have we walked as brothers for me not to see into your heart, Simu. Words against Naya will not take away Larani's scars. By insulting and impugning my sons, you cannot bring back your own! And by creating dissension among this people, you cannot restore life to Eneela."

Silence fell. Simu stared at Torka as though the headman had struck him with a rock.

"Fix blame if it will ease you, old friend," said Torka evenly. "Blame me, for surely I have often blamed myself. Blame Naya, for she has sometimes behaved foolishly and irresponsibly. Blame my sons, for neither one is perfect. But who is? Are *you*? I think not. So blame who you will, but know now, once and for all, that I will not let you tear my people apart!" Torka's tone softened. "Come now, old friend! The day is young. The sun is rising in a cloudless sky. The wind is a strong, blackfly-eating wind! There are stones to be gathered on Spear Mountain, and leaves and berries to be picked! The mammoth walks before us! Good hunting grounds lie ahead. What more could a man desire? Walk with your woman Summer Moon and with your newborn son and be grateful for what you *have* even if you cannot forget what you have *lost*! What has been done cannot be undone. Let us learn from our mistakes and get on with our lives!"

The wind blew out of the southern ranges, redolent of artemisia and distant steppelands, of forests of spruce and tamarack, and of groves of willow and cottonwood in which the leaves had already begun to turn gold. As Manaravak stopped on the loose scree of the south-facing ridge of Spear Mountain, he knew that he was scenting the good, rich smell of the hunting grounds that he and Demmi had discovered beyond the far ranges. It was a good scent, filled with promise of new and better days to come.

And yet the hackles rose on the back of his neck because there was another scent on the wind; it was so subtle only he and the dogs smelled it: the scent of something alive—of flesh and blood and fur.

"What is the matter, Manaravak?" asked Sayanah, clambering over the loose stones to join his brother and Jhon, and the sons of Grek.

"Nothing," Manaravak lied.

The scent was all around him. The dogs were worrying over it, circling and sniffing. Lower upon the ridge, Dak and Simu had raised their heads into the wind.

"What is it?" asked Simu.

"Can you make it out, Manaravak?" Dak called.

"No." Another lie. It was the wanawut. He was a man of the People at last and wanted no part of the wanawut now. But if the other hunters knew that the beasts were near, they would insist upon stalking the wanawut and killing them. As always, the thought upset him.

The distant scent was distressing the dogs.

"Something's out there!" exclaimed Jhon with excitement.

Manaravak eyed Umak's son; he would not be easy to deceive.

"Torka says that we will hunt tomorrow!" informed Sayanah. "Whatever is riling the dogs had better be wary of us!"

Manaravak raised a brow. "The provisions from the Lake of Watered Blood have not run out."

"No," agreed Sayanah. "But Simu does not like that meat, and Torka has been keeping an eye out for signs of game."

Tankh took the posture of a spearman about to be attacked and, using an imaginary spear, pretended to be killing something. "The animal I want is big and hairy and walks like a man. It will die in fear of me when I kill it with my new spear."

"No more!" Manaravak snatched the son of Grek by the front of his tunic. "Do not even think it. If the life spirits of the game will honor us by coming forth to die upon our spears, those spirits will be moose, elk, bison, and caribou.

But never is any spear of mine, or of my design, to be used against wanawut." Manaravak pushed Tankh away, and as the boy gasped for air, he added sternly, "A man of the People I am, but I have been one with the wanawut and will not raise a spear against them any more than I would against any of you."

"Not *ever?*" Sayanah pressed him.

Manaravak looked down at his younger brother. Memories, confusing and conflicting, were strong in him. He shook them away. "Not ever," he said.

11

The sun set, and darkness enveloped the encampment. As Honee, Naya, and Li worked together to transform Umak into the shaman, he found it difficult to stand still. Torka had asked him to make an especially fine show this night, and his females were outdoing themselves.

"There is much to be grateful for!" exclaimed Honee, daubing the tip of the little finger of her right hand into the black colorant that Li held up to her on a plate made of an antelope pelvis. The paint was a mixture of finely ground ashes thinned to a paste in hot water within which clean parings taken from the underside of a sealskin had been simmered. The resulting colorant went on smooth and thick. "The mammoth totem is leading us again, and—if we are to believe Demmi and Manaravak—we are going to the finest hunting grounds that any of us have ever seen!"

Umak exhaled a blast of impatience. "We should go back to the Lake of Watered Blood instead. It is an offense to the forces of Creation to abandon a camp in which there was so much food at hand."

Honee frowned. "You had no vision from the Seeing Wind to tell you that the People must stay."

"No, I did not. Perhaps I should have made one up!"

"A shaman does not lie!" reminded the woman, annoyed.

"Yes, Honee, yes!" Umak cut her off impatiently. "But Simu is right about this country. There are too many ghosts in it. He is not the only one to be ill at ease with them. I, too, feel their presence and chafe against it."

Honee made a face. "Manaravak does not chafe! Manaravak does not worry over ghosts! Manaravak has returned from the world beyond this world and has caused the People to fear that Umak's power has failed him! You must show them that this is not true."

"If the People want to name my brother Shaman, let them do so!"

"There is no need," said Naya softly. She knelt to Umak's right, festooning his ankle with a thong of feathers and small, polished bones that would click and rattle when he danced. "I will help my shaman make a special magic for *all* the People so not even Simu will have cause to question my man's powers."

"I do not care what Simu thinks of me!"

"But you must!" declared Naya. "Grandmother Wallah used to tell me that for a medicine to work, the People must have faith in its magic!"

"You speak wisdom, my dear girl!" Honee said, then turned to Umak. "Naya is right. Simu's doubts and fears can eat away at the faith of the People until there will be no magic left for any of us!"

Umak looked at Naya. "And how can the granddaughter of Grek restore Simu's faith in Umak's magic when Umak himself has been unable to do so?" he asked politely.

Naya hesitated for a moment. "This woman can make a drink that will cause the People to forget their fears while their bellies grow warm within the cold night and their spirits smile as they fly away across the world and back again at Umak's command." She stopped speaking. Their faces had gone blank. "It is true! I can do this for my shaman!"

Honee looked at Umak. Umak looked at Honee.

Li looked at them all and said quietly, "I do not want my spirit to fly across the world and back again."

"No, dear, nor would any of us," said Honee.

Naya felt insulted. "You *would* come back. I have come back safely many times."

"Of course, dear girl," Honee patronized. "But we are wasting time. There are still more feathers and bones to string."

"You don't believe me!"

"I . . . well . . . come, Naya, give this woman a useful hand now."

"No," Umak said, touched by the expression of hurt upon Naya's face. He rested his hand lovingly upon her head. "Honee and Li will assist me here. Mix leaves and lichens, mosses and berries if it will please you. What harm can it do?"

The women raised the communal fire high. The People ate, but the shaman fasted. Apart from the other members of the band, Umak stood with his arms raised to the night and his spirit open to the Seeing Wind. Salivating, he was painfully aware that his conjuring was no more than the wishful thinking of a man who had not eaten since midday. With a sigh, he knew full well that he would not eat until his performance was done, and so he came forth to dance before the flames.

He chanted. He whirled. He sang the history of the People, while Naya, Honee, and Li circulated among the gathering with bladder flasks of the ceremonial brew that the granddaughter of Grek had prepared in haste but in generous portions. All drank. All exclaimed of its excellence—except Larani. She took one sip. Visibly startled, she quickly handed back the flask and would have spoken, but Naya turned and stepped dancingly away to offer the flask to Summer Moon. By then the three females who resided at the shaman's fire circle had passed the flasks to everyone except Umak and the dogs.

The shaman was not certain when things began to go wrong. He sensed an immediate change in those who were watching his performance: The younger children became drowsier until, yawning and giggling happily, they curled up and fell asleep. The day had been long, so Umak would not have counted this as unusual had it not been for the disconcerting way in which their parents were observing him out of fixed, unblinking eyes. A few moments later, Jhon sat bolt upright, clasped his hands to his mouth, and ran from the gathering to become violently sick.

Honee watched him out of lackluster eyes and tittered after him almost malevolently. "Mustn't bolt your food. . . . Mother's warned you many times. Cough it up! Serves you right!"

Umak frowned. In the past, Honee had often warned the boy to eat more slowly, but it was not like her to take even the most trivial complaints of her children lightly. Yet when

Jhon came swaying back to the fire, his summer-browned face as pale as chalk, she tittered again and chastised him while offering another pull on one of the bladder flasks.

"Ugh!" He waved it away. "It makes me sick!" Seated cross-legged and shivering with revulsion beside Sayanah, he rubbed his temples as though to be rid of a headache while Sayanah greedily accepted the bladder from Honee and took a deep pull.

In the red, flickering glow of the fire, Umak saw his young brother grow wide-eyed with amazement and then, with a beatific smile on his face, swoon into a dead faint.

Umak waited for Torka to rise and see if Sayanah was all right, but Torka did not move.

"Dance, my son! Why do you stop?" asked Torka, his words oddly slurred.

What *had* Naya put in her ceremonial brew? Umak wondered. She had said that she could make the spirits of men fly away, and so she had! The realization was upsetting. Demmi sighed sleepily, then suddenly laughed out loud as she pointed a finger at him, and every conscious pair of eyes in the band followed her finger, and everyone who was not in a stupor laughed as though at the funniest joke in all the world.

Umak was annoyed and disconcerted. He altered his dance, wondering what he was doing wrong and why he had become an object of amusement.

Suddenly, with her baby asleep in her back carrier, Summer Moon was on her feet, dancing with him, mimicking his steps. When he told her to sit down before she angered the spirits and woke her little one, she smiled blankly at him and shushed him. Before he knew what was happening, Swan, Honee, and Lonit had joined her.

Umak stopped. The women kept on dancing. It was not his dance now; it was theirs. They were holding hands and sidestepping around the fire. All were smiling, suppressing laughter, looking at one another as though sharing some wonderful jest at his expense.

Honee called to Naya, and the granddaughter of Grek joined the circle. Umak knew that she was as intoxicated as any of them. Larani, sober, stayed away from the dancing, as did Demmi, who was sound asleep.

Umak turned from the women's side of the fire. The men of the band had begun to clap their hands in a sure, slow, steady rhythm.

"Women, you move like *plaku* dancers!" exclaimed Simu.

The words brought a sensual laugh from Summer Moon as, pausing before her man, she reached up and loosed the thongs that held her braids. When her hair fell loose, she shook her head, and beneath the fall of her tunic, her breasts shook as well. Her movement was so sexually provocative and out of character that Umak stared like a gape-mouthed boy as her baby began to cry.

Simu cheered, quickening the pace of his clapping. "*Plaku!*" he called out. "Would you be willing, Summer Moon? Would any of the women of this band be willing? After all that we have endured, where's the harm, eh?" There was fire in his question, and a deep, hungry, sexual excitement.

Umak was stunned. Performed in the land of their ancestors and wisely forbidden by Torka, the *plaku* was a ritual dance that ended in savagely erotic couplings. Was Simu seriously calling for the women of the band to strip off their garments and dance naked before their men until, at last, tradition commanded each woman to join for a single night of pleasure with a partner other than her own mate?

"No!" Panic broke loose within his veins. On a night of *plaku,* Naya would dance naked, but she would not dance for him. She would dance for Manaravak. He knew it. He felt it in his bones and blood and heart. His brother would have her, after all.

He looked directly at Manaravak now, standing tall and watchful behind Torka. His long lids were lowered in speculation. He was like a wolf as he looked across the fire at Naya.

"Never!" Umak raged the word and tore his eyes from Manaravak to stare at his father imploringly. "Torka, you must tell Simu that what he suggests is impossible. For the good of the band, you have wisely forbidden the ritual of *plaku*. Torka, what are you doing?"

The headman struggled to his feet. At last he managed to stand upright, to steady himself, and to focus his eyes. "*Plaku?*" He spoke the word as though unsure of it.

Umak felt sick. His father had drunk much too deeply of Naya's magic drink. He looked around. With the exception of Larani and the colt tethered nearby, everyone was drunk—including the dogs, since the boys had seen fit to feed them meat soaked in Naya's special brew. A terrible, sinking feeling settled in his gut.

"Be shtill, Shaman!" demanded Torka. "I am headman! I shay what ish done or not done in thish band!"

"But, my father, the *plaku* ceremony, it is not—"

"Be shtill, I shay! I have no shtomach for the ways of rude shons hor for rude shamans hor for *plaku* chere . . . cheremo . . . cheremoniesh. But if each woman feels now like dancing for her *own* man, I could not shay that it would not be a good thing."

And so it was that each woman of Torka's band danced for her man. They danced naked in the light of a fire that the men were too drunk to tend. They danced, and the men sang, and the colt whinnied nervously as dogs, bleary-eyed with an excess of Naya's brew, howled off-key . . . and did not hear something else howling—far away but not so far that Larani, who had taken Summer Moon's infant from that woman, did not stiffen and stare and try to make the others take notice.

It was no use. No one cared. The dancing was too intense. The sound that she heard—or thought she heard—was too fleeting. Besides, stalking animals made no noise. If they did, they would never eat.

Larani relaxed and rocked Summer Moon's infant. The night was fine and cool, with the wind feeding life into the fire's embers. Gusting as it was, she could not bring herself to venture near to the fire, and so she sat apart, to the lee of a grouping of large boulders that allowed her a view of the dancing.

She imagined how it would be if she were one of them—naked, beautiful in the firelight, desired by her man. She smiled tenderly. Old Grek was asleep with the children. She was not sorry. Such a night as this would be too much for him. Tomorrow she would tell him how it had been between them, and she would make things up that would cause him to smile proudly and believe that he was still as much a man as he had ever been.

She sighed. The women circled the fire again and again, facing their men, then turning away, sliding their feet slowly to the side, allowing the firelight to penetrate between their thighs as they raised their arms and displayed their breasts and rolled their hips while their men pounded out a quickening rhythm with the clap of their hands and the beat of their palms upon their thighs. Larani envied them.

The men were rising now. One by one they were undressing—even Umak. He was not drunk on Naya's brew but on the sight of the young woman. Honee was dancing by herself. Larani caught her breath. Umak was naked now. How fine he was. How fine they all were. How powerful and ready to fill their women as they faced their partners and took up their part in a dance that was not really a dance at all.

Her face flushed. She saw Torka extend his hands to Lonit. Simu was gesturing to Summer Moon in a way that set Larani's pulse throbbing. Dak stood looking first toward the sleeping Demmi and then, with a snap of his head, he aggressively placed his hands upon Swan's hips and took her down, ending her dance and beginning a new one then and there. Larani's face was burning now. Manaravak was standing alone. He had no partner. His eyes were on Umak.

Manaravak! How she longed to dance for him . . . to touch him . . . to open herself to him, body and spirit . . . to tell him that he need never be alone, that she would be his, all that he would ever need or desire, more woman than he could imagine if he would only . . . Only what?

The bitterness that she felt at this moment was appalling. She was certain that he would lie with Honee before he would so much as look at her. When Yona, Li, or Uni matured, he would name one of them as his own. She would stand aside, watching him pass, knowing that he would not even look her way, let alone see the love in her eyes, as he eagerly claimed his new woman.

Larani suddenly regretted not having drunk her share of the ceremonial brew. It would have been good to face this night without pain. She stared at the dancers. Naya was moving dreamily before Umak, working her hips for him, performing the sex act with an invisible partner for him, arousing him, inviting him . . . and Manaravak.

Larani went cold. *Stupid girl*, she thought. *Stupid, mindless girl! Have you learned nothing?*

She stared ahead, unable to look away as Naya danced before the twins. Honee circled the threesome, giggling until Larani longed to trip her, take her place, and lead Manaravak away from Naya's dangerous, mindless game. She trembled with wanting until the specter of herself dancing naked with her scarred face and arm and back made her catch her breath in misery.

As Larani watched, Naya fell to the ground and writhed

on her back. With her limbs parted and bent at the knees, she arched her hips, held herself open, and began to move—to dance—all the while reaching toward the brothers who stood above her, beckoning them down, inviting them to share her dance. As Larani watched in horror, Manaravak snarled with sudden viciousness and without warning pushed Umak away. He fell upon Naya, gripped her flanks, and with a single thrust penetrated deeply.

"Yes!" Naya cried.

But at that very moment Umak charged Manaravak from behind.

Larani hung her head and walked to the other side of the boulders. She did not want to see any more. She did not want to see Manaravak taking another woman.

Yet, with the sound of the dancers pounding in her ears, a fierce rebelliousness rose in her. Why should she not take part in this night of celebration? With old Grek in a stupor, who would know or care whether she danced or not? Who would see unless she let them see? Only the dogs. Only the wind. Only the uncounted and uncountable star eyes of Father Above! And he would not care if she danced. The sight of her could not possibly offend him. He and his daughter had made her what she was. Let them watch! Let Daughter of the Sky turn away in shame to see what she had done to a child of the earth who had never done her any harm! Let Father Above marvel at how much of a woman Larani still was.

And so, after setting the baby gently down into a sheltering crevice between two boulders, she stripped off her tunic. With the wind in her hair and the cool, starlit darkness caressing every curve of her body, Larani danced. She whirled. With tears of defiance shining in her eyes, she cupped her breasts and raised them to the night. They were beautiful . . . her body was beautiful . . . as she had once been beautiful. Once, but no more.

And so she danced alone and cursed the forces of Creation for maiming her, and Simu for not killing her when he had had the chance.

Manaravak's blood was spattered across Naya's face and body.

"What has happened here?" Torka demanded of Umak. "Why have you raised your hand against your brother?"

"I swore that I would kill him if he touched her, and by all the powers in this world and the next now I will do just that!"

Manaravak staggered to his feet. Blood ran from his broken nose and turned his fingers and the back of his hand black in the moonlight. "She invited it." Manaravak's words were tight with pain. The hostility in his eyes was terrible to behold.

But not half as terrible as the anger on Torka's face. "Enough!" Torka was adamant. "No son of mine will ever again raise his hand against his brother!"

"Then tell Manaravak to stay away from my woman."

"You have two!" Manaravak retorted.

"No longer!" declared Torka. "Get up, Naya."

Naya laughed. Umak reached to clasp her wrists and yank her to her feet.

"I have had enough of this endless bickering over the granddaughter of Grek!" the headman erupted. "By the forces of Creation, Umak, share the stupid, troublemaking creature and let me hear no more about it—or I swear to you, Naya will walk the wind forever!"

"No!" Umak raged.

Torka fixed Naya with a look of dislike that withered her on the spot. "I had hoped that you had changed, but you play my sons against one another as though they were a game. Because of your medicine drink, there has been a madness on my people tonight. I must think long and hard about this, Naya. But now my head throbs, my gut is heavy, and my body aches for want of sleep. I suggest that you and my sons seek sleep apart from one another so that you may think about what I have said. I will not warn you again."

12

The wanawut came while the band slept in a drunken stupor. Not even the dogs sensed their presence until it was too late.

Larani heard Life Giver trumpet in the hills to the east. She raised her head in time to see manlike shapes moving past the boulders in which she and the baby had been sleeping. The creatures moved as though in a dream—massive beasts, knee-deep in ground fog, ambling forward with their backs hunched.

She caught her breath in horror. Never had she been so close to wanawut. There were five of them, each nearly as big and furred as a bear, except for the one female among them. Noticeably pregnant, the creature was taller than Larani, and its bone structure and musculature were massive, revealing the potential of inordinate physical strength and endurance. Like its male counterparts, the female moved with knees bent and its short, stubby limbs bowed outward. Its arms were longer than its legs—so long, in fact, that although the animal stood more or less upright, it was able to knuckle the ground as it walked. A thick coat of stringy, mouse-brown hair covered every inch of its body except for the end of its bearlike snout, its disturbingly human-looking ears, the palms of its hands, and the two spatulate breasts that swung like a pair of dark, distended, overused bladder flasks.

Larani was sickened by the sight of the female thing and terrified by the muscular power of the other, larger animals that walked with it. They were moving toward the encampment of her people! They were advancing in the way of hunters—slowly, methodically, rousing no sound that might betray their presence to their unwary prey.

Her heart was pounding. Why didn't the dogs bark? She suddenly remembered that they were as sotted as her people. The only sober man in the entire camp was Umak, but after his earlier confrontation with Manaravak and Torka, she suspected that he might well have turned to drink in order to be able to sleep. If he had, who would sound alarm? What would happen if no one did? The answer was clear and irrefutable. *I must warn them! I am the only one who can! But if I cry out, who except the wanawut will hear me?*

Within the fold of Larani's arm, the baby began to squirm and fuss. In a near panic, she quickly offered a fingertip to the hungry infant, effectively silencing it. This baby, hungering for the milk of Summer Moon, would not long be satisfied to suck upon the thin, dry finger. In a moment it would begin to fuss again, and the wanawut would hear.

Her right hand slowly took up the skinning dagger that she had placed upon the stones next to where she had been sleeping. With it curled in her fist, she stood to her full height. For the sake of the infant, for her people, and for Manaravak, who lay asleep within the encampment and unaware of danger, Larani knew what she must do.

There was no time to waste. With a deep intake of breath to steady her nerves and strengthen her resolve, she slung off her dress. The cold struck at her skin, and her senses screamed in protest. She ignored them. Deftly, she wrapped the infant in her garment to muffle its cries as she bent to place the child within a protective crevice deep within the boulders. *Be safe little one,* she thought. *Be silent! If the forces of Creation are with us both, I will soon bring your mother back to feed you!*

She did not wait to discover whether the infant would be still or not. With her dagger in hand, Larani raced naked into danger.

"*Wanawut!*" She screamed the word again and again—a strident warning to her people that also called the attention of the wanawut to herself.

As the beasts turned, Larani thought that she would collapse with terror, but she did not. She displayed herself for them. She waved her arms and danced in great leaping strides, which took her away from the baby and farther still from any possible help from the band. "Come! Feed upon this woman if you hunger for the flesh of my kind this night! Ugly as you are, you should find me perfect for your tastes! Follow me! Catch me if you can!"

They stood dead still in the wind, watching her, listening to her taunts, weighing her value as meat. The largest animal stood erect. Every silver-tipped hair on its back was up. With a low huff of disdain and an enraged beating of fists against its massive chest, its lips curled back to show its teeth. Once again, Larani nearly fainted with terror. The wanawut had the teeth of a lion, and as one of its fists opened she saw that its hands were as big as the paws of a bear, and as clawed. She saw her fate glinting in the carnivore's gray eyes. In comparison, the burning hands of Daughter of the Sky seemed merciful.

"No . . ." Her mouth went dry. She was shaking so violently that her teeth chattered. "No! I will not stand here and wait for you. Come! All of you! Follow me, I say."

As Larani whirled around and began to race screaming toward the river, the female and two of the males took after her. But two others, including the huge silver-backed male, turned and headed straight for the encampment of the People.

"Torka! Wake up, Torka!"

Torka groaned at the sound of Lonit's voice. His head felt so heavy that he did not want to lift it from his bed furs.

Lonit was sitting up beside him, refusing to allow him to go back to sleep. There was an imperative quality to her voice that could not be denied. "Listen!"

Fighting against nausea, he sat up, holding his head and pressing in against his temples lest they explode. He listened and heard the sound of a woman screaming and the whinnying of the colt.

Torka was on his feet in an instant. Dizziness struck him, and he fell. Disoriented, he shook his head. Pain flared. It was all he could do to keep from vomiting. Cursing Naya and her foul drink, he forced himself to rise. He was nearly sick again as, moving across the darkness of their hut, he waved the door skin aside and stepped out into the predawn darkness. When the cold air touched his skin, it seemed to turn him inside out.

"Torka! Your spears!" Lonit called after him.

But he was on his knees, too violently, gut-wrenchingly sick to answer.

Larani's screams brought Demmi out of her drug-induced dreams. The screams were growing farther and farther away. Not so the frantic whinnying of Manaravak's colt or the sound of a man being sick.

Seated next to the lifeless rubble of the feast fire, Demmi felt unfocused. Who was sick? Had the screams been real?

Half-asleep, she raised her head and found herself facing two wanawut. Instinctively, her hand reached for a weapon, then froze. She had not brought her bola or even her skinning knife to the previous night's festivities.

The animal directly in front of her was the big silver-backed male that she had seen in the cave. Another, darker-furred male was leaning around her, scenting along the line of her hips, plucking at her tunic with curious fingers, and pinching her skin along with it.

"Ouch!" she cried, and silently cursed herself for lack of control. Almost instantaneously, the silver-backed beast furiously shoved the other wanawut away. The animal allowed itself to be pushed, but not before baring its teeth and issuing a roar of defiance—the sort that Demmi had heard many a predator make when being driven back from a potential meal by a dominant animal. The silver back responded with a roar of its own. She caught the hot scent of its breath and was nearly sick with dread.

"Demmi, do not move! They mean you no harm, Sister!"

Manaravak's command came from somewhere to her left. She was so paralyzed by fear that she could not have moved if she tried. Could he believe what he was saying? Was there a chance that he could possibly be right?

"Mother?" Kharn's query was a tremulous peep.

Her heart stopped.

Roused by the roar of the beast, Kharn looked up from where he had been sleeping with the other boys and stared across the fire toward her. Fear ebbed from Demmi as her maternal instincts came to the fore. Her son had called her Mother for the first time!

Demmi's eyes met Kharn's, then looked away lest the wanawut be drawn to him by following her line of sight. When she spoke, her voice was completely under control. "Do not say another word, my son. Breathe softly . . . slowly now . . . and begin to back away. . . ." Her warning was cut short. The silver back leaned in close and screeched at her.

She cowered before his appalling power. There was only one thing on her mind now: survival for herself, her unborn child, and her son.

Where was Dak? Where was everybody? Had the adults retired to their pit huts and left her alone with the children? Could Naya's ceremonial drink have made them so irresponsible? Demmi was suddenly cold as she realized that the wanawut had evidently overlooked the sleeping children as they came stalking into the dark, unguarded camp.

But if Manaravak was awake, then the other members of the band were probably awake, too! In a moment spears would fly, bolas would whir, the beasts would fall dead, and everything would be all right again. But no spears flew. No bolas whirred. Demmi realized that the dogs were not barking. Perhaps Naya's brew was not meant for dogs, and they would never wake up again.

Still curled submissively before the beast, the woman fought desperately against panic. The silver back was sniffing at her back, shoulders, and sides in quick, excited sucks of air. It was all she could do to keep from screaming as its hands began a hurtful exploration. She realized with horror that it was determining her gender.

Distracted by the frenzied sounds of the horse, the silver back twisted its upper body to stare in the colt's direction—the same direction from which Manaravak had called. At that moment hope shriveled and died within her; Manaravak, she realized, had gone to calm the horse rather than lift a spear against the wanawut threatening his sister and the band's children.

Slowly she raised and turned her head to see Manaravak poised halfway between his lean-to and the colt. Even in the predawn darkness she could see his indescribable confusion. The world seemed suddenly to sink beneath her. Manaravak could not make up his mind!

"Manaravak!" A sob broke out of her. "Why do you wait? Throw your spears! Or are you truly one of them, after all?"

Her cry had won the full attention of the beast. She stared straight into the familiar face. Demmi had seen it before—in the fog, in the cave, and in countless nightmares. The cold, gray eyes narrowed. The brow wrinkled. The lip seams rolled away from its teeth. The shaggy, grizzled mane bristled along its upper back and shoulders.

"Get back! Get away from me!"

The beast sucked in its breath in obvious surprise. It cocked its head. And then it uttered a series of low, dangerous growls. Demmi saw recognition in its eyes. The wanawut knew her! The beast remembered her words and what she had done! She had killed its mate, and now, in this moment, Demmi knew that she, too, was going to die.

"Dak!" She screamed the name of her man even though

she knew that no man could help her now. Her control shattered. "Run, Kharn!" she screamed. "Wake up, children! Run! Run for your life!" With the ferocity of a cornered animal, Demmi grabbed one of the hairy hands of the wanawut. Shaking her head like a badger burrowing for a vein, she bit through fur and skin and muscle until her teeth struck bone. The wanawut, startled, grabbed her by her head with its free hand and tried to pull her away. She would not be pulled. Claws pierced her brow and raked back along her skull, scalping her, but still she savaged the hand of the beast, ripping flesh and tendon until, with an outraged shriek of pain, the wanawut raised its arm so quickly that she was pulled straight off the ground. And still she held on, biting deeper and harder until the wanawut flung its arm sideways with such force that Demmi was hurled across the encampment.

In shock, with her own blood in her eyes and the flesh and fur of the beast still in her mouth, the pregnant woman landed hard on her back. Stunned, the breath went out of her as she heard her spine snap and her skull crack. Light and sound exploded within her head as a single word rang out.

"Demmi!"

It was Dak. She knew his voice. He was calling her name. She tried to answer but could not. She felt strangely cut loose from her body. Light was fading, and all sounds, external and internal, were rushing inward to pool within her shattered skull as the last, lingering remnants of Dak's voice cracked and fell into the blood-filled ruin of her brain like pieces of clear ice falling before a darkening sun that would radiate heat and light no more.

"No!" Manaravak hurled his spear. Even as it left his hand he knew that it was wide of its target, and even if it had struck true, he was too late to save his sister.

The silver back was already down with Dak's spear in its back. The other wanawut was racing off, bounding with a speed that surprised those who leaped out of its way. Now the encampment dissolved into confusion as Uni and the boys scattered from the fire. Old Grek sat up, bleary-eyed and uncomprehending, with Tankh and Chuk clutching at his armpits and trying to drag him away.

The silver back, up again, was reaching around, grabbing at the spear that had pierced its upper back. As it turned, it spotted Grek and his sons.

Manaravak's eyes refused to focus properly. Was the residue of Naya's drink blinding him, or was it his tears? If Demmi was dead, it was his fault! She had called for his help, and he had hesitated. No! He had done worse than that—he had known that the beasts were close to the encampment, but worried more about them than the safety of his people, he had said nothing! He had allowed himself and every man, woman, and child in the band to become intoxicated and vulnerable to their predations. And after the wanawut had entered the encampment and his sister had cried out to him, he had been unable to place his loyalty.

"Manaravak! What is wrong with you? Move!"

He was shocked by Lonit's command and by the ferociousness of her expression. She had just seen one of her daughters killed while her son had stood by and done nothing. While the wanawut towered over Grek and his sons, Torka was swaying on his feet. He had his spears in hand, but he looked sick and old and disoriented. The previous night of drinking had affected him badly. Manaravak was stunned by the sight. For the first time in his life, the young man realized that the calamities of the past year had cost Torka. By the time his unsteady hands levered a spear and sent it flying, Grek and his sons would suffer the same fate as Demmi.

Manaravak froze, transfixed. The wanawut, standing upright, had drawn the spear from its back, and as Tankh and Chuk yelled hysterically at Grek to get up, the beast cracked the shaft in half. Snarling, it threw the shattered pieces at the threesome. When the butt end of the shaft hit Tankh, panic set fire to the youth. He forgot his father and his brother. He stood up and would have run away, but his action instigated an instant reaction in the silver back. The long arm reached out and slashed the boy so hard across his face that his head snapped back as he went sprawling. There was something unnatural in the way Tankh fell. He did not get up. And still Manaravak could not move.

Umak raced out of the darkness from the opposite side of the encampment where he had chosen to spend the night with Jhon well away from his people. As Manaravak watched, Umak took deadly, sober, unhesitating aim with his spear. Jhon did the same. Simu and Dak closed on the beast with the women and children right behind them, whirling their bolas, hurling stones and clods of tundral soil, and shouting, "Away! Away!"

Companion, Snow Eater, and the younger dogs were up. Torka was in the fray now. He seemed to be himself again, running low in long, powerful strides that took him straight to Grek. Without hesitation, he hauled the old man safely away, with Chuk trailing behind, as Dak, Simu, Umak, and the boys kept at the beast with their spears, hurting it, wounding it.

The silver back was openly bewildered. In a rain of stones, surrounded by armed, shouting people and menacing dogs, it let loose a howl of agony as one of Umak's spears came in from behind to strike clean through its back. It grasped at the projectile point as it pierced through its chest. Another spear came hurtling out of the fading night to strike the wanawut through the throat. Manaravak felt its pain. It was down again, on its knees, grabbing for spears that were so deeply embedded that they would not pull free . . . spears designed by one who had never intended them to be used against such prey as this. Unable to restrain himself, Manaravak howled with the wanawut, sounding to it in the way of its kind to take away its pain, confusion and, by so doing, eradicate his own.

The first light of the sun was showing over the eastern ranges, but Manaravak hardly saw it. High above, a white-headed eagle circled and keened as it winged its way toward the southern mountains, but Manaravak hardly heard it. His people were keening now! The sound of their voices seemed to come from far away as Manaravak watched Dak turn from the slain wanawut. The man's face looked as though it had been flayed. Slowly, as though each step hurt him, Dak crossed the encampment, knelt by Demmi's broken body, and took his woman in his arms. It was a lover's embrace. With gentle fingers, he lovingly smoothed her hair, arranging it to cover the wounds in her mutilated scalp. He kissed the blood from her face. He placed an open, tenderly questing palm across her belly, and then, with a moan of agony, he laid his face against hers and sobbed her name.

"Demmi, come back to me, Demmi. You and the baby, *our baby*! Do you hear me? Forgive me, Demmi. Come back to me, please. How can I bear to lose you twice?"

It was a moment before he began to keen. He was not alone. His people surrounded him. Swan stood close at his back, Naya to the side, looking down in horror at the woman's corpse. With Torka and Lonit kneeling beside him, touching the body of their beloved daughter, Dak began to wail as Umak, in a broken, constricted voice, offered the death song for his sister and for the woman whom Dak had loved and spurned and yet had never stopped loving . . . or ever would.

"Demmi . . ." Her name bled from Manaravak's mouth. With it came all the cherished memories of youth, of laughter and song and sharing, of Demmi at his side, teaching him, loving him, risking everything for a brother who, in the end, had chosen to side with the wanawut and had let her die. He was so filled with shame that his senses seemed to be screaming *Forgive me! Forgive me!* But these were the words of man, and by his actions he had set himself apart from his own kind forever. When he saw Grek gather the body of his son Tankh in his arms and raise it to the sun, begging Father Above to restore life to the children of the People, Manaravak's heart felt as though it had been rent in two.

How could Father Above restore their lives when it was Manaravak who had taken them as surely as though he, and not the wanawut, had killed them? The question was more than he could bear. He was not conscious of howling. He knew only that his pain must be released, or he would die of it. His head went back. His arms went wide. His body shook as the sounds of his agony escaped his lips and ascended to the sky until a sharp, bruising pain to his shoulder silenced him.

A pale, curved object about the length of his forearm went hurtling past him with deadly speed and power. He heard it slice the air and knew that it would have struck a mortal blow had it been only a few inches higher and closer to his head. Grasping at his aching biceps and staring in astonishment at his people, Manaravak knew that one of them had thrown something at him. To silence him or to kill him? He saw the answer in their eyes. They were looking at him in revulsion and horror, as though a treacherous, murderous stranger had suddenly appeared to stand before them in the skin of someone they had known and loved and trusted.

He had betrayed their love. He had proved unworthy of their trust. They had called him Son and Brother and Man of the People; but in the end the formative years that he had spent with beasts had named him Wanawut.

Lonit's hands were folded around Torka's forearm. The expression of abject misery on her face told the story. Only a mother's love had saved him when Torka had taken it upon himself to claim a father's and a headman's right—to end the life of one who had proved to be a threat to his band. Manaravak's eyes widened as, disbelieving, he looked down and saw Torka's bludgeon lying broken upon the stones at his feet.

The etched whalebone—symbolic of the unity of the band and of the strength and purpose of his father's life—was broken . . . because of him. Demmi was dead . . . because of him. Old Grek and the People mourned again . . . because of him. Manaravak's heart, already torn by the agony of regret, cracked wide.

He was Manaravak, son of Torka, a man of the People, but on this dawn he had forfeited his right to live among them. He turned away, longing for death, deciding to seek it just as Honee cried out in terror.

"Where is Li? Has anyone seen Li?"

"Or Yona?" asked Chuk and, suddenly, with a cry of despair, began to call for his sister.

"Larani! Where are you, Larani?" called Simu, and for a man who had declared time and time again that he wished his daughter dead, he sounded inordinately concerned. Suddenly he dropped to his knees and wailed like a keening woman.

Larani! The image of that bright, scarred, lustrous girl pricked more sharply than the point of a spear. He was suddenly alert again, alive again. *Where* was *Larani? Where* were *the children?* The worst fears of his people could not match the horror of the truth: They had been stolen, taken by the wanawut, not to be meat but to be mated with beasts who had not enough females of their own.

"No!" Manaravak spoke the word of a man and did not see the expanding expression of rage that was twisting Umak's face.

"You! Animal! My daughter is gone because of you! How could you have stood by and watched and done nothing?"

Manaravak still had a spear in his hand—a spear that might have saved the life of Demmi or Tankh. A spear that could still be spent, if not for them, then for Larani and the children. When Umak charged him, he held the spear point out, jabbed forward, and warned his brother back until Dak tossed Umak a weapon.

Now, suddenly, the twin sons of Torka stood facing one another. No one moved.

"You should never have come back, Manaravak. I will kill you now. I *must* kill you now. You do not deserve to see another day!"

When Umak lunged, Manaravak leaped high and away; nevertheless, his brother's spearhead sliced his tunic and missed piercing his side by less than a hair's width.

Never had Manaravak seen such hatred on his brother's face. It twisted his strong, even features and made them ugly, carnivorous. And yet, even as Manaravak saw Umak position himself for another thrust, he felt only love for him, and with sorrow and regret, he whirled around and knocked Umak flat.

"*I must* see another day!" he exclaimed, and as a stunned, breathless Umak looked up at him out of eyes that had gone momentarily blank, he turned and ran.

He had misinterpreted the true nature of the wanawut, but he *had* lived too long among them not to have learned their ways. He would find them. And then, for Demmi and Tankh, and for Li and Yona and Larani, he knew what he must do.

◆━━━━━◆

13

◆━━━━━◆

Knife in hand, Larani plunged headlong into the river and gave herself to the current. She looked back over her bare shoulder. With a shock as penetrating as the cold water, she saw that the wanawut were still following. They could swim! She could not. They were covered with thick, insulating fur! She was naked. In a moment her body was so cold and aching that it was all she could do to hold on to the knife. Gasping for breath and straining to keep her head above water, she tried to paddle in the way that she had seen the dogs do at many a river crossing. It was no good; she was too cold. She allowed the river to take her as it would, reminding herself that she weighed little compared to even the smallest wanawut; perhaps the current would carry her more swiftly and keep her bobbing at the surface while the heavy-bodied, thick-boned beasts flailed about like rocks trying to float. It was a fleeting hope. As Larani was dragged under and pulled violently downstream, she remembered the massively fat bodies of the creatures that had swum so elegantly within the Lake of Watered Blood and had a fleeting image of the long, muscular arms of the wanawut reaching over the waters, slicing through them with ease while she was swept away.

The river was so cold. She gasped for air and breathed in water. Choking, she flailed her arms, kicked her legs, and somehow broke through to the surface to discover air. She filled her lungs just in time. The water took her down again. What did it matter? she thought. It was not the first time that she had been swept away by a river. After the initial feelings of suffocation, drowning had not seemed so bad—not nearly as bad as being captured and torn apart by the ravenous beasts that were pursuing her.

She did not know when she lost consciousness; perhaps she yielded to it too easily. When she awoke, the angle of the sun told her that the brief autumn day was already slipping past noon. What had happened to the dawn and the morning? How far had the river carried her? And where were the wanawut?

Shivering violently, she forced herself to sit up and look around. She remained as still as her cold-ravaged body would allow, straining to hear, barely daring to breathe until at last she was satisfied that there was neither sign nor sound of wanawut. To her amazement, she discovered that her dagger was still clenched between her stiff, benumbed fingers. Heartened by this, she crawled out of the shallows and crept across a rocky sandbar toward a thick grove of cottonwoods that grew along the embankment at the base of a south-facing bluff. Here, out of the wind, with the sun filtering through the trees, she made a nest and buried herself within the fallen leaves and lichens. It took a few minutes to shiver herself warm. It took longer than that to relax and feel life return to her chilled body.

Larani lay very still. Where were the wanawut? Had the river cast them onto this very shore, where, even now, they might be prowling, searching, determined to find her? Her fingers tightened around the sprucewood haft of her knife.

Let them come, she thought. *They will be sorry if they find me!*

Her defiance did not last. She suddenly recalled the big,

silver-backed male and the somewhat smaller one that had refused to be drawn away from the encampment. Had the People heard her warning screams in time? And what had happened to Summer Moon's baby? By now someone must have found it in the rocks. But who? Man or beast? Larani's dread was all pervasive.

I must know! I must get back!

But when she sat up, exhaustion knocked her down again. She lay breathless, shivering again, so sleepy that she could barely keep her lids apart. She must sleep. She must recover from her own ordeal before she could find the strength to face whatever may have happened to the baby and the other members of the band.

The crying of Summer Moon's baby led the women to the rocks outside the camp. With a sob of relief, Summer Moon picked up the infant and, bundling it in the warmth of Larani's dress, held her child close. Larani's dress and footprints, overlaid by the tracks of the wanawut, spoke loudly of her fate.

Lonit shivered. What would have happened had the daughter of Simu not screamed and led the beasts away? The band would have been forced to contend with five animals instead of two.

"She has saved many lives," said the headman's woman. "Let us hope that she has not lost her own. Come now. We have work to do."

They returned to the encampment in silence and set themselves to the task of laying out the bodies of the dead.

The men and boys were gone. With their spears, spear hurlers, and daggers, they had taken the dogs and followed Manaravak out of camp in a killing rage—in pursuit of him or the wanawut . . . or in search of Larani and the missing children? Lonit wondered if they really knew just what it was they were chasing. She could only hope it was more than hatred, futility, and death.

She felt ill and exhausted, doubting that she would ever see Manaravak again.

"Manaravak, my son, perhaps old Zhoonali, medicine woman of Cheanah's band, was right about you, after all. Perhaps it would have been better if you had not been allowed to live. You have known bad luck all your days and have brought sadness and turmoil to yourself and to your people from your first breath!"

"No, Mother! Do not say it!" Swan exclaimed, and leaned close to embrace Lonit.

But her mother waved her away. "What I say or do not say will change nothing, Swan." She knelt before Demmi's body, with Swan and Summer Moon on either side of her. Naya, Honee, Uni, and Kharn stood close at her back. "This day I have seen Manaravak stand back and watch Demmi die while making no move to help her. This day I have seen Umak try to kill his brother. This day a grandchild of mine has been stolen by beasts and may be lost to us forever. This day, had I not stopped him, Torka would have slain his own son. But my interference was useless. On this day, before the sun disappears beyond the western mountains, I know in my heart that Manaravak will die . . . at the hands of his own father."

Naya caught her breath. "They could not kill him. They *could* not! He is—"

"Be still," Lonit commanded coldly. She could not bear the sound of the young woman's voice. "It is you who has put the bad blood between my sons."

"Stop! Please, stop!" Honee's chin was wobbling. "My Li . . . she is so small and such a good girl. Such a . . . oh, do you think the men will find her before . . . before—"

"They will find her, Honee! And Yona, too, and Larani! We must believe that! We must not give up hope!" Swan's voice was overly loud; if there was hope in it, it sounded too much like despair.

Honee began to cry.

It occurred to Lonit that she should be weeping, too; but she had no tears left. She looked at the bodies of Tankh and Demmi. Poor Tankh. Poor young bear of a boy. They had laid him out beside Demmi, correcting the grotesque bend in his neck that had twisted his head completely around. Never again would Tankh strut proudly in the shadow of his father or blush in adolescent terror of taking a woman before he was ready. He would never take a woman at all.

Lonit's breath caught in her throat as her glance moved to rest upon Demmi. "I have lived too long. . . ." She sighed, and as the breath went out of her so did the will to live, and she slumped forward. Lying prone across the body of her daughter, she embraced Demmi as though she might capture what was left of her life spirit and will it back to life. "Demmi! My daughter! Come back to me! I cannot bear this sorrow! I am too old to carry the weight of so much grief!" Suddenly she drew back, startled.

"Mother? What is it, Mother?"

Was it Swan or Summer Moon who had just spoken? Lonit did not know, nor did she care. Demmi had moved beneath her!

With her heart suddenly pounding, she threw herself across her daughter's body once more and—yes!—there it was again. A strong rippling movement beneath the fur that covered Demmi's distended abdomen.

"Demmi!" Lonit looked up, touching her daughter's face, seeking signs of movement in the closed lids. There was none . . . until, suddenly, the ripple became a kick, and Lonit's heart lurched. "The baby!" she cried.

Demmi *was* dead, but her unborn child was alive, and in that child the life spirit of Lonit's wild, stubborn, intractable daughter was clinging to this world and speaking to her mother from the world beyond this world . . . begging to be free . . . to be reborn into the world of the living once more!

Lonit pulled back the furs that covered Demmi and savagely slit open her dead daughter's tunic with a dagger.

Naya moved forward. "I want to help," she offered.

"Get out of the way, you!" Lonit's voice was as cold as a storm wind. She shoved the young woman away.

"We have seen what your 'help' has brought to Iana and her baby," Summer Moon said hatefully. "Stay back, or you will regret the next step you take!"

Beside her, Swan took hold of Kharn's shoulders, and though the boy protested and squirmed against her hold, she turned him around and pressed his face into her skirt. "This is woman wisdom, not for the eyes of . . . 'men.' "

"Or for girls of your age, either, Uni," said Summer Moon, her tone gentle as she drew the girl close.

With one long, sure sweep of her knife, Lonit opened Demmi from hipbone to hipbone. The headman's woman was weeping, and then, abruptly, as her hands emerged from deep within Demmi's belly, she was laughing through her tears. Dropping blood and womb water, she raised an infant high for all to see. The baby's arms were moving! Its fists were waving!

"Demmi!" Lonit sobbed her daughter's name. And then, in the absence of the headman and the child's father, she named the child. "Demmit . . . Little Demmi . . . this people welcomes the return of its daughter into the world of the living! Be at once an all-new life spirit in this world and strong in the spirit of the one whose name you carry and from whose body you have come forth!"

The baby did not look strong. Its arms were limp now. Still connected to the umbilical cord, it lay breathless and blue in Lonit's hands.

Honee wore a look of dismay upon her tear-streaked face. "Take it to the river! Quickly! Cold water will shock it into life!"

Lonit's eyes scanned frantically across the encampment, measuring the distance between herself and the river. "It is too far! There is no time. It has already been too long in the womb of the dead! If this baby is going to live, it must breathe now!" Without hesitation, she lowered the motionless form, transferring the infant into the fold of her left arm as, with the fingers of her right hand she probed the tiny nostrils and opened the lax little mouth so that she might trespass deep in search of birth debris. This done, the woman of Torka placed her mouth over the infant's face and breathed life into Demmi's child.

The women smiled with delight. The baby was crying! The baby was screaming! It kicked its legs and shook its fists, and in a moment, its pale blue skin began to bloom with healthy, purple-red, highly oxygenated flowers that told all that this child's lungs and heart were as strong as its will to live.

Swan smiled a sad smile. "Listen to her demand her way. Truly, Mother, you have named her well. This little girl is Demmi all over again!"

"The little one is hungry. Here. I have milk enough for two. I will feed my sister's child," offered Summer Moon. As she accepted the baby from her mother's arms and looked down at the squalling face, her smile was very much like Swan's. "This may be Demmi's girl, but she has Dak's face. He will be glad for that."

Swan's face tightened. "He will not care. Though he may have said otherwise, I know his heart. It will be enough for him to know that it is Demmi's child. As it will also be for me. Demmit will be sister to Kharn—and to the baby that I will bear in the spring."

14

Larani was awakened by the sound of footfalls running through fallen leaves. She opened her eyes and stared through the bare, shifting canopy of the trees. The sun was still up. She had not slept long—only enough to replenish her exhausted body and to warm herself beneath the blanket that she had made of leaves and lichens. The wind had turned. The air was colder now; she could feel its chill against her face. But that was nothing when compared to the cold fear in her heart. Something was moving just beyond the trees. She heard the crush and rustle of leaves, the low, rhythmic huffs of breath. What . . . or who . . . was out there beyond the grove?

Wanawut! Terror ran wild within her. She held her breath lest it betray her presence. She willed herself to lie so still that her pulse seemed as loud as the Great Mad River at full flood.

Gripping her dagger tightly, Larani heard the sound of the river running wide beyond the grove, the wind in the trees, the brittle flurry of dry leaves, and the thin, almost painful sound of stalks and branches chafing against one another. Now and again a fish jumped in the river. Leaves fell constantly, sighing down, settling close. Insects moved in the ground cover and within her makeshift nest; she listened to their scuttlings and meanderings . . . and the manlike footfalls of the larger creature that had roused her from her dreamless sleep.

Larani willed herself to be hopeful. She heard one pair of feet, not three! Perhaps she was hearing a hunter of her band, someone sent after her when her tracks were discovered. Not even Simu would abandon her to beasts if there was a chance that she was still alive. Or would he? Yes, she thought miserably, he probably would consider it a kindness. But Dak would come looking for her. And Grek would never turn his back upon his new woman. Torka would lead a search party out from camp, with Umak and Manaravak at his side.

Manaravak! Come for me. Manaravak! Please come for me!

Light-headed from holding her breath, she experienced a momentary euphoria as she thought of him. But common sense prevailed. She was Grek's woman. 'She remained motionless, wondering why she wanted to live.

Then, suddenly, her eyes opened wide. Her senses were screaming, *Run. Run away!* But she knew that to run was to have the beast at her heels, for now she clearly heard more than wind moving in the trees and more than the footfall of a man: A wrathful screech destroyed the silence of the grove; a wanawut screamed in anger, a child began to cry; and a young girl wailed as if on the brink of madness when, from the top of the bluff, the distinctly different resounding howls of three wanawut voices answered as though summoning the lone beast and the captive children.

"Did you hear that?" Wheezing and gray-faced, Grek stopped in his tracks. "That was my Yona's cry! She is still alive! We must find her before it is too late!"

"The beast has gone downriver." Torka was terse and noncommittal. The men had lost the creatures' tracks far back, when the wanawut had entered the river. Much time had been lost looking for their sign. "And downriver is where we will find Larani and the others of the beast's kind!"

Simu's face had the stretched, pained, wide-eyed look of one who clings to a dying hope. "Yes, yes, I know, I know!" he exclaimed irritably. "My Larani led them straight into the river and away from us! Umak and Jhon heard her screaming, didn't you? Yelling at the top of her lungs to warn us! What a daughter my girl has turned out to be! What a brave and—"

" 'Your girl'?" Dak shook his head and leveled a look of abhorrence at his father. "Ever since the fire, all you have ever wanted was to see Larani die! You sicken me, Father. And worse than that, you shame me—and my sister."

"Enough!" Torka demanded. "We will accomplish nothing by standing here and insulting one another. What has happened cannot be undone. We must hurry! If Yona still lives, perhaps Li is alive, too."

"And Larani!" reminded Simu with a high-pitched enthusiasm that betrayed his own disbelief.

Torka felt pity for his old friend. How sad for him to have discovered the merit of the young woman too late. Ever since Larani's footprints had disappeared into the river—with the tracks of the wanawut right on top of them—Torka had lost all hope of ever finding her alive.

"Manaravak's tracks continue to lead the way," said Umak. As he strode out beside Torka with Jhon and Companion at his side, a murderous expression of pure loathing twisted his face. "He seeks his own kind at last and, in the seeking, will show us the way to find them . . . and him and the children."

Jhon looked up at his father. "You are going to kill him, aren't you?"

"Yes," affirmed Umak blackly. "I am."

"No," said Torka, and felt another part of himself die. "Manaravak is my son. When he was born beneath a black moon and a red sky, I defied the omens of the forces of Creation and let him live. I should have killed him then. It was my right to take his life. Now it is my obligation." He saw the tremor of compassion for him sweep through Umak and did not have the heart to add: *As it will be your obligation to take the life of Naya if we return to the band.*

Manaravak stopped. He, too, had heard the child scream and the beasts screech and howl. His spirit soared with triumph. They were at the top of a tall bluff that lay far ahead, beyond a grove of nearly bare-branched cottonwoods. At least one of the children was still alive! With the wind in his face and the howling of the wanawut in his ears, he threw back his head and howled back to them—brother to brother, kind to kind.

Larani lay still for a few more minutes, then sat up so slowly that the tumbling leaves disturbed by her movement made virtually no sound. She crept on all fours to the edge of the grove and peered out. She could see a single wanawut trudging toward the bend in the river where, atop the farthest escarpments of the massive bluff, the three wanawut that had earlier given chase to her stood beckoning.

The lone wanawut had a small child slung across its left shoulder.

"Li!" Larani exclaimed. Her heart bled for the child and ached mercilessly at the sight of Yona walking behind the wanawut. With her feet dragging and the fringes of her clothes waving in the wind like snarled, uncombed hair, Grek's proud, sometimes-nasty little girl looked bedraggled and soiled. With her head drooping, her garments torn, and one moccasin missing, she followed along in absolute dejection.

"Why do you follow, Yona? Run away!"

Larani soon had her answer. Yona was deliberately lagging, widening the space between herself and the wanawut until, suddenly, she made an attempt to run off. The beast turned, closed the gap, and knocked her down. In less time than it took Larani to gasp and Yona to scream, the wanawut grasped the girl by her hair and pulled her high off the ground, shaking her until she went limp. Then it dropped her hard. Yona sat stunned for a moment before trying to crawl away. When the beast dragged her back by a thigh, she screamed and screamed until, towering over her, the wanawut outscreamed her and, threatening with its fangs, yanked her up by her braids and shoved her along.

Larani knew she must try to free the girls before the wanawut set themselves to make a meal of them . . . although why this had not already happened was puzzling. Dark and ominous memories turned her gut: ancient tales of "wind spirits" that materialized out of the fog to steal the women and girls of the People so that they might raise them as their own and mate with them to produce creatures that were neither man nor mist but wanawut.

"Li, Yona, I will not leave you to such a fate as that!"

Larani did not hesitate. Child Stealer was now far enough away for her to react without alerting it to her presence. With grim deliberation, she rose and moved quickly within the grove, seeking the raw material for staves. Several tall, straight-trunked saplings served her purpose well. She felled them with her dagger, hacking away superfluous branches until she had five shafts approximately a quarter the height of her own body. The work went quickly, but her palms were raw and bleeding by the time each was sharpened at one end into a deadly point.

This done, she tucked the newly made staves under her arm and followed the beasts and the children, staying hidden within the shade of the cottonwoods until the three wanawut on the bluff disappeared and she was able to track Child Stealer without undue fear of being seen by its companions. She briefly wondered what had happened to the big silver-backed male and smiled with satisfaction when she realized that the hunters of the band must have killed it.

The wind was cold against her bare skin. Soon the sun would vanish beyond the western ranges. With the wind behind it, the air would grow frigid, and a naked woman would be too cold to succeed at the task to which she had set herself.

Larani paused beside a broad stretch of caribou lichen, set down her staves, and with her dagger began to cut away feverishly at the stalks of the wide, leathery, antler-shaped, gray-green "branches." She paid no heed to the pain in her blistered palms—pain was no stranger to her. She had learned to live with it long ago. Smiling with bitter irony, she thanked Daughter of the Sky for having allowed her to master a discipline that might now save Yona and Li.

At last, with her palms bleeding and oozing, she eyed the considerable mound of her gleaned treasure and judged it adequate for her intent. For a moment she hesitated. Then, with a deep breath of resolve, she used her dagger once more—to hack off her hair—whose treasured length had finally reached the point of hiding the scars on her scalp.

Twisting the strands into cording, she took up the lichens and bound them together, rapidly fashioning a crude cape that would shield her from the cold. It would be rough and abrasive against her skin, but it would serve well enough. Even so, as she slung it on and got to her feet, she knew what she must look like and cringed. Without her hair to cover her scarring, she felt truly naked for the first time.

"But what does it matter!" she spoke aloud to the wind. "Who will gaze upon me now except children who will be glad to see me and beasts that are uglier than I am!"

Grimly she walked on. She had her dagger. She had her staves. She had a cape of lichen to shield her from the cold. With these things and the wisdom of generations of the People at her command, Larani knew that she would not be totally naked or at a complete disadvantage when she set herself alone against the wanawut.

Umak paused. The Seeing Wind was rising in him, and he did not like what he saw. It was a vision of blood. . . .

"Umak! What is it, Umak?" old Grek pressed, glad for the opportunity to sit down.

The shaman did not move. He stood facing due north.

The wanawut were howling again. His little Li was with them if she still lived. Was it her blood he saw?

"Listen . . ." urged Simu. "Manaravak is howling with them!"

"He is one of them at last," said Dak.

Umak shook himself to cast off the weight of his emotionally draining vision. He failed; as he looked at Torka there was still blood in his eyes. "Do not kill him quickly, Father."

The saddest look that Umak had ever seen moved upon Torka's features as the headman spoke. "He did not ask for his fate. He was torn from his mother's arms to suckle the milk of life from the breast of an animal. But you have always lived among men. What beast speaks from your heart, Umak? Who has put the blood in your eyes and the hatred in your spirit for your brother?"

"Naya, my dear girl." Honee stared across the gloom of the shaman's hut to where the red-eyed, sobbing young woman was frantically ripping her medicine supplies apart. "What are you doing?"

"I am gathering up every medicine berry that I can find so that I can throw them all in the river where they belong! And how can you call me your 'dear girl,' Honee? I am a terrible girl!"

"You are dear to me, a sister of my fire circle."

"How can you say that? Because of me Li is gone, and Yona and Larani, too. Because of me Demmi and Tankh are dead, Manaravak has run off, and everyone in the band hates him and wants him dead. I am the one who is at fault. If I had not put so many berries in the celebration drink, everyone would not have been so drunk and the wanawut could never have gotten into camp. Manaravak and Umak would not have fought and—"

Honee shook her head. "So heavy the robe of sorrow and regret for one small woman! You meant to work good medicine, not bad. I do not blame you, Naya. We all drank past the sip that tells a body that it has drunk too much and should stop." With a wan smile, she gestured to Naya. "Come. Help me. I am sorting Li's belongings so that when she returns, her possessions will be in order, and she can change and settle herself and—"

"Li's clothes are always in order, Honee."

"Yes, but I thought that if we worked very hard and very

noisily and speak out Li's name often and loud, the spirits of this world and the next will hear us and . . . if they see that we are expecting our Li to come home . . ." She paused, aware of the edge of desperation that had broken her words, and went on calmly. "She will come home! Yes. The spirits will send her back to us. Won't they?"

15

The air was growing very cold. In the last lingering light of dusk, Larani reached the top of the bluff. She could hear the wanawut sounding somewhere below. Bending against the wind, she picked up sign that led her to the place where the wanawut had moved downward.

Sprawling flat against the stone so that her body might draw into itself the last of the sunlight that had been stored in the rock, Larani's half-frozen brow came down as she peered over the bluff's edge. The wanawut were at the base of a narrow stream canyon where, amid stunted spruce and bare-branched hardwoods, they had joined with Child Stealer to hunker out of the wind. She could make out the muted colors and textures of their furred bodies in the thickening shadows of the defile.

The beasts were sounding desultorily to one another, and Larani realized that they were expressing grief and sadness. Yona, apparently unhurt, cowered with her back to a good-sized boulder, her arms locked about her limbs and her knees pulled up to her chin. The single female was sitting apart and moaning, rocking on her haunches, holding Li to her breast, and mewing to the little girl as to a lost child.

Larani's mouth opened with amazement as she realized that the beasts were mourning their dead! At dawn they had been a pack of five; now there were only four: three males and one pregnant female with a human child clutched pathetically in its arms. As Larani watched the female fondling and cooing to Li, intuition told her that the animal had recently lost a young one of its own. Li would come to no harm in the arms of this beast. She would be mothered, nurtured, cherished—as Manaravak had been mothered and nurtured and cherished. He had been right about the wanawut all along! There *was* something profoundly human about these creatures. Compassion touched Larani and caused her fingers to relax around the haft of her dagger until one of the larger males rose to its feet and pounded its fists against its chest.

The animal seemed restless, angry. It circled twice, then stopped behind the pregnant female and leaned low to sniff at her bottom. With Li gripped to her breast, the female turned sharply and warned him back with a quivering snout and lips rolled up to show her teeth. The big male screeched furiously, dangerously. Unintimidated, she swiped at him with her free hand and boldly screeched back before resuming her mothering of Li, ignoring the pathetic protests of the little girl as her long, clawed, hairy fingers began to pick the feathers from the thong lacing of Li's braids.

The big male turned from the female. Two long strides placed it before Yona. It leaned close, sniffed at her, poked at her, and though she sat curled up tight, the wanawut managed to run a questing hand along her flank and under her buttocks.

Yona stiffened and, evidently beyond screaming, made small whimperings of despair. "No . . . no . . . no . . . please . . . no . . ."

Larani was sickened. Her position on the bluff placed her close enough to see the beast leer with sexual intent as it raised its massive hand, sniffed its fingers, and licked them. She knew that the animal could not possibly have found either smell or taste of a ripe and ready female in Yona. Nevertheless, the wanawut leaped to its feet, threw back its head, and beat its chest as it howled and displayed itself for the girl.

Larani's eyes went wide with disbelief. From within the long, gray-black hair that covered its belly and loins, the wanawut drew out the largest, most distended penis that she had ever seen.

Yona's reaction was instantaneous. She loosed a high-pitched, bloodcurdling scream. Startled, the big male stepped backward as the girl jumped up and ran around the boulder to hide beneath the close-growing trunks of several spruce trees.

The wanawut took off after her. He reached down into the maze of thickly foliated branches, but the girl eluded his grasp. His great, hairy hands angrily ripped away several branches. Panic-stricken, Yona managed to duck away, leaping from the cover of one tree trunk to another until she pressed herself against the back of a large tree against which many smaller ones grew close, forming a natural barrier to the violently questing hand of the beast. Infuriated, the wanawut took hold of the tree, and with all of its power, he pushed against the bole.

Larani heard the ripping of roots being pried loose as, with a single mighty shove, the spruce fell. Screaming again, this time in terror of being crushed by the falling tree, Yona leaped aside. Her reaction was too late, she fell beneath a maze of branches. Unharmed but stunned, she lay sprawled on her belly as the wanawut reached down and pulled her up by her back. He turned her toward him and held her in one hand while the other lifted what was left of her tunic and fingered her obscenely. Then, forcing her limbs wide, he seated himself and began to position her for rape.

Without a moment's hesitation or a single thought about her own safety, Larani leaped to her feet. With all of her strength, she hurled a stave down at the beast. The pointed end of the weapon buried itself in thick muscle just above his right shoulder blade. He leaped up in pain, grabbing at the stave and jerking it out. Another pierced his back. This one appeared to penetrate deeply. He whirled around, screeching in outrage as he tried to pull it out. Yona was free of him, stumbling away.

Larani shouted, "Run, Yona! Run into the thick trees in the narrow of the ravine. It will slow their pursuit. Don't look back!"

But Yona was too disoriented by her ordeal to obey. She was on her knees, head down, crawling away so slowly that Larani screamed down at her to hurry. Meanwhile, bleeding from wounds that had not proven fatal, the big male had lost interest in Yona and was glowering up at Larani with two staves in his hand and death glinting in his eyes.

Larani's heart sank. Instead of being weakened, the muscles along his upper back and neck were bunching, and every hair in his mane and along the curve of his spine was standing on end. While he glared at Larani, the female clutched Li even tighter and ran off to hide behind the boulder as the larger of the other two males came to check the wounds of his "brother." Growling, he turned and followed the gaze of the injured animal to fix his small eyes upon her.

Larani swallowed hard. Now two wanawut were staring up at her. Worse, the third male was taking advantage of their distraction. Excited by the sight of Yona's bare bottom, he sprang forward and grabbed her from behind. When he dropped to his knees Larani saw with horror that he was holding his penis, lancelike, ready to pierce the girl straight through.

"No!" Larani screamed in protest, stepping as close to the edge of the bluff as she dared while gesturing savagely. But her actions only served to ignite the fury of the big, injured male. With a howl of anger, he broke forward and began to pound his way up the ravine toward her, moving so fast that the sight nearly paralyzed her.

Larani willed herself to ignore his progress. In a matter of minutes he would be beside her and would tear her to pieces. Although she still had three staves and could hurl them all to drop him in his tracks, she knew that her next stave must be for the beast that was at Yona. If she could throw it hard and true enough, she might kill the thing—or at least hurt it enough to give Yona a moment's opportunity to run for freedom. It was the only chance the girl had left . . . even though Larani knew that by so choosing she was forfeiting her own chance for survival. She would not have time to throw another spear in her own defense before the other wanawut was upon her.

The stave flew and went wide of its target. Larani's anguish was short-lived; the wanawut was leaping at her. Instinctively, she hurled away the remaining stave. The beast's arms were wide, and its teeth were bared. Impelled by a killing fury, it was on her now. There was no time to avoid death. But—she still had her dagger; with a little luck, she might make the wanawut die with her! As the huge, hairy body of the beast overwhelmed her, she screamed in defiance and stabbed out and up with all her might just as something big and powerful grabbed her from behind, twisted her violently sideways, and threw her down.

Manaravak fell backward with Larani, and the wanawut landed on top of him. He had come onto the bluff only moments before and saw Larani hurl her stave and then stand to the attacking beast. The speed of the rushing wanawut had allowed Manaravak no time to do anything but race forward, come up behind Larani, and drop to one knee as he positioned his spear with its barbed stone head pointing up and forward while he jammed the butt end of the shaft hard against the ground.

The wanawut, with its eyes fixed upon Larani, had not seen Manaravak until it was too late. The momentum of its forward charge had not allowed it to turn away. Awkwardly, arms wide, still closing on Larani, it lunged forward, impaling itself through the heart upon Manaravak's spear. With a single gasp of shock, it fell, driving the spear straight through its chest and its back. As Manaravak desperately and vainly tried to heft Larani out of the way, the beast collapsed and lay spread-eagled over both of them.

The weight of the animal was terrible. So was the stench as its body, still twitching in death, released its bodily fluids. It required all of Manaravak's strength to heft the corpse up. With his left arm still curled protectively around Larani's waist, Manaravak rolled sideways.

In a moment he and the girl were standing over the dead wanawut. They were both stunned and shaking. Larani's dagger was still in her hand—wet to the haft with the dark, arterial blood of the wanawut. Disbelieving, she stared at the blade and then, with even more disbelief in her eyes, she looked up at him.

"Manaravak?" she whispered.

He nodded, unable to find his voice. When he had pulled her from her feet, her hideous cape of lichens had ripped and fallen away. She stood naked before him now. He had forgotten how extraordinarily beautiful her body was. Although her chopped-off hair revealed the full extent of her scars, he did not see them. His mind was filled with the wonder of the way she had stood alone, hurling her crudely fashioned weapons, boldly facing death as though she had no fear of it or anything else in all the world.

Suddenly she gasped. Another wanawut was coming up from the ravine.

With one foot braced on the back of the fallen beast, Manaravak gripped his spear and yanked it from the back of the dead wanawut. He turned and positioned himself to take on the other beast. "Run!" he commanded Larani.

"Never!" she replied. "Yona is down there! And Li! I have come this far to save them. I won't leave them—or you—to face the beasts alone!" She retrieved her staves and stood at his side, poised for an attack.

But the unmistakable sound of barking dogs was heard, and a man called out from the far end of the bluff. The wanawut stopped dead, caught the stink of death and dogs and armed men, and wisely turned to scramble back along the way it had come. Larani went after it.

Manaravak caught her by a wrist. "Where are you going?"

"The children are down there."

For a moment he thought to reply, "Wanawut do not hurt children." Then he remembered the scene in the encampment and heard Yona scream. The sound of pain and madness in the child's cries grew louder until, with a cracking sound, the screaming ceased.

Hackles rose at the back of Manaravak's neck. Side by side with Larani, he moved forward and looked down past the fleeing wanawut into the depths of the darkening ravine.

A sob shook Larani. "No!" she moaned, and turned away.

Manaravak's free arm enfolded her and pressed her close—as though an embrace could take away the horror of what they had both seen. He continued to stare down, deliberately filling himself with the sight of a mature male wanawut pumping to frenzied, slathering completion on a human child. Yona's head hung forward, bobbing up and down with every thrust of the animal who was joined to her. From the way her body sagged in the merciless grasp of the beast, it was clear to Manaravak that the girl was dead.

Shame and sorrow filled him. The barking of dogs was much closer now. Men were calling—running forward, if he was to judge from their voices. Standing with his back to the body of the slain wanawut and staring down into the ravine, he saw the other beast join its "brother" and pull it forcefully away from Yona's lifeless body. As she crumpled onto the ground, the two wanawut ran off into the trees, yipping and howling, with never a backward glance.

A terrible coldness filled Manaravak. He thought of the role his hesitancy back at the encampment played in Demmi's death and Tankh's—and now, indirectly, Yona's. His mind was numb, but with Larani pressed close against his side, the numbness suddenly burst into the flame of an epiphany that burned within his heart and spirit: He had been raised by a wanawut to live and think as an animal, but he was *not* one of them. He was a man, not a beast! He was Manaravak, son of Torka and Lonit; but before he could face his parents again, there was a debt that he must pay to them and to the dead—and to the beasts that had betrayed his trust.

"Li is still alive," said Larani, moving from his embrace, wiping away her tears and reaching for her cape to break the chill of the wind. As she refastened a few torn knots and slung it around her shoulders, she told him earnestly, "There are three wanawut left: the two males you saw and a female. She has Li. From what I saw, I do not think the female will hurt her, but she will never give her up without a fight."

"Then I will give her one." Manaravak's heart was colder than the wind that was blowing across the bluff. And yet, when he looked into Larani's face, something that he saw in her eyes warmed him, gentled him, soothed him more magically than any of Naya's potions or salves had ever done. *Love?* He was taken aback. *Yes!* It was love that he saw in Larani's eyes. A love as deep as the hatred that he now felt for the wanawut.

She looked back over her shoulder. Relief shone in her eyes. "Now we have a chance! Look! Torka comes with the others and the dogs!"

His expression was bleak. "I am afraid that they come for me as well as for the beasts and the children, Larani."

Her eyes went wide. "I don't understand!"

"They will explain. Now I must go. I must do this alone, for Demmi and Tankh and Yona . . . but most of all, for myself—and for my people."

When he turned and made to run away, she reached out and grabbed his arm. "No! Wait for the others! You are one man with only one spear! You cannot set yourself against three wanawut!"

"You did," he reminded her, and then, as amazed by his action as she was, he leaned down and kissed her. It was not a long kiss, but it was square on the mouth and pleased him intensely.

Her face flamed with a blush. Tears welled in her eyes as she lowered her head. His hand reached out and raised her face to his. He knew by her expression that she was ashamed of her scars, but when she tried to wave his hand away, he caught her fingers in his own and smiled. "You are not so bad ugly, Larani! You are brave. You are bold. To the eyes of this man, you are beautiful. Here, now. Give me your dagger and your staves."

"You must wait for the others. Manaravak, please, listen to reason. It is getting dark!"

"In the darkness Li will whimper in fear, a captive of the wanawut. In the darkness my people will be brought to pause. In the darkness it will take a wanawut to hunt wanawut. And if the forces of Creation are with me, Larani, one who has been raised as an animal will *be* an animal for the last time!"

16

In the darkness the hunters tracked Manaravak and the wanawut, but the night was thick and black, and soon they despaired of ever finding them. Reluctantly the men called back the dogs and made a cold camp, but only the dogs ate. Frustrated and somber, the men dozed fitfully and tried not to dream. Grek's heartbreaking lamentations could be heard coming from the bluff where he and the boys had remained behind with Larani and the body of Yona. When the sound of the old man's voice broke or grew faint, they heard Larani and young Chuk take up his mourning cries. After a while, as the glimmering stars shifted across the sky, the hunters heard the howling of wolves . . . and of wanawut . . . and of Manaravak.

"Listen!" Umak snapped to his feet beside Torka. "Despite all that Larani has said in his defense, he still howls with them!" He was trembling with hatred of his brother, with longing for his little daughter, and against his memories of what the beasts had done to Demmi, Tankh, and Yona. "If we find Li as we found the others, I will not stand back while you kill him, Father. I will wet my spear in his blood, and when he lies dead at my feet, you will hear *me* howl!"

Torka eyed his son out of weary eyes. "If we find Li as we found the others, we will kill him together, Umak. You have my word on that. And then we will break our spears and mourn together."

"Never will I mourn for Manaravak!"

"Then mourn for yourself, my son, and for me . . . for I have seen so much death since the rising of the last sun that it feels as if a portion of my own spirit has left my body to walk the wind forever."

In the moonless dark, Manaravak continued to follow the wanawut. He was exhausted. The beasts had been on the move all night, and they had traveled far. At first the dogs' barking had driven the wanawut on at near breakneck speed. He envied them their night vision. Nevertheless, years of living as one of them had sharpened his own senses, and he kept after them, out of the ravine and across low, tundral scrub. Occasionally he stumbled over stones and snags, but he always managed to stay on their scent and within the sound of their footfall.

He had not been surprised when they entered the river and sloshed along in the shallows at the water's edge, obliterating their tracks and scent and effectively slowing if not confounding the pursuit of the men and dogs. But Manaravak had not been slowed; he was well ahead of the hunters of his band, for, unlike them, he could anticipate where the wanawut would travel and the kind of country they would seek.

He kept after them, always hanging back just out of sight. He knew that they heard him; he made *certain* that they heard him as he alternately made the sounds of man and dog and every beast that his vocal cords could imitate. He called Li's name loudly so that if she was still alive, she would know that he was following and be less afraid. Now and then a wanawut would stop, turn back, and screech a warning in his direction and at the wolves that howled close by, speaking of territory and trespass and giving warnings of their own.

High, thin clouds swept in to obscure the stars. The night became as black as a pitch pool, but Manaravak did not mind. He had the wanawut on the move, and this was what he wanted. He hoped that the chase prevented them from thinking too much about their captive. In time they would tire. When they began to weaken, he would stand a chance against them.

After a while the dogs stopped barking, and Manaravak guessed that Torka had stopped to rest or called off the search until first light. But would the hunters have until the first light to save Li? Manaravak had heard no sound from the little girl for a long time. He thought of Yona and increased his pace, barking and howling fiendishly.

After a time he followed in absolute silence, wanting the wanawut to think that he, too, had given up the chase.

Breathing as silently as the rising wind of dawn, Manaravak watched the wanawut and continued to bide his time. They were resting at last. He rested also, but he did not sleep. He would sleep later, when and if he rescued Li. His eyes narrowed speculatively. The child was still alive, lying on her side, fast asleep in the protective curl of the female wanawut's arms. All of the beasts were sleeping deeply at last.

Manaravak smiled grimly: They had chosen a wind-protected hollow away from the river and within rolling tundral hills. It was a bad choice, one that they would never have made had they not been exhausted. They had given him the advantage of high ground from which to observe them.

He could hear the dogs again. The wanawut would have heard them, too, had they not been so fatigued that they had sunk into their dreams as though they had nothing to fear.

With his spear in one hand, Larani's staves in the other, and her dagger in his teeth, Manaravak began to creep toward his prey. Behind him the rising sun spread a soft, bluish light. It was going to be a beautiful morning—but not for the wanawut.

Manaravak was among the beasts now. Silent, barely having to breathe, he set down his spear and staves behind the sleeping female wanawut, and then he quickly leaned over her, grasping her muzzle in the bend of his left forearm, and squeezed it shut as he twisted her head up and hard to one side. As she struggled, she let loose of Li.

The child was instantly awake and scooting back on her knees while Manaravak tried to cut the throat of the wanawut with Larani's dagger. He could not get the angle he needed for a mortal wound. Blood splattered hot upon his face and salty within his mouth. His own blood was pounding in his head and heart.

Li opened her mouth to scream, but terror had stolen her voice.

"Run!" he commanded. The female wanawut was thrashing and twisting violently against his hold. She was so strong that he was forced to pivot around and straddle her in order to keep her down. It was all he could do to keep himself from being pitched sideways off her. He held on, feeling the contours of the animal writhing beneath him: breasts, swollen belly, hard with new life.

He willed himself to think only of Demmi and of what the beasts had done to her. He would not think of the animal that raised him. No! That beast was dead! This one was still alive—a slayer of his people, a predator that, along with the males of her pack, had destroyed the last illusions and vestiges of the love that he had felt for her kind.

Suddenly, unexpectedly, the wanawut managed to dig in with her heels, arch her back, and lever up so violently that Manaravak was jolted into the air. He lost his grip and, off-balance, nearly toppled sideways. Trying to regain his hold on the beast's muzzle, he found that she had a hold on him instead. Her teeth were deep in his left forearm, her jaws crushing, working, chewing.

The pain was excruciating. He cried out. Desperate now, his right hand sliced down and across her throat again and again. With all his power behind it, he felt the blade strike bone and then cut into the spine. The wanawut's jaws fell open as the beast collapsed beneath him and lay still, her eyes glazing, her lifeblood running from mutilated veins.

Stunned, he knelt back and stared at his left forearm. The many deep wounds were bleeding profusely. This arm would serve him no more this day . . . or perhaps ever again.

"Manaravak!"

Startled by Li's quivering voice, he turned to see that the girl had not run to safety. She was still on all fours, staring wide-eyed and in obvious shock at the two male wanawut that were coming straight at him.

It was the mad, enraged screeching of a wanawut that caused Torka and the others to break into a run. The dogs were well ahead of them, Companion leading the way. By the time the men crested the rise, the dogs were racing toward Manaravak. The sun was up and at their backs. Its light poured down into the hollow where Manaravak was fighting for his life.

He was not winning. He had already thrown three staves, which had evidently gone wide, for they were on the ground behind the advancing wanawut. The men could see that Manaravak's left arm was bloodied and virtually useless. He threw his last spear at the more aggressive wanawut. It fell short. Manaravak froze. And now the hunters froze as well.

Although he was obviously wounded and unsteady, he stood his ground, deliberately positioning himself between Li and the beasts, giving the child a chance to scramble wildly to safety.

Li was sobbing when she reached the top of the rise and threw herself into Umak's arms, burying her wet little face in his chest. "Don't let them kill him, Father! Please, don't let them kill him! He saved me. He came after me. All night I heard him following. I knew that he would not let me die!" She looked around. "Where is Yona?"

"She . . . we left her behind . . . in the care of Larani," Umak replied.

"By the forces of Creation, all he has left is a dagger!" Simu was clearly in awe. "Why doesn't he run?"

Umak trembled. With Li clinging to him, he was ashamed. Whatever he had previously felt about his brother was forgotten. He had just seen Manavarak risk his life to save his child. During the night, he had seen Manaravak do the same for Larani. A new understanding of his twin dawned within him. "He has not come to *join* the wanawut. He has come to kill them or die in the attempt."

"Never!" Torka, sharing Umak's insight, loosed a raging war cry and burst into a run, brandishing his spears at the beasts that were attacking his son.

Without hesitation Umak passed Li to Simu and ran after his father.

Simu's blood was up for killing, not for baby-sitting, but Umak had not given him a chance to refuse the child. He sighed, acknowledging the fact that he was stuck with her.

"Manaravak is of their blood, not ours," Dak told his father. "You have been right all along. Their ways are not our ways. Let them forgive and defend him if they wish. I cannot. Nor will I make a move to help them now."

Simu was surprised and pleased that Dak had chosen to speak to him again; but he was also disconcerted by his son's hardness of heart and sudden willingness to agree with his past position at the very moment when he had set himself to change it.

"If what I have seen Manaravak do this night is an indication of what 'they' are," Simu said, "then from this day forth I will call myself one of them and never again look back. A man who has the courage and the honor to risk all to make amends for past wrongs—that is a man I would call Brother in any camp, in any band. I am proud to know that the blood of Manaravak's ancestors flows through his sister into my new child. He has proved at last that he *is* a true son of Torka! If you cannot see this, then take care of Li so I may help my band brothers. I have always wanted to send a spear after one of those hairy, man-slaying, woman-killing—"

"They can kill every wanawut in the world if they want. It will not restore life to Demmi."

Simu eyed his son thoughtfully, sadly. "Nor will the death of Manaravak." With this said, he transferred Li into Dak's arms and ran into the hollow.

Surrounded by snarling, snapping dogs and with the prospect of a "pack" of spear-wielding hunters about to descend upon them, the wanawut turned and fled. Torka and Umak raced after them, past Manaravak, and with Simu following, eagerly took up the pursuit.

"Wait!" Manaravak's imperative call brought them to a pause.

Torka, heart pounding and blood up for the hunt, turned to see that Manaravak had retrieved his spear. The effort had cost him. He looked exhausted beyond measure. Nevertheless, there was a strength of purpose to his voice that could not be denied. "This kill must be mine."

"You are in no condition to kill anything except *yourself*," responded Umak.

"Be it so, then. If I am ever to be son or brother or man of the People, this kill *must* be mine."

Umak's eyes narrowed.

Torka appraised the shaman watchfully. Enmity still pulled at Umak's face and mind. But a brother was a brother, and a twin was even more than that. A sigh of relief went out of the headman when Umak nodded and extended his hand.

"Come, then, Brother," said Umak. "We will hunt these beasts and kill them together."

"No, Shaman." Manaravak refused his brother's hand. "I must hunt for Yona, for Tankh, and for Demmi."

Simu was incredulous. "But Li and Larani are alive because of you! You have proved that your heart is with your people."

"It is not enough." Manaravak's eyes were fixed on the country into which the wanawut had fled.

"You have been injured, Manaravak." Even as Torka spoke he knew that his words were falling on deaf ears. "You are only one man, with the use of only one arm. You cannot hope to win without our help!"

"I cannot win *with* it!" cried Manaravak. "Go now. Return to the encampment, mourn the dead, and leave me to do what I must do—what, perhaps, I was born to do—alone."

"You ask too much of me, Manaravak," said Umak. "You were not born 'alone.' In the belly of our mother we took life together. I feel your spirit locked tight within the fiber of my own life. I cannot stand back and watch you go to certain death."

A moment that seemed an eternity passed.

"I ask no more than what is my right as a man of the People," Manaravak said quietly. "I have no woman, no children, who will go hungry if I am not alive to hunt for them. The right to hunt alone is mine, as is the right to live on my own terms and to choose the manner of my own death if it comes to that."

"And if you fail?" pressed Simu.

"Look to the south, to the land beyond the mountains, and take the People there. I will be waiting, for it will be in that good country that my spirit will walk the wind forever!"

And so Manaravak left the hunters and the dogs and pursued the wanawut. He paused only long enough to cleanse his wounds with water from the icy stream, pack them with moisture-absorbing lichens, and bind his arm tightly with the leather thong of his brow band. He drank deeply before going on. He had lost a great deal of blood; the water seemed to drive back his weakness—or perhaps it was the pure, dark blood of resolve that strengthened him and drove him on. His arm ached mercilessly, but he willed himself to ignore the pain.

He did not know how far he had walked before he came upon the beasts. The sun had risen and set. He stared up into a night of extraordinary clarity and beauty. Had the stars ever been so bright, so close, as though he could reach up and set his hand to them?

For a long while he hunkered in silence, watching from high ground . . . waiting. The beasts slept within a thicket of wormwood. Only another wanawut would have thought to look for them within the low, broken scrub growth of fragrant artemisia that not only concealed their shapes but masked their scent.

"No more . . ." Manaravak whispered his repudiation of kinship with them to the wind and the night and to all the spirits of this world and the next. "I am a man!" he cried, and when his first spear flew from his hand, its point reflected the light of the stars and sparkled as though it were a piece of the sky flaming across the night. It carried his cry as it arced high. With all the power of the man behind it, when it fell to earth it struck true.

The larger wanawut, impaled straight through the heart, collapsed without a sound. Its companion rose and, as it turned, saw Manaravak standing silhouetted against the star-lit night.

"For Demmi!" His second spear flew. "For Yona! For Tankh! For Nantu!"

The beast had no time to react as the projectile point cut through its chest, pierced its heart, and sliced straight through its body. The animal staggered backward, and as it died it heard the sounding of its own kind until the howling became the anguished cry of a man.

———————◆———————

17

———————◆———————

Nothing would ever be the same again.

Torka knew it in his heart as he lay awake in the dark-ness of his hut and listened to the autumn wind and the high, distant honkings of migratory birds winging across the face of the moon. He could not sleep. Demmi's death had made an empty place in his spirit that allowed him no rest. He tried to ease his mind by taking Lonit's oft-given advice and being grateful for what was instead of longing for what might have been.

Manaravak had come back to his people with his spirit no longer belonging to the beasts of the wild. He was wholly a man—albeit a sadder and wiser one. The wounds in his arm were healing, as was the tension that had existed for too long between Umak and him.

Naya was a changed woman. She avoided Manaravak and tended his injured arm only when in the company of other women. Silent and circumspect, she was subservient to her elders and obedient to Umak in all things . . . and yet Torka could not stand the sight of her. He hated the girl. He could never forgive her for rendering his people vulnerable to predators on the night of the *plaku*, nor could he ever forget the sight of her dancing naked and spreading herself wide before his sons.

His eyes half closed in the darkness. It was only for old Grek's sake, and Umak's—who seemed able to forgive her anything—that he refrained from putting her out of the band. The time was no longer right for it. He could not bring himself to cast yet another shadow upon his people when they still had to recover from the tragedies of the past few days.

The birth of Demmit had given heart to Dak and had drawn all the members of the band closer in their need to nurture this new life that had come to them through such appalling death and terror. How Demmi would have laughed to see her own irascible spirit squalling up at her out of a miniature version of Dak's face! Everyone agreed that the baby girl was Demmi's gift to the band, a statement of life everlasting, and a promise of better days to come. . . . And yet, somehow, as Torka closed his eyes and heard the strident, healthy fussing of his new granddaughter waking up the band, he felt too much a part of the past to visualize the future.

A terrible feeling of desolation filled him, but he shrugged it off. It was not in his nature to brood—nevertheless, he had been doing nothing but that lately. Thinking of the way in which his daughter had died, he brooded some more.

The trumpeting of the mammoth jarred him from the edge of sleep. He was glad that his totem was still with him, keeping him from dreams that were too full of the past, too full of blood and death. He wanted no part of them. They made him feel old.

"Too many ghosts!" he declared, and as Lonit awakened and watched him in silence out of understanding eyes, he rose, took up his spear, and went out into the night, to walk the peripheries of the encampment alone. He strode up and down the river, seeking the mammoth and following it eastward, as far as the cold, bleak terminal moraines at the flanks of the mile-high, impenetrable eastern glaciers.

"Why do you lead me here, old friend? This is the end of the world, not the beginning."

The mammoth huffed and shook its head, then turned and plodded back toward the river.

In the cold, bitter night shadows of the Mountains That Walk, Torka smiled for the first time in longer than he could remember. He raised his spear in gratitude to the message of his totem. "I understand. I thank you. I will obey."

And the next day, under the shadowing wings of migrating waterfowl, he urged his people to break camp and relocate farther upriver.

"We must put the past behind us. In our new camp we will wait for the Great Mad River to freeze. In our new camp we will prepare for the long trek south."

Under clear, cold, wind-whipped skies, as the People assembled their sledges and ice walkers in preparation for long, dark days of winter travel, the land around the Great Mad River burned with the raw, savage colors of autumn.

Larani stood apart from the other women as they gathered dried grasses and lichens that would be used as kindling for winter fires. She caught her breath. Memories flamed within her as she stood up and stared at storm clouds gathering to the east.

"Be at ease, Daughter of the Sky. Those clouds have no lightning in them. There will be snow before nightfall, but no fire."

Larani turned. Manaravak was coming toward her. Again she caught her breath. He was not walking! He was sitting astride the colt and raising his bandaged arm in greeting as the wind blew his unplaited hair from his face. As he came closer he leaned back sightly. The redistribution of his weight seemed to trigger an unspoken communication to the young horse, for it paused. Larani's eyes widened.

Manaravak smiled. "It is good!" he exclaimed, patting the neck of the animal with his hand. "If Daughter of the Sky grows weary walking across the river in the time of the long dark, Horse will carry her."

Her eyes grew wider still. "What did you call me?"

"Daughter of the Sky!"

She flinched, certain that he was making fun of her. Her features hardened defensively. How magnificent he was, with the claw marks of the great bear marking his face with smooth, linear scars that enhanced his features rather than detracted from them—not like her own scars.

Shame made her blush. She wished that she had turned away, but it did no good to try to conceal her scarring. He had seen it all before, and now, with only a stubble of hair left, her scalp was bare to the sun—half of it a cap of thick, ropy scars that extended around her ear and across the side of her face like purple fingers. Her lips tightened. How she hated her scars! And now, perversely, she hated him as she remembered his kiss and his embrace. They had been things that a man did when he thought that he was about to die. They had nothing to do with now. Nothing.

"I am not the only one to carry scars," she reminded him coldly. "If I am Daughter of the Sky, then you must be Three Paws, for the great bear marked you well!"

He touched his face. "Yes, it is so. The forces of Creation have put their mark upon the son of Torka and the daughter of Simu."

Bitterness touched her. "Aren't we the lucky ones!"

His eyes narrowed and he observed her thoughtfully. "I have thought of you much, Daughter of the Sky. You look like fireweed in sunlight, and you are as strong."

Larani was certain that he had to be mocking her. Fireweed, indeed! "I *am* strong," she conceded, and hated the defensive, acidic sound of her own voice.

"And you are also Grek's woman!" Grek shouted angrily, possessively.

Startled, Larani turned back to see the old man stalking forward through the tall grasses like a breathy bison doing its best to charge despite the infirmities of age. By the time he paused before her, panting and wheezing in a cloud created by his hot breath condensing in the cold air, Manaravak and the horse were gone, trotting off to circle the encampment, with Jhon and Sayanah racing behind and every member of the band staring in amazement at the sight of a man riding upon the back of an animal.

"He said he would do it. No one believed it, but look at him, Grek!"

"You are my woman, Larani!" His tone was harsh, his big hand hurtful as it closed on her wrist and jerked her around to face him. Never before had he been angry with her, but he was angry now.

"Yes, Grek," she affirmed, surprised by his jealousy but not offended by it. "I am your woman." *Who else would have me?* she thought.

Then she frowned, suddenly worried. His face was gray, his eyes sunken, his lips dry and ashy and somehow blue. He was clearly exhausted, and yet he had just chased off a man half his years.

Tears stung beneath her lids. *Poor Grek.* She worked her wrist free and slipped her arm through the crook of his. "I am proud to be the woman of Old Lion . . . and prouder still to hear you roar for me!"

His features wrinkled with disbelief. "Yes?"

"Yes!" she told him, and knew that it was a truth half told. There was too much pity in her pride: pity for the old man, pity for herself. In that pity lived the ache of longing for what could never be . . . for a young man on horseback, with the wind in his hair, and his sudden bursts of joyous laughter a song that echoed through every part of her being.

"Hmmph!" the old man snorted, pausing to look back.

Larani followed his gaze. Manaravak and the colt were still being chased by Sayanah, Jhon, and the dogs. The boys laughed with boisterous merriment as they made grabs for the horse's tail. Jhon made good on his effort. The horse nickered in protest and pranced briefly in place, then turned so quickly that the son of Umak lost his hold and went down on his buttocks. Sayanah guffawed at his expense. In that moment, Manaravak kneed the colt, and just as it burst forward into a run, he leaned down and, with his good arm, whisked Sayanah off his feet.

"Manaravak!"

Larani heard Lonit cry out in dismay, but in less time than it took her to blink, Sayanah was swung up and around onto the colt's back. Breathless with delight, the boy waved triumphantly at the astonished onlookers. An exclamation of approval went up from everyone. Larani found herself smiling. Never had she seen anything so wonderful!

But when Manaravak kneed the horse into a tight turn, Sayanah slipped over the horse's rump to land hard on his buttocks right next to Jhon. Now it was Jhon's turn to guffaw at Sayanah's expense. Unfailingly good-natured, Sayanah, unhurt, shrugged sheepishly. The two boys helped each other to their feet, and everyone was laughing as the dogs ran in to knock them down again.

Grek grimaced with begrudging approval. "It is a good thing to hear laughter among this people once again. But look at Umak. See how tightly he holds Naya to him? He is still jealous of his brother."

Larani did not reply. At this moment she did not care about Naya or Umak. She was looking at Manaravak—loving him, wanting him, and trying to blink away her tears of desire.

"Why do you cry?" he asked, leaning down, scowling with concern.

"The wind," she lied. "It must have blown something into my eyes."

He looked around, nodding. "Yes, the wind has turned. It speaks of weather. Come, let us get out of the cold and leave the 'children' to their games."

It snowed that night—cold, granular snow that beat a triumphal fanfare for the arrival of winter. The next morning, the women found it necessary to crack through a layer of ice before they could drag their woven sinew nets through the bone-chilling water to collect sluggish fish that had become entrapped in the new stone weirs. When the children went to check the ptarmigan traps, they had to look doubly close, for the recently acquired winter-white plumage hid the birds well within the snow. The men of the band slipped soft leather linings of duck down into their boots and donned hooded outercoats of sealskin made in the camp beside the Lake of Watered Blood.

Days passed. Nights grew long. Despite a cold, dank weather pattern of rain and snow, Manaravak continued to work with the colt, patiently training it to accept the weight of side packs and the drag of a sledge. Simu and the boys were always eager to help him.

The People settled into a snug, warm camp of small, individual family shelters and waited for the river to freeze. When the morale-eating spirits of boredom began to settle upon the band, Torka commanded the raising of a communal lodge in which everyone could gather to pass the time with games and song and general conviviality; but he soon discovered that the ghosts that he had felt lingering in the last encampment had followed them to this one.

In the low, greasy light of the central fire pit, with the aromas of roasting fish, fowl, and moose mingling with those of dripping fat and burned tundral sods, he would find himself looking across the flames to see Demmi and Yona smiling at him from among the other women and girls. He would blink, and they would vanish, but they always came back. And when Chuk pitted himself against both Sayanah and Jhon in a rousing bout of wrestling, Torka saw Tankh and Nantu standing close to Grek, cheering alongside the old man.

It was impossible to keep the ghosts away. After a while, he no longer winced when he saw them. The time came when he actually welcomed their presence. He began to think that when a man had lived long enough, the dead became as much a part of him as the living.

He nodded, content with the moment, and with the night and the sound of the wind blowing across the world outside the communal hut. His beloved Lonit answered the request of the gathering by telling a story. While his people were carried away on the wondrous tide of their imagination, Torka went to his lean-to and returned with the halves of his broken bludgeon and the small skin bag in which he kept his incising tools. There were new details to be carved into the old bone weapon: the happy addition of a new member to the band as well as the tragic deletion of others. Slowly, quietly, he took out his tools and sought to occupy his hands with this useful and necessary work while the tale telling went on . . . but there was barely any room at all. Troubled, he tried not to recall the incident that had shattered the once magnificent weapon or to be upset that there was barely room enough to carve the barest essentials into the time-yellowed surface. He set to work, and after a moment, he looked up and smiled. The ghosts were watching him with approval, and Lonit, seeing what he was doing, began to recount the coming of the People across the Sea of Ice.

On and on went the tale, with Sayanah urging "more" until, at last, Lonit told of how Torka had led the People into the Forbidden Land, where the wanawut had been waiting.

"No!" protested Summer Moon, nursing a baby at each breast. "That is too sad to tell. I do not want to hear it."

"Nor do I," agreed Swan. "Tell us a story that will make us smile, Mother."

"Wait." Torka's contentment was shattered. "What are you saying, Daughters?"

Swan shrugged. "Only that this has been a happy night. I do not want to hear a story that will make me sad."

Summer Moon nodded. "These last days have given us enough sadness to last us the rest of our lives. I do not want to hear about them again!"

"But you must remember!" Torka was adamant. "If not for yourself, then for the little ones. When their children's children ask how they came into the new country beyond the Great Mad River, they will know how it was with us—who we were, why and how we came, and what we endured to keep the People strong."

Silence fell.

"Tell the story, Woman of My Heart," commanded Torka gently.

"But Torka . . ." She paused. To refuse the command of her man in the presence of others was unthinkable. Yet when her eyes met his, they spoke the criticism that her lips would not form. *It is too soon. The wounds have only just begun to heal. Do not open them again.*

He ignored her. "Tell it now so we will not forget. It *is* a sad story, but it is also a story of love and bravery and sacrifice."

And so it was told. By the time the last word was spoken and the sputtering flames had died, Torka knew that he had made a mistake. He should have heeded the warning in Lonit's eyes. It was much too soon for the tale to be told. She had done her best to soften it, to make it seem as though it had all happened to people who lived long ago and far away, but her listeners knew better.

Li quivered against recollections too terrible for such a young child to recall. Uni sobbed that she missed Yona. Jhon and Sayanah grimly looked at Chuk and remembered how his brother had died. The adults grew somber and reflective, and when Grek moaned in a tragic exhalation of grief, Naya lay her face upon her knees lest the others see her shame and sorrow. Umak's eyes narrowed resentfully at the sight of her discomfort, then widened with ill-contained rage when he saw that Manaravak was looking at her. A twisted look of longing for Demmi distorted Dak's face, and only when Swan lovingly reached across the fire to place his newborn daughter into his arms did his features relax a little—but then he glared at Manaravak, with all of the old hatred back in his eyes.

Torka flinched when he saw Dak's look, and at the way that Umak was glowering at Manaravak, who, in turn, was staring openly at Naya. Suddenly, the headman's hatred for the girl congealed into pure loathing.

"I wonder if the shores along the Lake of Watered Blood are still rich with meat?" asked Umak, staring at his twin.

Although the shaman's query seemed off the subject, Torka knew that it was not. It was a deliberate prod, perfectly placed. He looked at his eldest son and was furious with him.

"That land is far away," Torka said. "It was bad country. Death walked in the wind and swam in its restless waters. The great mammoth did not browse in it, nor were my lost children there!"

"No." Umak was looking at Torka now. "They were *here*, with your totem and the wanawut. Death walks in this land, too, Father—worse than anything we encountered in the country to the north. If we had stayed by the Lake of Watered Blood, we—"

"We could not stay. Your Visions should have shown us that, but they did not—any more than they spoke truly of the fate of your brother and sister or gave warning to us of the coming of the wanawut!"

Umak was shocked by his father's open hostility. "I . . . the Seeing Wind . . . it comes to a man as it will. I cannot—"

"No! Your ability to commune with the spirits has been weakened by another magic. *Her* magic." He pointed at Naya. "Because of her you have failed us, Shaman. And do not look at me like that. It is the truth, and you know it—as do you, Grek."

Naya looked up, bewildered, as Torka continued.

"Speak no more to me of the Lake of Watered Blood. I am headman. This band walks where I say, where *my* 'vision' leads! We follow Life Giver, and we will not look back. We look ahead to the new country that lies to the south."

Umak was shaking in his attempt to maintain control. "A country that we have never seen."

"*I* have seen it!" Manaravak's tone was guarded, uncertain.

"That is enough for me!" declared Torka.

Umak jumped to his feet. "Is it? Will you name him Shaman then?"

His words stunned the already shaken gathering.

"Torka?" There was a plea for reason in Lonit's voice.

Torka was staring at Umak. He knew that he had shamed his son. He saw the hurt on the young man's face, and all his instincts screamed at him to moderate his words and ease the pain that he had inflicted. Somehow he could not. His words had been spoken in anger, but they had also been the truth. "The forces of Creation name a man Shaman, Umak; I do not. It was Life Giver who saved Manaravak and, with Demmi, showed him the way to the new country to the south so that he might return to his people and lead us there."

Manaravak was openly amazed by the dispute. "I have no wish to be Shaman, Father," he protested. "Please sit down, Brother, I—"

"Do not tell me what to do! Come, Naya. I will not have you insulted. Jhon, help your mother with Li. I have had enough of this night's gathering."

"Go, then!" Torka shouted. "And consider yourself lucky that you still have Naya at your side to be insulted, for only a father's consideration for a son has kept me from sending her out of this band to walk the wind forever!"

Naya gasped.

Umak stiffened. "Send her away, and I will go with her."

Torka had no doubt that the threat was real. Since it had been made before the entire band, shame was on his head if he allowed it to pass without taking action. Torka was suddenly furious. The sight of Naya standing wide-eyed and innocent enraged him further. "That woman has brought bad luck to this people. She will not cross the river with us into the new country!"

It was as though a bolt of lightning had exploded in the midst of the gathering. Naya's hands flew to her face. Grek looked as though someone had just pierced him through the gut. Honee exclaimed in dismay, and Manaravak looked at his father with incredulity.

And Umak's face went blank with shock. It was as though he had died right there on the spot and then, instantaneously was reborn. "Is it so?" The question was as cold as the darkest day in the dead of the coldest winter.

Torka was suddenly tired. He had not wanted this. Again the need to salve the situation was strong in him, but by the time he framed the words needed to put it right, Umak had turned and ushered his family out of the communal hut.

"Umak! Brother! Wait!" Manaravak followed him.

The hide weather baffle was still swaying from the force of his hurried passage when all heard Umak's shout:

"Get out of my sight! By Father Above and Mother Below and all the forces of this world and the next, how I regret the day that I put myself into the path of Three Paws and made the killing thrust to save your life!"

There was absolute silence within the hut. Everyone waited for Manaravak to return. When he did not, Torka spoke again and tried hard not to show how deeply upset he was. "We . . . we will talk more of this tomorrow."

"You cannot put my Naya out of the band," said Grek, rising shakily as Chuk reached to support him.

Torka stared at the old man. He was so appallingly shaken, so afraid, so clearly devastated that, in fear of Grek's collapse, Torka said, "I would not do anything to hurt you, old friend, and certainly not without the calling of a council. We will do that and talk more . . . tomorrow."

Grek repeated, "You will not put my Naya out of the band."

Lonit forced a smile. "It is late. We are all tired, and tempers have needlessly flared. We should return to our own huts and get some sleep. There have been enough words spoken for one night."

Torka was grateful. She had eased the strain of the moment. But as he watched Larani and Chuk lead the old man away while the others rose, unnerved, and made their farewells, desolation stirred within his bones. What had he done? Why had he done it? As he remained sitting before the cooling embers of the fire, he tried with all his heart not to compare Umak and Manaravak to the broken halves of the whalebone bludgeon that lay within his hands—a bludgeon that he had shattered.

"Torka?"

He looked up. Lonit had risen, and with a hand on Sayanah's shoulder, she stood at the entrance to the hut, waiting for him.

"Come, Man of My Heart."

"Later," he replied softly. "You go on ahead."

"You aren't really going to make Naya walk the wind, are you, Father?" asked Sayanah.

"Go, boy. Take your mother back to our hut."

Sayanah hesitated until Lonit pressed his shoulder and silently urged him to obey.

Torka did not move, could not move. For a long time he remained alone, staring into the darkening gloom of the now unlighted hut. But he was not alone. The ghosts were back at the fire circle, but this time they were not smiling.

◆━━━━◆

18

◆━━━━◆

That night while the People slept, the wind turned and drove snow before it, and the first deep, true cold of winter came down. The level of the Great Mad River dropped. In the shallows, the ice was so thick that it touched bottom. Soon the People would be able to cross the waters and begin their journey to the south—all the band except one family. Umak, taking advantage of the snow to cover tracks, led Naya, Honee, his children, Companion, Snow Eater, and two of the younger dogs away from the encampment. But first he paused and looked back upon the huts of his friends and family.

"Father, please, I don't want to go!" Jhon told him.

"Nor do I," Umak said, and silenced further protests from the boy with a raised hand. "But we *must* go, for Naya's sake. There is no choice."

Jhon glared at Naya through the guard hairs of his ruff. "It's your fault, all of it."

"No more from you!" Honee warned him. "We are more than a family now; we are a band unto ourselves. If we are to survive our trek to the Lake of Watered Blood, there must be no dissent among us."

"We will survive," assured Umak. "The trek is long, but it will be an easier journey over the frozen barrens than across the bogs of summer."

Jhon growled with discontent. "We have not much food

with us. What if the legless animals have all gone away and there is nothing to hunt or eat when we get there?"

"I had a feeling we would return," Umak said. "I have left caches of meat and fat, with hides rolled tight around all that we will need to get us through the winter."

Jhon was not mollified. "My friends are here. I don't want to go! Why don't we just stay and let Torka do what he—"

"No woman of mine will ever be cast out of the band while I am able to prevent it. If Torka commands it, I will stand against him. I will not shame him or myself by such a confrontation—despite everything, he is my father, and I love him. I would give my life for him—but not Naya's. And so it is better to go."

Looking not much larger than a child in her heavy winter traveling furs, Naya was sobbing softly. "I'm sorry, Jhon. I have tried so hard to be a good and obedient woman. I have thrown away my berries and have told everyone that I am sorry about all that I have caused. I have done everything that anyone has asked of me. I don't understand why they can't forgive me."

Umak's reply was grim in its finality. "Some things cannot be forgiven, Naya."

Her voice was broken and pathetic as she sniffed back her tears. "C-can't you make some m-magic to make them forget?"

"Manaravak has stolen the magic and turned Torka and the People against our man with it!" exclaimed Honee.

Li's voice was so fragile that the wind almost blew it away. It was unfortunate that it did not succeed. "Can't Manaravak and Horse come, too? I love Manaravak, Father. He saved me from the wanawut when you did not!"

What came over Umak at that moment was jealousy, hatred, and sibling rivalry gone mad. The words of the child loosed a tide of rage in the man. At that moment the horse nickered, drawing Umak's attention. Slowly, purposefully, he walked forward, gesturing for his family to wait. They did not see him draw his dagger as he approached the horse. With his back to Jhon, Umak stroked the animal's snowy neck, and when the horse nickered with pleasure and raised its head, he slit its throat. He turned then and, with his dagger sheathed, walked back to his waiting family and led them on without a word. The dogs followed.

The shaman glanced back through the wind and falling snow and saw the horse sink to its knees. It would die alone, slowly, as Umak had intended . . . as he wished Manaravak would also die.

On and on they walked, and as the snow fell and the wind blew hard from the north, Naya began to cry again. "I am sorry, Umak."

"I know," he told her.

"If it means anything, I *do* love you."

"And I love you, Naya," he replied, but there was a sadness and an inconsolable grief within his heart as he spoke—for this love had cost him everything.

When Manaravak rose with the dawn to find Horse dead and Umak's fire circle abandoned, he understood immediately what his twin had done and why. With a shout of rage, he took up his spears and followed.

Alerted by his cry, the others came out of their pit huts to stand in the wind and snow, scanning the encampment as comprehension of the unseen events dawned upon them.

Summer Moon's face was pale with dread. "They will kill each other!"

Sayanah was on his knees, stroking the neck of the dead horse. Tears ran down his face. "Why did he do it? *How* could he do it? I will kill Umak myself for this!"

"He is your brother!" Lonit scolded.

"No more!" The boy wept, flinging himself across the body of the horse as though it were a beloved friend—for, indeed, that was what it had become to him.

"Father, you must bring them back!" Swan pleaded. "You must make Manaravak understand that what our shaman did was done only out of anger and that you—"

"He is no shaman of mine!" retorted Simu.

Dak eyed his father sharply. "Would you have acted any differently had you been insulted by the headman before the entire band and told that your woman was to be abandoned?"

Torka was stung by Dak's open repudiation, but before he could respond, Simu snapped, "That woman should have been abandoned many moons ago!"

"No!" Grek was having difficulty breathing. With his bed furs drooping around his shoulders and the deformity of his hunched back exposed beneath his hair, he came stumbling barefoot from his hut. Larani called after him, carrying his shoes. He was oblivious to her. "My little Naya . . . she is gone?"

"Yes, old friend," replied Torka. "Umak has taken her and the rest of his family."

Grek's right arm pressed across his chest. He seemed to be in pain, but his concentration was focused entirely upon Naya's predicament. "We must find her! We must bring Little Girl back! If Manaravak and Umak fight, they will not yield until one or both of them is dead. If both die, who will look after my Naya? I must bring her home!"

"Bring Naya back into this encampment, Old Man, and I will personally wring her neck and yours!" warned Simu. "Can't you see it even now? Do you think Manaravak is slogging out in this weather to spear Umak for killing a horse or because of a few hot words? By the forces of Creation, man, he's after Naya—after your bad-luck, sniveling little granddaughter! There's bad blood in that girl! There was from the start!"

Simu did not expect the hard right that uncoiled from Grek's armpit. It contained all of what was left of the old man's strength. Had the effort not taken Grek off balance and knocked him down, it would have done more than glance a stunning blow off Simu's left cheek. As it was, Simu cried out in pain as he grabbed at his jaw and was spun around and nearly off his feet by the considerable force of the impact.

On the ground and gasping for breath, Grek was wheezing like a dying ox. Chuk and Larani ran to his side.

"You touch my grandfather again, and you'll regret it, Simu!" Chuk threatened.

"Me? Touch him? The old bison dropped himself in the snow! Don't look at me to blame! I'm the one he punched, and if he tries it again, I'll—"

"You'll what?" Larani snarled at her father as she knelt protectively over Grek and pulled the old man's furs around his shoulders. "Get away from us, you miserable, unforgiving, grudge-nurturing excuse for a man!"

Simu gasped in shock at his daughter's words.

It was Lonit who put order into the moment. She came stomping out of her family pit hut, wearing half-laced winter moccasins and her traveling coat. Her snow prod and walkers were strapped to her back, her mittens strung to her belt, her dagger sheathed at her side, and her bola in her hands. From the way she was stretching the thongs, she looked ready to use the weapon against anyone who got in her way. "I don't know about the rest of you, but I am going to pack a few traveling rations and go after my sons. Someone has to stop them from killing each other! You men can stay here and squabble with Larani and my daughters if you like! As for this woman, I am going to try to talk some sense into my sons . . . if they have any sense left!"

They would have left Grek in charge of the women and children, but this time he would not allow it.

"Little Girl is out there! I will go!"

"And if you slow us down on the trail, Old Man?" Simu asked.

"Then go without me. But know that if you do, I *will* follow, even if I must abandon the women and children. Where my Naya is, there also will be Grek to see that she comes to no harm."

"She is with Umak, old friend," assured Torka. "Nothing will happen to her as long as she is with him."

Grek measured the headman out of old and weary eyes. "No, I know Umak will not hurt her. It is not the shaman I fear or even Manaravak. It is Simu. And it is you, Torka. It is you."

And so Dak agreed to be the woman watcher while Torka led the others off into the wind and snow. They moved quickly, certain that Umak would be headed back toward the Lake of Watered Blood—and equally certain that they must find him before Manaravak did.

No one knew just when Larani joined them. By the time her fur-clad figure was noticed striding along behind, it was too late to send her back.

"Why are you here, woman?" Grek was not pleased to see her. "I do not need you on this trek!"

"It is growing so much colder. I could not think of the coming night without shivering at the thought of trying to sleep without you beside me. I will not slow you down, and I will not complain."

She was as good as her word. Like Lonit, she matched the men stride for stride. Grek seemed to have found an inner well of strength until, several hours out from camp, it began to run dry. But by then the wind had risen to a gale, and the snow was driving so hard that they could not see their hands in front of their faces and were forced to stop.

"Why did you follow, Larani?" Torka took the young woman aside as they prepared to raise shelters against the storm.

"He is old," she said of Grek. "Older than he knows. If he falters, you will have to leave him. I would not have him endure that shame alone. I will be there for him so that you may go on for the sake of your sons . . . and for the People, so that they might become one again."

With Lonit bundled close beside Torka beneath the combined warmth of their traveling robes, the headman slept in a hollow that he had dug into the snow, with his back curled tightly to the wind.

He was not certain exactly what wakened him. He had no idea how much time had passed since his fellow travelers and he had stopped and made a temporary refuge against the storm. He lay awake. The howling beat of the wind was as bitter as his mood. Where was Manaravak? Was Umak safe from his own brother? Had the wanawut in Manaravak's spirit not been killed, after all?

Torka shivered. The ghosts were with him again, and Larani's words were a haunting that ate away at his last hope of returning to sleep: *For the sake of your sons . . . and for the People, so that they might become one again.*

The image of his broken bludgeon filled his mind. Some things, once broken, could not be made whole again. Restless, he moved out from beneath the weight of the two robes and, still fully clothed, yielded to the need to walk, to move about, to cast off the ghosts. But they would not be cast away. The all-too-familiar desolation swept his soul as the spirits of the dead seemed to ride the wind around him and within him. So many ghosts! So many beloved faces!

With a start, he imagined Naya among them . . . small and wide-eyed and as confused as she had been on the night he had condemned her in the communal hut. Worse, he himself had created the situation that allowed for enmity between his sons. In his gladness to have his long-lost son at his side, he had been too lenient with Manaravak in those first years home, allowing this wild twin to display behavior that he would never have tolerated in Umak. When he had at last seen the error of his ways and had attempted to make amends, it had been too late, and his failure to deal with Naya's mindless flirtatiousness had driven the final wedge between them.

He had also sanctioned the mating of Umak and Naya while a kernel of doubt existed regarding Umak's paternity. If Navahk had been Umak's father and Naya's grandfather, then a taboo had been broken, and perhaps all that had happened to the People since then was payment exacted by the spirits.

With a clarity of mind that he had not experienced in many years, he reproached and vilified himself. He was sickened with the realization of how many drastic errors in judgment he had committed since Three Paws had walked across the autumn tundra and into his life. He closed his eyes, not wanting to remember the mistakes, the deaths, the injuries— and yet how could he forget? In less than the rising and setting of a single sun he had made enemies of his sons again, condemned a young woman to death, and set the people of his band at odds. "It is I, not Naya, who should be set out from among the People to walk the wind forever," he said.

The wind shifted. He paused. Something had crested one of the hills before him. It was a towering, snow-covered mountain of living power. Huge and silent, it filled him with awe. Torka moved forward and did not stop until he and the mammoth stood face to face. Life Giver huffed, extended its trunk, and breathed upon him, swaying softly.

Torka raised his hands and touched the tusks of the great totem. How worn they were, how discolored and cracked and worn away at the tips. "You grow old, Life Giver, as old as this hill upon which we stand . . . as old as the wind and the sky . . . as old as this man who stands before you." Was this what it was to be old? Was this what Grek felt and fought against? "When does it end for us . . . where . . . how?" he asked the mammoth. "For how many moons must we walk among the living and see them die? How many of your children do you grieve for, old friend? And for how many moons have I heard you calling in my dreams . . . summoning . . . always to the east. But to what? And why do my sons tear me apart in their need to lead me to the north and to the south? I am only one man, and unlike a whalebone bludgeon, I cannot be broken in two and still survive!"

The mammoth huffed again, but not gently this time. Triumphantly it raised its tusks skyward. It shook its twin-domed, shaggy head as though in affirmation of Torka's distress, and then it turned and walked away, eastward, toward the soaring, lifeless mountains of ice that stretched away toward the place of the rising sun.

Torka was suddenly cold to the very marrow of his spirit as a wondrous and terrifying understanding dawned upon him. The coldness became euphoria as he threw back his head and shouted aloud to the wind and the sky and to all the spirits of this world and the world beyond this world.

"For the sake of my sons and for the People, the bludgeon has been broken. And by this breaking—*only* by this breaking—will a solution be presented to the People!"

"Torka?" He whirled around.

"I heard the mammoth," Lonit said, coming up behind him. "The others have been awakened, too, and are eager to go on. But the words you cried out just now . . . what did they mean?"

He was smiling when he walked to meet her, and as he slung a loving arm around her shoulders and drew her near he felt young again for the first time in more moons than he could remember. "You will see, Woman of My Heart! Soon now!"

It was said in the days to come that everything that happened after this was a gift of the spirits, for a white hare appeared in the snow on the hill after the mammoth walked away. It had bright black eyes and burn scars on its ears. Torka smiled when he saw it. He knew that it would lead him to Manaravak . . . and it did.

"My son, I ask you to set down your spears and return to the encampment by the Great Mad River. I ask you to trust in the wisdom of one who has not always been wise."

Manaravak sensed the change in his father. His eyes narrowed warily. "I will not forgive or forget what my brother has done."

"I would ask that of no man."

Three days later, alone by his own command, Torka caught up with Umak and his family and posed the same question.

"I will not walk with a people who threaten the life of my woman," replied Umak coldly. "Nor will I live again in the same camp with a brother who cannot look at her except with hungry eyes."

"I do not ask this of you, and never again will you hear me—or any other man in your band—speak against Naya."

Umak's expression registered disbelief.

Torka met his gaze squarely, unflinchingly. "In the past I have spoken against you, Umak, but I have never lied to you." He paused. The old doubt about Umak's paternity was there, but only for a moment. What did it matter now? The mammoth had led him through all that, and now in the light of a new understanding, he reached out and laid his hand upon Umak's shoulder. "You *are* my son, Shaman," he repeated. "I ask for your trust. I ask for you to send the Vision into my spirit so that you may know that I speak with a true heart. Return with me to the camp above the Great Mad River—for just a little while."

And so it was that beneath a clear, cold sky, the People of Torka stood on two sides of the high, hot fire that the headman raised with his own hands.

Manaravak and Umak did not look at one another. Naya stood close to Honee with her head down and her eyes staring straight at the ground. No one spoke—not even the ghosts around the fire.

Torka knelt and lifted the sheath that held his bludgeon. He drew the weapon out, holding it so that it emerged as one piece, and then, with great solemnity, he took a half in each hand and held them out—one to Umak, the other to Manaravak.

"Now!" he declared. "For the last time is Torka headman of his people! From this moment the People must walk separate paths and seek new ways in new lands. Umak and those who will choose to walk with him will go to the north. Manaravak and his followers will trek to the south after the great Mammoth."

Lonit cried out in despair. "No, Man of My Heart! The People are *one!*"

"But, Torka, what of you?" Grek was openly confused.

"I will follow the mammoth, as I have always done."

There was not a member of the band who was not stunned by what had just occurred.

"Lest enmity divide us forever, this must be so," Torka told them. "The coming generations must be strong, and the many will remember the song of the few—of how, in time beyond beginning, a hunter named Torka and a woman named Lonit were Father and Mother of generations as they walked across the Sea of Ice and through the Corridor of Storms to make a new people within this Forbidden Land!"

For a long while the People stood in shocked silence until the headman spoke again, to ease their fear and answer their questions.

"Once each year, when the tundra burns with the colors of autumn, the People will convene in this camp beside the Great Mad River. Here the children from the south and north will join together as brothers and sisters. Here the storytellers will share the new tales. The headmen will join in peace, set aside whatever dissent once turned their hearts against each other, and tell the old tales. From this day the headmen will keep the halves of the bludgeon sacred so that whenever men and women of the People gather to sing the life song that is carved into the bone, there will Torka be . . . and all of you, alive with Demmi and Tankh and Yona, with Wallah and Iana and Nantu and Eneela, and with all those who have walked with us out of the country of our ancestors and into the new land."

For a long while the People remained in silence around the fire. Not until the flames had begun to die down did Torka insist that the time had come for his "children" to decide who would walk with whom.

"I will take Swan, Kharn, and Demmit and walk with Umak," said Dak, his announcement coming as no surprise to anyone but Umak.

"I thought you had lost faith in my shaman's magic!"

"What does faith in magic have to do with faith in a friend?" Dak wanted to know.

Simu frowned in thought, then, with a shrug, threw in his lot with Manaravak. "I'm not sure what sort of a headman an ex-wanawut will make, but I won't walk with a band that has Naya in it if I have a choice!"

"But Simu . . ." Swan was visibly upset. "If you and Summer Moon do not come with Umak, where will I get milk for Demmit?"

Dak's face tightened. "I will not walk with Manaravak— not after I saw him stand by while my Demmi was killed by beasts."

"I will take the baby if you wish . . . until next autumn," volunteered Summer Moon.

Dak thought for a long moment before he agreed. "Until next autumn."

"I, too, will walk with Umak," said Grek. "I cannot be in a band separate from Naya."

His decision prompted a stifled intake of Larani's breath and a look of disappointment on her face—and on Manaravak's. But Larani nodded and worked hard to make a cheerful smile for him.

"I walk with Grek. It does not matter where. I am his woman."

The old man harrumphed, then told her to pack their things. As she walked off obediently to do as she was told, his face twisted into a jealous scowl. There was no missing the guarded look of longing that transformed Manaravak's face as his eyes followed Larani.

It took time to break down the pit huts and assemble everyone's traveling supplies. When the last tearful good-byes were finally said, when the sledges were loaded and the dogs were under harness, a grim-faced Umak led his followers away from the Great Mad River—but not before Naya suddenly turned on her heels and ran back across the encampment to Manaravak.

"For you!" she declared. Not caring who saw her or what they thought, she stood on her tiptoes to plant a kiss on his cheek. Then she pressed a gift in his palm. "Here. This is yours. I return it to you. May it bring you luck and happiness in the new land across the river!"

"Naya!" Umak's roar pricked the fine hairs at the base of her neck.

She knew that he was coming after her. She heard the gasps rise from the band and felt Manaravak stiffen as, with his two strong hands upon her waist, he set her aside and made ready for his brother to attack him.

"No!" Naya cried. Not quite certain what had come over her, she placed both hands on her hips, and with her feet planted squarely apart, she turned to face her man. "You must not do this, either of you! You must try to love each other again!"

Umak stopped in his tracks.

Naya was frightened, but a strange and pleasant calm was coming over her. "Please, Umak, I only wish to say good-bye to a 'brother' for whom I have caused a great deal of trouble. Regardless of what has happened between us, I am *your* woman, Umak!" She walked forward, stood on tiptoes again, took his face in her hands, and kissed him on the mouth. "Although why you still want a fearful, silly girl like me, I really do not know!"

"Nor do I!" he exclaimed with a scowl, but he kissed her back—a kiss that made Uni, Li, and the boys giggle.

Naya stepped back and smiled. She cocked her head as she looked at him and, with a start, realized how much she loved him. "I am a much better woman without my berries," she said. "I know what I am doing now!"

"Do you?" he pressed.

"Yes," she replied. "I do. And I will try to be a good woman for you from this time on."

"Good luck to you on that one!" Simu called out, but Umak did not hear him; he had taken Naya by the hand, and as he led her away from the encampment he did not look back.

For a day and a night, Umak led his band of followers toward the distant Lake of Watered Blood. They camped at dark and walked on at dawn. The next night it snowed, and they raised lean-tos against the weather.

Within the hide shelter of Grek, Larani lay awake, listening to the wind plucking at the tent thongs, to snowflakes scudding against the tent cover, and to the old man sleeping soundly beside her. She sighed. For once he was not snoring. She closed her eyes, grateful for the silence and the song of the wind and snow that lulled her to sleep. Her dreams were of her girlhood, of long-gone days when Swan and Naya and she had played together and had shared the secret longings of their hearts.

"Manaravak . . ."

Her dreams were full of him now—such fine dreams . . . until Grek woke her.

"You have been a good woman for me, Larani."

She did not speak. She lay still, patiently waiting for him to touch her, to begin to handle her in his earnest, clumsy way—trying so hard to please them both and never quite succeeding.

He did not move. "You did not want to walk with me, did you, Larani?"

"I am your woman," she told him, although she knew that he wanted to hear more than this from her.

He was quiet for a while; his breathing shallow, strained. Then: "When the time of the long dark is over and we journey back across the land to the Valley of the Great Mad River, you will not be sorry to return . . . to see him again?"

"Him?"

"You speak his name with longing in your dreams, Larani."

He sounded so sad, so old—and so full of hope that she would speak to prove him wrong. She turned toward him and touched his face with loving hands. "I am your woman, Old Lion. Whom else would I walk with? Who else can touch my spirit in the way you do?"

She kissed him then. It was a gentle, loving, woman's kiss, and in her heart she knew that she did love him—not as she loved Manaravak, not in the way he longed to be loved, but he need not know that. When she drew back, he smiled, so she kissed him again and would have made love to him, but he held her away.

"No, Larani. Your man is tired. I would sleep awhile. Then Grek will love you, yes, and you will not be sorry that you have chosen to walk with Old Lion!"

She slept, too, and awoke before dawn. Grek was still sleeping soundly—so soundly that she was glad for him, knowing how much the trek was wearying him. She rose, dressed, and prepared for the day's walk. When all was ready, she spoke his name. Outside the snow had stopped falling, and the others were up and readying to walk on.

"Grek, it is time to get up," she told him.

When he did not answer, she kissed his brow, and then drew back with a start. His brow was cold—but not half so cold as her heart as Larani lay her hand upon the old man's cheek and knew that he was dead.

Lonit wept that night.

"How will I live until the next Moon When the Grass Goes Yellow?" she lamented. "Without my Swan and Umak, or Jhon and Kharn and the babies!"

"Patiently," Torka told her, and kissed her mouth.

"Do you think that they will be all right, Father?" pressed Sayanah.

"With Umak to lead them, and Dak at his right hand, and old Grek to tell the stories and—"

"I will miss Jhon!" said the boy.

"We will all miss him," Torka agreed, "but think of the fine time that you will have when you meet again when the grass is tall."

Beyond the headman's pit hut, Manaravak stood against the stars. He looked off to where Simu sat contentedly with Summer Moon and the babies. He knew his father had made a wise decision. Better a band cut in half than no band at all. But he was still alone . . . still without a woman of his own.

To the north end of the encampment, the dogs started barking. Manaravak turned and narrowed his eyes to see what was causing the dogs to bark so enthusiastically.

In robes of snow-crusted sealskin and a snow prod in her hand, Larani was coming toward them against the star-strewn sky.

Manaravak froze. She would have to pass him before she entered the encampment. The dogs were jumping all over her. Taken off guard by the exuberance of their welcome, she laughed with pleasure and knelt to receive their greeting. Manaravak went to greet her.

"Daughter of the Sky, how is it that you walk from the band of my brother and from the side of your man?"

"I have no man," she said, and told him how Old Lion had died.

Struggling to get to her feet amid the licking, leaping, lolling dogs, she nearly fell.

He extended a hand. She reached for it, but when the dogs half knocked her down again, he caught her in his arms and helped her up. She fell against him, and suddenly he was lifting her high, looking up at her and grinning with delight, pushing back her hood so that he could see with his own eyes that it was really Larani and not a trick of the spirits of the night.

She tried to stop him. "Don't! Oh, please, don't look at me, Manaravak. Until my hair grows back, I am ugly. I am—"

"You are Larani! That is enough for me, *all* for me. I have never wanted more!" he told her, and with one hand cupping her head, he pulled her into a kiss that would have allowed her no retreat, even if she had desired one.

19

Time passed along the shores of the Great Mad River. The men hunted. The women sewed. And on a night of such cold, crystal clarity that it seemed as though the stars would crack away from the sky and fall to earth, a great fire was raised. Sparks flew high. The voices of the People rose in joyous song as their feet beat a strong and strident rhythm that went deep into the frozen earth. Wolves responded with songs of their own. The followers of Manaravak wondered if their brothers and sisters to the north with Umak could hear them and, if they could, if they would know that they were celebrating the union of their new headman and Larani.

The time of the long dark settled upon the world. The surface of the river froze fast. In the clear, cold light of a blue aurora, the band crossed the river without mishap. The southern ranges beckoned, and Manaravak was eager to lead his people to the cave where Demmi and he once found warmth and shelter. With his new woman, Larani, close at his side, he spoke with confidence and rising excitement of the fine land to which they would travel.

But even as they moved on across the far shore, Torka remained where he was. The mammoth had not crossed the river. It was standing, trunk up, beckoning, summoning him . . . back, back to the eastern ranges.

"Torka! Come!" Simu called.

How could he? How could he leave the eastern lands

behind? The spirit wind was whispering all around him. He turned right, then left, then right again, and with every turn he heard the voices of loved ones—so *many* loved ones: Demmi . . . Iana . . . Tankh . . . Nantu . . . Yona . . . Eneela . . . Wallah . . . old Umak . . . and old Grek.

"Father!" Manaravak's call caused him to turn and look toward his son. He was startled to see himself. He blinked and looked again. This time he saw Manaravak—bold, strong, confident, a hunter who was ready to take on even the forces of Creation if they stood in his way or in the way of his band.

Manaravak's band! Yes. Slowly, over the past rising and falling of the moon, Manaravak had changed. He had cast off the last vestiges of his animal nature. Seeing the change in him, even Simu was satisfied with Manaravak as headman.

Torka stood tall. A strange and calming resolve was growing in him. He felt neither old nor weak, but somehow he knew that his life was over. Life Giver walked to the east, and though his people would either be south with Manaravak or north with Umak, Torka knew that he must follow his totem into the face of the rising sun.

"Father!"

He was surprised to see that Manaravak had come to stand before him.

"Come! We have a long way yet to travel before we reach the cave and—"

"I will not go to the cave with you, Manaravak. I will follow the mammoth. It is time for me to seek the place of the rising sun."

"What are you saying? You have been seeking the rising sun all your life. You have seen where it has led you—straight into the impassable eastern ranges of ice! Nothing gets through those mountains, Father! They are solid ice so high that not even hawks and eagles can surmount them. Come. You have taught me that in new lands men must learn new ways. It is time for you to travel southward now. You have responsibilities to the band, to Mother, Sayanah, the children—"

"*Your* band," Torka interrupted, scanning the southern horizon. "*Your* mother . . . *your* brother . . . *your* children . . . *your* future. Now *you* are headman, Manaravak. Now

you must respect *my* rights as a hunter of the People,
as I honored yours when you went alone after the wanawut. With you to hunt for my woman and son, I claim
my right to choose my own life—and my own death. My
spirit walks to the east with the great mammoth. I must
follow."

For many hours Torka walked without resting and without looking back. The mammoth plodded on. The wind
was with him. He was not sure when the little longspur
alighted on his head and, shivering, sought warmth by
burrowing deep into the long, silken guard hairs of his
ruff.

"Greetings, Longspur, totem of my daughter. You are
very welcome to walk with me."

The bird made small chirps of contentment, then fell
silent. Torka knew that it slept, safe and warm . . . as Demmi
used to sleep contentedly, riding high upon his shoulders in
the far country beyond the Forbidden Land. He half closed
his eyes, daydreaming. With no effort, he could imagine
that Demmi was walking beside him, a little girl holding
his hand.

A shooting star flamed across the night—a brief, in-
candescent lance of beauty that struck him to the heart.

"A good sign!"

Lonit's exclamation startled him out of his daydreams.
She was walking beside him, taking his arm, and smiling.

"What are you smiling at?" he shouted as he came to an
abrupt halt. "Go back to the band at once!"

"You are my band!"

"But Lonit, the mammoth walks eastward into the great
white range."

"This woman has seen mountains before!"

"Lonit, Woman of My Heart . . ."

"Yes!" she interrupted hotly. "Lonit and Torka, always
and forever! This woman is not afraid. I have brought my
lamp and my memories and enough kindling in my heart to
keep us both warm for a long time. Did you think that I
would let you make this last trek without me?"

For a long while they stood looking at each other. The
wind was rising. The mammoth looked back. When it raised

its trunk and beckoned, the longspur took wing and flew ahead. Arm in arm, Torka and Lonit followed, into the vast, impenetrable northern icefields of the Pleistocene, walking into the wind, always and forever, Father and Mother of the People . . . and of all generations that would follow.

AUTHOR'S NOTE

This novel has sought to follow the first migration of man into the "New World." Although the characters are fictitious, their long trek eastward "into the face of the sun" is not. Sometime at the dawn of prehistory, the ancestors of today's native Americans took up their spears, strapped side packs onto their dogs, and began the most monumental trek that has ever—or perhaps will ever be—accomplished by man . . . until he sets himself to the ultimate migration and commits us all to a future among the stars.

Forty thousand years ago, when the Age of Ice lay upon the world and the level of the earth's oceans was three hundred feet lower than it is today, the stars were cold, mystic signposts that guided bands of Paleolithic hunters from one frigid, wind-swept hunting camp to another. Somewhere on the bleak barrens of coastal Siberia, one or more of these bands followed the great migratory herds of the Pleistocene right out of Asia as, always in pursuit of big game, they hunted their way across the Bering land bridge, inadvertently following the megafauna of the Ice Age deeper and deeper into North America.

This novel—and the previous three books in THE FIRST AMERICANS Series—has shown how man first came into the Americas by way of the high Arctic, eventually traversed the upper reaches of the Yukon, penetrated the high passes of the Richardson Mountains, reached the shores of the MacKensie River and—facing the impenetrable mile-high walls of the Cordilleran and Laurentide ice sheets—at last turned south along the eastern spine of the Rocky Mountains and headed straight into the heartland of Ice Age America. Eventually, the descendants of these First Americans would people two continents from Alaska to the Patagonian isles of Tierra del Fuego.

As to those who came first, their antiquity is so great that even in legends and lore of their descendants they are only inferences of memory, spirit dancers moving to ghostly rhythms that vibrate in long-forgotten cadences and sing to us in long-forgotten tongues. We will never know their specific names or deeds. Their thoughts, hopes, and dreams are lost to us. Their language has melded into so many others that it has ceased to exist. No Amer-Indian Homer has recounted their earliest epic journeys. The earth and stars are the only "living" witnesses to their triumphs and tribulations. Yet, although the stars remain silent and their children have forgotten them, the earth speaks when it is probed, and in the ancient legends and ethos of all tribes who call themselves the People, the song of the ancient ones is sung . . . to those who would listen.

The behavior of the characters within this novel, their manner of dress, hunting methods, and general customs and attitudes toward life and death have been drawn from that song. The story has been shaped with great care out of "gold" gleaned by the author from increasingly rich deposits of "ore" that historians, archaeologists, explorers, cultural anthropologists, and paleoanthropologists have been "mining" over the past decades. The body of their work is a treasure for us all.

The conflict between Umak and Manaravak has been based not upon Cain and Abel of Judeo-Christian tradition but upon the Creation legend of the widely dispersed Amer-Indian tribes, whose story singers speak of twin war gods who shattered the unity of the first people. Studies of the life ways of ancient man are beginning to prove that the disbanding of small, nomadic family groups of hunter-gatherers occurred most often at fifteen-to-twenty-five-year intervals— or just long enough for sons to grow up and challenge the authority of their father.

The use of hallucinogens among native Americans is well-known. As an intoxicant and "dream enhancer," the Amanita or fly agaric mushroom seems to have been chewed since "time beyond beginning," in spite of the potentially deadly properties of the Death Cup. Man's knowledge and use of the intoxicating properties that result from the process of fermentation appear to have been with him always. There must have been a progenitor in the Arctic of the plant we know as mescal. Naya's wonderful berries are from a pre-Ice Age and hence fictitious species of small deciduous Arctic shrub not unlike mescal (Sophora secundiflora), which preceded peyote (Lophorophora williamsii), a cactus, onto the southern plains. Like peyote, the mescal bean (or berry) contains alkaloids that cause similar physiological and psychological effects when eaten. Reaction to these alkaloids varies greatly among users. Hallucination is common. Sexual arousal occurs in some users. Nausea can be an unpleasant side effect. Necklaces of mescal "buttons" are often included in the "kits" of peyote users.

Once again, my thanks must go to the staff at Book Creations, who have given so much invaluable, time-saving editorial assistance . . . especially to Editorial Director par excellence, Laurie Rosin, and to two most diligent editors, Judy Stockmayer and Marjie Weber, who "hung in there" till the end despite the rigors of the journey to which the author subjected them. Thanks also to the many readers who have written to express their hope that the People may yet walk many miles into the wind and discover many a new land.

May it be so!

William Sarabande
Fawnskin, California

THE WORLD OF
THE FIRST AMERICANS

A monumental epic, **The First Americans** chronicles all the passion, danger, and adventure from the dawn of the Ice Age. It was a time when humans walked the world and when nature ruled the earth and sky. For the people who lived then, it was a time of mystery but also of wonderment and discovery.

BEYOND THE SEA OF ICE

In Book One of this breathtaking series, a crazed mammoth rampages through Torka's village and kills all but three people. Torka and two fellow hunters, unaware of the band's decimation, are stalking game far from the encampment and battling their own superstitions.

The brothers nodded, one to the other, acknowledging their unspoken thoughts. An Arctic hunter's ability to communicate without sound was a sixth sense, as it was with all predators whose survival depended upon their ability to hunt in packs. To speak was to alert prey to their presence, and to break the concentration of others when game was being stalked was unthinkable.

It was hunger, coupled with exhaustion, that put the word on Nap's tongue. He did not know that he spoke until the wind blew his voice back into his face and slapped him with it.

"Caribou . . ."

The enormity of his transgression hit him at once. He sucked in a half-strangled gasp of alarm, as though he might draw back his utterance, but it was too late. The word was out, running free upon the wind.

Torka and Alinak stood stunned to silence. Nap had just broken one of the most ancient taboos of the Arctic. They all knew that to name a thing was to give it the spirit of life. And life spirits had wills of their own. If called forth without the proper ceremony or chants of respect, they were dishonored and would seek to punish those who had shamed them. In the case of game, they might not come forth at all, thus punishing the transgressors through starvation. Or they might transform themselves into crooked spirits, half-flesh, half-phantom . . . clawed, fanged, invisible, and malevolent . . . big enough to make prey of men and eat them . . . slowly.

Torka did not have to tell Nap that what he had done was unforgivable. His lapse might well cost all three of them their lives. And if, by some chance, they *did* manage to get safely back to the winter encampment of their band, Nap's reputation as a hunter would be sullied forever. Yet, as the initial flaring of his anger cooled, Torka could not condemn Nap for his blunder. They were *all* exhausted, *all* hungry and dangerously near starvation. It was said that starvation fed the light of vision. It was also said that hunger made men careless. Any one of them might have blurted the word of longing and thus, inadvertently, broken the ancient taboo. But if Nap *had* loosed a crooked spirit, it would be a separate entity from the one that Torka sensed stalking them. *That* phantom had been following them for hours. And whatever it was, Torka was now more certain than ever that it was no herd of caribou.

The three hunters stood immobile. They all saw specters, listened for the voice of danger, and imagined that they saw death stalking them in the wind-driven mists.

Torka stood with his fleshing dagger in one hand and his stabbing spear balanced and at the ready in the other. He could taste bile at the back of his throat as he recalled the words of old Umak, the grandfather who had raised him and taught him to hunt after his parents had been killed: *There is a light that burns at the back of a man's eyes when death is near, stalking, waiting for the hunter to make the final error. The hunter must face into this light. Only by facing death may his spirit overcome it.*

The light that burns, Torka could feel it now. It seared the back of his eyes and transformed his vision. The world was ignited by it, bright, as white and bold as the great white bear of the north, and he thought: *Whatever is out there, the wind is in its favor now. It will have our scent. And if it is a bear, it will be mad with hunger after months of living off its own fat. It will come for us, even here upon high ground. It will come.*

But what if the prey was a crooked spirit? Or worse, what if it was a bear? He had seen what the great white bear could do. When Torka was a child he had seen his father slashed and torn by those great paws. He had seen his father die as many others were mauled, until at last the huge, short-faced, lumbering marauder had been driven off. Later it had been found dead from wounds it had suffered in the encampment. The surviving members of the band had eaten it, but the bear had ruined ten spears and taken the lives of three hunters and one woman, Torka's mother, to the spirit world with it.

The memory roused anger and a fully formed resolve that drove away his fear. Umak had stood against that bear. Umak's courage had enabled him to place the killing spear. Not even the great white bear had been bolder than Umak. *And I am Torka. I*

*am the son of Umak's son. I can be bold. I, too, am mad with
hunger after months of living off my own fat.*

The wind was gusting now, its power ebbing as morning
claimed the tundra and banished the terrors of the dark. Torka's
black eyes stared into the settling ground snow, searching for a
bear that was not there. Nap and Alinak frowned into the
distance, expecting crooked spirits to take shape and come at
them to take their lives. But to their infinite relief, there was only
the familiar, empty tundra spreading out before them, with the
mountains circling the far horizon and, on that horizon, the
frozen jewel of a shallow little lake glinting in the cold colors of
the morning. The lake was at the base of the shouldering rise of
a terminal moraine, no doubt the result of the recent thaw and
ensuing freeze. A huge embankment of loose stones and rocky
debris rose at the foot of a glacier. And mired at the edge of the
lake, its shape a dark scab upon the ice, was a corpse whose color
was unmistakable. Red. Deep red, the color of blood rising from
a wound.

The hunters exhaled in disbelieving unison. The terrors of the
night and caution were forgotten. Hunger took complete control
of their senses as they realized that at last they had food enough
to gorge upon until they were sated and still have more than
enough to bring back to their starving people.

*Nap and Alinak are also savaged by the killer mammoth. Torka
returns to the village to find that only his grandfather Umak and
a young girl, Lonit, have survived. The threesome travel into a
realm of mystery and danger, where they come upon the boy
Karana, abandoned by his father, the headman Supnah, to die.
Karana joins Torka's tiny group.*

CORRIDOR OF STORMS

*The four travelers arrive at a winter camp where many bands
gather to hunt the great mammoth. Here Torka and his followers
meet the evil magic man called Navahk, who maintains his
power by frightening the people with stories of the wanawut, a
vicious man-eating monster.*

"Who has seen this wanawut?" Supnah's tone reeked of
skepticism. "Who has found its hide or bones or any portion of

its carcass upon the tundra? Who has seen its tracks or spoor or looked upon the living flesh of this wanawut . . . this spirit of the wind and mists that brings fear to the hearts of my people through the mouth of Navahk?'' The headman's challenge was as powerful as the man.

Beside him, the boy Karana was startled and amazed. He was not certain if he had heard correctly. Had the headman actually spoken out to the magic man? Had Supnah, for the first time in his life, openly impugned his brother before the entire band?

Yes! It was so! The boy smiled for the first time since Supnah had insisted that he leave Torka to dwell with him and Naiapi, his third woman, as the headman's son again. He had not wanted to go, but Torka had allowed no argument from him. And although he had balked, he had actually been delighted when Navahk had glowered at him and proclaimed that the dead could not return to dwell among the living without dire consequences to all. Supnah had coldly replied that his son was alive, not dead, no thanks to his brother's mistaken portending. Then Karana had enjoyed smirking at the magic man but had not enjoyed his forced residence within Supnah's pit hut. He disliked Naiapi as much as she disliked him, although her little daughter, Pet, half smothered him with sisterly affection. She was looking at him now from across the fire, but he pretended not to notice. He wanted no part of her; she was one of only a handful of toddlers who had not been abandoned to the winter dark, because her mother, having just lost a sickly newborn, had breast milk to suckle her after the infant died. He had told her that she was not his sister, but Supnah had insisted that, although they had been born out of different mothers, they were nevertheless of his blood, and he cherished them, so must they cherish each other.

Sullenly, Karana had kept his thought to himself. *If you cherished me, how could you have sent any of us? No matter what Navahk said, you were headman and did not have to listen. In starving times Torka found enough food to feed his people and took in a strange band's child. We were hungry, but we survived. And now Karana is Torka's son forever. Karana will never be Supnah's son again.*

The boy sighed. He had loved Supnah once and been proud of the bold hunter. Yet there was now a bittersweet emptiness within his heart where filial love should have been. There was no way to tell the headman that he was, in fact, Navahk's spawn. When Karana had returned to his people, Navahk, for reasons the boy still could not fully understand, had sought him out and smiled maliciously as he had burned him with that unwelcome truth. It both revolted and shamed him.

Yet now, as he stared at the magic man in the flickering shadows of red and black and gold, he realized that he had always sensed the truth—even in those long-ago days of his childhood, when others would remark upon his resemblance to his father's brother. The similarity did not end there. He would amaze himself, as well as the people of his band, by knowing when the weather would turn, when the game would come, and where it would be found. He had often felt the magic man watching him, measuring him out of sharp, resentful eyes. His mother had warned him to keep his portending to himself and to be wary of Navahk. He was a dangerous, ugly man, she had warned. But Karana had been baffled because Navahk was even more beautiful than his mother, and she was the headman's woman, envied by all the females of the band.

A lump formed at the back of the boy's throat. His mother had perished the winter he had been abandoned. Her reasons for distrusting the magic man had died with her, and Karana was certain that if he were to tell Supnah the truth about his parentage, the headman would never believe him. Since the death of their parents, Supnah had been like a father to his much younger brother. To speak against Navahk to the headman had always been like shouting into the north wind at the height of a gale.

So it was that now Karana stared at Supnah, then at Navahk, incredulous. The headman's words struck the magic man like a well-placed spear, actually making him stagger. Supnah had never challenged Navahk, not even when the magic man had told the headman to abandon his own son.

A dark, intense warning sparked within Karana each time his eyes met his father's. He chafed each time the headman drew him close and called him son. *Torka is my father now. Torka will always be my father!* he wanted to shout. Loyalty and love made them father and son, not blood; blood was a thin, red thing that dried and blew away on the wind.

Karana knew that all too well, for he had watched the other children slowly starve and freeze to death, one by one, crying for mothers and fathers who never came. He had been unable to help them, for he, too, was starving and dying—and all because Supnah had not been bold enough to challenge the spirits of the storms that spoke to him through his brother's mouth.

Navahk plots against Torka and Karana and pursues Lonit, who has matured into a beauty. As a mob beats Torka and the boy and leaves them for dead, Navahk attacks Lonit. Using their last reserves of strength and courage, Torka's few allies manage to save the victims and take them to a new continent that has never known the footsteps of man.

FORBIDDEN LAND

Lonit becomes Torka's woman and bears him two daughters. In this untamed wilderness, Torka's success is based upon his willingness to cast aside old beliefs. But while Lonit is in labor for the third time, all he can do is wait.

Lonit was young and strong, and it was not within her nature to cry. She willed herself to run with wolves across the open miles of her imagination. Her blood surged, and her heart pounded fast and hard. She was no longer a woman. She *was* a wolf! She was a strong and sleek wild animal, just like the wolf that had once leaped upon her and nearly claimed her life. Her arm bore the white lightning mark of a jagged scar inflicted by the tearing fangs of that wolf. Her man wore the skin of the beast, and its paws and fangs were around his neck. But now, as she ran, she was pursued by a terrifying white lion with a great black mane, a lion that roared within her.

"Torka!" From out of her very soul, Lonit howled his name in unspeakable anguish as another contraction transformed the supple muscles of her abdomen into a single oiled, ash-blackened strap that tightened, boring in and down upon her unborn child, crushing it—no!—and forcing it from her body at last!

The baby was coming! She could feel the head burrowing deep, ripping her tender flesh, tearing her apart like a wolf trying to free itself of a trap—and failing. Never had she suffered such agony. Not at the birth of her firstborn child, Summer Moon, nor at the birth of her second daughter, Demmi.

Beyond the winter hunting camp of her band, the wolves broke and scattered, disappearing into the far hills and the farthest reaches of her fevered mind. Her little girls ran with them, and her man followed. Only the pain remained. She tried to call out after the ones she loved—the wild wolves, her children, her man. But even as she attempted to form their names, light exploded within the little hut. Briefly she thought of the sun. She wondered if the intensified pain were its child; for with pain, always there was light, bright . . . glaring . . . blinding.

"The child comes!" Xhan was shouting. "You must kneel again now. You must try harder!"

Lonit was beyond trying. She was not even a woman anymore. She was a spirit, running away into the face of the rising sun with the ghosts of the caribou. Why did the women not leave her alone? The child would come or not come. Her body would allow it life or not; either way, she had no control. None.

"Push!" demanded Kimm.

Slumped in Kimm's arms, Lonit could not even try. The ebbing pain would come again. The next time, she knew it would kill her, and she would be glad.

Wallah knelt before her, shook her head, fixed Lonit with frightened eyes, and, with a sigh of regret, slapped her once, twice, and then again.

"You will *not* give up now, Lonit! The life you carry is the first to come forth in this new land. It will be a bad thing if it dies, and a worse thing if it takes you with it! Look at me, Woman of the West! You have never been lazy before! You must work *harder*!"

In a stupor of pain and exhaustion, her entire body was trembling as she crumpled forward, bent double against the agony of yet another contraction. Blood and fluid gushed again from her body, and still the child would not be born.

"Stand back and away!" Zhoonali's command was for Wallah as the old woman took the matron's place and reached out with taloned hands to part the curtain of black hair that had fallen before Lonit's face.

"This goes on too long. A woman can only take so much. You are young and strong. You have given life before, and if the forces of Creation allow it, you will give life again. But now the spirits have spoken with the voices of wolves—a very bad omen. The life in your belly must be taken now, before it *is* life."

Lonit blinked. The contraction was easing a little, just enough to give her time to focus her thoughts. The old woman's words had been spoken so softly, but with threat. She began to understand that Zhoonali was speaking of killing her unborn child.

"No . . . ." She sighed the word, moving back from the old woman and wrapping her long, slender arms protectively about the great, swollen mound of her belly. This was *her* baby! When her pains had first begun, a new star had shown itself above the western horizon. *A new star!* A tiny, glimmering, golden eye with a bright whisk of a coltish tail! It was the best of omens! The magic man, Karana, had said so.

Karana. Where was Karana? He should be here now, outside the hut of blood, making magic smokes, dancing magic dances, chanting magic chants for one who was as a sister to him. Had he left the encampment again, to seek the counsel of mammoths? Were Zhoonali and those loyal to her right about him? Was he too young and unreliable for the responsibilities of his position?

Lonit moaned. Within her belly, the baby moved. With or without omens or the presence of the magic man, her child lived, and Zhoonali had no right to speak of ending its life. The child would live or die according to the will of the forces of Creation. Apart from this, only its father and the magic man had the right to deny it a place within the band. This baby was Torka's child—perhaps Torka's *son!* And what man with only daughters at his fire circle would deny life to a son!

Pain was rising in her again, cresting, then crashing as Lonit felt her back and hips rent apart. It was excruciating, but she had no wish to evade it. This time when she gritted her teeth and closed her eyes, she did not think of wolves or spirits. She thought of her man. She thought of his child. *Their* child. And with a fully human cry, she bore down on the pain, pushing so hard that the world seemed to crack open all around her. She screamed until it seemed that her pain screamed back at her as she fell gratefully into darkness, into a thick, all-encompassing black lake of oblivion in which she would have drowned . . . but for the cry of a child. Her child!

"A male child!" The voice of Wallah was as full of pride as though she announced the birth of one of her own.

Relieved, Lonit managed a brief moaning tremor of a laugh. At last. She would look upon her infant and hold it to her breast! She had given birth to a son! Karana was right; the new star *had* been a good omen! Torka would be so proud!

She tried to open her eyes but failed; her lids were too heavy. It did not matter. The long ordeal of childbirth was over. The pain was over. The midwives were cleansing her, stroking her back. Old Zhoonali was gently kneading her belly, seeking to purge it of the afterbirth.

Strange: Her abdomen still felt swollen, and she could have sworn that the baby still moved and kicked within her.

Then she heard Zhoonali sadly say, "The infant son of Torka is strong and sound. The first infant born in this new and forbidden land is more beautiful than any boy this woman has ever seen. It is a pity that this child must die."

Lonit bears twins sons, Manaravak and Umak. Because twins are considered bad luck by Zhoonali, the elderly midwife steals Manaravak and exposes him on a cliffside to die. Before Torka can search for the infant, the wanawut, a huge, pre-Neanderthal hominid, finds the baby and takes him away to her cave.

WALKERS OF THE WIND

After being raised by the wanawut for ten years, Manaravak is reunited with his family. But a deadly rivalry erupts between him and Umak over the affections of lovely Naya, who enjoys being the center of attention. Addicted to an aphrodisiac berry that causes hallucinations, the girl unwittingly worsens the competition and strife.

Naya ran on, clasping a tiny hand across her mouth lest her laughter reveal her knowledge that she was being watched and followed by . . .

"Umak! *And* Manaravak!"

As long as the twin sons of the headman were near, no harm could come to her.

Why did they follow? For how long had they been watching her? Had they seen her dance naked beneath the sun? Had the sight of her childlike little body been so amusing that the sound she had heard was not a sneeze but an attempt to stifle their own laughter?

Without warning, the thong ties of Naya's right boot came loose, tripped her, and sent her sprawling. She lay still, unhurt, and cast a glance back over her shoulder. Yes. The twins were still within the grass now, with the dog between them. The corners of Naya's lips turned upward with satisfaction because Demmi was not with them. The twins' older sister was too big and too bold for a proper female. No doubt she was off tracking the bear with the other hunters. Summer Moon, the headman's eldest daughter, showed none of these faults, and neither did Swan, the youngest of the threesome. Demmi was Manaravak's constant shadow, and Naya half hoped that the young woman would run afoul of the great bear and never return to the People.

Manaravak! His name formed upon Naya's tongue, as complex and beautiful as the man to whom it belonged—a man who would be her man someday, when and *if* she ever grew up! With the berry necklace held between her teeth, she sat up, tied her moccasin thongs, and ran on toward the lake.

Below the crest of the ridge, the hunters paused as their headman dropped to one knee and laid his hand upon the earth.

There it was again—the sign of the bear, and of something else. He watched, listened, and waited, but no matter how hard he tried to define the warning within his brain, it refused to reveal itself.

"Torka? What is it?"

He raised a hand to silence the hunter Simu. A moment passed. Whatever had raised the hackles on his neck was gone. And now a real and immediate danger threatened them all: the great, plundering bear. All day he and the others had been searching for it. He rose and walked across the ridge until he knelt again, and with his left hand upon the earth and his right hand curled around the hafts of his spears, he saw that bear sign was fresh. The newly scattered scree revealed a massive imprint that lay bared to the sun, unmarred by the crossing of insect tracks or by the settling of dust. Beneath that massive print lay another—a much smaller, human imprint that turned him cold with dread.

At his back, his daughter Demmi stood beside Simu and his sons, Dak and young Nantu. Silent and motionless in the wind, the foursome awaited his word.

It came: "Here the great one slipped, fought for footing, and fell. She slid and then rose again, followed by her cubs, into the country of much grass."

Demmi came forward to kneel beside Torka. "Is there sign of Manaravak?" Her voice was tight with stress.

Torka looked into Demmi's worry-shaded dark eyes. He saw much of his beloved woman, Lonit, in the face of his daughter: the wide brow; the narrow, high-bridged nose; the round, deeply lidded eyes that were so like those of an antelope. These features Lonit had shared with all three of her girls, as well as with Umak, the firstborn of her twins. Of Torka's children only Manaravak and Sayanah, seven winters old and the son last born to Lonit, resembled the headman. Their fourth daughter had lived just long enough to be named, but Torka had looked upon her face and known that if the forces of Creation allowed her to be born into the world again, she would carry the look of her mother. A cold, fleeting mist of mourning chilled him.

Demmi leaned closer and put a strong, sun-browned hand over his own. "Father, is there sign of Manaravak?"

The mists within Torka's mind cleared. He nodded but could barely find the heart to speak as he looked into her distraught face. Demmi, even more than Lonit, had taught Manaravak to speak, live, and think as a human being when he had first returned to his people from the wild. From the moment that she had set eyes upon her long-lost younger brother, the girl had been fiercely protective and possessive of his affection. It was not unusual for them to know each other's thoughts, as though their ability to communicate transcended the bonds of flesh, as though their blood was one blood, and their spirits one spirit.

Demmi said, "It is not like Manaravak to leave my side—"

"*Your* side?" Dak's query was pincer sharp. "He left us *all*, woman! Forgive me, Torka, but if we had needed Manaravak, where would he have been, eh? And you, Demmi, what is the matter with you? Soon Manaravak will take a woman of his own! It is about time that you stopped mothering him."

She glared at Dak coldly. "I am of the People. Manaravak is my brother. Ours is a bond of blood and heart and spirit. You . . . what are you to me? I sit at your fire only because this is a small band that needs children to assure its future, and it seems that a woman cannot make them by herself!"

"Demmi!" Torka sent her shrinking back like a scolded child. "Enough! This is no time for you and Dak to set to your endless bickering." Beneath his headband of lion skin, Torka's brow furrowed as he appraised the young hunter. Dak was as solidly put together as a well-made sledge and, like Simu, his father, every bit as useful to the band. He was an exemplary hunter and had proved to be a caring father to Kharn, the little son Demmi had borne to him three long autumns before.

"Come, Dak," Torka invited. "Kneel beside me and Demmi. Use your eyes *and* your head, man. Do you see it? The track of the man is overlaid by the imprint of the bear. Your woman has just cause for concern on Manaravak's behalf."

Dak glowered down at the ground, leaned low, then nodded solemnly. "The bear *follows* Manaravak!"

"Yes," confirmed Torka. "And Manaravak follows Umak, who follows Grek, the women, and children."

"And now we will follow them all!" blurted Nantu.

"Nantu is right," said Torka, rising and loping forward into the wind without looking back. "Come. Hurry! We have no time to lose!"

Torka, who has always insisted that the People are One, must now divide his band to prevent his twin sons from killing each other. As Manaravak and his followers go in one direction and Umak and his adherents trek in another, Lonit and Torka walk eastward, into the face of the rising sun. Torka has passed the responsibility of leadership to his boys, and now he and his "always and forever woman" seek their destiny alone, having been the parents of countless generations of Americans.

In Volume Five of THE FIRST AMERICANS series, THE SACRED STONES, the descendants of Manaravak and Umak—gentle food gatherers of the Southwest and the buffalo hunters of the Plains—face a fierce enemy who carries the blood of the evil Navahk. Demanding human sacrifices, the People of the Watching Star introduce violence into a land of peace, to bands who have never been forced to defend themselves.

Eyes closed, Ysuna lay partially awake in Masau's arms, awash in the warm, familiar streams of her subconscious mind. She saw herself walking alone within the misted fibers of her mind. She was a tall figure, clothed only in light and in her sacred collar as she moved slowly through wide, dark corridors of time beneath the huge, unblinking eye of the Watching Star.

Suddenly she found herself sweeping through long strands of human finger bones, which clicked and sang like shards of volcanic glass in the wind. The sense of wonder was strong in her now as the curtains of bone fell away and dissolved into the night.

At last she stopped at the base of a great canyon. Even in the darkness she could see a waterfall plunging from one of many soaring cliffs that towered thousands of feet above the canyon floor. The air was sharp with the smell of roses and unfamiliar trees. Her nostrils expanded and drew in the scent of grazing animals—deer, pronghorn, horse, tapir, peccary. And mammoth! She caught her breath as a sense of wonder nearly overwhelmed her.

Then, suddenly, from directly behind her a lion roared.

"Do you imagine that Thunder in the Sky did not see who took the lead upon the last hunt? It was not you, Ysuna! And do you believe that the spirit of this lion—and of this wise man who died at Maliwal's hand by your command and was eaten by this lion—will allow you to forget us?"

Ysuna moaned against the dream. The headless lion prepared to leap. And now, as the great cat sprang out of the tree, it had the head of the old man. With fangs bared, Ish-iwi came for Ysuna and screamed for vengeance.

"I will have the sacred stone that you stole from me!"

"No!" she cried, and clutching her collar of sacred stones and human hair, she wheeled and fled deeper into the dream, racing headlong into the vastness of the canyon.

The lion did not follow, but the ghost of the old man called after her. "Run as you will, Ysuna. You have eaten of the heart and flesh of the meat eater that has eaten me. My spirit is within you now, and in the end I will have of you what I will."

Ysuna trembled within the dream. She saw herself moving deeper and deeper into the canyon. Mammoth walked ahead of her, as many mammoth as there were stars in the sky. She salivated, tasting blood and salt again. She slowed her steps and followed the mammoth until he appeared—Great Ghost Spirit . . . Thunder in the Sky . . . a white mammoth, the source of all wonder. Her heart was pounding.

In her dream a man and woman rode astride the high, swaying shoulders of the mammoth. Their backs were to her, so she could not see their faces; but she could tell that they were young and strong, beautiful and without fear. She was certain that the man was Masau. Who else but Mystic Warrior would be bold enough to ride upon the back of the god? And when the woman turned and looked back through the swirling, wind-combed black hair, she knew that she had to be looking at herself. The mammoth plodded on, leaving her behind as they followed Thunder in the Sky and the two who rode upon his back. She called out for the god to wait, but he did not. Behind him the ghosts of his many brides materialized to follow in a silent, diaphanous column until, once more, Ysuna was alone in the darkness of her dream.

Shivering, she knelt and looked down to see herself and the stars reflected in a pool of blood. Startled and appalled, she stared not at youth or at Daughter of the Sun. Her reflection showed the withered form of an ancient hag.

"No!" She screamed in horror and jumped to her feet.

Somewhere far away beyond the entrance of the canyon, a lion roared and an old man laughed.

Her hands flew to her collar of sacred stones. "No!" she cried again, and even as she spoke she felt the power growing in her.

The stars began to fall around her, and Thunder in the Sky appeared on the opposite side of the pool. He was alone now, a great white mammoth, massive and magnificent.

She stood motionless, then her head went high as she felt his power. She named him god and totem, and as she did he raised his massive head and pierced the night with his tusks.

The world shook. Falling stars turned red. Suddenly, as Ysuna screamed, the great mammoth collapsed and dissolved into the pool.

She stood alone in a rain of blood. She knelt again, made a cup of her hand, dipped it into the pool, then drank. The taste of blood was the taste of the white mammoth. She sluiced its hot saltiness through her teeth and savored the feel of its oozing down the back of her throat.

She looked into the pool, and instead of seeing the hag, Ysuna found a woman of eternal youth and beauty . . . an immortal clothed in the skin of a white mammoth. Masau, Mystic Warrior, stood at her side, and a golden grassland stretched out forever behind him, treed with the lodges of a people whose number exceeded that of the stars in the sky.

And in THUNDER IN THE SKY, the sixth volume of THE FIRST AMERICANS, a struggle for the future of humanity begins. On one side is the young shaman Cha-kwena, who has led his tiny band along the trail made by a magnificent white mammoth, the totem he believes will lead the People to a land of safety and abundance. But they are pursued by a race of vicious and relentless hunters who want to steal his magic and kill the sacred mammoth . . .

Read all six volumes of this stirring series, available wherever Bantam paperbacks are sold!